Praise for *The Sun Down Motel*

"There are very few novels that leave me feeling genuinely spooked. . . . St. James's *The Sun Down Motel* is very much one of those books, taking twists and turns that are equal parts compelling and creepy."

—PopSugar

"St. James knows that true terror, as she effectively illustrates in *The Sun Down Motel*, goes beyond things that go bump in the night. . . . St. James deftly melds an engrossing mystery with a tense supernatural thriller. . . . St. James keeps the tension high with myriad surprising twists."

—The Associated Press

"This creepy supernatural thriller will send shivers down your spine."

—*Good Housekeeping*

"A truly nightmarish trip back and forth in time and into the supernatural. . . . Guaranteed to keep readers rapt. . . . What a story!"

—*Booklist* (starred review)

"This novel is a creepy delight."   —*The New York Post*

"When are we too old for ghost stories? As long as they are as taut and twisty as St. James's latest novel, make that never. . . . Readers of this thoroughly entertaining thriller won't be disappointed."

—*Minneapolis Star Tribune*

Praise for *The Broken Girls*

"[*The Broken Girls*] mixes a creepy supernatural tale . . . with a gripping mystery. [It] also works well as a story about unshakeable friendship, parenting issues, obsession, and sexism folded into a satisfying plot that straddles two eras of time."   —The Associated Press

"Clever and wonderfully chilling. It held me hostage in a very modern ghost story until the early hours."

—Fiona Barton, *New York Times* bestselling author of *The Suspect*

"Part hauntingly Gothic and part suspenseful crime drama, *The Broken Girls* is a bona fide page-turner. [A] story of friendship, revenge, and redemption."

—Karen White, *New York Times* bestselling author of *Dreams of Falling*

"Haunting and memorable, *The Broken Girls* is a mesmerizing blend of past and present, a sometimes heartbreaking and always compelling quest for the truth about secrets that shouldn't stay buried. Masterfully done!"

—Karen Dionne, international bestselling author of *The Marsh King's Daughter*

"A creepy supernatural mystery. . . . In this page-turner, the secrets Fiona uncovers lead to a terrifying conclusion that has less to do with the paranormal and more to do with the evil that men do."

—Shondaland

"St. James is a unique author who usually combines elegant writing with a mystery to be solved that is complicated by ghostly elements. Spooky and Gothic but fascinating too."

—*Kirkus Reviews*

"[A] creepy supernatural thriller."   —*Publishers Weekly*

"This modern Gothic tale . . . is a real page-turner and just creepy enough to keep readers satisfyingly on edge. Perfect for a dark and stormy night."

—*Library Journal*

"A vivid, riveting story you won't soon forget."

—Deanna Raybourn, *New York Times* bestselling author of
A Murderous Relation

ALSO BY SIMONE ST. JAMES

The Haunting of Maddy Clare
An Inquiry into Love and Death
Silence for the Dead
The Other Side of Midnight
Lost Among the Living
The Broken Girls
The Book of Cold Cases

The Sun Down
MOTEL

NO VACANCY

SIMONE ST. JAMES

BERKLEY
New York

BERKLEY
An imprint of Penguin Random House LLC
penguinrandomhouse.com

Copyright © 2020 by Simone Seguin
Readers Guide copyright © 2020 by Simone Seguin
Excerpt from *The Broken Girls* by Simone St. James copyright © 2018 by Simone Seguin
Penguin Random House supports copyright. Copyright fuels creativity, encourages diverse voices, promotes
free speech, and creates a vibrant culture. Thank you for buying an authorized edition of this book and for
complying with copyright laws by not reproducing, scanning, or distributing any part of it in any form
without permission. You are supporting writers and allowing Penguin Random House to continue
to publish books for every reader.

BERKLEY and the BERKLEY & B colophon are registered trademarks of Penguin Random House LLC.

ISBN: 9780440000204

The Library of Congress has cataloged the Berkley hardcover edition as follows:

Names: St. James, Simone, author.
Title: The sun down motel / Simone St. James.
Description: First edition. | New York : Berkley, 2020.
Identifiers: LCCN 2019026692 | ISBN 9780440000174 (hardcover) |
ISBN 9780440000181 (ebook)
Subjects: GSAFD: Suspense fiction. | Mystery fiction.
Classification: LCC PR9199.4.S726 S86 2020 | DDC 813/.6—dc23
LC record available at https://lccn.loc.gov/2019026692

Berkley hardcover edition / February 2020
Berkley trade paperback edition / October 2020

Printed in the United States of America
12th Printing

Cover photos: Motel sign © Tom Hogan/PlainPicture; Clouds © Menno can der Haven/Shutterstock;
Border © LoudRedCreative/Getty Images
Cover design by Sarah Oberrender

For the odd girls, the nerdy girls, and the murderinos.
This one is yours.

Fell, New York
November 1982
VIV

The night it all ended, Vivian was alone.

That was fine with her. She preferred it. It was something she'd discovered, working the night shift at this place in the middle of nowhere: Being with people was easy, but being alone was hard. Especially being alone in the dark. The person who could be truly alone, in the company of no one but oneself and one's own thoughts—that person was stronger than anyone else. More ready. More prepared.

Still, she pulled into the parking lot of the Sun Down Motel in Fell, New York, and paused, feeling the familiar beat of fear. She sat in her beat-up Cavalier, the key in the ignition, the heat and the radio on, her coat huddled around her shoulders. She looked at the glowing blue and yellow sign, the two stories of rooms in two long stripes in the shape of an L, and thought, *I don't want to go in there. But I will.* She was ready, but she was still afraid. It was 10:59 p.m.

She felt like crying. She felt like screaming. She felt sick.

I don't want to go in there.

But I will. Because I always do.

Outside, two drops of half-frozen rain hit the windshield. A truck droned by on the road in the rearview mirror. The clock ticked over to eleven o'clock, and the news came on the radio. Another minute and she'd be late, but she didn't care. No one would fire her. No one cared if she came to work. The Sun Down had few customers, none of whom would notice if the night girl was late. It was often so quiet that an observer would think that nothing ever happened here.

Viv Delaney knew better.

The Sun Down only looked empty. But it wasn't.

With cold fingers, she pulled down the driver's-side visor. She touched her hair, which she'd had cut short, a sharp style that ended below her earlobes and was sprayed out for volume. She checked her eye makeup— not the frosty kind, like some girls wore, but a soft lavender purple. It looked a little like bruises. You could streak it with yellow and orange to create a days-old-bruise effect, but she hadn't bothered with that tonight. Just the purple on the delicate skin of her lids, meeting the darker line of her eyeliner and lashes. Why had she put makeup on at all? She couldn't remember.

On the radio, they talked about a body. A girl found in a ditch off Melborn Road, ten miles from here. Not that *here* was anywhere—just a motel on the side of a two-lane highway leading out of Fell and into the nothingness of upstate New York and eventually Canada. But if you took the two-lane for a mile and made a right at the single light dangling from an overhead wire, and followed that road to another and another, you'd be where the girl's body was found. A girl named Tracy Waters, last seen leaving a friend's house in a neighboring town. Eighteen years old, stripped naked and dumped in a ditch. They'd found her body two days after her parents reported her missing.

As she sat in her car, twenty-year-old Viv Delaney's hands shook as she listened to the story. She thought about what it must be like to lie naked as the half-frozen rain pelted your helpless skin. How horribly cold that would be. How it was always girls who ended up stripped and dead like roadkill. How it didn't matter how afraid or how careful you were—it could always be you.

Especially here. It could always be you.

Her gaze went to the motel, to the reflection of the gaudy lit-up blue and yellow sign blinking endlessly in the darkness. VACANCY. CABLE TV! VACANCY. CABLE TV!

Even after three months in this place, she could still be scared. Awfully, perfectly scared, her thoughts skittering up the back of her neck and around her brain in panic. *I'm alone for the next eight hours, alone in the dark. Alone with her and the others.*

And despite herself, Viv turned the key so the heat and the radio—still talking about Tracy Waters—went off. Lifted her chin and pushed open the driver's-side door. Stepped out into the cold.

She hunched deeper into her nylon coat and started across the parking lot. She was wearing jeans and a pair of navy blue sneakers with white laces, the soles too thin for the cold and damp. The rain wet her hair, and the wind pushed it out of place. She walked across the lot toward the door that said OFFICE.

Inside the office, Johnny was standing behind the counter, zipping up his coat over his big stomach. He'd probably seen her from the window in the door. "Are you late?" he asked, though there was a clock on the wall behind him.

"Five minutes," Viv argued back, unzipping her own coat. Her stomach felt tight, queasy now that she was inside. *I want to go home.*

But where was home? Fell wasn't home. Neither was Illinois, where she was born. When she left home for the last time, after the final screaming fight with her mother, she'd supposedly been headed to New York to become an actress. But that, like everything else in her life to that point, had been a part she was playing, a story. She had no idea how to become a New York actress—the story had enraged her mother, which had made it good enough. What Viv had wanted, more than anything, was to simply be in motion, to go.

So she'd gone. And she'd ended up here. Fell would have to be home for now.

"Mrs. Bailey is in room two-seventeen," Johnny said, running down the motel's few guests. "She already made a liquor run, so expect a phone call anytime."

"Great," Viv said. Mrs. Bailey came to the Sun Down to drink, probably because if she did it at home she'd get in some kind of trouble. She made drunken phone calls to the front desk to make demands she usually forgot about. "Anyone else?"

"The couple on their way to Florida checked out," Johnny said. "We've had two prank phone calls, both heavy breathing. Stupid teenagers. And I wrote a note to Janice about the door to number one-oh-three. There's something wrong with it. It keeps blowing open in the wind, even when I lock it."

"It always does that," Viv said. "You told Janice about it a week ago." Janice was the motel's owner, and Viv hadn't seen her in weeks. Months, maybe. She didn't come to the motel if she didn't have to, and she certainly didn't come at night. She left Vivian's paychecks in an envelope on the desk, and all communication was handled with notes. Even the motel's owner didn't spend time here if she could help it.

"Well, she should fix the door," Johnny said. "I mean, it's strange, right? I locked it."

"Sure," Viv said. "It's strange."

She was used to this. No one else who worked at the motel saw what she saw or experienced what she did. The things she saw only happened in the middle of the night. The day shift and the evening shift employees had no idea.

"Hopefully no one else will check in," Johnny said, pulling the hood of his jacket over his head. "Hopefully it'll be quiet."

It's never quiet, Viv thought, but she said, "Yes, hopefully."

Viv watched him walk out of the office, listened to his car start up and drive away. Johnny was thirty-six and lived with his mother. Viv pictured him going home, maybe watching TV before going to bed. A guy who had never made much of himself, living a relatively normal life, free of the kind of fear Viv was feeling. A life in which he never thought about Tracy Waters, except to vaguely recall her name from the radio.

Maybe it was just her who was going crazy.

The quiet settled in, broken only by the occasional sound of the traffic on Number Six Road and the wind in the trees behind the motel. It was now 11:12. The clock on the wall behind the desk ticked over to 11:13.

She hung her jacket on the hook in the corner. From another hook she took a navy blue polyester vest with the words *Sun Down Motel* embroidered on the left breast and shrugged it on over her white blouse. She pulled out the hard wooden chair behind the counter and sat in it. She surveyed the scarred, stained desktop quickly: jar of pens and pencils, the black square that made a clacking sound when you dragged the handle back and forth over a credit card to make a carbon impression, puke-colored rotary phone. In the middle of the desk was a large, flat book, where guests were to write their information and sign their names when checking in. The guest book was open to November 1982.

Pulling a notebook from her purse, Viv pulled a pen from between its pages, opened the notebook on the desk, and wrote.

Nov. 29

Door to number 103 has begun to open again. Prank calls. No one here. Tracy Waters is dead.

A sound came from outside, and she paused, her head half raised. A bang, and then another one. Rhythmic and wild. The door to number 103 blowing open and hitting the wall in the wind. Again.

For a second, Viv closed her eyes. The fear came over her in a wave, but she was too far in it now. She was already here. She had to be ready. The Sun Down had claimed her for the night.

She lowered the pen again.

What if everything I've seen, everything I think, is true? Because I think it is.

Her eyes glanced to the guest book, took in the names there. She paused as the clock on the wall behind her shoulder ticked on, then wrote again.

The ghosts are awake tonight. They're restless. I think this will be over soon. Her hand trembled, and she tried to keep it steady. *I'm so sorry, Tracy. I've failed.*

A small sound escaped the back of her throat, but she bit it down into silence. She put the pen down and rubbed her eyes, some of the pretty lavender eyeshadow coming off on her fingertips.

It was November 29, 1982, 11:24 p.m.

By three o'clock in the morning, Viv Delaney had vanished.

That was the beginning.

Fell, New York
November 2017
CARLY

This place was unfamiliar.

I opened my eyes and stared into the darkness, panicked. Strange bed, strange light through the window, strange room. I had a minute of free fall, frightening and exhilarating at the same time.

Then I remembered: I was in Fell, New York.

My name was Carly Kirk, I was twenty years old, and I wasn't supposed to be here.

I checked my phone on the nightstand; it was four o'clock in the morning, only the light from streetlamps and the twenty-four-hour Denny's shining through the sheer drapes on the hotel room window and making a hazy square on the wall.

I wasn't getting back to sleep now. I swung my legs over the side of the bed and picked up my glasses from the nightstand, putting them on. I'd driven from Illinois yesterday, a long drive that left me tired enough to sleep like the dead in this bland chain hotel in downtown Fell.

It wasn't that impressive a place; Google Earth had told me that much. Downtown was a grid of cafés, laundromats, junky antique stores, apartment rental buildings, and used-book stores, nestled reverently around a grocery store and a CVS. The street I was on, with the chain hotel and the Denny's, passed straight through town, as if a lot of people got to Fell and simply kept driving without making the turnoff into the rest of the town. The WELCOME TO FELL sign I'd passed last night had been vandalized by a wit who had used spray paint to add the words TURN BACK.

I didn't turn back.

With my glasses on, I picked up my phone again and scrolled through the emails and texts that had come in while I slept. ˙

The first email was from my family's lawyer. *The remainder of funds has been deposited into your account. Please see breakdown attached.*

I flipped past it without reading the rest, without opening the attachment. I didn't need to see it: I already knew I'd inherited some of Mom's money, split with my brother, Graham. I knew it wasn't riches, but it was enough to keep me in food and shelter for a little while. I didn't want numbers, and I couldn't look at them. Losing your mother to cancer—she was only fifty-one—made things like money look petty and stupid.

In fact, it made you rethink everything in your life. Which in my crazy way, after fourteen months in a fog of grief, I was doing. And I couldn't stop.

There was a string of texts from Graham. *What do you think you're doing, Carly? Leaving college? For how long? You think you can keep up? Whatever. If all that tuition is down the drain, you're on your own. You know that, right? Whatever you're doing, good luck with it. Try not to get killed.*

I hit Reply and typed, *Hey, drama queen. It's only for a few days, and I'm acing everything. This is just a side trip, because I'm curious. So sue me. I'll be fine. No plans to get killed, but thanks for checking.*

Actually, I was hoping to be here for longer than a few days. Since losing Mom, staying in college for my business degree seemed pointless. When I'd started college, I'd thought I had all the time in the world to figure out what I wanted to do. But Mom's death showed me that life wasn't as long as you thought it was. And I had questions I wanted answers to. It was time to find them.

Hailey, Graham's fiancée, had sent me her own text. *Hey! You OK??*

Worried about you. I'm here to talk if you want. Maybe you need another grief counselor? I can find you one! OK? XO!

God, she was so *nice*. I'd already done grief counseling. Therapy. Spirit circles. Yoga. Meditation. Self-care. In doing all of that, what I'd discovered was that I didn't need another therapy session right now. What I really needed, at long last, was answers.

I put down my phone and opened my laptop, tapping it awake. I opened the file on my desktop, scrolling through it. I picked out a scan of a newspaper from 1982, with the headline *POLICE SEARCHING FOR MISSING LOCAL WOMAN*. Beneath the headline was a photo of a young woman, clipped from a snapshot. She was beautiful, vivacious, smiling at the camera, her hair teased, her bangs sprayed in place up from her forehead as the rest of her hair hung down in a classic eighties look. Her skin was clear and her eyes sparkled, even in black and white. The caption below the photo said: *Twenty-year-old Vivian Delaney has not been seen since the night of November 29. Anyone who has seen her is asked to call the police.*

This. *This* was the answer I needed.

I'd been a nerd all my life, my nose buried in a book. Except that once I graduated from reading *The Black Stallion*, the books I read were the dark kind—about scary things like disappearances and murders, especially the true ones. While other kids read J. K. Rowling, I read Stephen King. While other kids did history reports about the Civil War, I read about Lizzie Borden. The report I wrote about that one—complete with details about exactly where the axe hit Lizzie's father and stepmother— got my teacher to call my mother with concern. *Is Carly all right?* My mother had brushed it off, because by then she knew how dark her daughter was. *She's fine. She just likes to read about murder, that's all.*

What my mother didn't mention—what she hated to talk about at all—was that I came by it naturally. There was an unsolved murder in my family, and I'd been obsessed with it for as long as I could remember.

I looked at the newspaper clipping again. Viv Delaney, the girl in the photograph, was my mother's sister. In 1982, she disappeared while working the night shift at the Sun Down Motel and was never found.

It was the huge, gaping hole in my family, the thing that everyone knew about but no one spoke of. Viv's disappearance was a loss like a missing tooth. *Never ask your mother about that,* my father told me the year before he left us all for good. *It upsets her.* Even my brother, the eternal pain in the ass, was sensitive about it. *Mom's sister was killed,* he told me. *Someone took her and murdered her, like that guy with the hook. It creeps me out. No wonder Mom doesn't talk about it.*

Thirty-five years my aunt Viv had been missing. My grandparents—Mom and Viv's parents—were dead. There were no pictures of Viv in our house, no mementos of her. The year before Mom died, when I was home for the summer, I'd found a story online and seen Viv's face for the first time. I'd thought maybe enough time had passed. I'd printed the clipping out and gone downstairs to show it to her. "Look what I found," I said.

Mom was sitting on the sofa in the living room, watching TV after dinner. She took the clipping from me and read it. Then she stared at it for a long time, her gaze fixed on the photograph.

When she looked back up at me, she had a strange look on her face that I'd never seen before and would never see again. Pain, maybe. Exhaustion, and some kind of old, rotted-over, carved-out fear. In that moment I had no idea that she had cancer, that I would lose her within a year. Maybe she knew then and didn't tell me, but I didn't think so. That look on her face, that fear, was all about Vivian.

Her voice, when she finally spoke, was flat, without inflection. "Vivian is dead," she said. She put down the clipping and got up and left the room.

I never asked Mom about it again.

It was only after Mom died that I got mad. Not at Mom, really—she was a teenager when Viv disappeared, and there wasn't much she could have done. But what about everyone else? The cops? The locals? Viv's parents?

Why hadn't there been a statewide search? Why had Viv been allowed to vanish into nothingness with barely a ripple?

The first person I asked was Graham, who was older and remembered more than I did. "Grandma and Granddad were divorced by then," Graham said. "When Viv disappeared, Grandma was a single mother."

"So? That meant she didn't look for her daughter? Granddad, either?"

Graham shrugged. "Grandma didn't have much money. And Mom told me that she and Viv used to fight all the time. They didn't get along at all."

I'd stared at him, shocked. We were sitting in my mother's rental apartment, in the middle of boxing up her things. We were taking a break and eating takeout. "Mom told you that? She never told me that."

My brother shrugged again, leaning back on a box and scrolling through his phone. "They didn't have the Internet back then, or DNA. If you wanted to find a missing person, you had to get in your car and go driving around looking for them. Grandma couldn't take time off work and go to Fell. And Granddad was already remarried. I don't think he cared about any of them all that much."

It was true. Mom hadn't had a good relationship with her father, who had left their family to sink or swim. She hadn't even gone to his funeral. "What about the cops, though?" I said.

Graham put his phone down briefly and thought it over. "Well, Viv had already left home, and she was twenty," he said. "I guess they thought she'd just taken off somewhere." He looked at me. "You're really into this, aren't you?"

"Yes, I'm really into this. They didn't even find a body. It isn't 1982 anymore. We have the Internet and DNA now. Maybe something can be done."

"By you?"

Yes, by me. There didn't seem to be anyone else. And now that Mom was gone, I could ask all the questions I wanted without hurting her feelings. Mom had taken all of her memories of Viv with her when she died, and I'd never hear them. My anger at that was helpless, something that the therapists and counselors said I needed to work through. But my anger at everyone else, my outrage that my aunt's likely abduction and death were written off as just something that happened—I could work through that by coming to Fell and getting my own answers.

I clicked the other scanned article I had on my computer. It was headlined simply *MISSING GIRL STILL NOT FOUND*. The details were sketchy: Viv was twenty; she had been in Fell for three months; she worked at the Sun Down Motel on the night shift. She'd gone to work and disappeared sometime in the middle of her shift, leaving behind her car, her purse, and her belongings. Her roommate, a girl named Jenny Summers, said Viv was "a nice person, easy to get along with." She was also described—by who was not cited—as "pretty and vivacious." She had no boyfriend that anyone knew of. She was not into drugs, alcohol, or prostitution that anyone could tell. Her mother—my grandmother—was quoted as being "worried sick."

She was a beautiful girl, gone.

On foot. Without any money.

Vivian is dead.

Viv's case hadn't received national or even statewide media attention. The local Fell newspapers weren't digitized—they were still physically archived in the Fell library. When I started digging, all I found were true-crime blogs and Reddit threads by armchair detectives. None of the blogs or threads were about Vivian, but a lot of them were about Fell. Because Fell, it turned out, had more than one unsolved murder. For such a small place, it was a true-crime buff's paradise.

The second article was in Mom's belongings. I'd found it when I'd gone through her dresser after she died, tucked in an envelope in the back of a drawer. The envelope was white, crisp, brand-new. Written on the back, in Mom's lovely handwriting, was: *27 Greville Street, apartment C.*

Viv's address, maybe? The piece of newsprint inside the envelope was nearly disintegrating, so I'd scanned it and added it to the first one I found.

Vivian is dead.

Mom had wanted no memories of her sister, no discussion of her, and yet she'd kept this article for thirty-five years, along with the address. She'd even put it in a new envelope sometime recently, recopied the address, which meant she'd at least pulled the article out of the old envelope, maybe read it again.

Viv was real. She wasn't a spooky tale or a ghost story. She had been real, she had been Mom's sister—and somehow, looking at that crisp white envelope, I knew she had mattered to Mom, a lot, in a way I had lost my chance to understand.

This was all I had: two newspaper articles and a memory of grief. Except now I had more than that. I had a little money and I had a very clear map from Illinois to Fell, New York. I had an address for Viv's apartment, maybe, and the Sun Down Motel. I had no boyfriend and a college career I had no passion for. I had a car and so few belongings that they fit into the back seat. I was twenty, and I still hadn't started my life yet. Just like Viv hadn't.

So I'd left school—Graham really was blowing this out of proportion—and got in my car for a road trip. And here I was. I'd look around town and dig up the local articles in the library. I'd go see the Sun Down for myself, since my Internet search said it was still in business. Maybe someone who lived here had known Viv, remembered her, could tell me about her. Maybe I could make her more than a fading piece of newsprint hidden in my mother's drawer. Her disappearance was the big mystery of my family—I wanted to see it firsthand, and all it would cost was a few days out of school.

Try not to get killed. That was my big brother, trying to scare me. It wasn't going to work. I didn't scare easily.

Still, I closed my laptop and tried not to think about someone hurting the girl I'd seen in the photo, someone grabbing her, taking her somewhere, doing something to her, killing her. Dumping her somewhere lonely, where maybe she still was. Maybe she was only bones now. Maybe that person, whoever they were, was dead now, or in prison. Maybe they weren't.

Vivian is dead.

It wasn't fair that Vivian was forgotten, reduced to a few pieces of newsprint and nothing else. It wasn't fair that Mom had died and taken her memories and her grief with her. It wasn't fair that Viv didn't matter to anyone but me.

I was in Fell. I didn't belong here. I had no idea what I was doing.

And still I waited, without sleeping, for the sun to come up again.

Fell, New York
August 1982
VIV

Coming here was an accident. A detour sent her bus into Pennsylvania, and from there she hitched, trying to save cash. The first ride was only going to Binghamton. The second ride told her he was going to New York, but an hour later she realized he was driving the wrong way.

"We're not going to New York," Viv said to the man. "We're driving upstate."

"Well," the man said. He was in his forties, wearing a pale yellow collared shirt and dress pants. He was clean-shaven and wore rimless glasses. "You should have been more clear. When you said New York, I thought you meant upstate."

She'd been clear. She knew she had. She looked out the window at the setting sun, wondering where he was taking her, her heart starting to accelerate in panic. She didn't want to be rude. Maybe she should be nice about it. "It's okay," she said. "You can let me out here."

"Don't be silly," the man said. "I'll bring you to Rochester, where I can at least get you a meal. You can get a bus from there."

Viv gave him a smile, like he was doing her a favor, driving her away from where she wanted to be. "Oh, you don't need to do that."

"Sure I do."

They were on a two-lane stretch of road, and she saw the sign for a motel ahead. "I need to stop for the night anyway," she said. "I'll just stay here."

"That place? Looks sketchy to me."

"I'm sure it's fine." When he didn't speak, she said, "I don't mean to be a bother."

Her throat went dry as the man pulled over. She thought she might throw up. She couldn't have said what she was afraid of, what made her so relieved that he did as she asked. *What else would he have done?* she chided herself. He was probably a nice man and she was being ridiculous. It came from being on the road alone.

Still, once he stopped the car she opened the door, putting one foot on the roadside gravel. Only then did she turn and get her bag from the back seat. The entire time she had her back to him, she held her breath.

When she had finished wrestling the bag into her lap, she felt something warm on her thigh. She looked down and saw the man's hand resting there.

"You don't have to," he said.

Viv's mind went blank. She mumbled something, pulled out from under his hand, got out of the car, and slammed the door. The only words she could manage—spoken as the car pulled away, when the man couldn't hear her—were "Thank you" and "Sorry." She didn't know why she said them. She only knew that she stood at the side of an empty road, in front of an empty motel, her heart pounding so hard it felt like it was squeezing her chest.

Back in Grisham, Illinois, Viv was the problem daughter. After her parents' divorce five years earlier, she couldn't seem to do anything right. While her younger sister obeyed the rules, Viv did everything she wasn't supposed to: skipping school, staying out late, lying to her mother, cheating on tests. She didn't even know why she did it; she didn't want to do half of those things. It sometimes felt like she was in someone else's body, one that was angry and exhausted in turns.

But she did all the things that made her bad, that made her mother furious and embarrassed. One night, after she'd been caught coming home at two in the morning, her panicked mother had nearly slapped her. *You think you're so damned smart*, her mother had shouted in her face. *What would you do if you ever saw real trouble?*

Now, standing on the side of a lonely road far from home, with the man's taillights vanishing in the distance, those words came back. *What would you do if you ever saw real trouble?*

The August sky was turning red, the lowering sun stinging her eyes. She wore a sleeveless turquoise top, jeans with a white and silver belt, and tennis shoes. She hefted her bag on her shoulder and looked up at the motel sign. It was blue and yellow, the words SUN DOWN in the classic old-style kind of letters you saw from the fifties and sixties. Underneath that were neon letters that probably lit up at night: VACANCY. CABLE TV!

Behind the sign was a motel laid out in an L shape, the main thrust leading away from the road, the foot of the L running parallel to it. It had an overhang and a concrete walkway, the room doors lined up in the open air. An unremarkable place decorated in dark brown and dirty cream, the kind of place people drove by unless they were desperate to sleep. At the joint of the L was a set of stairs leading to the upper level. There was only one car in the parking lot, parked next to the door nearest the road that said OFFICE.

Viv wiped her forehead. The adrenaline spike from getting away from the man in the car was fading, and she was tired, her back and shoulders aching. Sweat dampened her armpits.

She had twenty dollars or so—all the cash she had left. She had a bank account with savings from her job back home at the popcorn stand at the drive-in, plus her small earnings from modeling for a local catalog. She'd stood in front of a camera for an afternoon wearing high-waisted acid-wash jeans and a bright purple button-down blouse, placing her fingertips into the pockets of the jeans and smiling.

Her entire savings totaled four hundred eighty-five dollars. It was supposed to be New York money, the money that would send her to her new life. She wasn't supposed to spend it before she even got anywhere. Yet like everything else about this trip so far, she seemed to have miscalculated.

This didn't look like an expensive place. Maybe twenty dollars would get her a bed and a shower. If not, maybe there was a way to sneak into one of the rooms. It didn't look like anyone would see.

Viv approached the office door and put her hand on the cold doorknob. Somewhere far off in the trees, a bird cried. There was no traffic on the road. *If the guy on the other side of this door looks like Norman Bates*, she told herself, *I'm turning around and running.* She took a deep breath and swung the door open.

The man inside did not look like Norman Bates—it wasn't a man at all. It was a woman sitting on a chair behind an old desk. She was about thirty, lean and vital, with brown hair in a ponytail and a face that had hard lines. She was wearing a baggy gray sweatshirt, loose-fit jeans, and heavy brown boots, which Viv could see because she had them propped right up on the desk. She was reading a magazine but looked up when the door opened.

"Help you?" the woman said without moving her feet off the desk.

Viv put her shoulders back and gave the woman her catalog-model smile. "Hi," she said. "I'd like a room, but I only have twenty dollars in cash. How much is it, please?"

"Usually thirty," the woman said without missing a beat or changing her pose. The magazine was still at chin height. "But I'm the owner and there's no one else here, so I'm not going to turn down twenty bucks."

Feeling a rush of triumph, Viv put her twenty-dollar bill down on the desk. And waited.

The woman still didn't move. She didn't put down her magazine, and she didn't take the twenty. Instead her gaze moved over Viv. "You passing through, honey?" she said.

It seemed a safe enough question. "Yes."

"Is that so? I didn't hear a car."

Viv shrugged, trying for vacant and harmless. Most people fell for it.

The woman finally closed the magazine and put it on her jean-clad lap. "Were you hitching on Number Six?"

"Number Six?" Viv said, confused.

"Number Six Road." The woman's eyebrows lowered. "If I was your mother, I would tan your hide. Hitching on that road is dangerous for lone girls."

"I didn't. My ride just dropped me off here. He picked me up outside Binghamton. I was heading for New York."

"Well, honey, this isn't New York. This is Fell. You're going the wrong way."

"I know." Viv wished the woman would just give her a room. She needed to put her heavy bag down. She needed a shower. She needed something to eat, though without the twenty she didn't know how she would pay for it. She pointed to the big book sitting open on the desk, obviously a guest registry. "Should I write my name in there?" Then, her suburban Illinois good-girl training coming through: "I can pay you the thirty if I can just get to a bank tomorrow. But they're all closed now."

The woman snorted. She tossed the magazine—Viv saw that it was *People*, with Tom Selleck on the cover—onto the desk and finally swung her feet down. "I have a better idea," she said. "My night guy just quit. Cover the desk tonight and keep your twenty bucks."

"Cover the desk?"

"Sit here, answer the phone. If someone comes in, take their money and give them a key. Keys are here." She opened the desk drawer at her right hand. "Have them sign the book. That's it. You think you can do that?"

"You don't have anyone else to do it?"

"I just said my guy quit, didn't I? I'm the owner, so I should know. Either you sit at this desk all night or I do. I already know which one I'd rather it be."

Viv blew out a breath. The work itself didn't bother her; she'd worked plenty of service jobs back in Illinois. But the idea of staying awake all night didn't sound very fun.

Still, if she did it she held on to her twenty. Which meant she could eat something.

She glanced around the office, looking for a signal that there was a catch, but all she saw was bland walls, a desk, a few shelves, and the window on the office door. There was the muffled sound of a car going by on the road, and the sky was getting darker. Surprisingly, Viv smelled the faint tang of cigarette smoke from somewhere. It was sharp and burning, not the old-smoke smell that could come from the woman's clothes. Someone was smoking a cigarette nearby.

For some reason, that made her feel a little better. There was obviously *someone* in this place, even if she couldn't see them.

"Sure," she told the woman. "I'll work the night shift."

"Good," the woman said, opening the desk drawer and tossing a key on the desk. "Room one-oh-four is yours. Wash up, have a nap, and come see me at eleven. What's your name?"

That smell of smoke again, like whoever it was had just taken a drag and exhaled. "Vivian Delaney. Viv."

"Well, Viv," the woman said, "I'm Janice. This is the Sun Down. Looks like you've found yourself somewhere to stay."

"Thank you," Viv said, but Janice had already gone back to Tom Selleck, putting her boots on the desk again.

She picked up the key and her twenty and left, pushing open the office door and stepping onto the walkway. She expected to see the smoker somewhere out here, maybe a guest having a smoke in the evening air, but there was no one. She walked out onto the gravel lot, turned in a circle, looking. In the lowering light of dusk the motel looked shuttered, no light coming from any of the rooms. The trees behind the place made a hushing sound in the wind. There was the soft sound of a shoe scraping on the gravel in the unlit corner of the lot.

"Hello?" Viv called, thinking of the man who'd put his hand on her leg.

Nothing.

She stood in the lowering darkness, listening to the wind and her own breathing.

Then she went to room 104, took a hot shower, and lay on the bed, wrapped in a towel, staring at the blank ceiling, feeling the rough comforter against the skin of her shoulders. She listened for the sounds you usually heard in hotels—footsteps coming and going, strangers' voices passing outside your door. Human sounds. There were none. There was no sound at all.

What kind of motel was this? If it was this deserted, how did it stay open? And why did they need a night clerk at all? At the movie theater, the manager had sent everyone home at ten because he didn't want to pay them after that.

She wasn't getting paid, not exactly. But it would still be easier for Janice to turn the lights out, lock the office door, and go home instead of trying to find someone to sit there all night.

Her feet ached, and her body relaxed slowly into the bed. Lonely or not, this was still better than hitching on that dark highway, hoping for another stranger to pick her up. She started to hope there was a vending machine somewhere in the Sun Down, preferably one with a Snickers bar in it.

The man in the yellow collared shirt had put his hand on her thigh like it belonged, like they had an agreement because she was in his car. He'd curled his fingers gently toward the inside of her thigh before she pulled away. She felt that jolt in her gut again, the fear. She'd never felt fear like that before. Anger, yes. And she'd slept a lot since her parents' divorce, sometimes until one or two in the afternoon, another thing that made her mother yell at her.

But the fear she'd felt today had been deep and sudden, almost like a numbing blow. For the first time in her life, it occurred to her how erasable she was. How it could all be over in an instant. Vivian Delaney could vanish. She would simply be gone.

I'm afraid, she thought.

Then: *This seems like the right place for it.*

She was asleep before she could think anything else.

Greville Street was barely three blocks long, a street of low-rise apartments ending in a dead end covered by a warped chain-link fence. The buildings looked like they were made from children's blocks stacked on angles, a boxy style in concrete and vinyl siding that had gone out of favor sometime around 1971. I drove slowly past the short, squat driveways to each building, looking for number twenty-seven.

I parked next to a dusky gray Volvo with a rounded rear and balding tires, feeling a little like a time traveler. I'd come here to see where my aunt had lived, maybe get a glimpse into what her life had been, but I hadn't expected to stand on a street that looked almost unchanged from 1982. If the address was correct, she'd stood exactly where I did now, looking at the same landscape.

There was no one around except for two kids riding bikes up and down the street, ringing the bells on their handlebars and laughing. I walked to the front door of number twenty-seven and found that it was unlocked, so I went in.

There was a short hallway lined with tenants' mailboxes and a set of stairs. The mailbox to apartment C said ATKINS, H. I had poked my head around the edge of the stairwell, looking up and wondering how not to look like a stalker, when a girl appeared in the upstairs hallway.

She was about my age, with a slight, firm build and dark blond hair that fell straight to her chin. She had taken the front hank of her hair and pinned it back from her forehead in a single bobby pin, and she looked at me with eyes that were clear and intelligent in an expressive face. She was wearing a large knitted poncho, basically a square placed over her shoulders with a hole for the head.

"Are you here for the ad?" she asked me.

"I—"

"There's only one person coming," she said. "The roommate for apartment C."

That gave me pause. "Apartment C?"

"Sure. Come on up."

I didn't even think of turning around.

Instead I followed Poncho Girl up another set of stairs and through a door. The apartment inside was surprisingly big, with a linoleum-floored kitchen, a TV room, and two bedroom doors opening from opposite ends.

"I'm Heather," the poncho girl said as she closed the door behind me. She stuck out her hand from beneath the folds of wool. It was a slender hand, porcelain white, and when I shook it, it gave my skin a little chill.

"Carly," I said.

"I'll give you a tour."

The next thing I knew it was ten minutes later and I had seen every room. I knew that the hot water was fussy and the Wi-Fi reception was unreliable and the rent was two hundred per month. I also knew I was a bit of a jerk, because I still hadn't told Heather the truth.

"Two hundred a month isn't very much money," I pointed out.

Heather rubbed a hand on the back of her neck. She had faint purple circles beneath her eyes, as if she were very tired, but she still gave off a tight vitality that was hard to look away from. "Okay, I can't lie," she said, the words in a rush. "I don't really need the money. My father pays for this place while I'm at Fell."

"At Fell?"

"Fell College," she said. "It's weird, I know. A local girl going to a local college, moved out into an apartment paid for by her parents. Right?" She tilted her chin like she wanted me to answer, but she kept talking without giving me the chance. "I needed the experience, or so the parental units tell me. To feed myself and fend for myself, something like that. And I like it, I do. But I'm alone all the time, and this apartment makes noises. And there's no one to talk to. I'm a night owl and I don't sleep at night. I think I posted the ad for a roommate just so I can have someone here. It isn't the money really. You know?"

"Okay," I said, because she seemed really nice. "I've never heard of Fell College."

"No one has," Heather said, shrugging her thin shoulders beneath her poncho. "It's a local place. Not a college in the usual sense, really. It's obscure, and we locals go there. Makes us feel like we're going to college without leaving town."

"Isn't the point of college to leave town?"

"The point of college is to go to college," Heather said with utter logic. "And I'm surprised you aren't one of us. I took you for a fellow student."

I looked down at myself: worn jeans, old boots that laced up the ankles, black T-shirt that said BOOKS ARE MY LIFE beneath a stretched-out hoodie, messenger bag. Add my dark-rimmed glasses and ponytail and I was pretty much a cliché. "I am a student, actually. But not at Fell College. I'm . . ." I looked around, cleared my throat. "Okay, I can't lie, either. I didn't actually come here about the roommate thing. You just assumed."

Heather's eyes widened. "Then why are you here?"

"Um, because I like grim Soviet Bloc architecture?"

She clapped her hands once, the motion making the poncho ripple. Her eyes sparkled. "I like you! Okay, then! Tell me why you're really here. The details." She closed her eyes tight, then opened them again. "You're mooning over an ex-boyfriend. There's a guy who lived in B who wasn't bad, but he moved out last week."

"No," I said. "No mooning."

"Curses. Okay. You're an archaeology student, and on a dig you found a map that led you here and you want to know why."

I stared at her. "That's actually sort of close, but my reason is weirder."

"I live for weird," Heather said.

I stared at her again, because she meant it. No one in Illinois lived for weird. No one I'd met, anyway.

"My aunt lived here, I think," I told her. "She disappeared in 1982. My mother died and never told me about her, and I left school, and I'm here to find out what happened." It didn't sound stupid. In this apartment, telling this particular girl, it didn't sound stupid at all.

Heather didn't even blink. "Um, 1982," she said, thinking. "What was her name?"

"Viv Delaney."

She shook her head. "It doesn't ring a bell. But then again, there are so many."

"So many what?"

"Dead girls. There are lots. But you said she wasn't dead, right? She disappeared."

"Y—yes."

"And she lived here, in this apartment?" Heather looked around at the apartment, as if picturing it like I was.

"Yes, I think she did."

"Have you found the tenant records?"

"Do you think I could?"

Heather looked thoughtful. "The landlord is a friend of my dad's. I could probably ask him if he has any records from 1982. And the archives in the Fell Central Library might have something. Nothing is digitized here. We're stuck in a time warp."

"I'm looking for people who might have known my aunt," I said. "I have her roommate's name. According to Google, she might still live in town. I want to find her and talk to her. And my aunt worked at the Sun Down Motel. Maybe someone there remembers her."

Heather nodded, as if all of this were not at all strange. "I can help you. I've lived in Fell all my life. True crime is kind of a hobby of mine."

I couldn't believe I was hearing this. "Me, too."

Her smile wasn't exactly even, but I still liked it. "Gosh, that settles it. Don't you think?"

"Settles what?"

"I think you should stay here," she said. "It's fate. Come stay here for as long as you need to, and I'll help you look for your aunt."

Fell, New York
November 2017
CARLY

Heather, it turned out, wasn't lying when she said she knew a lot about Fell. "My dad is a dork," she told me plainly. "His idea of a vacation is to drive to Americana Village and walk around. He's a nerd about history, so I grew up learning a lot about the history of this place. Being a dork runs in the family."

It was hours later and we were back in apartment C. I'd retrieved my things from the hotel and put them in the second bedroom. We'd ordered pizza, and night was starting to fall, even though it was only dinnertime. I was sitting on the sofa and Heather was lying on her back on the floor, still swathed in the poncho. She'd had a bicycling accident two years ago, she said, that gave her daily back pain. "One vertebra is smushing down into the one below it," was her explanation. "They say I have to have surgery, but I can't do it. I'm too neurotic." Since I'd seen the shelf of prescription pills in the bathroom when I dumped my things, I didn't ask questions.

"I'm talking about 1982," I reminded her now, dropping a crust back into the pizza box. "I don't need to know about old forts and cannons."

"Ha ha," Heather said from the floor. She had her knees bent and her feet flat, her pale hands resting on her stomach as she stared at the ceiling. "Fell doesn't have any forts or cannons. It's a strange place. Sort of morbid, like me."

"I read a few things online. This place has some unsolved murders."

"We have plenty of them. It isn't just the unsolved murders. It's the solved ones, too. I don't know the stats, but with our small population we're probably some kind of per capita murder capital of the country. Or at least of New York." She lifted a hand and I placed a pizza slice into it. "I can't explain it. It's just a weird place, that's all. Tell me about your aunt."

I told her about Viv, about her disappearance in the middle of the night from the Sun Down. I gave her my two newspaper articles.

"Hmm," Heather said, leafing through them. "No boyfriend, no drugs. 'Pretty and vivacious.' Ugh. We can find the roommate in the phone book if she's still in Fell." She handed the articles back to me and lay staring at the ceiling again. "So she worked a night shift and disappeared. You'd be amazed how many people do that—disappear as if into thin air. They leave doors open behind them, food on the counter, their shoes by the door. It doesn't seem possible, but it is."

"I know," I said. "Do you think the cops will let me look at their records?"

"I have no idea, but anything's possible with a case that old, I guess. A few of the Internet sleuths have tried to get records from the Fell PD and not gotten anywhere, but this is different. You're the victim's family."

"Are you training to be a detective?" I asked, putting my folder away.

Heather laughed. "Hardly. My anxiety couldn't handle it. No, I'm taking medieval literature. That's more my style."

"They teach medieval literature at the college in Fell?"

"It's practically *all* they teach. The school's full name is Fell College of Classical Education. Greek literature, Latin, classic art and sculpture, Russian literature, that sort of thing. It's a small, private college started a hundred years ago as a vanity project by the richest man in town. We only have three hundred students. I've never had a class that had more than ten people in it."

"Are you getting a degree?"

"Pray tell," Heather said in an amused voice, "what exactly can one do with a degree in medieval literature? Usefulness is not exactly Fell College's forte. You should apply. I like it there."

"I was taking business studies," I told her.

"*Carly.*" Her voice was shocked, like I'd said I was taking porn star classes. "You can't take business studies. You're a Fell girl. I know it already."

I handed her another slice. She was small under that poncho, but she could pack pizza away. "Town history, remember?"

"Okay," she said, lowering the slice. "The Sun Down Motel. Let me think. There was a time in the early seventies when people thought Fell would be a tourist destination, even though we don't have lakes or mountains or anything to see. There were plans for a big amusement park that would bring thousands of people a year, so businesses got built—the Sun Down, a few other motels, some ice cream shops and restaurants. Then the amusement park plan fell through and none of it happened. Most of those old businesses are gone, but the Sun Down is still there."

"It didn't go out of business?"

"It's pretty dodgy," she admitted. "Maybe it gets by taking in drug dealers and such. I wouldn't know. A few kids in high school liked to go there on weekends to drink, but my parents are prudes and never let me go."

I pulled my laptop toward me on the sofa and opened it, my mind working.

"They say it's haunted," Heather said.

"Really?" I asked in surprise.

"Well, sure," Heather said. "Isn't every hotel haunted since *The Shining*? People have probably died there, I bet."

I looked at my Google Map of Fell, with a pin in the spot where the Sun Down was. If it was built in the 1970s, then it was still relatively new in 1982. Had it been unsavory then? Had it been haunted?

Aside from Graham's stupid stories and the odd scary movie, I'd never really thought about ghosts, whether they were real. But sitting in Viv's apartment, living where she'd lived before she disappeared . . . I thought about it. I thought about ghosts and whether she was here somewhere, looking through the window or trapped in a doorway, watching us. If she'd been killed, would she come back? Would she come to this place or somewhere else? If every person who disappeared came back, wouldn't the world be full of ghosts?

I scratched my nose under my glasses and said, "Heather, are you tired?"

On the floor, she sighed. "I'm never tired. I told you, I have insomnia."

"Don't you have to study or something?"

"I've read my textbook twice. One has to read *something*."

I smiled. "Well, since one doesn't have to study, would one like to go to the Sun Down Motel with me?"

Her head appeared above the rim of the vintage coffee table. "Really?"

I shrugged. "I don't know what I'll find, but I've come this far. I may as well go, and now is as good a time as ever."

She lit up, like I'd suspected she would. "One would be delighted."

I closed my laptop. "Let's go."

Fell, New York
September 1982
VIV

She didn't *want* to stay in Fell, exactly, yet somehow she did. She worked another shift at the Sun Down, and another. Janice paid her some money, and Viv found an apartment on Greville Street that had cheap rent and a roommate named Jenny. Jenny was a night shift nurse at a local nursing home, working the same hours as Viv. She was tired, single after a bad breakup, and not in the least curious. The two girls came and went, slept all day and worked all night.

"I don't get it," Jenny said one evening. She was preparing to iron a blouse, fiddling with the knobs on the iron as it heated up. "You were on your way to New York City. Why didn't you go?"

Viv turned the page of the *People* magazine she was reading, leaning against the kitchen counter. "That's just something I told my mother," she said. "I didn't really want to go. I just wanted to leave home."

"I get that," Jenny said. She had ash blond hair, cut in feathered layers like Heather Locklear. She licked the pad of her finger and lightly touched the face of the iron to see if it was hot enough yet. "But this is Fell. No one wants to be here. I mean, come on. People leave."

"You haven't left," Viv pointed out.

"Only because this job is good. But trust me, I'm going." She licked her finger again and touched the iron. This time there was a sizzling sound and she jerked her finger away. "I'm going to meet a rich, gorgeous guy and marry him the first chance I get. The women's libbers say it's wrong, but I still think it's the best thing a girl can do."

"That's it?" Viv asked her. "Get married?"

"Why not?" Jenny shrugged and tugged the blouse onto the ironing board, started to work on it.

Viv didn't want to get married. She'd dated boys, made out with them. She'd even let Matthew Reardon put his hand down her pants. But she'd only done that because they were on their third date, and he expected it. His fingers smelled like cigarettes, and she hadn't liked it much. Her entire life in Illinois had been about doing what other people expected, never what she actually wanted.

"Don't you want to do something with your life? Something big?" she asked Jenny.

Jenny didn't look impressed. "If you wanted to do something big, you should have gone to New York, don't you think?"

Maybe. It was stupid to think you had some kind of destiny in life. It was extra stupid to think that Fell, New York, was somewhere you wanted to be. But Grisham belonged to Viv's family, and New York City belonged to everyone else. Fell, in its shadowy way, was hers.

She bought a car, a used Cavalier, the first car she'd ever owned herself. She took two hundred dollars out of her bank account to buy it, and she didn't feel the panic she thought she would.

There was a movie theater downtown, a hole in the wall called the Royal that showed second-run movies for a dollar. Viv went to the early show before her shift sometimes, sitting in the half-empty theater. She watched *E.T.* and *An Officer and a Gentleman* and, on one memorable night, *Poltergeist*. She ate sandwiches from the Famous Fell Deli, down the street from the theater, and sometimes she got a milkshake from the Milkshake Palace, around the corner, for fifty cents. She cut her hair, which she'd worn long like all of the other girls in Grisham. *Good girls don't have short hair*, her mother always said. Viv cut her light brown hair to shoulder length and teased the top and the sides with hair spray.

She called her mother, who was furious even though Viv hadn't ended up in the den of sin that was New York City. "I'm not sending you money," her mother told her. "You'll just spend it on drugs or something. I guess you'll see what it's like to be a grown-up now. Why can't you be like Debby?"

Debby, Viv's little sister, the good daughter. At eighteen, Debby wanted to be a teacher; she wanted to stay in Grisham, work in Grisham, get married in Grisham, and most likely die in Grisham. She looked at Viv's angry restlessness as something alien. "I'm working extra shifts at the ice cream shop and saving for college," Debby said when she got on the phone. "I think you're crazy."

"You can be as perfect as you want," Viv told her. "Dad still isn't coming back. And he still doesn't care."

"That's mean," Debby said. "He's going to call. He is."

"No, he isn't," Viv told her. "He has a new wife, and his new wife is going to have new kids. I'm not waiting around for life to go back to the way it was, and neither should you."

Debby said something else, but Viv didn't hear it. She took the phone from her ear and made herself hang up, listening to the click it made in the cradle as it disconnected.

The world was different at night. Not just dark, not just quiet, but *different*. Sounds and smells were different. Number Six Road had an eerie light, greenish under the empty expanse of sky. Viv's body got cold, then damp with unpleasant sweat; she was hungry, then queasy. She wasn't tired after the first few nights, but there were times she felt like there was sand under her eyelids, blurring her vision as her temples pounded. Three o'clock in the morning was the worst time, almost delirious, when she could half believe anything could happen—ghosts, elves, time travel, every *Twilight Zone* episode she'd ever seen.

And she sort of liked it.

Night people were not the same as day people. The good people of Fell, whoever they were, were sound asleep at three a.m. Those people never saw the people Viv saw: the cheating couples having affairs, the truckers strung out on whatever they took to stay awake, the women with blackened eyes who checked out at five a.m. to futilely go home again. These weren't people suburban Viv Delaney would ever have seen in a hundred years. They weren't people she would ever have talked to. There was an edge to them, a hard collision with life, that she hadn't known was possible in her soft cocoon. It wasn't romantic, but something about it drew her. It fascinated her. She didn't want to look away.

And it was in the depths of night that the Sun Down itself seemed alive. The candy machine made a deep whirring noise in the middle of the night, and the ice machine next to it clattered from time to time like someone was shaking it. The leaves swirled in the pool, which was empty of water and fenced in, even though it was the last month of summer. The pipes in the walls groaned, and when one of the buttons on the phone in front of her lit up—indicating someone in one of the rooms was making a call—it made a featherlight *click* sound, audible only in the perfect, silent hush of night.

The smell of cigarette smoke came back again and again when she was in the front office. Always the sting of fresh smoke, never old. At first she thought it must be coming through the vents from one of the rooms, so she took a folding chair and moved it around the room, standing on it beneath each vent so she could close her eyes and inhale. Nothing.

She stood next to the office door for an hour one night, staying still, nostrils flaring, waiting for the smoke to come. When it did she rotated, left then right, trying to figure out the direction it came from. She had gotten nowhere when the front desk phone rang and interrupted her, the sound shrill in the night air.

She picked up the phone, her voice almost cracking with disuse. "Sun Down Motel, can I help you?"

Nothing. Just the faint sound of breathing.

She hung up and stared at the phone for a minute. She'd had a similar call before, and she wasn't quite sure what to do about it. Who called a motel in the middle of the night and breathed into the phone?

The next night found her standing in front of the office door again, waiting for the smoke. If someone had asked her in that moment, she could not have told them what she was looking for. A man? A malfunction in the duct system? An illusion in her own mind? It wasn't clear, but the smoke bothered her. It was eerie, but it also made her feel less alone. If she had to put it into words, perhaps she'd say that she wanted to know who was keeping her company.

She was interrupted that night by someone actually coming through the office door—a real person, one not smoking a cigarette. He was a trucker getting a room to catch a few hours' sleep before continuing south. Viv took his thirty dollars and he inked his name into the guest book. After him came another man, also solo, wearing a suit and trench coat, carrying a suitcase and a briefcase. He, too, paid thirty dollars and wrote his name in the guest book: Michael Ennis. He might stay an extra night, he explained, because he was waiting for a phone call to tell him where to travel next, and he might not get it tomorrow.

"Sounds exciting," Viv said absently as she opened the key drawer and took out the key to room 211. She was putting him several doors away from the trucker; she always gave people their space. Night people didn't like to have neighbors too close.

He didn't reply, so she raised her gaze and saw him looking at her. His look was calm and polite, but it was fixed on her nonetheless. "Not really," he said, in reply to her comment. "I'm a salesman. I go where my bosses tell me to go."

She nodded and gave him the key. She did not ask what he sold, because it was none of her business. When he left, she could not have said what he looked like.

The next night, she tried a different tactic: She stood outside the office door, her back to the wall, and waited for the smell of smoke. She suspected it came from outside the door now, not through the vents, so she moved closer to the supposed source. It was a beautiful night, silent and warm, the breeze just enough to lift her hair from her neck and fan her sweaty cheeks.

It took less than twenty minutes this time: The tang of fresh cigarette smoke came to her nostrils. Jackpot. She shuffled down the walkway, following it slowly away from the direction of the rooms and around the other side of the building, toward the empty pool. She lost the smell twice and stood still both times, waiting for it to come back. Silently tracking her prey.

She edged out toward the drained and emptied pool, stopping next to the fence that had been around it all summer for reasons unknown. She looked around in the dark, seeing nothing and no one. Maddeningly, the smell came and went, as if whoever created it was moving. "Hello?" she said into the blackness, the concrete and the empty pool and the trees beyond, the deserted highway far to her left past the parking lot. "Hello?"

There was no answer, but the hair prickled on the back of her neck. Her throat went tight, and she had a moment of panic, hard and nauseating. She hooked her fingers through the pool's chain-link fence to hold on and closed her eyes until it passed.

She smelled smoke, and someone walked past her, behind her back, in five evenly paced steps. A man's heavy footsteps. And then there was silence again.

Her breath was frozen, her hands cold. That had been someone, *something*. Something real, but not a real person. The steps had started and stopped, like a figure crossing an open doorway.

Viv had heard ghost stories. Everyone has. But she had never thought she'd be standing holding a chain-link fence, trying not to vomit in fear as her knuckles went white and something *other* crossed behind her back. It was crazy. It was the kind of story you told years later while your listeners rolled their eyes, because they had no idea how the terror felt on the back of your neck.

Behind Viv's shoulder, the motel sign went dark.

The garish light vanished, she heard a sad *zap* as the bulbs gave up, and she turned to see the sign dark, the words SUN DOWN no longer lit up, the words VACANCY. CABLE TV! flickering out beneath them. She walked toward the sign, unthinking, a hard beat of panic in her chest. She had no idea where the switch to the sign was, whether someone could turn it off. She had never had to turn the sign on or off in her weeks here—the evening clerk always turned it on, and the morning clerk always turned it off. The loss of its bright, ugly light was like an alarm going off up her spine.

She turned the corner, opening up her view of the interior of the motel's L. She stopped and cried out, because the lights were going out.

At the end of the short leg of the L—room 130 and the one above it, room 230—the lights on the walkway in front blinked out. Then the lights in front of rooms 129 and 229, and on, and on. As if someone were flicking out a row of switches one by one, leaving the entire motel in darkness.

Viv stood frozen, unable to do anything but watch as the Sun Down Motel went dark. The last lights to go out were the office, closest to her at the end of the long row of the L, followed by the neon sign that said OFFICE. And then she was standing in front of a black hole on the edge of the road, without a sound or a shuffle of feet, without another soul for miles.

She could hear her breath sawing in and out of her throat. *What the hell is going on?* Her mind didn't go to mundane explanations, like an electrical malfunction or even a blackout; it was three o'clock in the morning, the sodium lights on Number Six Road were still lit, and she'd just heard the smoking man's footsteps behind her. No, this was no malfunction, and something told her it was just starting.

And now a muted clicking sound came from the motel. *Click, click.* Viv peered through the dark to see one of the motel doors drift open, then another. The doors were opening on their own, each revealing a strip of deeper darkness of the room inside, as if inviting her. *Come in to this one. This one. This one . . .*

Her panicked gaze went to her car. She could get in, go to the nearest pay phone. Call—who? The police, maybe. Or go to an all-night diner and sit there until whatever this was went away. The problem was that her purse, with her keys in it, was in the office.

The wind was soft and cool in her hair, making her shiver. The doors had finished clicking open and were quiet. There was not a single sound from Number Six Road behind her.

Do it. She could. Go to the office door, push it open. Her purse was next to the chair behind the reception desk. Four steps into the office, swoop down and grab the purse, then turn and leave.

She made her feet move. Her sneakers shuffled against the gravel again, and she found herself lifting her feet to move more quietly. As if whatever it was could be fooled into thinking she wasn't coming. As if whatever it was couldn't see her already.

Still, she found herself running toward the door, trying to keep her steps light. *In and out. Just in and out. I can do it quick and—*

Her foot hit the step to the walkway, and something banged overhead. One of the room doors, banging open. Viv jumped and made a sound in her throat as footsteps pounded the walk above her, short and staccato, a full stomping run. The steps pounded down to the bottom of the L, then turned the corner. A voice rang out into the night air—a child's. *I want to go in the pool!*

Viv twisted the knob to the office door and ducked into the darkness. She stumbled through the office, her breath in whooping gasps, her hands flailing for her purse, her keys. Her eyes stung, and she realized it was because the smell of smoke was so strong, as if someone had been smoking in here for hours.

She had just found her purse in the dark, her hands clutching the bulge of dark purple fake leather, when she heard the voice. A man's voice, crying out from the other side of the desk.

For God's sake, call an ambulance! the voice said, as close as if the man was standing there. *Someone call an ambulance!*

Viv dropped her purse, the keys flying out and landing on the floor in a tinkle of metal. She gasped another breath, snatching them up and rising to run to the door. She ran to her Cavalier and wrenched open the driver's door, launching herself inside. She threw her purse onto the passenger seat, got behind the wheel, and slammed the door.

The motel in front of her windshield was still dark as she turned the key and pumped the gas, her foot hitting the floorboard. Nothing happened; the car didn't start. She pumped the gas and cranked the key again, a sound of panic in her throat, tears tracking down her cheeks, but still nothing.

She raised her gaze as a figure stepped in front of the car. It was a woman. She was young, thirty maybe, and had dark blond curly hair pulled back from her face and falling down her collarbones, dark eyes, a face of perfect oval. In the shock of the moment, Viv saw everything clearly: the woman's slim shoulders, her long-sleeved dress in a pattern of large, dark purple flowers, the belt tied in a bow at her waist. She was staring through the windshield at Viv, and her eyes . . . her eyes . . .

Viv opened her mouth to scream, then froze. No sound came out. She inhaled a breath, fixed for a long moment in the woman's gaze.

The woman wasn't real, and yet—Viv saw her. Looked at her. And the woman looked back, her eyes blazing with some kind of ungodly emotion that made Viv want to scream and weep and throw up all at once.

She gripped the steering wheel, feeling her gorge rise.

There was a *bang* as the woman's palms slammed the hood of the car—a real sound, hard and violent. The woman stood with her arms braced, staring through the windshield at Viv. Her mouth moved. Viv could hear no sound, or perhaps there was none. But it wasn't hard to translate the single word.

Run.

Viv made a strangled sound and jerked the key again. The engine didn't turn. She twisted the key and stomped the pedal, tears streaming down her face as a frustrated scream came out of her mouth. When she dared to look up again the woman was gone, but the motel was still dark, the night around her even darker.

The engine was flooded. The car wouldn't start. She had nowhere to go.

Viv pushed down the locks on her doors and crawled into the back seat, curling into as small a ball as she could, crouching behind the passenger seat so she couldn't see through the windshield anymore. Like someone escaping the line of fire. She stayed there for a long time.

When the lights went on again and the sign lit up, she was still weeping.

Fell, New York
November 2017
CARLY

After all of my research, I wasn't sure what I expected at the Sun Down. I'd seen an image of it on Google Earth, and it looked like an everyday roadside place: a strip of rooms, a sign. I knew full well that my family history, and my odd fixation, gave it a halo of importance in my mind. But to anyone else, I figured the Sun Down would be mundane.

The Sun Down was not mundane.

I stepped out onto the gravel lot and looked around. The building was shaped like an L, with doors facing an open-air walkway. It was full dark now, and the blue and yellow sign blinked down on us with its shrill message about cable TV and vacancy. There was a single car in the lot, an old Tercel parked in the shadows of the far corner. There were no other cars parked in front of the motel's doorways, no sign of anyone at all.

Heather got out of the passenger side and we stood in a breath of silence. No traffic passed on the road behind us. Beyond the motel were only trees and darkness with a half-moon high in the sky. I zipped the collar of my coat up and stared at the building, transfixed, taking in the dim lights on the walkway, the uneven patterns they made, the blank reflections on the motel windows. For a place that was built for people to come to, it had an air so deserted and quiet I felt for a minute like I was somewhere unearthly, like a graveyard or an Icelandic landscape.

Heather seemed to feel the same, because she stood next to me in silence. She had left the poncho behind and was now swathed in a black puffy coat, practically a parka. I had the idea that Heather was perpetually cold.

"Not creepy," my roommate finally said, her voice low in the night air. "Not creepy at all."

My gaze traveled to the OFFICE sign, which was lit up. In theory, someone must be inside, but I found I didn't really want to know. "Let's look around," I said instead.

We circled the building, looking at the walkways and the closed doors. The walkways were dated, and the doors still had knobs with keyholes; it was practically the same place my aunt had seen thirty-five years ago. Around the other side of the building we found an empty pool, surrounded by a dilapidated chain-link fence. It was darker here, but even without the extra light I could see that the pool hadn't just been closed for the season. The edges of the concrete were chipped and cracked, and the entire pool was filled with dirt and old leaves. The pool had closed years, maybe decades, ago and was never going to open again.

I made myself think past the creep factor, think past the clammy cold in my spine, and remember my aunt Viv. *If you were going to disappear from this place, where would you go?*

The most obvious answer was the road. Viv had left her car behind, but someone could have shoved her into their car and driven away. But that opened up a new list of questions. How had the person done it? Had they knocked her unconscious? The newspaper reports didn't mention any blood or sign of a struggle. Had the person lured Viv out of the front office somehow? Begged for emergency help, perhaps, or pretended to need her for something? Had the person planned to take Viv specifically, or was it done on the spur of the moment?

I walked away from the pool and started to circle back around the front of the motel. I wished now I'd come in daylight, so I could see the landscape better. Maybe in daylight the motel wouldn't loom quite so weird and sinister.

I was lucky, actually, that the Sun Down was still almost exactly as it was in 1982. If it had been bulldozed and replaced with a strip of big-box stores, I wouldn't be able to map out where Viv could have gone. What if she hadn't left by car? Could she have run somewhere on foot?

"Heather," I said, "do you remember what's around here? Say, if someone were walking?"

"Oh, God, let me think," Heather said, following my footsteps. "I think it's just woods and maybe farmland over that way, behind the motel. You'd have to go miles before you hit anything."

"What about either way up the road?"

"You'd hit a gas station that way," Heather said, pointing along Number Six Road in the direction out of Fell, "but again it's a mile. And I don't know if it was there in 1982. That way"—she pointed in the direction of Fell, the road we'd just driven up to get here—"there's a turnoff toward Coopersville two miles up, and past that are a few old houses and a Value Mart before you hit the edge of town."

"I wonder if I can find a 1982 map," I said.

"Probably in the city library," Heather agreed. "Someone died in that pool, by the way."

I turned and looked at her. "What?"

"Seriously, Carly." Her pale cheeks were reddened by the cold breeze, her blond hair tousling around its bobby pin. "I mean, come *on*. I'd bet a thousand dollars. Someone died, and they emptied it and closed it off and no one ever went there again."

I pressed my lips together. "Maybe they closed it because they don't have enough customers to keep opening it," I said. "Like, none."

"Duh," Heather said, "they have no customers because someone died in the pool."

I opened my mouth to answer her, but a voice called out, "Hey there! Can I help you?"

We turned and saw a man standing in front of the office. He was watching us, though he had not come off the walkway to get any closer. With the light from the sign over his shoulder, we could only see that he was tall, beefy, and somewhat young.

"Sorry!" I called out to him. "We're just looking around."

The man shifted his weight uneasily. "That isn't a good idea," he said. "No one is supposed to go near the old pool area."

"Okay," I said, trying to sound agreeable. I started toward him, Heather following behind me.

When we got closer, I could see he was about thirty, with dark hair cut close to his scalp. He was wearing a white shirt and a blue polyester uniform vest with dark dress pants. The vest had the words *Sun Down Motel* in yellow over the left breast. "Do you need a room?" he asked us.

"No," I said. "Sorry, we're just curious."

That seemed to confuse him. "About what?"

"I like old motels," I said, inspired. "You know, these midcentury ones. I think they're neat. It's sort of a hobby of mine."

We stepped onto the walkway. The man's gaze moved between me and Heather. "I've never heard of anyone with a hobby like that," he said.

I looked at his uniform vest and felt my fascination ramping up. This was the place where Viv had worked for months before she disappeared. She'd likely stood in this exact spot. Had the vests been the same in 1982? I had the feeling of Viv nearby, looking over my shoulder, like I'd had in apartment C. I was so close, with just the thin shimmer of time between me and her. In Fell, that shimmer seemed to barely exist. "Can I see the office?" I asked him.

He looked even more confused, but Heather gave him a polite smile, and he shrugged. "I suppose."

The office was dated, the walls dull brown, the reception desk large and heavy. I stared in shocked awe at the big landline telephone with its plastic buttons for various lines, the leather book with handwritten guest entries, the worn office chair, the coat hook in the corner, even the space heater next to the desk that looked like a fire hazard with its yellowed cord. "Jesus. What is it with this place?" I asked myself in a murmur.

"What was that?" the man said.

"Nothing, sorry." I tried giving him a smile. "Have you worked here long?"

"A few months, I guess." Now the man's look had turned a little sullen and curiously blank, as if he was rapidly becoming uninterested in us.

"Do you like it?" Heather asked.

"Not really." He looked around, like someone might hear. "It's okay, I guess," he amended. "We don't get very many customers."

I tried to get more information from him, but it got harder and harder. His name was Oliver. Yes, it was very quiet out here. No, he had no idea how old the motel was. No, he didn't think they'd ever renovated it, but he didn't really know. Heather wandered to the office door, where she looked out the little window at the world outside while we talked.

By the time I'd given up on Oliver and we were driving back to town, the fascination and excitement had drained out of me, leaving only frustration. "I don't know what I'm doing," I admitted to Heather. "I mean, what did I think I would learn, going there, standing in that office? How did I think that would help me?"

"You wanted to feel closer to her," Heather said, as if the answer were simple. "You wanted to see what her life was like."

"Well, I guess I accomplished that, since nothing at that motel has changed since 1982."

We were quiet for a minute, the dark road going by outside our window. Heather bit her lip.

"What?" I said.

"I'm not sure I should show you."

"Well, now you have to show me. What is it?"

She hesitated, then took a piece of paper from her pocket and un-folded it.

Help wanted. Night shift desk clerk. Start immediately. Please inquire. A phone number.

"No way," I said, staring at it in disbelief. "No freaking way. They're hiring for my aunt's actual *shift*?"

"I know, it's weird," Heather said.

"Weird doesn't even describe it." I sighed, running a hand over my ponytail. "Why am I actually tempted to apply? Am I insane?"

"It would be creepy, right? But it would also be kind of cool."

It was exactly what I was thinking. Spend my nights at the Sun Down? I was the kind of girl who would spend the night in a supposedly haunted house, just to see what would happen. That sounded like my ideal vaca-tion. "Maybe they won't hire me."

"Um, I don't think they're exactly overrun with options."

My heart was beating faster. Excitement, or fear? "We could stay in touch through the night. Do regular check-ins."

"You can bring my Mace with you. I have extra."

"Heather, my aunt vanished from that same spot. On the night shift."

"Sure, but that was thirty-five years ago. Do you think whoever did it is still hanging around? He might not still be alive, and if he is, he's old now."

"I'm not supposed to be here very long. Yet I think I want to do this. I want to stay. Why?"

"Because you're a Fell girl," Heather said with a nod. "I called it when I met you."

"This place is dark."

"Some of us like the dark. It's what we know."

I made a turn next to an old theater called the Royal, which had boarded-up windows. The marquee still advertised a showing of *You've Got Mail*. "I could work a few shifts, find what there is to find, and bail," I said. "I can do it for a few nights, right? Do whatever Viv did. See things through her eyes."

"You've come this far," she said. "Are you going to turn around now and go back to college? It doesn't seem right, leaving your aunt in the lurch like that."

Viv. Whatever I was afraid of, Viv had gone through worse. She'd gone through something awful, something terrifying, and in all this time, no one had ever solved it. No one had even found her body. I was the only one to do it. To do anything.

Which meant I needed to work nights at the Sun Down Motel.

"Okay," I said. "I'll do it. What could possibly go wrong?"

Fell, New York
September 1982
VIV

A week after the night the motel went dark, Viv had to call the police for the first time in her career at the Sun Down.

She'd thought about quitting after that terrible night. She'd thought of packing her bags and going back to Illinois. But what would she say when she got there? *I saw a ghost, so I ran home?*

She was twenty years old. *What would you do if you ever saw real trouble?* her mother had said. Going back to her old bedroom, to working at the popcorn stand at the drive-in, was out of the question.

Besides, part of her wondered who the woman in the flowered dress was. Something about the woman's anger, her obvious anguish, spoke to her.

So she went back to work at the Sun Down.

The night of the police, she brought a bologna sandwich with her to work—Wonder Bread, bologna, one Kraft single, a dab of mustard. The best meal you could have in the middle of the night when you made three dollars per hour. It usually sufficed just fine, but tonight the bologna didn't cut it. She found herself thinking about the candy machine.

The candy machine was behind a door marked AMENITIES, on the first level next to room 104, in a tiny room it shared with the ice machine. The candy machine worked, and it had candy in it; Viv figured it must be refilled during the daylight hours. It carried Snickers, and they were twenty cents, and Viv had two dimes in her pocket.

She took her jacket from the hook and put it on over her uniform vest. Pulling the zipper up, she stepped outside the office and turned the corner. The Sun Down actually had a few guests tonight, so she wasn't entirely alone. There was a couple on their way to visit family in North Carolina; there was a young guy who looked dead on his feet, as if he'd been driving for days. There was a man who had taken a room alone with no luggage.

Still, she felt the low-level fear she always felt when she turned the corner and saw the long leg of the L stretching away from her, the rows of doors, the feeble beams from the overhead lightbulbs, some of them burned out like broken teeth. Her spine tightened and she remembered the feeling of the sign going out, the buzzing blinking into silence, the doors opening one by one. The footsteps, the voices, the smoke. And the woman.

Run.

She looked around the parking lot, at the building. She saw no sign of the woman now, but she imagined she could feel her. Maybe it was nothing; she didn't know. *I can't leave her*, she thought.

Viv had bought a spiral notebook and a pen at a stationery store after that night. At first she just thought about it, glancing at the book every once in a while, but eventually she started writing. She wrote down what had happened that night, what the woman looked like, what the voices had said. It got the thoughts out of her own head, made them real. The notebook became her only company on the long nights—that and a used copy of *The Hotel New Hampshire*, which she doggedly kept reading though she didn't fully understand it.

She was thinking vaguely of the novel, of whether she'd take it out of her purse and try again, as she entered the AMENITIES room for her Snickers bar. Summer had turned into early fall, the heat falling away, the nights getting cooler and breezier. She sidled into the tiny room, which was big enough for only one person, and contemplated the candy machine.

Outside, a new-looking Thunderbird pulled into the parking lot. A woman got out, putting her keys in her purse. Viv peeked around the door and watched her. The woman was in her late twenties, wearing pale blue jeans and a white blouse with small red polka dots on it. A silver belt and ankle boots completed the outfit. Her dark hair was cut short and teased, sprayed back from her temples and away from her forehead. She had blue eyes under dark slashes of brows and a curl to her lip that was sensual and full of attitude. She looked like Pat Benatar's not-so-cool sister—pretty and fashionable, rebellious but not quite rock-'n'-roll.

She didn't head for the motel office to check in but instead walked to the door to room 121, the room Viv had given the man with no luggage.

Viv ducked behind the door and watched. The man in 121, she recalled, wasn't bad-looking, but he was near forty. What was this girl doing meeting him at a motel? The hookers who came to the Sun Down were washed-out women with stringy hair and tight clothes, who spent a few hours in a room and paid in crumpled fives and tens. This woman looked nothing like that. She looked like she could have come from Viv's suburb in Grisham. Viv watched as the woman knocked once on the door of room 121. The door was opened by the man Viv had checked in; he had taken off his coat and was wearing dress pants and a shirt unbuttoned at the throat, his shoes off. He smiled at the woman. "Helen," he said.

The woman cocked her hip, giving the man a pose, though her smile was warm. "Robert."

Robert held out his hand. "Come in."

Behind Viv, the ice machine made a whirring noise and kicked to life, making Viv jump. She ducked back into the AMENITIES room before they could see her looking. She scrambled for her two dimes and shoved them into the candy machine, and was just digging behind the machine's flap for her Snickers bar when the door swung shut and she was suddenly in the dark.

Viv froze. She could see absolutely nothing—she tried waving her hand in front of her face but saw only blackness. She waved her arms in front of her, touching the front of the candy machine, feeling her way along it. The ice machine continued to click and whirr behind her like it was speaking an ancient language, and ice cubes clicked into its plastic container with a chattering sound. Viv felt frantically for a light switch, her breath in her throat.

There was no light switch, just blank wall. She found the outline of the door beneath her fingertips and followed it to the doorknob, which she turned and pushed. A glimpse of parking lot, a rush of sweet cold air—and the door swung closed again.

"Hey," Viv said aloud, her voice cracking. Then: "Hey," a little bit louder. She found the doorknob again, grasped it. It wouldn't turn.

The ice machine shut off abruptly, and now all she could hear was her own breath sawing in and out of her lungs. "Hey," she said again, louder, though she didn't know who she was talking to. She banged the side of her fist on the door once, wondering if anyone in any of the rooms would hear her. If they did, would they bother to come out?

She banged again and was shoved backward by a force against her chest. She stumbled, the hard bone of her shoulder blade hitting the edge of the candy machine, pain flaring upward. She flung her hands back and tried to scrabble for purchase.

Run, a voice said, a breath of wind, a hiss of air.

The door flung open, so hard it hit the wall behind it with a bang. Then it hung limply, creaking in the September wind.

Viv bolted out of the door and into the parking lot. She was gasping for breath, but one thing rang around and around in her mind, like an alarm going off without stopping: *Those were hands. Those were HANDS.* Two hands, two palms, their distinct shape against her rib cage as they shoved her. Viv stumbled, put her hands on her knees, trying not to throw up with fear.

That was when, through the panicked ringing in her ears, she finally heard the shouting.

The office was quiet and tidy, just as she'd left it. She came through the door on numb feet and dropped into the chair behind the desk, her hands shaking, looking for something Janice had pointed out on her first night.

She found it tacked to the wall next to the desk: a piece of paper labeled *FELL POLICE DEPT. In case anyone gets rowdy*, Janice had told her. *They know who we are.* Viv picked up the office phone.

There was no dial tone on the other end of the line. Instead, there was a man's voice. "Helen, just tell me what's going on."

Viv went still.

"I have no idea." The woman's reply was calm, her voice low and sexy as whiskey. "Someone is arguing in the parking lot. Two men. They look like truckers. The night shift girl said she'd call the police."

That was me, Viv thought. *I said that.*

"How late will you be?" the man said.

"I have no idea," Helen replied. "I could be all night."

Viv went very still, trying not to breathe and listening. *I have no idea how, but I'm hearing the phone line from room 121.*

Then she thought, *I should hang up.*

"I just want you home safe," the man said. "I'm waiting for you. I'll stay up."

"You know that isn't a good idea," Helen said, her voice tired. "I'll call you when I'm free, okay?"

Viv listened as they said a few more words, then hung up. She felt a little bit sick. *I should have hung up*, she thought. *Why didn't I hang up?* She pictured herself calling the man back—though she didn't have a phone number—and saying, *Your wife is lying to you!*

But of course she wouldn't do that.

Instead she toggled the phone a few times to make sure the line was clear, then dialed the number for the Fell Police Department.

A bored, gravelly male voice answered. "Fell PD."

"Hi," Viv said. "I, um, I work at the Sun Down Motel. At reception."

"Yeah."

"There's a fight going on in our parking lot. Two truckers. They're, um, fighting."

This didn't impress him. "They armed?"

"I don't think so?" she said, hating how she sounded like a stupid girl, which of course he assumed she was. She thought of the woman with the whiskey voice, how effortlessly dignified she was, and she made an effort to change her tone, sound more worldly. "I didn't see any weapons. But they're having a fistfight and punching each other right now."

"'Kay," the man said. "Hold tight. Chances are they'll sort it out themselves, but we'll send someone anyway."

Ten minutes later, the fight was still happening. The guests had stayed in their rooms and Viv was standing by the office door, poking her head out and biting the hangnail on her thumb. Her shoulder throbbed. She caught a faint whiff of cigarette smoke. *Not now*, she pleaded silently to the smoking man, *Not now*.

A police cruiser pulled into the parking lot, silent, cherry lights off. It pulled up in front of the two trucks that were parked in the lot, next to the fighting men, and a cop got out. Viv breathed a sigh of relief, and then she realized the cop was too small, too slight, the hair tied up at the back of her neck. It was a woman.

She took another step out onto the walkway to see more closely. A woman cop? She'd never seen one except on *Cagney & Lacey*.

But this cop was real. Unlike Cagney and Lacey she was wearing a uniform, dark blue polyester with a cap on her head. Her belt was heavy with a gun holster, a nightstick, and a radio, but it fit her hips snugly and she walked with a swagger that looked powerful and confident. As Viv watched, she walked straight to the fighting truckers and pulled one man off the other, breaking them up.

The truckers obeyed. They looked angry and one spit on the ground next to the cop's feet, but they stopped fighting and stood still as the cop spoke to them. Viv watched her take out a notebook and pen and start writing down information, like she wasn't at least fifty pounds lighter than each man.

When the cop finished writing, she took the radio from her belt and talked into it. Both truckers retreated to their trucks. The one who had spit turned and added a second gob, aiming it so it hit close to the cop's heel without hitting her. The cop didn't seem to notice, or care.

She turned and saw Viv standing at the corner of the office. Caught gawking, Viv raised a hand in a shy hello. The cop nodded and started in her direction as Viv ducked back into the office.

"Crazy night," the cop said as she followed Viv through the office door. Up close, Viv could see that the cop wasn't more than thirty, with dark brown hair tied neatly back under her cap. She wasn't precisely pretty, but she had high cheekbones, dark brown eyes, and a tired air of complete confidence. Viv retreated behind the desk and touched her teased hair, suddenly self-conscious about her white blouse on its third wear and her ugly uniform vest.

"Crazy," Viv said, thinking, *You have no idea. No idea at all.* She pressed her shaking hands together and hid them under the desk. She could still feel the imprint of the two palms on her chest, shoving her backward. She worked hard to take a deep breath.

The cop yanked a chair from its spot against the wall next to the rack of ancient and wilted tourist brochures and plopped down in it, pulling out her notebook and crossing her legs. "It says here it was called in by one Vivian Delaney. Is that you?"

"Yes, ma'am," Viv said.

The cop gave her an amused look. "I'm no more a ma'am than you are, honey. My name is Alma Trent. Officer Trent. Okay?"

"Yes, okay, Officer Trent," Viv said. Why was it so comforting to have a cop around? It was an instinctive thing. *She can't protect you from ghosts,* Viv reminded herself. *No one can.*

Officer Trent tilted her head a degree, studying Viv. "How old are you, anyway?"

"Twenty."

"Uh-huh," Alma Trent said. She had a no-bones way of speaking, but her eyes weren't unkind. Without knowing she was doing it, Viv glanced and saw she wore no wedding ring. "You from around here?" the cop asked.

"Huh?" Stupid, she sounded so stupid.

"Here." The cop made a circle with her index finger. "Around here. Are you from it?"

"No, ma'am. Officer Trent. I'm from Illinois." Viv closed her eyes. "I'm sorry I sound like this. It's been a long night. I've never talked to a policeman—woman—before."

"That's a nice sort of person to be," Officer Trent said, again not unkindly. "The kind who has never talked to the police, I mean. You're the night girl, I take it?"

This time, she sounded slightly less idiotic. "Yes."

"On shift every night?"

"Yes, though I get one night a week off."

"Worked here long?" The questions were rapid-fire, probably to help Viv keep her thoughts straight. It was working.

"Four weeks," Viv said, and then she realized she couldn't remember the last time she'd looked at a calendar, taken note of what day it was. "Five, maybe."

"You called us in before?"

"No."

"First time, then." It was conversational, but Officer Trent's gaze didn't leave Viv. "No disturbances until now?"

"No." Unless you counted the lights going out, the ghosts coming out, and whatever had been lurking in the AMENITIES room. *Run.* Viv cleared her throat and tried not to shudder. "It's usually quiet here."

"Yeah, I'll bet," the cop said. "We sometimes get calls about hookers and dealers out here. You see anything like that?"

Was she supposed to tell on her employer? What if she got fired? She saw hookers and dealers every day; if Alma Trent didn't know that, she wasn't a very good cop. "I don't know," Viv said. "It kind of seems like none of my business."

"A philosopher, I see," Officer Trent said. "You'll fit right in at the Sun Down." She gave Viv a smile and leaned back in her chair. "I work nights, so it's usually me who gets the call. Drug deals, drunk and disorderly, fights, domestics, runaway teenagers. That's the kind of thing that happens out here. If you've been here five weeks, I think you have the idea."

Viv sat up in her chair. For a second, the ghosts were forgotten. "You work nights? Do you like it?"

Alma shrugged. "I'm the only woman at the station, so they put me on nights and they won't take me off," she said matter-of-factly. "They probably want me to quit, but I haven't yet. Turns out I sort of like the night shift. To tell the truth, I barely remember what daytime looks like, and I don't miss it."

"I'm barely even tired anymore," Viv said.

Alma nodded. "They say it's bad for you, but then again, everything's bad for you. Soda, cigarettes, you name it. If you don't have a body like Olivia Newton-John's, then you're doing something wrong. Personally, I don't buy it. I think it's instructive to be awake in the middle of the night every once in a while. To really see what you're missing while you're usually sleeping."

"Not everything you see is good," Viv said.

"No, definitely not." Alma smiled. "You seem like a nice girl. The Sun Down is a little rough for you, isn't it?"

"The people aren't so bad." *The living ones, anyway.* She chose her words carefully. She didn't even know Officer Trent, but it felt good to talk to someone, even for a few minutes. "I left home. I just wanted to be alone for a while, I guess."

"Fell is a good place for that." Alma stood up.

She had walked most of the way to the office door when Viv said, "Who died in the pool?"

Alma stopped, turned. Her mouth was set in a line. "What?"

Viv took a breath, smelled smoke again. *For God's sake, call an ambulance!* The voice had been right here in this room, not two feet away. Alma Trent had to know. "Someone died in the pool, right? A kid."

"Where did you hear that?" Alma's voice was sharp, cautious.

Viv made herself shrug. "A rumor."

There was a long beat of silence as Alma looked at her. Then she said, "You shouldn't believe every rumor you hear. But yes, a boy died in the pool two years ago. Hit his head on the side of the pool, he went unconscious, and he never woke up. But I don't know how you could have heard that, since Janice never talks about it and Henry can't have told you."

"Henry?" Viv asked.

"The man who worked here at the time," Alma said. "He was the one who called it in. He had a heart attack six months later." She pointed to Viv. "He was sitting in that very chair."

Viv was silent. She thought she might be sick.

"Someday you're going to tell me how you knew that," Officer Trent said. "Those aren't the worst things that have happened here. But I think you guessed that, too." She nodded. "Have a nice night, Vivian Delaney. Call me if you need me again."

Fell, New York
November 2017
CARLY

They hired me. There probably weren't very many other applicants; maybe there weren't any at all. But I found myself at eleven o'clock at night four days later, sitting in the Sun Down's office with a miserable man named Chris, learning the job of night clerk. Chris was about fifty, and he said he was the son of the motel's original owners. He wore a blue plaid flannel shirt and high-waisted jeans, and he was as unhappy as any guy I'd ever met, even in high school. Misery came off him like a smell.

"Keys are in here," he said, opening the desk drawer. "We never changed to an electronic card system, because that costs a lot of money. We have problems with electronics in this place, anyway. We tried a booking computer for a while, but it never worked, and eventually it just stopped turning on. So we still use the book." He gestured to the big leather book on the desk where guests wrote their names.

"Okay," I said. My job as a barista had been way higher tech than this. "Landline, too, huh?" I gestured at the old phone.

Chris glanced at it. "You can use your cell out here if you get reception. We don't have Wi-Fi unless you steal one of the local signals when the weather is right. Again, the electronics problem, and Wi-Fi costs money.

Nancy comes at noon every day to make up any rooms that have been used—you'll never see her. Dirty laundry goes in the bin in the back. Laundry is picked up and dropped off every week, again during the day. You won't see them, either."

I was still stuck on the Internet thing. "There's no Internet? None at all?"

That got me a look of disdain. "I guess that's a problem for someone your age, right? I bet you'd like to get paid to stay up all night and Twitter."

I gave him my best poker face. "Yes," I said. "It's a dream of mine to make minimum wage to sit in a motel office and Twitter. Like, totally. When I get extra ambitious, I Facebook."

"This country is going to the shitter in a handbasket," Chris said.

"It's 'hell in a handbasket,' actually. The saying."

"Whatever. Wear this." He handed me a dark blue vest with the logo on the breast. "Honestly, I won't know if you actually wear it, but you're supposed to. We were going to update them, but—"

"That costs money," I filled in for him.

I gave him a smile, but he just looked sad. "My parents paid a song for this place," he said. "Dad bought the land off of some old farmer and had the motel built for cheap. The land was supposed to be the real investment, with the motel just a way to make money to pay the taxes. I guess they were going to sell when the value went up." He sighed. "It never did, because they never built that damn amusement park. Now my parents are dead and the place is mine. I tried to sell it around 2000, but no takers. So here we are. The few thousand bucks a year it makes is cheaper than paying an agent to sell it."

I took the polyester vest, feeling its thick plasticky texture between my fingers. "Then how do you make a living?" I asked.

"I sell car insurance. Always have. Stateline Auto in town. If you need insurance, call me." He looked around, his eyes tired. "Frankly, I hate this place. I come out here as little as possible. Every memory I have of this place is bad."

I wanted to ask what that meant, but the expression on his face had shut down. So I said, "If you want to save money, why have a night clerk at all?"

"We tried going without one in the nineties, and frankly the hookers took over. They stayed here all night, did damage I had to fix, and took off without paying. Profits actually went *down*, if you can believe it. Turns out having someone here makes people behave, at least a little." He pointed to a pinboard on the wall next to the desk with a note on it. "Call the cops if you need to. Most people are just jerks who back down when you tell them to knock it off. We've never had anyone get violent with a night clerk."

"Except for the one who went missing," I said.

Chris blinked at me. "What?"

"The night clerk who went missing in 1982."

"How the hell did you hear about that?"

"It was in the papers," I said, which wasn't a lie.

"Oh, God," he said, running a hand through his thinning hair. He seemed horrified. "Don't bring that up, okay? I thought everyone had forgotten about that. That was in my parents' time. You weren't even born."

"Did you know her?" I asked him.

"I was a kid, so no."

"What do you think happened to her?"

"Who knows? It's ancient history. Please don't bring it up. We don't need even fewer customers than we already have."

That was the end of my interview with Chris about my aunt's disappearance. Score zero for Nancy Drew.

When Chris left, I dropped the blue polyester vest on a chair and went to work. I started with the desk, opening all the drawers and rifling through them. Except for the room keys, each of which was on a ring on a leather tab with a number stamped on it, there was nothing interesting.

Next, I moved to the desktop. It was chipped wood with a Formica top. There was a blotter, pencils and pens, the old telephone with big square buttons across the bottom to open different lines. None of the buttons were lit at the moment. On the corner was the guest book, a large leather binder with pages inside. I hovered my hand over the guest book, then stopped.

For a crazy minute it seemed like time had folded in on itself, like there was no gap between 1982 and this moment. This was the desk Viv Delaney had sat at; this was the exact phone she had used. The blue polyester vest may have been the one she wore. She had sat in this chair, looked at this pinboard with the police phone number pinned to it. *What year is it?* a voice in the back of my mind asked. *Is it 1982 or 2017? Do you really know?*

I picked up the guest book and opened it. There were four rooms occupied tonight: two men, a couple, and a woman. I didn't recognize any of the names. I found an old notepad and a pen, scribbled them down, and pulled out my phone. I already knew there was no signal in here, but I put on my coat, slipped out the office door, and roamed the walkway, then the parking lot, looking at the screen to see if a signal would appear.

When I stood almost next to the sign (VACANCY. CABLE TV!) the signal icon popped up. I quickly tried to Google the names on my paper, but not even the first search would load. The signal was too weak.

I stuffed the paper into my pocket. I texted Heather, knowing she would be awake. We'd stayed awake the past two nights, watching movies and getting me prepared to take the night shift once I knew I had the job.

No files, no computer, no Internet, and my boss says not to ask him about Viv. I'm striking out so far, I texted her.

Her reply was immediate. *Carly, it's eleven thirty.*

Right. I was just here to work a few shifts and find what I could find before quitting. I had plenty of time left in the night. *Carrying on*, I texted, and put the phone back in my pocket as the signal went dead again.

The wind sliced down my neck, and the sign made a weird electric buzzing sound overhead. I moved away from it and walked to the parking lot, looking up at the motel. The rooms were dark except for two that had lamps on, the curtains drawn. The motel itself looked asleep in the darkness, yet it had that eerie vibe I'd felt when I first came here. I rubbed my hands together and wondered how I would spend the next seven and a half hours here. I wondered what the heck I thought I was doing.

On the second level, the door to one of the unoccupied rooms swung open, showing the darkness within.

I squinted. There was definitely no one staying in the room, no one in the doorway. Yet the door hung open now, banging gently in the wind.

The lock must be broken, or the knob. I crossed the parking lot and climbed the stairs, huddling deeper into my coat because it seemed colder up here. Late fall in upstate New York is no joke. My ears were stinging and my nose was starting to run.

I grabbed the knob to the room door—it was room 218—and pulled it closed. I tried turning the knob and found it was unlocked, and I had no key. I opened the door again and found it had a disc on the inside of the knob that locked it. I turned the disc and closed the door again.

Two doors down, room 216 opened.

That was it—just the soft squeak of the door opening, then nothing. The wind blew and the door creaked, waving.

Something inside my mind said, *This is not right.*

Still, I walked to the doorway and grabbed the knob, this time taking a second to sweep a glance through the dark room. Bed, dresser, TV, door to the bathroom. Nothing else there.

I turned the disc and shut the door, making sure to pull it all the way closed. It swung back open again, even though the knob didn't turn. I grabbed it and banged it closed again, harder this time. It stayed shut for a stretch of maybe ten seconds, then creaked open again.

There was a faint sound from behind the door, as if someone were standing there. A rustle of cloth. The soft tap of a footstep. I caught a whiff of flowery perfume.

"Hey," I said, and reached my hand out. Before I could touch the door it slammed shut, so hard the door frame nearly rattled.

My breath had stopped. My arm was still out, my hand up, my fingers cold. A wash of freezing air brushed into my face, down my neck. I couldn't think.

While I stood frozen, the door to 210 opened.

My chest squeezed inside my coat. I made my feet move, bumped back against the railing. Dull pain thudded up my spine. My hands were like ice as I tried clumsily to turn my body, to back away. There were heavy footsteps.

A man stepped out of room 210 and into the corridor. He was a few years older than me, maybe. Brown hair, cropped short. Worn jeans and an old dark gray T-shirt. Stubble on his jaw. Laser blue eyes. His hair was sticking up, like he'd been sleeping.

I stared at him, dumbfounded. He was real, but I'd looked at the guest book, and he wasn't supposed to be here. Room 210 was unoccupied. Which meant I had no idea who he was.

"Hey," the man said to me as if he belonged here. "Who the fuck are you?"

I exhaled a breath that steamed in the cold. I took a step back. "Um," I said, "I'm—"

"Banging doors in the middle of the night," he finished. "I'm trying to sleep in here."

That wasn't me. At least, I don't think so. "You're not supposed to be here," I said to the man. I pointed to the doorway behind him. "In that room."

He scowled at me. "What the hell are you talking about?"

"I'm calling the cops," I said. I was impressed with how I sounded, considering I was terrified out of my mind. Too late, I remembered that the pepper spray Heather had given me was in my purse, back in the office. I moved my feet back again and turned to leave.

"Wait," the man said after me. "I'm staying here. It's legit. I have a key and everything." There was a clinking sound, and I turned to see him hold up a familiar leather tab with a key dangling from it.

I paused. "What's your name?"

"Nick Harkness."

"You're not in the guest book."

"I never signed the guest book. It's legit." He put the key away and reached into his back pocket. "You want to check me out? Here." He pulled out his wallet and tossed it to the ground between us, where it made a heavy sound against the concrete floor. "My ID, everything," he said. "I didn't mean to freak you out."

I paused. Was it a mistake to bend down and pick up the wallet? Everyone knows a serial killer can get you in an unguarded moment. I toed the wallet toward me and grabbed it as fast as I could. His ID was in there, as advertised. He had sixty dollars, too.

"Okay," I said, mostly to myself. I closed my eyes and massaged the bridge of my nose beneath my glasses. "Right, okay, fine. This is under control."

Nick Harkness watched me, but he didn't make a move. "You okay?" he asked.

"Sure, I'm great," I said. "I'm just great. I'm the night clerk."

Nick blinked his ice blue eyes in disbelief. I remembered that I was wearing my coat and I hadn't put on the blue polyester vest. "*You're* the night clerk," he said. It wasn't a question.

"Yeah, I am. Sorry about the noise. I didn't realize you were sleeping."

"You didn't think you'd wake people up by banging doors in the middle of the night."

His tone dripped with sarcasm, and I wanted to fling his stupid wallet at his head. *Something was opening and slamming the doors, you idiot, and I've had a shitty night.* But I couldn't quite get mad as I looked at him again, standing there in the November cold in his T-shirt. Something about his face. It was a good-looking face. It was also edged with exhaustion, as if he slept as little as I did. "You could try not to be a jerk," I told him. "I was just doing my job."

A muscle ticked in his jaw, and he looked away.

"The doors," I said. "Have, um, have you noticed any problem with them?" When he still didn't say anything, I said, "They were opening and closing, and I think . . . It was really strange."

Now I sounded ditzy and lame at the same time, but he didn't seem to notice. He still looked away and absently scratched his stomach. The motion made his shirt lift. Under the T-shirt, his stomach was very flat. "Christ," he said, almost to himself.

"Right," I said. "You were sleeping. Here's your wallet back. I'll go."

"You new here?" he asked. He didn't reach to take the wallet I held out.

"Sort of." Yes.

"You're new," Nick Harkness said. He dropped his hand from his stomach, which made his shirt drop, unfortunately. "Jesus, I didn't think they'd actually hire someone. The last guy left weeks ago, and Chris never even comes out here. I thought he'd given up."

"It's temporary. At least, I think so. Do you . . . You've been here for weeks?"

"Chris and I have an arrangement."

"What arrangement?"

Nick gave me another glare—he was good at it—and said, "An arrangement where I stay here and call the cops if there's trouble, and he leaves me the fuck alone. Is that enough detail for you?"

Jesus. Now I really did toss the wallet, dropping it to the floor the way he had done with me. "Well, someone could have told me instead of scaring the shit out of me," I said. "It would have been nice. I can see why you're staying here alone. Have a nice night."

I turned, but he called after me. "Let me give you a word of advice, New Night Clerk. If you think you hear the doors up here, don't come up and fix it. Stay in the office and don't come out. In fact, don't come out of the office for anything. Just close the door and sit there until your time's up. Okay?"

I turned back to tell him he was rude, that it was uncalled-for, that he shouldn't treat people that way. But for a second I could see past him into his room. The words stopped in my throat. I just stared.

He didn't notice. "Okay, go," he said to me. "Go."

I turned and walked back to the stairs, my numb hands gripping the rail so I wouldn't stumble on the way down. My eyes were watering with cold, my blood racing in my veins.

Two things kept moving through my brain as I walked back toward the office.

One, he knew about the doors. He knew.

And two, when I'd seen past him into his room, I'd seen a bed, a TV, a lit lamp. The bed was made, but the pillow had an indent, as if he'd been lying there.

And on the nightstand next to the bed was a gun, gleaming in the lamplight. As if someone had just put it down. As if he'd been holding it before he opened the door.

W ait a minute. Back up," Heather said. "Tell me that last part again."

I took another bite of my peanut butter toast. It was the next day, after I'd come home from my first shift at the Sun Down and fallen into bed, dead asleep for nine straight hours. Now I was in pajama pants and my favorite T-shirt, a baby blue one that read *EAT CAKE FOR BREAKFAST* on the front. I would have liked to eat cake for breakfast, except that I only had toast and it was five o'clock in the afternoon. "I know," I said. "Maybe he was a cop or something."

"Carly." Heather glared at me, a little like Nick had. She was wearing her black poncho, and we were sitting across from each other at the apartment's small kitchen table, Heather with her laptop in front of her where she was listlessly working on an essay that wasn't due for another six days. "No cop is staying at the Sun Down Motel for weeks on end. Dead girls, remember? The goal is that you are *not one*. Men with guns are the first thing to steer clear of. You should have Maced him."

"I don't think he would have hurt me," I said. "I didn't need the Mace. I went back to the office and I sat there, like he told me to."

"All night?"

I dropped my toast crust onto my plate. I didn't quite want to admit that I'd been too scared to venture out of the office after that encounter. The doors, that rustle of fabric and whiff of perfume, Nick Harkness—it had been too much. I'd been in a fog of fear, vague and unfocused, like I knew something was going to happen and I didn't know what. It was a piercing, lonely feeling, one I'd never had before. "I found an old computer in a cabinet in the office," I told Heather. "I spent a few hours trying to boot it up and make it work. I answered the phone three times. One was a wrong number, and two others were heavy breathing." I looked up at her. "Who makes heavy-breathing phone calls in 2017?"

Heather winced. "No one good. Did you get the computer to work?"

I shook my head and took a sip of my coffee. It had felt strange at first to eat breakfast when everyone else ate dinner, but I almost liked it. "Chris, the owner, said they tried a computer booking system, but the motel has an electronics problem. I got it hooked up to a monitor, but it wouldn't actually turn on. Then I found an old copy of *Firestarter* under a shelf, so I read that for a while until it was time to go home."

"Hmm," Heather said, clicking away at her laptop. "Maybe tonight will be more eventful."

I stared at her across the table. "Did you miss the part where the doors opened on their own? Several of them?"

"I told you the motel was haunted," she said matter-of-factly. "I guess the rumors are true. How many people do you think have died in a place like that? There must be plenty. Like the person who died in the pool."

"We have no evidence anyone died in the pool."

"I'm right. You'll see."

I took my glasses off and set them on the table. Then I rubbed my eyes slowly, pressing my fingertips into my eye sockets. The world went pleasantly blurry, and I didn't have to see the details anymore.

I had to go back there tonight. I couldn't let a few opening doors defeat me. I had to think of Viv, maybe lying in a grave somewhere for thirty-five years, with no gravestone and no one to care. I could find some of the answers at the Sun Down—I felt it.

No, the creepiness and the boredom were not going to keep me away. I'd had some sleep. I was going to win.

"If that guy is a cop, maybe he'll help me," I said, unable to quite stop thinking about Nick Harkness. Ice blue eyes. I'd never met a guy with ice blue eyes.

"He definitely isn't a cop," Heather said.

I dropped my hands and looked at her. She was a blond blur until I put my glasses back on. "How do you know that?"

"I Googled him," she said, turning her laptop so I could see the screen. "He's from Fell. Except he doesn't live here anymore, because fifteen years ago his father shot Nick's brother to death, and after his father went to prison, he left town."

There was no one in the motel office when I got there at eleven. The lights were on, the door unlocked, but there was no one behind the desk. It looked like whoever was working had just stepped out the door, but there was no coat on the hook in the corner and I already knew there was no car parked in front of the office door. There was no car in the lot at all except for mine and a truck I recognized from the night before. Nick Harkness's truck, I now guessed.

I pulled off my messenger bag and shrugged off my jacket. "Hello?" I said into the quiet.

No answer. I caught a whiff of cigarette smoke—maybe whoever I was relieving was having a smoke somewhere. But I hadn't seen anyone outside.

I poked my head back out of the office door and looked left and right. "Hello?"

A whiff of smoke again, and then nothing.

I pulled back into the office and walked back to the desk. I checked the guest registry—someone named James March had checked in. He was the only new guest since last night. It was written next to his name that he was in room 103. So, just down the corridor. Maybe it was James March who was having a cigarette, even though we had a yellowed sign over the office door that said NO SMOKING IN MOTEL.

I sat at the desk and pulled out a sheaf of printouts from my messenger bag. Before coming to work, I'd spent a few hours on the Internet, using up the precious toner on Heather's small printer. I'd added to my collection of articles about Fell—the few I'd been able to find before coming here. And I'd added articles about Nick Harkness. There were plenty of those.

According to the articles, Nick was twenty-nine. His mother had died in a swimming accident when he was young, and he'd lived with his father and older brother, Eli. His father was a lawyer, well known in Fell.

"He'd become erratic," Martin Harkness's partner at the firm said afterward. "He was angry, sometimes forgetful. We didn't know what was wrong with him, but he wasn't himself. I don't know how we could have stopped it."

One day, Martin came home from work carrying a handgun. Eli was in the living room, and Nick—who was fourteen—was upstairs in his room, playing video games. From what the police could piece together, Martin shot Eli twice point-blank in the chest. Upstairs, Nick opened the door to the Juliet balcony, swung down to the ground, and ran to a neighbor's to get help.

When asked why he'd run, Nick had replied, "I heard the gunshots, and then I heard Eli screaming and Dad coming up the stairs."

When the cops came to the Harkness house, they found seventeen-year-old Eli dead on the living room floor and Martin in the kitchen, drinking a glass of water, the gun on the counter next to him. "Where's Nick?" he said.

Since Martin was well known in town, there was a frenzy in the local media. *PROMINENT LAWYER SNAPS*, headlines read. *WHY DID HE KILL HIS OWN SON?* No one had any answers. "It needed to be over," was the only comment Martin ever made about the murder. "All of it needed to be over." He pleaded guilty, leaving no new revelations to report. After a few weeks, the papers moved on to other things.

I read through the pages again, looking at the photos. There was a school picture of fourteen-year-old Nick, with the blue eyes and the cheekbones I recognized. *The family's only surviving son*, the caption read. He'd lived with relatives in town for a few years, then had left at eighteen. What was Nick doing back in Fell, staying at the Sun Down Motel alone for weeks? Why was he here? What did he want?

The lights flickered, went out, then on again, the fluorescents overhead making a zapping buzz. I stood and walked to the door, peeking out the window at the motel sign. It was on—and then it flickered off, then on again.

Shit. A power problem? I grabbed my coat and put it back on, pulling the office door open and stepping out. Behind me, the lights flickered again as if we were in the middle of a thunderstorm, even though the air was cold and still. From down the hall came a rhythmic thumping, a metallic clunking sound that I couldn't quite place. It sounded mechanical, accompanied by a high-pitched, motorized *whirr*. I stepped out and realized it came from behind a door labeled AMENITIES. It was probably an ice machine, malfunctioning with the power problem.

The wind slapped me in the face, and I pulled my coat closed. There was another whiff of cigarette smoke, and something brushed by me— actually *touched* me, knocked me back a step. In the yawning, empty darkness, a man's voice said, "Goddamn bitch."

I stumbled back another step. *Goddamn bitch.* I'd heard that—really heard it. A strangled sound came from my throat, and I turned to look back at the motel.

The lights were going out. Starting at the end of the L, the corridor lights were blinking out like a row of dominoes. The darkness sat heavier and heavier, gained more and more weight. *A fuse problem*, I tried to tell myself, though I'd never seen a fuse in my life. The darkness marched down one side of the L, then straight up the other, step by step, ending at the office. The light over the door blinked out, and then the sign. I was alone. There was no sound.

That was when I saw the boy.

He was around eight or nine, on the second level. He was sitting on the walkway floor, cross-legged in the dark, looking at me with a pale face through the latticed bars of the panel beneath the railing. He was wearing shorts and a T-shirt with colors splashed brightly on it, as if he were heading for the beach. As I watched, he put his hand on the panel and leaned forward.

"Hey!" I shouted at him in surprise. There weren't any kids staying here according to the guest book, certainly none who were underdressed for the cold. I took a step toward the staircase. "Hey! Hello?"

The boy stood, turned, and bolted, running lightly down the corridor away from me. I heard his small, even footsteps on the stairs. I forgot about the smoke and the disembodied swearing and the rest of it and jogged down the length of the motel, hoping to catch the boy as he descended.

The boy hit the bottom step and vanished around the corner, toward the nothingness of the dark woods. "Hey!" I shouted again, as if I could make him turn around. I had a shiver up my back, along the back of my neck. *Was that real? It looked real. What if it was a real boy?*

I was at the bottom of the stairs now, and from above me I heard a familiar *click*. The same click from last night when the doors opened. I stepped back, tilting my head back and looking up through the slats of the railing. It was a single *click* this time, followed by the other sound I'd heard that night—the rustle of fabric. There was a footstep, the double-*click* of a woman's heeled shoe. Then another.

I took another step back, looking up. The light from above the door to room 216 was out, but I could vaguely see. The door was open, like it had been last night. As I watched, a woman walked out into the corridor.

She was bathed in shadows, but I could see enough. She wore a dark, knee-length, long-sleeved dress. It looked purple, or maybe blue, with a flower pattern. On her feet she wore low heels with modest closed toes. She was slender, her calves slim beneath the hem of the dress, her arms pale and graceful. Her hair was curly and spilled over her shoulders. She put her hands on the rail and looked down at me, and for a second I could see the dark liner around her almond-shaped eyes, the pale oval of her face. She looked like any one of a million women in family photographs a generation ago, except that she was looking at me, and she was not real.

Her eyes were white-hot, harsh, angry, and incredibly sad. She was looking at me, and *she was not real.*

She opened her mouth to speak.

I made a terrified sound in my throat, and then a hand grabbed my arm—a big, strong, *real* hand. I spun and saw Nick Harkness standing there, staring at me, his blue eyes blazing.

"What the hell do you think you're doing?" he shouted.

I gaped at him. "I—" I looked up, but the woman was gone. I felt panic and unspeakable relief. "Did you see that?" I said to Nick.

He didn't answer. His hand was still on my arm. I heard the *snick* of a door opening overhead, then another. Then another. The doors were opening one by one.

"Come on," Nick said, tugging me toward the parking lot.

"Where are we going?" I managed.

"We're leaving. I don't know what's going on, but I'm not sticking around for it. Are you?"

Fell, New York
September 1982
VIV

S he tried not to listen in on people's phone calls once she learned the phone trick, but it was hard.

Jamie Blaknik, for example. He was a young guy in jeans and a worn-thin T-shirt who smoked cigarettes, ignoring the NO SMOKING IN MOTEL sign and messing with Viv's ability to detect the smoking man every time he checked in. The smoky-sweet smell of him told her he was most likely a pot dealer, the kind of guy she had never talked to before—the kind of guy who would give her mother a rage fit if she ever brought him home. He was attractive in an edgy, I-won't-be-nice-to-you way, and Viv's neck and cheeks always got hot when he checked in and gave her that smirk across the desk. *Nice night*, he'd say, and she'd nod like an idiot, until one night she smiled at him when he walked in and he smiled back.

"Nice night," he said, pulling a roll of bills from his broken-in jeans pocket and unwrapping a few twenties.

Viv looked at his tousled brown hair, his gray eyes—which were actually rather nice—and his unaffected slouch that went in an easy line from his shoulders to his hips, and said, "You come here a lot."

"That bother you?" he said in an easy drawl as he picked up a pen and scribbled his name into the guest book.

"No," Viv replied. "What is it about this place, though? Do you like the view?"

He looked up at her from the guest book and gave her a smile that had a thousand possible meanings to it. She just wished she knew which one. "Yeah," he said with a touch of humor in his voice. "I like the view."

"That's nice," she said, holding his gaze. "I'm not going to bother you. Just so you know. It doesn't matter to me what you're doing."

Jamie straightened. "Okay," he said, holding out his hand for his key. He wore a leather bracelet on his wrist, wound with one of woven cloth. "That works for me. I don't bother you, you don't bother me."

"Right." She rifled through the key drawer to pick him a key.

"Unless you want to party," he added. "If you do, just come on over to my room and knock on the door."

Whoa! That was a step beyond what she was ready for. But Viv handed him his key and batted her lashes, just theatrical enough for him to know she was kidding. "Oh, I couldn't do that," she said. "I might get fired."

He laughed, and his laugh was just as pleasant as the rest of him. "Have it your way, Good Girl," he said. "The party's happening anyway. Have a good night."

He left, and when the light blinked on the phone a few minutes later with its whispered *click*, she lifted the receiver and listened to the low, pleasant hum of his voice. *Hey, man, I'm checked in. You on your way?* He made and took a dozen phone calls from customers, and Viv—who had never even seen a joint in real life, let alone held or tried one—listened to all of it, learning the lingo of the measured bits of weed and how much they cost, appreciating Jamie's droll sense of humor at his line of work.

On another night a prostitute called her babysitter in between taking her clients, checking in on her four-year-old daughter, Bridget, as Viv listened in. *Make sure she drinks her milk. Let her have a little popcorn but not too much. Did she go to sleep right away or did she get up? Sometimes she has to go potty two or three times. Call you later, I gotta go.* The woman left at five thirty, tying back her long hair as she walked to her car in tight jeans and flip-flops. It was still dark but there was something about the light at that time of morning, something that let you know dawn was coming soon. It was a different darkness than midnight darkness. In the darkness of five thirty, Bridget's mother almost looked pretty, her hair shiny and long, her shoulders back. Alone in the office, Viv watched her walk, the effortless way her hips moved, with perfect envy.

"Don't you see creepy things in that job?" Viv's roommate, Jenny, asked her one night as they both got ready for work. Jenny was eating yogurt, dressed in her hospital scrubs as Viv stood at the kitchen counter, making her bologna sandwich. The TV was on, showing the ten o'clock news with the volume on low. Viv was wearing high-waisted jeans and a white T-shirt that was cut loosely, billowing from where she had tucked it into her pants. She'd added a slim red belt she thought was pretty in the belt loops.

She looked at her roommate, startled. "Creepy things?"

Jenny shrugged. She'd just redone her perm last week, and Viv quietly envied the perfect curls in her hair, wondered if she could scrape up the budget for a perm herself. "You know, creepy things. Perverts. Homos."

Viv was more worldly now, after nearly two months at the Sun Down. She knew what homos were, though admittedly she had no idea how to identify one and no idea if she'd ever seen one. "I see lots of hookers," she said, pleased that she'd used a worldly word like *hookers*. "No homos, though."

Jenny nodded, taking a scoop of yogurt, and Viv felt like she'd passed a test. "The homos probably go to the park. Still, it must be creepy, working that place at night."

Viv thought of the ghost woman telling her to run, the shove in the AMENITIES room. "Sometimes, yes."

"Just be careful," Jenny said. "You'll end up like Cathy Caldwell."

Viv wrapped her sandwich in waxed paper. "Who is Cathy Caldwell?"

Jenny waggled her eyebrows dramatically and put on a Vincent Price voice. "Murdered and found under an overpass two years ago. Stabbed to death!" She dropped the dramatic voice and went back to her regular, bored one. "She lived down the street from my parents. My mother calls me every week. She thinks I'm going to be Cathy Caldwell any day because I work nights. It must be rubbing off on me."

"Was she working a night shift?" Viv asked.

"No, she was coming home from work," Jenny said, dipping her spoon into her yogurt. Viv could smell its sour-milk scent. "It terrifies my mother. She thinks she's going to get a midnight phone call: *Your daughter is dead!* Oh, and don't go jogging, either. *That* will turn you into Victoria Lee, who was killed and dumped on the jogging trail on the edge of town."

Viv stared at her, sandwich forgotten. Something was tightening in her chest, like a bell tolling. "What? You mean there's a murderer in Fell?"

"No." Jenny seemed sure of this. "Victoria's boyfriend did hers. It just makes us all scared of jogging. But Cathy Caldwell . . ." She widened her eyes and waggled her eyebrows again. "Maybe it was Michael Myers. Or, like, that story about the babysitter. *The killer is inside the house!*"

Viv laughed, but it felt forced. She remembered the man who had put his hand on her thigh when she was hitchhiking. How she'd realized that he could leave her in a ditch and no one would ever know.

"Okay, no jogging trail," Viv said to Jenny. "I don't jog anyway. I've never had anyone bother me at the motel, though." Even Jamie Blaknik the pot dealer was nice, in his way.

"No one has bothered you *yet*," Jenny said in her practical, no-nonsense way. She looked Viv up and down. "I mean, you're pretty. And you're alone there at night. We single girls have to be careful. I don't leave the nursing home at night, even to smoke. You should carry a knife."

"I can't carry a knife."

"Sure you can. I don't mean a big machete. I mean a small one, you know, for girls. I was thinking of getting one myself. And then if one of those old guys at my work gets creepy—*whammo*." She mimed jabbing a knife into the countertop. Viv laughed again. The only stories Jenny told about being a night shift nurse in a retirement home were that it was boring, and old people were weird and useless. Jenny didn't seem to like very many people, but tonight Viv was in her good graces.

Jenny left for work, and Viv bustled around the apartment, getting her last few things together to go to the Sun Down. The TV was still on, and the segment on the news featured a beautiful brunette anchor with the words on screen in front of her: *SAFETY TIPS FOR TEENS.* "Always go out with a friend if it's after dark," she was saying from her beautifully lipsticked lips. "Use a buddy system. Never get into a stranger's vehicle. Consider carrying a whistle or a flashlight."

Viv turned the TV off and went to work.

At her desk at the Sun Down, wearing her blue vest, she pulled out her notebook in the deserted quiet. Using the meticulous penmanship learned since first grade in Illinois, her letters carefully swirled with feminine loops, she wrote: *Cathy Caldwell. Left under underpass. Victoria Lee. Jogging trail. Boyfriend?*

She tucked her pen into the corner of her mouth for a minute, then wrote: *Buy a whistle? A flashlight? A knife?*

Outside, she heard a car come into the parking lot. She'd expected this; Robert White, the fortyish man cheating with the woman named Helen, had checked in half an hour ago. Alone, with no luggage, as before.

Curious, she put her pen and notebook down and slipped out the office door, taking a quick trip to the AMENITIES room. Helen's Thunderbird pulled in and parked next to Mr. White's car, and as Viv watched through the crack in the AMENITIES doorway, Helen got out. She was wearing a one-piece wrap dress of jewel blue that set off her short, styled dark hair. This time Mr. White opened the door before she could knock. They smiled at each other and then he followed her into the room, closing the door behind him.

Viv was about to go back to the office, to her desk and her notebook, when she saw the second car.

A dark green sedan pulled into the back of the lot, behind Helen's

Thunderbird. Viv waited, but no one got out. Now, with the door closing behind Helen and Mr. White, Viv saw the passenger window of the second car roll up as a camera lens ducked back into the car.

Viv waited, her gaze fixed on the sedan, but nothing else happened. The door stayed closed and the mystery car stayed parked at the back of the lot. Whoever was in the car was watching, waiting however long it took for Helen to come out again. The person in the car had a clear view of the AMENITIES door and would see her when she came out.

She couldn't hide here all night, so she dug in her pocket and pulled out twenty cents. She put it in the candy machine, got a Snickers bar, and left the AMENITIES room, closing the door behind her. She held the candy bar in her outer hand and angled herself subtly just so—in theater they called it *cheating out*—so that the person in the car could clearly see her Sun Down Motel vest and the Snickers. *Just an innocent employee hitting the candy machine*, she thought. She walked back to the office and closed the door behind her, then positioned herself at the edge of the window, looking at the car again. Maybe she imagined it, but she thought there was a flicker of movement behind the passenger window. Which didn't make sense, because there was no reason for someone to take a picture of her. No reason at all.

It was a strangely busy night. A trucker stopped in and asked for directions, and when Viv couldn't help, he pulled out his paper map and the two of them looked at it together, trying to figure out how he could get back to the interstate. There was another phone call with only breathing at the other end of the line. The linen company had left a bin of clean linens behind the motel, and Viv had to figure out how to open the UTIL-ITIES door and push it inside. Through all of that, her attention kept wandering back to the scene in the parking lot: the closed motel door, the two cars parked in front of it, and the third car in the back of the parking lot, watching. She wondered if the man in the third car was going to stay there all night. She wondered if he was bored. She wondered if he had seen her.

It was just past two a.m. when another car pulled into the lot and a man walked into the office.

He was alone. He wore a suit and a trench coat, carried a briefcase and a suitcase. Viv remembered her manners and put on a smile as she raised her gaze to his face. She faltered, because he looked oddly familiar. He was in his thirties, decent-looking, clean-shaven. He looked like a thousand other men. Still, there was something in his eyes that she had seen before.

"Evening," the man said, though it was the middle of the night by now. He approached the desk and set down his suitcase and his briefcase. "I'd like a room, please."

Viv kept some of the smile on her face. "Sure thing," she said. "A room is thirty dollars a night."

"I know." The man smiled at her, and Viv felt a rush of something—that familiarity again, mixed with something strangely like fear, as if she were remembering a bad dream she couldn't quite grasp. *This man should never smile*, she thought wildly before she pushed the thought away. There was nothing wrong with his smile. He looked perfectly fine.

"Oh?" she asked him politely when he didn't elaborate.

His pause was just a second too long, the smile still on his face. "You don't remember me?" he said. "I stayed here a few weeks ago. I remember you. Oh, well, I guess I'm just that memorable."

Now something clawed up the back of her memory. "Yes, I remember," she said. "You're a traveling salesman."

"I am," the man said, smiling again. "And just like last time I need to stay tonight, but I may need to stay longer after I talk to my bosses tomorrow. I go wherever they tell me, you see."

Viv nodded, turning the guest book and pushing it toward him. "That's okay," she said, fighting the urge she had at the base of her spine to get rid of him, get him out of here. She needed to be polite; it was her job. "That's fine."

"Thank you." The salesman took the pen from her—his fingertip nearly brushed hers, and she gritted her teeth—and swiftly wrote his name. Then he handed over thirty dollars. "I'll be back tomorrow if I need to stay another night."

Viv nodded and took the key to room 210 from the drawer. "Here you go. Have a nice night."

"Thank you . . ." He paused dramatically. "What is your name?"

She was cornered. "Vivian," she said, unwilling to ask him to call her Viv.

"Vivian," the salesman said. He tipped an invisible hat to her, then picked up his cases and left the room.

Viv stood in the silence, her temples pounding. When he had gone she peeked out the office window, watched him climb the stairs to the upper level.

Helen's car was gone, and so was the car in the back of the parking lot. Damn it—she'd missed it. The only piece of excitement promised for the rest of the night.

She walked back to the desk and looked at the guest register. The salesman had written his name in big, bold letters: *JAMES MARCH.*

She flipped back in the book, remembering back to the night with the smoke and the voices. She paged back and back until she saw that same bold, black handwriting.

MICHAEL ENNIS, he'd written.

No one here tells the truth, Viv thought. *Not ever.*

N ick had a black pickup truck, a big machine that made a lot of noise and smelled a little of aftershave. Even in my panicked, half-delirious state, the testosterone was like a bong hit. I crouched in the huge leather-upholstered seat as we roared off down Number Six Road. It was comforting and unsettling at the same time. I wasn't alone anymore. There was a man taking care of things now. And yet.

And yet.

We pulled into the parking lot of an all-night Denny's. I had no idea what direction we'd driven or how long we'd traveled. It felt like minutes and hours at the same time. "Wait here," Nick said, and got out.

I watched him walk toward the restaurant. My hands were shaking, my back cold with half-dried sweat. He moved with an ease that made my stomach swirl and made me tense at the same time. *You don't know this man*, my hopped-up instincts told me. *The last time you saw him, he had a gun. His father is a murderer. You're alone in his car in the middle of the night.* I'd left my messenger bag at the motel, with my cell phone and the Mace Heather had given me. I put my hand on the passenger door handle, pressing it experimentally. Of course it gave. I wasn't locked in. There was no such thing as locking someone in your truck.

Then again, there was no such thing as little boys who vanished or the woman in 216.

I gulped breaths in the quiet of the truck, trying not to let panic overtake me. I could get out, go ask for help in the restaurant. But what kind of help did I want? The police? Did I just want to get out of here? To go home?

Where was home? In that moment, I couldn't even picture Illinois. I had no idea what it looked like. The only thing I could picture was my apartment with Heather and the Sun Down Motel. Should I call Heather? Would it panic her if I did?

The driver's door cracked open and I jumped. I hadn't even seen Nick come back. He swung into the truck, but he didn't touch the ignition. Instead he handed me a take-out cup and kept one for himself.

I inhaled. It was hot chocolate. I peeked through the gap in the lid and saw there was whipped cream on the top of the drink. I stared for a second, so surprised I didn't even sip it.

"I didn't know if you liked coffee," Nick said. I turned to see him watching me stare at my drink. "I forgot to ask. I figured chocolate was a safe bet."

"Thank you," I said, my voice rusty.

He looked at me for another long minute. The harsh light from the restaurant was dimmed by distance and the shadows of the truck's cab. It made his face look half lit, half sliced with darkness. It was hard to figure out how old he was in this light, even though I knew his age from the newspaper stories—he was twenty-nine. He looked handsome and jaded and a little bit crazy. I probably looked crazy myself, and I'd bet the light glinting off my glasses wasn't very flattering.

"What's your name?" he asked, his voice harsh.

I blinked, surprised. I realized I'd never told him. Well, if he was a serial-killer-slash-date-rapist who specialized in women who had just seen ghosts, it was too late now. I'd just throw my hot drink at him and run. "Carly," I said, sipping my chocolate. It was heavenly, the whipped cream melting into the hot drink and making it teeth-achingly sweet.

"Carly," Nick said, "tell me you just saw what I saw."

"I saw it," I said. "I saw that little boy. And I saw that . . . woman." She was a woman, yet she wasn't. She was something else.

"Jesus." He rubbed a hand over his face, and I heard the rasp of his beard. He was wearing a dark blue plaid flannel shirt over a T-shirt, and once again no jacket. I realized he must have run straight out of his room when the commotion started.

"You've been staying at the motel for weeks," I said. "Has anything like that happened before?"

"No." He dropped his hand, stared ahead out the windshield. "There are noises. Always noises, even when the place is empty. There are strange smells, and the door thing. You saw what the doors do. That happens a lot. The lights go on and off. And one night, that woman was on my bed. Sitting on the foot of the bed. I woke up and she was just there, looking at me. The bed didn't sag or anything—she had no weight. She was there, and then I blinked and she was gone. I could smell her perfume, and something bad. Coppery, like blood. That was about two weeks ago."

My heart was thumping again just listening. I couldn't imagine being so close to that woman, so close to whatever she was. "And you stayed?" I asked him, incredulous. "After you saw that, you still stayed?"

"I know. But I have my reasons."

"Your reasons are crazy, whatever they are," I said.

But he shook his head. "They're not." His voice had the slightest ragged edge to it—you could only hear it if you were listening closely. Whatever his reasons were, he believed in them. "You shouldn't talk about crazy," he said. "You know damn well we're going back there as soon as we finish this drink."

I opened my mouth, the words ready to go. *No way. I'm never going back there again. Forget about my wallet and all my stuff, and forget about the job. Forget about Viv. No freaking way.*

But I didn't say any of it, because he was right. Whatever had gone on at the Sun Down, we'd run away in the middle of it. And damn it, I wanted to know how it had ended.

I wanted to know what the Sun Down looked like right now. Were the ghosts gone?

I tilted my cup and swallowed down some hot chocolate. The whipped cream was like soft, sweet comfort in my throat. I couldn't reconcile the man next to me with whipped cream. I wiped my mouth and said, "I Googled you."

He didn't speak, but I felt him tense in the air between us.

"I had to," I said. "You're staying at the motel where I work. At night. You stay off the books. And you had a gun on your bedside table."

"I keep that for protection." He opened his free hand. "Some good it did. I didn't even grab it when I left the room. I don't have it right now." He glanced at me. "I've been gone a long time. You don't know what it's like to have unresolved shit in your past, shit that weighs you down and draws you back to a certain place."

Oh, he was wrong. So wrong.

"I do," he continued. "I guess you know what happened to me. Some people can get past something like that, eventually move on. I never could. I've been an open wound all these years. Drugs, alcohol—nothing helped. So I thought I'd come back, see this place as a grown man. Face my past. I checked into the Sun Down for one night—one night. And do you know what happened?"

"What?"

"I slept." He gave me half a smile, and for a second I could see the high school kid I'd seen in the newspaper stories, the kid who had been good-looking and decent and ready to take life on. "I mean, I really *slept*. It's been years since that happened. I'm a night person. I've had insomnia for so long I don't even remember when it started. And I checked into the Sun Down and slept for eleven straight hours. Just like that." He snapped his fingers, the sound loud in the truck.

"In Fell, though?" I asked. "The place where it all happened? It's the only place you can sleep?"

"I can't explain it, either." He looked out the window. "Eli is buried here. My mother is buried here. I sure as hell never made a home any-where else. Maybe this fucked-up place is as close to home as I'm ever going to get."

I was quiet, thinking about Heather saying, *Some of us like the dark. It's what we know.*

"So I stayed," Nick said. "I paid Chris a stack of money, and he left me alone once he saw I wasn't dealing or doing any other shit. Just sleeping. Every time I lie down in that place, day or night, I fall asleep. You want to know what I've been doing for most of the past month? Catching up on a decade's worth of sleep."

"And when you woke up one night, the woman was on your bed."

"She was," Nick agreed. "And after that, I fell asleep again. It's a weird thing to do, but I did. That's what that place does to me, and I'll take it. I don't care about sounds or smells or strange women. I'm going back to the Sun Down tonight, because it's the only place I've found in the world where I can sleep."

I bit my lip. In the upside-down night world, it made a crazy kind of sense. "I'm not leaving, either," I said. "I do have shit from my past that brings me here, as it happens. My aunt disappeared from the Sun Down in 1982, and no one ever found her body. I want to know what happened to her. That's why I'm there."

It was a testament to the strangeness of the night that Nick didn't seem fazed. "Was she working there when she disappeared? Like you?"

"Yes. I came to Fell to find out what happened to her, because it looks like no one else ever bothered to. And they had this job available at the motel. So I took it."

He nodded, like that wasn't weird. "Was that her? In the dress?"

I shook my head. I was ninety-nine percent sure, but it had happened so fast. "I don't think so. The clothes were all wrong, and her hair was the wrong color and style. I don't think that was Viv."

"I saw the dress when she was in my room," Nick said. "It's like a 1970s thing. At least, that's what it looks like to me. It makes her too old to be your aunt." A muscle in his jaw twitched. "But she's someone. That much I know for sure. She's *someone.*"

I stared ahead of me out the windshield at the ugly parking lot. I had seen things tonight that everyone I knew would say were impossible. But in the dark cab of this truck, they were real. Not only real, but understandable. Possibly even solvable. My eyes burned and my chest was tight. I felt like the night wouldn't be long enough, that I wouldn't have enough hours. That I certainly wouldn't sleep. I felt like I'd never be tired again.

She's someone.

"We can start with the dress," I said. "We can find out what era dresses like that are from. We can look at the local newspaper archives. She died, we know that much. Right? There aren't ghosts of living people." I glanced at him.

Nick was watching me. He took a sip of coffee and shrugged. "I have no idea, but my guess is no."

"So she died in the seventies, maybe. At the motel. That would be in the news. If she was local, there might be family still here. We could talk to them." I glanced at him again. "I could talk to them if you don't want to. The boy, too—he must have died at the motel. I didn't see what he was wearing, but if a kid died at the Sun Down, it must have been in the news."

"I thought you wanted to look for your aunt." Nick's voice was almost gentle.

Acid burned down my throat. "I do," I said. "That's what this is. I'm looking for her. Because I think . . ." I took a breath. "I think that whatever got the woman and the boy could have gotten Viv that night back in 1982. Which means she could be there with them." I leaned back against the passenger seat. My eyes were still burning, but they were dry. "I might see her next," I said. There was no way around it, but it was hard to contemplate: seeing the face from the newspaper clippings, those pretty eyes and that wide smile, coming out of one of the doors at the Sun Down. Hearing Viv's steps like I'd heard the woman's. Seeing her sitting on the end of a bed.

The thought was terrifying. And yet.

And yet.

This was what I was here for, wasn't it?

She's someone.

I was in the right place. And now it was time to go back to it.

It wasn't until we pulled into the parking lot that I remembered about the motel's other guest. James March, whose name was written in the guest book.

The lights were back on at the Sun Down, including the sign, sending its message out over Number Six Road. The corridor lights were back on, feeble and pale in the darkness. My phone said it was 1:23 a.m.

Nick and I got out of the truck and stood in the parking lot. The Sun Down looked like any normal motel, but we both knew it wasn't. It was just . . . sleeping, maybe. Napping. *Come on in,* the building seemed to say with its jagged up-and-down lights, its blue and yellow neon cheeriness. *Get some sleep. Take it easy until the sun comes up again. And if you see someone sitting at the end of your bed, pay them no mind. That's just one of my secrets. And I'm not going to tell.*

The rooms were all dark. The sign over the office door was lit, and the light was back on inside, but that was the only light in the building.

"Room one-oh-three," I said to Nick.

He came around the truck, hunched a little into his flannel shirt. I remembered again that he didn't have a coat. "What?" he said to me.

"There's a guest in room one-oh-three," I told him. "A man. Or at least there was before all the commotion started."

Nick followed my gaze toward room 103, which was dark like the others. "Hmm," he said, and strode across the parking lot toward the door.

"We shouldn't disturb him in the middle of the night," I said, hurrying to follow him.

"If he heard any of that shit earlier, he's already been disturbed," Nick replied.

"Do you think he slept through it?" I asked.

"I have no idea," Nick said. "I'll ask him."

But there was no answer to a knock on the door to the room. There was no light on, either. Instead, when Nick pounded harder on the door, it drifted open, as if it had been barely latched shut.

I looked at Nick as we stood in the dark, open doorway. He frowned at me, said, "Stay here," and slowly walked inside. "Hello?" I heard him call.

A minute later, he came out again. "There's no one in there. It doesn't look like anyone's been there, either. The bed isn't touched, and neither is anything else."

"His name is in the register," I said. "Maybe he left."

Nick came out to the corridor and looked over the parking lot, which held only my car and his truck. "What car was he driving?"

I thought back. There was a car. There had to have been a car. But I remembered pulling up to the motel office, finding it empty with the lights on. I'd thought that was strange at the time. I'd looked out to the parking lot and seen my own car, plus Nick's truck. Like I was seeing right now.

I turned and walked down the corridor to the motel office. The door was unlocked, the lights on. Inside, the office looked like I'd left it, with my messenger bag on the floor next to the desk. I inhaled when I came into the room, searching for the smell of cigarette smoke. There was none.

Nick's footsteps came behind me as I walked to the desk. I opened the guest book and flipped to tonight's page. The name was there: James March, room 103. The handwriting was dark and spindly, and I didn't recognize it. I walked around the desk and pulled open the key drawer. I rifled through the keys, and except for Nick's key to room 210, they were all there. The key to room 103 was right there in the drawer.

I picked it up by its leather tab and held it out for Nick to see.

"He could have returned it," Nick said. "The office door was unlocked, and so was that drawer."

"There wasn't a car," I said.

"What did he look like? Did you check him in?"

"I have no idea, and no."

"Who checked him in, then?" Nick asked.

"There was no one in the office when I got here tonight," I replied. "It was open, the lights on, and this name was in the guest book. That's all I know."

Nick pulled the guest book toward him and looked at the name written on the page. "James March," he said. "If he isn't here, then where is he?"

Fell, New York
October 1982
VIV

There was a diner called the Turnabout on a stretch of the North Edge Road, close to the turnoff for the interstate. It was on the outskirts, when you were in the territory of overnight drivers and truckers, where you could find a place that was open until midnight.

The Turnabout wasn't a fancy place, and the coffee wasn't particularly good, but Viv found that she didn't mind it. For three dollars she could get a meal, and there were people here—real people who knew each other, who sometimes sat around and talked. She'd forgotten what it was like to be around people who weren't just passing through.

Tonight she sat in a booth and waited, fidgety and impatient. She had her notebook and pen with her, along with a manila folder stuffed with papers. She'd spent a week gathering everything, and tonight she would find out if she'd wasted her time.

You can't do this.

Yes, you can.

To say it was a rabbit hole was an understatement. Ever since Jenny, her roommate, had made those comments about Cathy Caldwell and Victoria Lee, Viv had felt an uncomfortable itch, a need to know. It felt like curiosity mixed with something lurid and mysterious, but Viv knew it was deeper than that. It felt almost like a purpose. Something she was meant to find.

She'd left the apartment early every day and gone to the Fell Central Library, digging through old newspapers. It wasn't hard to find articles about Cathy and Victoria; their murders had made the news. After a week each girl had dropped off the front page of the *Fell Daily*, and then you had to find updates—what few there were—in the back pages, with headlines like *PO-LICE STILL MAKE NO HEADWAY* and *QUESTIONS STILL REMAIN*.

The waitress poured Viv another coffee, and Viv anxiously glanced at the door. Because Alma Trent had said she'd come.

She did. She came through the door five minutes later, wearing her uniform and nodding politely at the waitress. "How are things, Laura?"

"Not so bad," the waitress said. "You haven't been here in a dog's age."

"You haven't had to call me," Alma said practically. "But I'd sure like a cup of coffee." She slid into the booth opposite Viv. "Hello, Vivian."

Viv nodded. Her palms were sweating, but she was determined not to be the speechless idiot Alma had met before. "Thanks for coming," she said.

"Well, you said you had something interesting for me." Alma glanced at her watch. "I'm due on shift in forty-five minutes, and if I'm not mistaken, so are you."

Viv put her shoulders back. She was wearing a floral blouse tonight, and she'd put on a yellow sweater over it. She'd considered wearing darker colors to make herself look more serious, but she liked the yellow better. "I wanted to talk to you about something. Something I think that could help you."

"Okay," Alma said politely, accepting a cup of coffee from the waitress and stirring some sugar into it.

"It's about Cathy Caldwell and Victoria Lee."

Alma went very still.

Viv opened her folder. "Well, it isn't only about them. It's—just listen, okay?"

"Vivian." Alma's voice was almost gentle. "I'm only the night-shift duty officer. I don't work murder cases."

"Just listen," Viv said again, and there must have been something urgent in her voice, something that was almost alarming, because Alma closed her mouth and nodded.

"Cathy Caldwell was killed in December 1980," Viv said. "She was twenty-one. She worked as a receptionist at a dental office. She was married and had a six-month-old son. Her husband was deployed in the military."

She knew all of these things. She recited them like they were the facts of her own life. Alma nodded. "I remember it."

"She went to work one day and left her son with a babysitter. She called the babysitter at five o'clock and said she was picking up groceries on the way home, that she'd be fifteen minutes late. At six thirty, the babysitter called her mother, asking what she should do because Cathy wasn't home yet. The mother said she should wait another hour, then call the police. So at seven thirty, the babysitter called the police." She looked at Alma, then continued. "The police searched for her for three days. They found her body under an overpass. She was naked and had been stabbed in the side of the neck three times. The stabs were deep. They think he was trying to get her artery. Which he did."

"Vivian, honey," Alma said. "Maybe you shouldn't—"

"Just *listen*." She had to get this out. It had been boiling in her mind for days as she scribbled thoughts into her notebook. Alma quieted and Viv pulled a hand-drawn map from her file folder.

"The article said that Cathy's usual grocery store was this one here." She pointed to a spot on the map, halfway between the X marked with Cathy's work and the X marked with Cathy's home. "No one saw her there that night. Her car was found just out of town, parked at the mall, so there was a theory she went shopping instead. But that wasn't like Cathy at all. And you see, it makes sense. Because he dumped her at the overpass, here"—she indicated another X—"and then he drove her car to the mall, which was ten minutes away. Just because her car was there doesn't mean she was ever there."

"I get it," Alma said. "You've been playing amateur detective."

The words stung. *Playing amateur detective.* It didn't feel like that. "I'm getting to a point," Viv said, but Alma kept talking.

"We get people like this sometimes," Alma said. "They call in to the station with their theories. Especially when it comes to Cathy. People don't like that it wasn't solved. They feel like her killer is out there somewhere."

"That's because he is," Viv said.

Alma shook her head. "I didn't work that case, but I was on the force when it happened. We all got briefed. The leads were all followed."

Viv was losing Alma, she could tell. "Just hear me out this one time," she said. "Just until you have to go on shift. Then you'll never hear from me again."

Alma sighed. "I hope I hear from you again, because I like you," she said. "You seem like a bright girl. All right, I'll drink my coffee and listen. Carry on."

Viv took a breath. "There was a theory about Cathy. They found that one of her tires had a repaired puncture in it. So he could have punctured her tire, then taken her when he pulled over to help her. But the article said they couldn't determine when the puncture repair was done." She flipped a page to another set of neatly written notes. "I used the Fell yellow pages and called every auto repair shop. They all said they had no record of fixing Cathy's tire. But it was two years ago now, so it's possible she came in and the record is long gone."

There was silence, and Viv looked up to see Alma looking at her. "You called auto repair shops," Alma said. It wasn't spoken as a question.

Viv shrugged like it was no big deal. She wasn't about to admit that she'd been hung up on three times. "I just asked a few questions. The other thing is that if Cathy was stabbed in the neck she would have lost a lot of blood. Like, gallons. And the articles didn't say there were gallons of blood under the overpass."

Alma's eyebrows went up. "So you surmise that she was killed elsewhere."

"I looked up the weather records," Viv said, ignoring Alma's dry tone. "There was a thunderstorm with heavy rain the day after Cathy disappeared. So he could have killed her outside somewhere, and the rain washed the blood away." She ran a hand through her newly short hair. "If you were going to kill someone with a lot of blood, where would you do it? Not the overpass, for sure. There are cars going by there. My guess is the creek." She pointed to the creek on her map, the bank two hundred yards from the overpass. "None of the articles say if they checked the creek. Or if Cathy had mud on her. I bet that's in the police records, though. If Cathy was muddy."

"You looked up weather records, too?"

"Sure," Viv said. "They're right there in the library." She flipped to another page in her notebook. "Personally, I think the tire puncture is a coincidence. If he didn't get her on the side of the road, and he didn't get her at the grocery store, then that leaves one place." She pointed to an X on the map. "Cathy's work. He got her when she got into her car."

Alma sipped her coffee. She seemed to be getting into it now. "It's a theory, sure. But so far you aren't telling me anything I don't already know, or anything I can't look up at work."

"Victoria Lee," Viv said, ignoring her and flipping to yet another page, pulling out another hand-drawn map. "She was eighteen. The article said she'd had 'numerous boyfriends.' That means everyone thought she was a slut, right?"

Alma pressed her lips together and said nothing.

"It does," Viv said. "Victoria had an on-again, off-again boyfriend. They fought all the time. She fought with her parents, her teachers. She had a brother who ran away from home and never came back." That was almost all she knew about Victoria. There had been considerably less coverage of her in the newspapers next to pretty, upstanding young mother Cathy. After all, Victoria's killer had been arrested. And next to Cathy, Victoria was a girl who deserved it.

"August of 1981," Alma said, breaking into Viv's thoughts. "I remember that day well."

Viv looked up at her and nodded. "Victoria liked to go jogging. She left home here"—an X on the map—"and went to the jogging trail here." Another X. "She didn't come home. Her parents didn't report it until late the next afternoon. They said that Victoria went out a lot without telling them. They figured she found some of her friends."

"We spun our wheels for a while," Alma admitted. "The parents were so certain she'd been out partying the night before. So we started there, questioning all her friends, trying to figure out what party she was at. It was a full day before we realized the parents just assumed, and Victoria wasn't at a party at all. We had to backtrack to the last time anyone had seen her, which was heading to the jogging trail."

Viv leaned forward. None of this was in the newspapers, none. "The article said they used tracking dogs."

"We did. We gave them a shirt of hers, and we found her. She was twenty feet off the jogging trail, in the bushes." Alma blinked and looked away, her hands squeezing her coffee cup. "The coroner said she'd been dead almost the whole time. She got to that jogging trail and he just killed her right away and dumped her. And she just lay there while everyone screwed around."

They were silent for a minute.

"Was it really her boyfriend?" Viv asked.

"Sure," Alma said. "They'd had a big fight. She nagged him a lot, and he called her a bitch. There were a dozen witnesses. Then Victoria went home and fought with her parents, too. The boyfriend, Charlie, had no alibi. He said he went home after their fight, but his mother said he came home an hour later than he claimed he did. Plenty of time to kill Victoria. He couldn't say where he was. He eventually tried to claim he'd spent that hour with another girl, but he couldn't produce the actual girl or give her name. The whole thing stunk, and he was convicted." She frowned. "Why are you interested in Victoria? It isn't like Cathy. It's solved."

Viv tapped her fingers on her notebook. She couldn't say, really. The papers had portrayed it as an open-and-shut case. But it was those words Jenny had said: *Don't go on the jogging trail.* Words of wisdom from one girl to another. Like it could happen again.

"They were so close together," she said to Alma. "Cathy in December of 1980, Victoria in August of 1981. Two girls murdered in Fell in under a year. Maybe it wasn't the boyfriend."

This earned her a smile—kind, but still condescending. "Honey, the police and the courts decide that. They did their job already."

The court. Was there a transcript of the trial? Viv wondered. How could she get one? "It doesn't feel finished," she said, though she knew it sounded lame said out loud. "Why the jogging trail? Why there of all places? He knew her. He could have killed her anywhere. He could have phoned her and lured her somewhere private, say he wanted to apologize or something. And she'd go. Instead he killed her where anyone could walk by."

"Who knows why?" Alma said. "It was a frequented spot, but it was raining that day. He was angry and irrational. He killed her quickly, dumped her in the bushes, and went home. You're young, Vivian, but it's an old story. Trust me." Alma set her empty coffee cup on the table and gentled her voice. "You're a nice girl, but you aren't trained for this kind of thing. I don't know why you think it's connected to Cathy. Is that what you're getting at?"

She couldn't have said. Because they were both cautionary tales, maybe. *Don't be like her. Don't end up like her.* It was a gut feeling. Which was stupid, because she was just a clueless girl, not a cop or a judge. She had no area of expertise.

Except being a potential victim. That was her area of expertise.

"There weren't two murders," Viv said. "There were three."

She pulled a newspaper clipping from her file and put it in front of Alma. *Local family still search for their daughter's killer*, the headline read.

"Betty Graham was murdered, too," Viv said.

Alma looked at the article, and for the first time her expression went hard. "I'm not going to talk about Betty Graham," she said. "I shouldn't be talking to you at all."

This was why she had done all this research. This was what mattered. To Viv, it was all about the woman in the flowered dress. Who, she now knew, was Betty Graham.

"Betty was unsolved," Viv said, pushing her. "Before Cathy. In November of 1978."

Alma's face was fully shut down now. She shook her head. "That's what this is all about, isn't it? I get it now. You heard about Betty and where her body was dumped. That's what set all of this off."

"A schoolteacher," Viv said. "Killed and dumped. The articles say her body was 'violated.' What does that mean? Does that mean rape? They didn't say Cathy was violated."

"Vivian, this isn't healthy. These kinds of topics aren't normal. A nice girl like you, you should be thinking about—"

"Parties? Boys? Movies? Cathy and Victoria cared about those things, I bet. Betty, too, maybe." She tapped the article sitting between them. "Her body was dumped at the Sun Down Motel."

Alma's voice was tight. "It wasn't the Sun Down Motel. Not then."

"No, it was a construction site. He killed her and dumped her body on a dirt heap at a construction site."

"It was years ago."

Maybe, but Betty is still there. She's still at the Sun Down. I've seen her, because she never left.

She's still there, and she's telling me to run.

Betty had been twenty-four. Unmarried with no boyfriends, no enemies, no wild habits. Gone from her own house in the middle of a Saturday, never seen alive again. Betty's parents were still grieving, still looking. "We just want to know who would do such a thing," Betty's father was quoted in the article as saying. "We can't understand it. I suppose it won't help in the end. But we just want to know."

The photo of Betty was of the woman she'd seen at the Sun Down. Her hair was tied back and there was a smile on her face for the camera, but it was her.

"What does 'violated' mean?" Viv asked again.

Alma shook her head. "You should drop this, honey. These are dark things. They aren't good for you."

"Dark things are *real* things," Viv said. She'd sat reading articles in the Fell library, her stomach sick. She'd gone home and wept soundlessly on her bed, the sobs coming as drowning gasps, thinking about the woman in the flowered dress, how she was still there where her body was dumped, as if she couldn't leave. "Listen," she said to Alma yet again. They were both due on shift in ten minutes. "The last person to see Betty alive was a neighbor who saw what she thought was a traveling salesman knock on Betty's door. She opened the door and let him in." Her blood pounded so hard in her temples that she heard her own voice like an echo. "There's a traveling salesman who comes to the motel. He uses fake names every time he checks in."

That made Alma go still for a minute as she thought it over—but only for a minute. "So you've seen a traveling salesman, and you think it could be Betty's killer?"

"A traveling salesman who comes to the Sun Down, where her body was left. And doesn't say who he is."

"Okay." Alma looked at her watch. "Look, I'll tell you what: Get me something, anything I can look up, and I'll look it up for you. Hell, no one gives a shit what I do on my shift anyway. Next time this guy comes in, get me something. Try to get a name, make and model of car, a license plate, the company where he works, anything. Chat him up a bit. Be nice, but be careful. You're a good-looking girl and not everyone is as nice as you are."

"I know." She knew that now.

"Okay then, we have a deal. I have to go to work now. See you later, Vivian. And if nothing comes of this—please drop it. If not for yourself, then for me."

Viv nodded, though she knew she would never drop it. It was in her blood now. She gathered her papers and notebook and went to work.

There was no one in the office again, though the lights were on and the door was unlocked. She put on her uniform vest and sat at the desk.

Next time this guy comes in, get me something.

She hadn't told Alma about the ghosts. About the woman in the flowered dress. About the fact that every time the traveling salesman checked in, the motel woke up and became a kind of waking nightmare.

As if the Sun Down didn't like him at all.

Next time this guy comes in, get me something.

Run.

Maybe it was nothing. It was probably nothing, and she was just a stupid girl who didn't know what she was talking about.

"Betty?" she said aloud into the silence.

There was no answer. But when she breathed in, Viv caught a faint trace of fresh cigarette smoke.

What does "violated" mean?

The man in the car, his hand on her thigh.

What does "violated" mean?

Get me something.

Betty, then Cathy, then Victoria. Three women murdered in Fell in the past few years. Their bodies dumped like trash. Even if one of them was solved, that still left two whose murderer was still out there. The salesman was the only lead she could think of, the only place to start.

She had a problem: She didn't know when the salesman would come again. She was stuck for however long, until he chose to check in. If he chose to check in ever again.

When he was here before, he'd left no trace of who he was. Except . . .

Viv thought it over and smiled to herself.

Maybe she wasn't stuck after all.

Fell, New York
November 2017
CARLY

Libraries were my places. I was that girl who maxed out her library card every week, starting with *The Hobbit* and *The Witch of Blackbird Pond* and moving up from there. I could kill an hour by wandering into an unfamiliar part of the Dewey Decimal System and checking it out. Computers, card catalogs, microfiches—I could navigate them all.

So the Fell Central Library was immediately familiar. It was set in the middle of downtown in a building that was large-ish and supposed to be prestigious based on its fake marble and columns. Inside it was musty and boxy, a huge cube with high windows and open stairs to the upper level. I bypassed the circulation desk on the main floor and headed for the back of the building, taking a guess at where the media archives room would be. I passed a few retirees, a thirty-year-old woman obviously studying feverishly for an exam, and a handful of students my age who probably went to Fell's tiny college. They likely assumed I was one of them, since I was wearing jeans, my lace-up boots, and a sweater under a waist-length jacket, my hair in its usual ponytail.

I hefted my messenger bag and wandered the stacks. The back of the library was pleasantly dusty and dim, far from the windows and full of empty corners. It suited my exhaustion, since it was four o'clock in the afternoon—the middle of the night for me. I'd had to rouse myself from bed to get to the library while it was still open. I hadn't had the heart to wake Heather and drag her with me since she slept so rarely, and was still asleep in our apartment.

I had to go upstairs to find what I wanted, but it was indeed at the back of the library: a glass door with the words FELL ARCHIVE ROOM on them. Inside the room I had the place to myself—just me, a couple of computer terminals, a few long tables, and a few shelves of books and magazines. I didn't even bother asking a librarian; I just sat down.

Twenty minutes later I'd figured out the archive system. It was time to learn about Fell.

I started with the obvious searches: *Viv Delaney, Viv Delaney missing, Sun Down Motel*. I'd only ever had the two articles I'd found in my mother's belongings, those two scraps of newsprint, but in Fell's database there was another article that mostly repeated the same information I already had, as well as one more titled *WHO WAS VIVIAN DELANEY? Local girl's disappearance leaves questions behind.* I entered my credit card number and hit Print on that one.

The *Sun Down Motel* search gave me different results. I narrowed the search parameters to 1980–1983 and didn't get many hits, so I expanded the years and then deleted the parameters entirely. What I got from that was, in its bits and pieces of glory, a chronological history of the Sun Down Motel.

It was built in 1978 on a plot of land called Cotton's Land because it had belonged to a farmer named Cotton before he sold out. It opened in early 1979—still the cold season, before the tourist season began. There wasn't much fanfare about its opening except for a photo of the motel, taken from just past the sign on the edge of Number Six Road. In front of the motel stood a woman, a man, and a young boy, their hands on his shoulders. The caption read: *Janice and Carl McNamara, with their son Christopher, in front of their new motel, called the Sun Down. The motel is now open for business and features a pool, cable TV, and rooms at twenty dollars per night.*

I looked closer at the little boy, recognizing Chris, the depressed guy who had hired me. *Frankly, I hate this place. I come out here as little as possible. Every memory I have of this place is bad.*

I looked at the photo for another minute. The Sun Down, on that day in early 1979, looked exactly like it did when I'd worked there last night—same doors, same fixtures, same sign. Except for Carl's big collar, Chris's gingham shirt, and Janice's ultra-high-waisted pants—which were coming back in style anyway—I *lived* in this picture. Even the motel office sign behind Carl's shoulder was the same one I saw every night. The parking lot was empty, the trees tall and dark in the backdrop. There was something creepy and comforting at the same time about the familiarity, as if Carl and Janice had never died, as if Chris hadn't grown up miserable and wishing the motel had never existed. As if the woman in the flowered dress could open one of the room doors and step out to the railing, asking politely when the pool would open.

I printed the photo and flipped to the next mentions. The Sun Down hadn't done well, even from the first—there was a marijuana bust there in December 1979, and a runaway girl was found there with her boyfriend in February 1980.

I scrolled to an article in July 1980 and froze.

BOY DIES IN TRAGIC POOL ACCIDENT, the headline read. It was buried in the back of the paper on July 13, 1980, two paragraphs in the "Local News" section. William Dandridge, known as Billy, age nine, had been staying at the Sun Down with his parents—they were driving to Florida—when he'd hit his head on the side of the pool. He'd been in the hospital for four days, his brain slowly swelling and dying, before he'd finally gone. His parents refused to speak to the press. When asked if the motel was going to hire a lifeguard, Janice McNamara had only said, "No. I think we'll just close the pool."

I stared at the monitor, my eyes going dry behind my glasses. That boy—I had seen him. Sitting on the motel's second level, his hand against the panel as he leaned forward. I'd watched him run away.

It was him. And now I knew who he was.

"Excuse me," a voice said at my shoulder. "Is this yours?"

I turned to find a man holding a stack of papers out to me. He was about my age, with soft golden brown hair worn a little long and brown eyes. He wore a black sweater and jeans, and behind him I could see a jacket and backpack on a table. I hadn't even heard him come in.

I looked at the papers. It was the stack of articles I'd printed out—they were likely sitting in the printer on the other side of the room. The article on top was the headline that read *WHO WAS VIVIAN DELANEY?*

"Thanks," I said, taking the stack of pages from him.

"Did you figure it out?" he asked. His voice was low but not quite a whisper. This was a library, but so far we were alone in this room.

"Figure what out?" I asked him.

He pointed to the headline. "Who was Vivian Delaney?" he said. "I have to admit, I kind of want to know."

I looked up at him again. I wasn't used to seeing guys in daylight anymore, I realized. I scrambled to recall how people who weren't me or Heather spoke to each other in the middle of the day. "She disappeared in 1982," I told the man. "No one ever found her."

"No shit," the guy said. "She disappeared from Fell?"

"From the Sun Down Motel. She was working a night shift there."

"I know that place." He pulled up a chair and sat on it next to me, then seemed to remember himself. "I'm Callum MacRae, by the way," he said, holding out his hand.

"Carly," I said, shaking it. Now that I was level with him I could see that he had even features, dark brown eyes set beneath symmetrical brows, a perfect nose and cheekbones, a good chin. Something about him radiated class—the sweater, maybe, which I could now see was far from cheap and fit him to every seam. Or the easy way he took over and leaned in, like it was his right. Or the crisp way he smelled, like he'd put expensive cologne on a day or two ago, its tang just barely discernible. It was a nice package, and he gave me a smile, but I still kept my guard up. I'd spent time in college, and he was an inch too far into my space. If this guy was a creeper, I'd have no problem making a scene.

"Sorry," Callum said, though his tone said he wasn't really. "I'm interrupting you. But I'm a geek when it comes to the history of Fell. Are you at FCCE? Doing a project?"

I was tired and stupid for a second. "What's FCCE?"

He smiled again, more widely. "I guess you aren't a student, then. It's the Fell College of Classical Education."

Oh. Right. "No, I don't go there. Do you?"

"Not really," Callum said. "Sort of. My mother is one of the profs there, so technically I get to go for free. It's a perk they have for their profs. I try to go, but to be honest I don't make it there very often." He shrugged. "It's boring, at least to me. I find this more interesting." He tapped my pages. "I guess it's a stupid question to ask if you're doing a project, since you're looking up Fell newspapers from 1982 and not Chaucer or something. I was just surprised to see someone in here. The only person who ever hangs out in this room is me."

I looked around. "You hang out in the archive room of the Fell Library?"

"It sounds weird, I know. But they haven't digitized the *Fell Daily* before 2014. I guess you know that, since you're here. You can't get older issues online."

"I know." It was a big part of the reason for this whole adventure, actually. I had wanted to come to Fell to read the archives, a century ago when I was a seminormal Illinois girl with a weird reading hobby and a skeleton in the family closet.

"There were two other Fell papers," Callum continued. His face had lit up, and I knew that whatever this was, it was his thing. "The *Fell Gazette* and the *Upstate New York Journal*. The *Gazette* was daily, the *Journal* weekly. The *Gazette* folded in 1980, the *Journal* in 1994. Neither of them are digitized, either, and they're full of amazing stuff. A lot of those two aren't even in the microfiches here. They're all paper issues in the stacks, if you can believe it. And I know I'm totally boring you, but I'm going somewhere with this, I promise." He smiled again, and I felt myself smiling back. "The library doesn't have the budget for the digitization project. When I heard that, I decided to do it myself. As a volunteer."

My eyebrows rose. "Wow. You come in here every day and digitize papers? For free?"

"Yeah, I have permission. It's not costing the library anything except for the scanner they bought and the computer they let me use. The librarians all know my mother because she's an FCCE prof. They know I want to do this. So here I am."

"But why?" I asked him. "Shouldn't you be in school or something?" I cringed inwardly, because I sounded exactly like my mother. "I didn't mean that the way it came out. I meant that if you really like this kind of thing, you could go to journalism school. Or intern at a paper."

"I could do that," Callum admitted, "but then I'd have to write about what they assign me and not what I want."

I sighed and adjusted my glasses on the bridge of my nose. "I get that, actually."

"I thought you would, because you're here, too. Sitting in the archives room alone, just like I do." He leaned forward. "This is Fell. Did you know that when they dug to make the parking lot of the Sav-Mart on Meller Street, they found six bodies? All children, all two hundred years old. That was in 1991. It wasn't a graveyard—there was just a pit with six kids in it, all dead of typhoid. There weren't even any coffins. Someone just dug a hole and put them in."

"Holy shit," I said. "Were they siblings?"

Callum held up a finger. "No," he said, relishing the moment. "Not siblings. They were Europeans, too. So what happened? If there was an outbreak, there's no record of it. Fell has a graveyard that dates back to 1756 and has European settlers in it. So why weren't these kids there? Who just dumped them in a hole and ran? No one knows. I found the story in the *Journal* when I was digitizing last week. They wrote one story, that's it. It's the craziest thing. Just 'someone found the bodies of six kids, no one knows why they're there. Also, it's going to rain this weekend.' That's what I mean about Fell."

"Yeah, I'm getting the idea," I said.

"You're not a local, I can tell." Callum leaned back in his chair. "Fell attracts weird types. People who are a bit morbid. No offense."

"None taken." I gestured to the article on the table between us. "Viv Delaney was my aunt. My mother was her only sibling, and she's dead now. I want to find out what happened, because she deserves some kind of justice. But nothing's going the way I thought it would."

He didn't ask what that meant. He just nodded. "Okay, then. You're not getting the full story on this microfiche. Let's find some of the papers from 1982."

Three hours later, Heather and I were sitting in our apartment, me on the sofa and her cross-legged on the floor. The coffee table was covered in printouts and photocopies, my spiral notebook sat open and scrawled in, and both of our laptops were open.

"This is a bonanza," she said. "I've always done my true-crime stalking on the Internet. I guess the Fell archives room is the place to be."

"I know." I wrapped a blanket over my lap. Not all of the articles I'd pulled were about Viv; in fact, very few of them were. Her disappearance was a blip in the life of Fell, just another thing that happened in 1982. "Here's what I don't understand," I said, picking up an article. Viv's photo looked back at me from the page, a picture I hadn't seen before. She was alone. Her shoulders were turned from the camera but she was looking back as if someone had called her name, her chin tilted down. The photo was slightly blurry, as if taken from a distance, but it was still clearly her. The other photos had been posed snapshots of Viv smiling, but in this picture her expression was serious, her mouth in a firm line, her brows slashes above her eyes, which were focused on something with deadly intensity. She wore a blue sweater with a handbag over her shoulder, and her bangs were flipped with a curling iron, her hair cut just above her shoulders. No matter how fuzzy the photo or how dated the hairstyle, Viv had been a pretty young woman. "The articles don't mention a search for her. Literally nothing. It seems like the cops asked around, put a few articles in the paper, and didn't try much else."

"Maybe we should talk to cops," Heather said. She held up a piece of paper. "This article quotes Edward Parey, chief of Fell PD. Let's see if he's still alive."

"Do you think he would talk to us?" I asked her.

Heather shrugged as she typed. "Why not? We're harmless. What does he think we're going to do?"

"If he's still alive, he's probably retired. Maybe he doesn't want to talk about old cases."

"Or maybe he does. If I'd been chief of police, and I'd retired, I'd be bored out of my mind." She clicked through a few pages. "Doesn't look like he's died. It would help if we knew someone who knew him, though."

"Maybe Callum can help."

Heather looked up at me, blank.

"The guy who helped me in the archives room today. I told you."

"Oh, right. Another one of your men."

I couldn't help it; I laughed.

"Well, you have a lot of them," Heather pointed out.

That made me laugh more. "I like that you don't know how pathetic I am," I told her. "I don't think I talked to an actual, literal man in college. One of them might have spoken to me at a party and I nearly choked on my drink. Then I went home and read *The Deathly Hallows* again so I could tell myself that was why I was crying."

"My God, we're truly soul sisters," Heather said. "Men are not my bailiwick." At my carefully blank expression, she said, "Relax. Men are my bailiwick *in theory*. I just don't like . . ." She moved her hands around, miming a bubble. "I don't like anyone touching me. Anywhere, ever."

"I get that," I said.

"Carly, *no one* gets that. Not my parents, not boys, not shrinks. Not anyone."

I thought again about the lineup of medications on our bathroom counter and said, "I do. Not wanting someone's hands on you. I get it."

There was a slow arc of seriousness for a long moment. She looked at me, and I could see she wanted to say something important. But in the end she didn't, and she looked away with a small sigh.

And I wasn't lying. I did get it. I thought about Callum MacRae, as nice as he was, and I got it. Then I thought about Nick Harkness, and my first thought was that I could picture wanting his hands on me. I could picture it easily, even though he'd never do it.

I smoothed the photocopied page in my lap and looked down at Viv again. At how alive and unrehearsed she was in this picture, like she was just going about her business instead of posing for a camera. And then it struck me that maybe she hadn't even been aware this picture was taken. Like someone had taken it and she hadn't seen.

I looked at the bottom of the picture and read: *Photo by Marnie Mahoney.*

Fell, New York
October 1982
VIV

Helen and Robert were at the Sun Down again. So was the green sedan that followed them. It was still there at seven in the morning; it had been there all night. It was raining and the sun was only a faint grayish tinge through the pour of water. Viv wondered how the man in the green sedan could get any good photos in this light.

Her shift was finished, so she shed her polyester vest and put on her coat. Sometimes Janice showed up to relieve her at seven, and sometimes she didn't. Viv always left either way. There weren't any real rules at the Sun Down.

There was no sign of Janice, so Viv locked the office door, though she left the neon sign on. She put her hood up to fend off the rain and took the path away from the parking lot, heading toward the pool. She circled the edge of the motel property, her feet in their sneakers splashing in the cold puddles. She trotted along the thin strand of trees that bordered Number Six Road and skirted to the back of the parking lot. By the time she approached the green sedan, from the other side of the motel, her feet were soaked and there was rain running down her neck.

The car was parked at the back edge of the parking lot, the same place as before, its right tires on the line where concrete met dirty gravel. The inside was dark, and in the rain Viv couldn't see through the windows. She walked up to the front passenger side and knocked on the window.

A shadow moved inside the car, but nothing else happened. Obviously he wanted her to go away, so Viv bent at the waist and said loudly to the glass, "They'll be out in ten minutes. They're getting ready to leave right now."

Another second of nothing, and then the shadow moved again and the window started to crank down. Viv caught a whiff of a smell that was surprisingly nice, like clean perfume. A woman's voice said, "What the hell are you talking about?"

Viv stood frozen with surprise, but she recovered herself quickly. "The couple in room one-oh-nine," she said. "That's who you're waiting for, isn't it? You're waiting to take pictures. You've been here all night."

Silence from the car, then a breathed "Shit" that Viv could hear over the rain.

"They usually don't stay this long," Viv continued. "They leave by four, though you already know that. The man just called his wife to tell her he's on his way home. She'll come out any minute. She always leaves first."

"Shit." This one was louder. "Get in the back seat, for God's sake. I'm trying to make a living here."

Viv opened the back door and slid into the car. She pushed her hood back, dripping on the pleather, and looked at the woman in the front seat.

The woman turned in the driver's seat and looked back at her. The other woman was black, slender, with natural hair in a short Afro. She looked to be in her late twenties. She was wearing a blouse in an understated floral print and neat jeans. She had no makeup and gold studs in her ears. If she was tired after being awake all night, her face showed no sign of it.

Viv hadn't expected a black woman. She'd expected a man, a detective type from one of her TV shows. Detectives weren't black women, not even on *Cagney & Lacey*. Then again, why not? Fell was full of surprises. Viv was almost used to it by now.

Next to the woman on the front passenger seat was a bag of bulky camera equipment and a lunch bag that had obviously contained her dinner. The woman's dark brown eyes looked straight into Viv's, and Viv saw someone who was tough, wary, and not a little annoyed, because she knew exactly what Viv was thinking.

The woman's eyes narrowed with recognition. "You're the office girl."

"Yes," Viv said. "And you're the one following Helen while she cheats on her husband."

"That bother you? Are you going to call your boss about it?"

"No," Viv said. "It doesn't bother me at all. And I don't know where my boss is."

The woman's face turned harder. "So you came into my car exactly why? Because you don't have anything better to do?"

Viv held her gaze. "No. I came because I need a favor."

"A favor?" The woman shook her head, almost laughing. "Shit and double shit," she said. "This is not my night. I didn't know you made me, office girl. I obviously need to be more discreet."

"They have no idea you're here," Viv offered. "I'm sure of it."

"Uh-huh. And how do you know what Romeo says in his phone calls?"

"There's something defective about the phone line," Viv replied. "When someone makes a call, I can lift the receiver in the office and listen to it. I do it all the time."

The woman's eyes widened for a brief second. "Huh. That's handy."

Viv shrugged. "It depends on what you want to hear. But if you want something in return for a favor for me, I can tell you everything either of them has ever said on the telephone at the Sun Down."

There was a moment of silence as the woman thought this through. The quiet settled throughout the car. Viv wondered if she'd played her cards wrong. Maybe she had. She hadn't planned on selling out Helen and Robert to get what she wanted, but she was starting to learn that you had to do what you had to do.

"Okay, I'll bite," the woman said finally. She held out her hand. "My name is Marnie."

Viv shook it. "Viv. I think that—"

"Shh." Marnie dropped her hand and grabbed her camera. "Get down in the seat, will you? Out of sight."

Viv saw that the door to room 109 had opened and Helen was coming out. She was dressed in jeans again, with a long-waisted black and white shirt under her coat. She put a piece of paper over her head—Viv recognized the yellowed *Welcome to the Sun Down!* card that was on the nightstand in every room—and hurried through the rain to her car.

Watching Helen made Viv think about her parents. After the divorce, her father had remarried in less than a year. Had he cheated? Her mother had never said anything. Then again, her mother was so humiliated she would rather die than tell the truth. The entire divorce had gone down in stony silence—her father was there, and then he was gone. There was no discussion, nothing but her father's absence and her mother's panicked insistence on perfection from both of her daughters, as if being perfect would make all of the problems go away.

If there had been cheating, neither parent would ever tell her. Even though she was an adult now. She would never have the truth.

Viv slid down in the back seat as Marnie aimed her camera and clicked it over and over. She captured Helen getting in her car, driving away. Then she put the camera down. "Damn, that woman is cold," she commented.

"Who hired you?" Viv asked, sitting up in her seat again. "His wife or her husband?"

Marnie glanced at her. "I'm not supposed to tell. But I've been sitting in this car all night, so too bad. A lawyer hired me. He represents the husband. The man thinks something is going on."

"You should have plenty of evidence by now."

"I do. But I give the lawyer a roll of film and he asks me for another one. He wants it ironclad, he says. Sounds to me like that bitch is going to get put out on her ass. And for what? A few nights with Mr. White in there? Don't get me wrong, the man is far from ugly. But a girl can find a not-ugly man any day of the week, and an unmarried one, too. He must be some kind of Superman in bed."

Viv looked out at the rain and thought about Helen. "I don't think she's looking for romance. I don't know what she's looking for, but that's not it."

"I don't give a shit what she's looking for," Marnie said practically, putting her camera gear back in its bag. "Personally, I'm looking for a check. And I just earned one. Now I get to sleep before my next gig."

"This is what you do all the time? Every day?" Viv asked. "It seems dangerous. I mean, for a woman. I thought you'd be a man."

"You did? Well, we're all disappointed sometimes. You thought I'd be white, too, right? You can say it."

Viv shrugged. She had.

"I don't do this all the time," Marnie said, indicating the parking lot, the motel. "I do other work, too. I take glamour shots and sometimes I work school photo days. Real estate agents need pictures of the houses they're advertising. On slow days I can pick up five or six houses at four bucks a shot. It isn't creative, but it's work."

Viv had never heard of anyone doing any of that for a living. It seemed her time at the Sun Down Motel was one learning experience after another. "The pictures you take of the motel. Do you still have them?"

"Once I develop them, I keep a copy of every one. Even the ones I'm not supposed to. You never know what's going to be useful. Why do you ask? Shit, here he comes. Get down. I don't want him to see you."

Viv looked out to see Mr. White leaving his room and locking the door behind him. He was slim, fit, and vigorous, and he plainly wore a wedding band on his left hand. He was dressed in a dark suit and light shirt, his tie knotted, salt-and-pepper hair combed back from his forehead. He opened an umbrella and in a flash of panic Viv realized he would have to check out. "There's no one in the office," she said. "I'm off shift and Janice hasn't come in yet. It's locked."

Marnie was pulling her camera out of her bag again. "Did he pay up front?"

"Yes."

"Then don't worry about it." She aimed the camera, snapped a few shots of Mr. White walking to the office. He seemed like any average man going to work on an average day, except he was leaving a motel at seven o'clock in the morning after a night with a woman who wasn't his wife.

"I don't really need the pictures of him," Marnie said as the camera clicked. "Just her. But here he is, so I may as well. To each her own, you know? White men aren't my thing."

She tossed the words off so easily, and Viv felt the pain of embarrassment in her chest. Even though her mother saw her as a delinquent, the fact was that she was twenty years old and a virgin. She had no idea what kind of man was "her thing." You had to have tried a few men, at least, to know that. She wondered if she'd ever be as worldly as Marnie, or Helen, or even Alma Trent, who seemed to know everything. Still, she tried it on by saying, "He isn't my type, either."

Marnie clicked her camera as Mr. White tried the locked office door, then gave up. She laughed softly, not unkindly. "You're a sweet girl," she said as she followed the man through her lens. He walked back down the walkway, tossed the key back into the motel room, closed the door, and jogged to his car. "Tell me what you're doing in my car in the rain," Marnie said.

Still slid down in the back seat, her coat rucked up around her ears, Viv let the words *This is stupid* trickle through her mind.

But deep in her gut, she knew they were a lie. The burning inside her chest that had started when she first learned about Cathy's and Victoria's murders, of Betty Graham's body being dumped at the future Sun Down, hadn't subsided. In fact, it had gotten worse. She wasn't sleeping during the day, and instead she spent her time at the Fell Central Library, going through more and more old papers, looking for something, anything at all. But she had hit a dead end. The appearance of Helen and Mr. White tonight, with the green sedan in faithful attendance, had been a godsend that sent her spirits up. It was the thing she'd been waiting for.

Next time this guy comes in, get me something.

This wasn't stupid. Not at all.

"Have you heard of Betty Graham?" she asked Marnie.

The woman in the front seat went still for a second. "What do you know about Betty Graham?" she asked, and her voice had an edge of suspicion. "And why are you asking?"

"Her body was dumped here," Viv said. "At the Sun Down, before it was built. Did you know that?"

"Yeah, I knew that." Marnie lowered her camera as Mr. White drove away. "A lot of people know that. It was a big deal when it happened. My question is, why do *you* know that?"

Because I've seen her, Viv thought. She'd seen the woman in the flowered dress again three nights ago. She'd heard the soft click of heels outside the office door, and when she'd gone to the door and opened it, she'd smelled a faint scent of perfume. The woman in the flowered dress was standing twenty feet away, her back to Viv, the hem of her dress rippling in the wind, her pretty hair lifted from her neck. She hadn't turned around.

Viv had gathered her courage and said, *Betty?*

The woman hadn't answered. And then she was gone.

"I'm interested," Viv said, to try to placate the suspicious tone in Marnie's voice. "I work here, and I heard about this famous murder in Fell. With the body dumped where I work. So I'm interested."

"Uh-huh." Marnie's tone said that cynicism was her usual default. "And what does this have to do with me?"

"The last person to see Betty Graham alive saw her with a traveling salesman," Viv said. "He knocked on her door and she let him in. No one saw either of them leave. No one knows if he killed her or even who he was."

Marnie turned in her seat and looked at Viv. "Go on."

"There's a traveling salesman who comes to the motel," Viv said. She pointed out the window, to the Sun Down, sheeted with rain. "He checks in here. To this place. Over and over. And he uses a fake name every time."

It wasn't the same as with Alma. Marnie stared at Viv like Viv was reading a page from a book she'd never thought to hear aloud. "You are shitting me," she said, her voice almost a whisper. "Little girl, you are shitting me."

"He was here the last time Helen was here," Viv said. "The last time *you* were here. Taking pictures. So I want to know if he's in any of your pictures. His face, anything. And I want to know if his car is in your pictures. Because if I can get a license plate, I can find out who he is. Who he really is."

The words Marnie said were teasing, but her voice was dead serious. "This is what you're doing, then? Playing Nancy Drew and solving the murder in the middle of the night?"

Viv held the other woman's eyes and didn't look away. Her answer was simple. "Someone has to."

Marnie seemed to think things over. "Okay," she said, "I can take a look at my shots. They're all developed."

"Can I look for myself?"

"You have a spine on you, you know that? But I get it. What happened to Betty Graham shouldn't happen to anyone, and whoever did it is still walking around. If there's a chance this guy is him, then I suppose I can go through some photos with you."

"It isn't just Betty," Viv said. "There are others."

Marnie shook her head, her lips pressed together. She said, "You mean the girl left under the overpass. The one with the baby."

There was a feeling in the back of Viv's neck like a tap that had been turned too tight, that was finally being twisted loose. Of something finally flowing that had been twisted off for too long, maybe forever. Marnie *knew*. Like it was common knowledge for every woman in Fell. Like the women here all spoke the same language. "Her, and another one. Victoria."

"The jogging trail girl." Marnie eyed Viv up and down again. "Are you a cop, or what? You say you work at the Sun Down, and you really don't look like a cop."

"I'm not a cop. I just spent some time in the library, looking up dead girls. I think there are a lot of them in Fell."

"You think there are a lot of them in Fell." Marnie repeated the words back. "You think? I've lived here all my life. Every woman was afraid when Betty Graham died. Every single one. We locked our doors and didn't go out at night. Our mothers called us ten times a day. Even my mother, and Betty was white. Because we were all Betty. For a few weeks, at least. You know?"

Viv swallowed and nodded. "We're all still Betty," she said. "At least I am."

Marnie shook her head again. "You're a strange girl, but I like you. Get in the front seat."

Viv got out of the back seat and got in the front, which Marnie had cleared of photography equipment. "Are we going somewhere?"

"I'll get you your photos," Marnie said, putting the key in the ignition and starting the car. "But if you're so interested in dead girls, let's take a little tour."

t took them four days to even realize Viv was missing," I said. *"Four days. Can you believe it?"*

I was in the AMENITIES room with Nick. It was two o'clock in the morning. The candy machine wasn't working, so Nick had agreed to take a look at it. He'd gone into the motel's maintenance room—I hadn't even known there was one—and come out with a toolbox. Now I was sitting on the ice machine while he poked at the candy machine in the tiny, closet-sized room. We'd found an old brick and propped the door open with it, because the door kept trying to close on its own.

"What do you mean?" Nick said. "No one called the police?"

"No. The papers said she *likely* went missing during her shift on the twenty-ninth of November. She talked to the guy who was on the shift before her, and that was the last anyone saw. Four days later, when the cops started looking for her, they found her belongings in the Sun Down office."

Nick unscrewed something and the front of the candy machine popped open. "I'd say the staff wasn't very observant, but then again I've been here for weeks. There's barely any staff at all."

"I know. Most of the time no one relieves me at seven in the morning. It makes me think that if I disappeared during my shift, no one would know."

"I would know," Nick said.

My cheeks went hot. I couldn't think of anything to say.

He was looking at the candy machine and he didn't notice. "I thought she had a roommate," he said.

"The roommate's name was Jenny Summers." When Nick was focused on the candy machine, I could stare at his profile without him noticing. His profile was pretty much perfect when you looked at it closely. His blue eyes were set under a more or less semipermanent scowl, especially when he was concentrating. His nose was just right. He hadn't shaved in a few days, and he had a dark brown shadow of beard along his jaw and under his cheekbones. When he turned the screwdriver, mysterious and amazing things happened in the muscles and tendons of his forearms, and his biceps flexed under the sleeve of his T-shirt. It was time to admit I had a crush on the mysterious occupant of room 210.

Nick paused, and I realized I'd stopped talking in order to ogle him. I recovered and remembered what I was saying. "I looked up Jenny Summers today," I said. Nick's frown eased a degree and he went back to work. "Her name is still Jenny Summers—she hasn't changed it. And get this—she's in the Fell phone book. Because Fell has an actual, physical phone book."

"I know," Nick said, picking up his screwdriver again and flipping a switch on the inside of the candy machine. Nothing happened. "There's one in the motel office."

"There is," I said, pointing at him in congratulations, though he wasn't looking at me. "I found it in the desk drawer. There's also a copy at the library. It's like the Internet never happened in this place."

"You have to get used to it," Nick said.

He crouched down to pick a different screwdriver out of the toolbox, and the pose made his shirt ride a few inches up his lower back. I stared fixedly at that slice of skin and said, "Anyway, Jenny Summers is listed in there. I called her and left her a message, telling her I'm Viv's niece. I also tried to contact the cop that worked on the case. I want to know why no one knew she was gone for four whole days."

"She didn't have friends, a boyfriend," Nick said. "When you're all alone, it can happen."

"That's the other thing," I said. Beneath me, the ice machine made a random rumble, like a belch, and the inner workings clicked. It was weird, thinking about this machine making ice year after year when no one ever needed it. I waited politely until it was finished before I continued. "The news stories all described Viv as pretty and popular. And she really was pretty. But no one who is popular disappears for four days without anyone noticing. I mean, I'm not even popular, but I at least had to tell my roommate I was leaving college for a while. She would have thought I'd been taken by the *Silence of the Lambs* guy if I didn't come home."

"That's now," Nick pointed out. "We're talking about 1982. It was different then."

"Maybe. But why describe a girl as popular when no one even notices she's disappeared? That doesn't sound very popular to me."

Nick scrubbed a hand through his hair. "I don't know. Maybe the reporter who wrote the story just assumed she was popular."

"Because she was pretty? They just looked at a photo of a good-looking girl and decided she must be popular? Like a woman who's pretty can't have problems. She can't have any depth. She can't have any life except a perfect one."

Nick glanced at me, amused. "Nice rant, but I didn't write the article."

I was talking his ear off, I knew, but I couldn't seem to help it. I should probably shut up about Viv, but I was obsessed, I'd already told Heather all of this, and the longer I talked to Nick, the longer I could look at him. "Do you really think you can fix the candy machine?" I asked.

"No," Nick said honestly, standing up again. The slice of skin disappeared, but a different slice appeared when he raised his arm and grabbed the first screwdriver, which he'd left on top of the machine. Was his stomach honestly that flat? "I can't even figure out how it works in the first place. It has to be a few decades old. Have you ever actually gotten candy out of this thing?"

"No. I came in here to get a chocolate bar, because the machine says they're twenty cents, which is insane. I put two dimes in and it just ate my money and made strange noises. So I figured it was broken."

"Well, it's been broken for a while. There's dust on these M&M's. This Snickers doesn't look too bad." He held it out to me, so I took it and he turned to the machine again, using the screwdriver to pry open a panel on the side. "I wonder if it's jammed."

"Jammed with what?"

"Your guess is as good as mine. I don't see anything in there. But this machine is definitely not dishing out candy. Breaking in is your only option."

I sighed. "All this work, and all I got was a dusty Snickers bar."

"Don't knock it," Nick said. He inspected the panel he'd just opened. "Yeah, this is definitely broken. I'm surprised the thing is plugged in."

I ripped open the Snickers bar. Because why not? It wasn't *that* old—like, not decades old. A year or two, maybe. "My guess is that a repair person costs money. We do not spend money at the Sun Down. Not on new phones, not on electronic keys—nothing."

"My room is like a museum," Nick agreed, putting the panel back on the side of the machine. "The lampshades are the color of cigarettes and the bedspread has those fabric knobs in it. I don't care, because I'm sleeping for the first time since I was a teenager. Oh, shit—something's happening."

The candy machine, reassembled now, made a whirring noise. My two dimes clinked somewhere deep in the mechanism. There was a *thump*, and a second Snickers bar appeared in the gap at the bottom.

We both stared for a second in surprise.

"Um, congratulations?" I said. "Looks like you fixed it."

Nick looked as shocked as I felt. "Looks like I did." He picked up the Snickers bar. "Which cop did you call?"

"What?"

"You said you called the cop that worked your aunt's disappearance. Which one?" He glanced at me. "Carly, I know every cop in Fell."

Right. Because his brother had been murdered, and he almost had been, too. "Edward Parey," I said. "He was chief of police."

Nick shook his head. "He won't help you. Parey was chief when my brother died, and he was an asshole then. I doubt he's improved."

When my brother died. He said it like his brother had passed away naturally. His expression gave nothing away.

"Okay, then," I said. "He's likely a dead end. I'll find someone else."

"I know a few names you can call." Nick scratched the back of his neck, thinking. "Don't mention my name, though. I got into a lot of trouble as a teenager and none of them are fans of mine."

"What did you do?"

"Stole stuff, got in fights. Got drunk a lot. I went off the rails after the murder, became a bad kid. You probably shouldn't associate with me, really."

"I'm sorry," I said, because I realized I'd never said that to him. It wasn't adequate, but it was something.

He gave me a curious look, as if I'd said something strange. Then he said, "Did you call Alma Trent?"

I shook my head. "Who's Alma Trent?"

"She's the cop who used to work the night shift. She worked it for years—decades. She has to be retired by now. She was a beat cop, but she might have met Viv if she worked nights."

"Does Alma Trent hate you?" I asked him.

That made him smile a little. "She mopped me off the floor of a party or two, but she was okay about it. I got a few lectures about letting my life waste away. Alma didn't put up with any shit." His smile faded. "Jesus, I just realized I've been back in Fell for a month and I've barely left this motel. I don't know if any of these people I knew are still around."

I poked at my Snickers bar, dropping my gaze. "Come with me," I said. "When I talk to some of these people."

He was quiet, and I looked up to see that his blue eyes had gone hard. "That isn't a good idea," he said slowly.

"You said you came back to face your demons, right? To get over the past. You can't do that by staying at the motel. Maybe getting out will help."

"It isn't that easy," Nick said. He turned back to the machine and closed the front, picking up the screwdriver again. "For you, maybe, because you're a stranger. But not for me. I know these people. A lot of them knew my father, knew Eli. I'll face them when I'm ready, but not before."

My cell phone rang at eleven thirty in the morning. I was deep under my covers in the dark, asleep and dreaming—something about a road and a lake, the stillness of the water. I didn't want to swim. I rolled out of my covers at the sound of the phone, a sheen of cool sweat on my skin.

I picked up the phone from my nightstand. "Hello?"

"Is this Carly Kirk?" a woman asked.

I frowned, still in a fog. "Yes."

"This is Marnie Clark returning your call."

Marnie Clark, formerly Marnie Mahoney. The photographer who was credited with the photo of Viv I'd seen in the paper. I'd taken a shot and Googled her. She'd gotten married in 1983, but she was still in Fell, just like Jenny Summers, Viv's old roommate. No one, it seemed, ever left Fell. Or if they did—like Nick—they eventually came back.

"Hi," I said to Marnie, sitting up in bed. Outside my room I could hear Heather banging around in the kitchen. "Thank you for calling me."

"Don't thank me," the woman said. Her voice wasn't angry, but it was firm. "I don't have anything to tell you about Vivian Delaney."

"I saw a photo in the paper," I said. "Your name was on it."

"That's just a photo, honey. I was a freelance photographer in those days. I took a lot of pictures. The papers bought some of them. Other people bought other ones. It was how I made a living."

"It looked like a candid photo," I said.

"Yeah, it probably was. Unless she sat for a portrait for me, it would have been a candid. But I don't remember it. And I don't remember her."

I rubbed a hand through my hair. "Maybe you don't understand. Viv was my aunt. She disappeared in 1982. No one has ever found her and—"

"I know what happened," Marnie said. "I know she disappeared. I saw it in the papers, and I had a photo of her, and I offered it to them for sale. They bought it. I cashed the check. That's all I have to say."

"I just thought—"

"You're on the wrong track, honey," the woman said. "Whatever you think is going to happen, it isn't. You have to accept that."

"What?"

"I'm just giving you some advice here. It's been thirty-five years. I've lived in this town all my life. Gone is gone. You get me? It's hard to take, but sometimes gone is just gone. That's all I have to say about Vivian Delaney, or anyone."

"Listen," I said. "Maybe we can meet for coffee or something. I just want to talk."

But there was no one on the other end of the line. Marnie Clark had hung up.

Fell, New York
October 1982
VIV

It seemed fitting that the rain was still coming down as Marnie drove them through town. She wound through the streets of downtown Fell and to the other side, where the small split-level homes tapered off into farmland and scrub, pocked by warehouses and run-down auto body shops that never seemed to be open. She pulled up next to an overpass and parked on the gravel, the windshield facing the dark tunnel in the rain.

"This is where Cathy Caldwell was found," Marnie said.

Viv pulled her hood up over her head and got out of the car, her sneakers squelching on the wet ground. Cars passed on the highway overhead, a small two-lane that fed onto the interstate miles away. Other than that, the world was quiet except for the rushing of the rain. There was no one around, no other cars on this road, no buildings in sight.

Viv looked at the overpass, the shadowed concrete place beneath it. It was just an overpass, one of thousands, an ugly stretch of concrete spattered by a few lazy squiggles of spray-painted graffiti, as if the teenagers of Fell couldn't be bothered to come out here very often, no matter how bored they were. Beneath the gray sky the mouth of the overpass looked dark, like it was waiting to swallow prey. The road beyond was slick with water in the hazy light.

Viv passed beneath the lip of the overpass and the rain stopped beating on her hood. She pushed it back and looked around. There was a concrete shoulder on either side of the road, and the ground at her feet was littered with trash, a broken beer bottle, and cigarette butts. There was a deflated piece of rubber that she realized with shock must be a condom—a used one. She looked away, blinking and smelling old urine.

Cathy's killer had dumped her body here. This place, of all places. *This* place. Viv pushed down her disgust, her outrage at the thought of being left here to lie naked and dead, and tried to think. Why this place?

First of all: There was no one to see. That much was obvious. Since Marnie had parked the car, no one had driven through here. The only potential witnesses were the cars passing overhead, and those drivers would have to be leaning out their windows to see. How long did it take to dump a body? One minute, two? She had already stood here longer than that.

Second of all: The overpass was full of shadows. A body might be mistaken for a sleeping drunk or an addict. Compared to a ditch or an open field, there was the chance for a longer time before the body was discovered. Yet the body *would* be discovered—that was also clear.

Third of all: This was a place for the people who knew where it was. The drunks, the teenagers, the condom users. This wasn't a place that someone would randomly find on a stroll. He dumped the body here because he'd driven through here before. Probably many times. In one direction or the other—this was a road he'd taken.

Cathy, being taken as she got into her car to go home from work. At a time when her husband was away. Her body dumped here.

Viv walked back to the car and got in. Marnie was sitting in the driver's seat, and Viv realized she'd been watching her the entire time.

"Well?" the other woman said.

Viv ran a hand through her hair, her careful curls that were wet now, her pretty makeup that had been rubbed off long ago. "He picked her," she said. "He followed her. He knew where she worked, knew that her husband was away. And after he killed her he picked this place. He planned it—and he's local."

"Well, hell. All that from five minutes standing there?" Marnie seemed to think this over. "He's local because he knows this place," she said, putting the pieces together. "A stranger wouldn't know."

Viv pointed through the overpass. "What's that way?"

"It goes out of town, heading south to New York."

New York. Viv remembered wanting to go there, wanting to be on this very road. Planning to pass through Fell and take this very route. She could still do it. She could still go.

Someone who came and went from Fell would take this road. Someone like, say, a traveling salesman.

She turned to Marnie. "Let's go to the next place."

Marnie took her to a tree-lined street on the edge of what passed for Fell's suburbs, a neighborhood of twenty-year-old bungalows. Viv had been born in a house like this before her father got a better job and they moved into a brand-new house in Grisham, surrounded by freshly dug lawns and newly planted trees. This street was well kept and unpretentious, and was probably pretty on a summer day, though now it was soaked and dark in the early-morning rain.

Marnie pulled the car up to a curb and turned the engine off.

"What's this place?" Viv asked her.

"You asked about Betty Graham," Marnie said. "She let a traveling salesman into her house on a Saturday afternoon." She pointed. "That's Betty's house."

Viv stared through the windshield as the rain pelted the car. The house was small and tidy, with a neat front walk and well-tended shrubs in the garden beneath the windows. It was past eight o'clock in the morning now, and as they watched a man came out the front door. He wore a plaid overcoat and a matching brown hat, and he looked to be in his late

fifties. He checked his watch, then got in his car and drove away. Somewhere nearby, a dog barked.

"They sold the place, obviously," Marnie said. "You'd think they'd
have trouble selling it, but they didn't. Maybe because Betty wasn't killed
in the house."

"She wasn't?"

Marnie shook her head. "There was a broken lamp in the living room.
That was the only sign anything had happened there at all. No blood, no
nothing. He got her out of there somehow." She pointed to a house across
the street. "That's the neighbor who saw the salesman. She saw him go in
the house. No one saw anyone leave."

"How is that possible?"

Marnie shrugged, though the motion was tight, her shoulders tense.
"You'd have to ask him that. All anyone knows is that Betty disappeared,
and then her body showed up on the construction heap that was the Sun
Down Motel."

The woman in the flowered dress. She'd lived here, but she didn't
haunt this place. She haunted the motel instead.

"How do you know so much about all of this?" Viv asked her.

"The Fell PD hires me sometimes to take photos of crime scenes. Usually burglary scenes—smashed windows, broken locks, ransacked rooms,
footprints in the garden. The PD is so small that they don't have someone
full time to do pictures, and they don't have enough equipment for two
scenes at a time. That's where I come in. Freelance, of course." She started
the car again. "I've never shot a body, but I've worked with cops. I listen
to what they talk about, the things they say among themselves. Cops gossip just like everyone else. And if they aren't paying attention to you, you
can listen."

"They don't think the same man did these," Viv said. It wasn't a
question.

"Not even close. It's a small police department. It isn't like the movies,
with a staff of detectives to look at this stuff. Betty and Cathy didn't travel

in the same circles or know any of the same men. And Victoria's boy-friend was convicted of her murder, so they don't include her at all."

She pulled away from the curb and drove slowly forward, her wipers going in the rain. "What if they're right?" Viv asked her. "What if these girls all got killed by different men for different reasons?"

"Then we don't have a killer in Fell," Marnie said. "We have more than one. Which one gives you the best odds, honey?"

The jogging path where Victoria Lee was murdered was nearly dark in the rain, the last dead leaves drooping wetly from the trees, the ground thick with soaked mulch. The entrance was off a side street, blocked by a small guardrail that everyone obviously stepped over. There was no sign.

"Victoria's house is that way," Marnie said, pointing to a row of the backs of houses visible on a rise behind a line of fence. "She would have come around the end of the road and up the street here toward the trail."

"This is wide open," Viv commented, looking around. "Anyone could have walked by."

"Not that day," Marnie said. "It was raining, just like it is today. A thunderstorm, actually. No one uses the path in the rain."

Viv swung her leg over the guardrail and walked onto the jog-ging path, her hood up, the rain soaking the fabric. "She went running in the rain."

"After an argument." Marnie followed Viv over the guardrail. She didn't bother with the fiction of a hood; she just got wet, let the water run down the jacket she wore. "She didn't get far. Her body was found about thirty feet down the path."

The sound of the rain was quieter under the trees, hushed in the thick carpet of brush along the path. Water dripped and trickled onto Viv's forehead, and her shoes squelched in the mud. She pushed her hood back and looked around. It was like a cathedral in here, dark and silent and scary. You couldn't see the place where the trees cleared and the yards and houses beyond, even though it wasn't far away. Standing here felt like being in a forest that went for miles. "Where does the path lead?" she asked Marnie.

"It runs just over a mile. It's old city land that was supposed to be used for a railroad that was never built. That was probably a century ago. The land sat for a long time while the city argued over it, and in the end they just left it, because it's long and narrow and they can't use it for much else. In the meantime the people who live around here made a path. It ends just behind the Bank and Trust building on Eastern Road."

Viv walked farther down the path. "The newspapers didn't say that Victoria was an athlete," she said. They'd only said that Victoria got in a lot of trouble in school, as if that might be a reason her boyfriend had grabbed her and strangled her. As if somehow she deserved it. They didn't say it outright, but Viv could read it between the lines—any girl could. *If you're bad, if you're slutty, this could happen to you.* Even the articles about saintly, married Cathy Caldwell speculated whether her killer could be a secret boyfriend. *Sneak around behind your husband's back, and this could happen to you.* Viv wondered what the newspapers would say if Helen the cheating wife died.

"She wasn't a runner," Marnie said. "She was just trying to keep slim. You know, for all those guys she supposedly dated."

So a girl no one had really liked had come down this path, running in the rain because she was angry and needed to move. Viv left the path and fought her way through the brush, which was wet and darkened the knees of her jeans. Her shoes were hopelessly wet now, her socks soaked through.

He did it quick, she thought. Victoria was running, angry. She wasn't sweet or pliant. He'd have to physically jump her, grab her, stop her. Get her on the ground. Get her quiet. His hand over her mouth, on her throat. Maybe he had a knife or a gun.

Would Victoria have fought? She could have at least tried to scream— there were houses not far away, including her own. There was a good chance there were people in hearing range. All it would have taken was one scream.

But if the man who grabbed her was her boyfriend, someone familiar, would she have screamed?

Viv turned in a circle, the thoughts going inescapably through her mind: *What would I have done?* Because this could have been her, storming out of the house at eighteen after a fight with her mother. Or leaving work. Doing what women did every day.

It could still be her now. It could be her tomorrow, or the next day, or the next. It could be Marnie, it could be Helen. It could be Viv's sister back home in Illinois. This was the reality: It wasn't just these girls. It could always, always be her or someone she knew.

She looked back at the path. *Would I scream?* She didn't think so. She would have been so terrified, so horribly afraid, that she would have done whatever the man said. *Don't speak. Don't make a sound. Come over here. Lie down.* And when he heard someone coming and put his hands on her neck, it would all be over.

"You think the boyfriend didn't do it?" Marnie called to her from the path.

"I don't know," Viv answered honestly. "It's like you said. If he did it, then there's more than one killer in Fell."

"You're ignoring the possibility that he did Betty Graham and Cathy Caldwell. Maybe it's Victoria's boyfriend who is the serial killer."

Viv closed her eyes as water dripped through the trees. It was possible, she had to admit. The timeline worked. "So he started with strange women, then killed his girlfriend."

"And he hasn't killed anyone since. Because the cops caught the right man."

The rain was cold on Viv's skin, but she welcomed it. She felt hot, her blood pumping hard. "Victoria was eighteen when she was killed. Was her boyfriend older?"

"He was twenty."

"Still, it puts him in high school when Betty was killed. He would have had to pull off posing as a salesman."

"If the salesman actually did it. Which no one knows."

It was possible. Victoria's boyfriend could have spent years as a monster in secret, killing a teacher and a young mother before he was twenty. Viv kept her eyes closed. "You don't think that's true," she said to Marnie. "If you did, you wouldn't have brought me to all of these places. You think there's a killer still on the loose."

Marnie was quiet for a minute. "All I know is I'd like to leave this damn jogging path. It's giving me the creeps."

Viv opened her eyes again and walked farther into the brush. It was true—this was likely a fool's errand. Victoria's killer was in prison. There was no mystery here. Except there was. How did Victoria's boyfriend know where she was? She wasn't an athlete or even a habitual runner. Why had he come here to this place? If he jumped her at the beginning of the path, was he waiting for her? If so, how did he know where she would go?

She kept walking until she hit the edge of the trees. She looked out onto a rain-soaked stretch of scrub with fences and houses beyond it. These were the same houses that Marnie had pointed out as being Victoria's street.

She peered through the rain. The stretch of backyard fences was broken in only one place: a narrow laneway, a shortcut from the street, so that people didn't have to walk all the way to the end of the street and around if they didn't want to. Viv pressed forward, leaving the trees and heading for the laneway.

She heard footsteps behind her, Marnie's voice. "Hey! Where are you going? It's wet out here."

The laneway was a dirt path leading between two yards. Weedy but well used. A shortcut the locals took when they wanted to come to the jogging path.

And from it, while she stood out of sight, she could see the street. A short suburban lane, maybe fifteen houses packed in a row.

Viv was still staring at the street when Marnie caught up to her and stood at her shoulder. "What the hell?" she said.

"Look," Viv said.

Marnie was quiet.

"Which house is Victoria's?" Viv asked her.

"I don't know."

"I bet it was one of these," Viv said, pointing to the row of houses in view. "I bet that's how he knew when she left the house, where she was going. He stood right where we are now. And if she went around the end of the street and back . . ."

"Then he could take this shortcut and beat her there," Marnie said.

Maybe. Maybe. So many maybes. But if Victoria's boyfriend had killed her, then he must have had a way to head her off at the jogging path.

And if her boyfriend could have stood here and watched the house, then so could a stranger.

Viv pulled her notebook from her pocket and made notes, bowing over the page so the letters wouldn't get wet. She wrote addresses, names. She made a map. She made a list of what she had to do next, because she knew. Marnie waited, no longer complaining about the rain.

When she finished, Viv put the notebook away and turned to Marnie again. "Okay, I'm finished. Can we look at your pictures now?"

Fell, New York
November 2017
CARLY

Jenny Summers, who had been my aunt Viv's roommate in 1982, worked at an old-age home in downtown Fell. It was a flat square building of burnt red brick, surrounded by low evergreen shrubs, a metal sign embedded in the front lawn: KEENAN RETIREMENT RESIDENCE. Jenny refused to talk on the phone, but she'd asked me to come to her work so we could talk on her break. I stayed awake when I was supposed to be sleeping and said yes.

Heather came with me, her poncho and parka traded for a quilted coat because the day was slightly warmer than usual. She'd pinned her hair back from her forehead in her usual style and wore dove-gray mittens that complemented the coat. She wore a black skirt that fell to her ankles and black boots.

"Are we Good Cop and Bad Cop?" she asked as we got out of the car. "Can I be Bad Cop?"

"I don't think anyone falls for that anymore," I said, zipping up my coat and leading the way to the front door. There was hardly any traffic in the middle of the day, and the breeze smelled almost good, if chilled. Black birds wheeled in the sky overhead, calling to each other.

"You're probably right," Heather admitted. "Besides, it would work better if you brought one of your men with you instead of me."

I made a face at her as we opened the door. "No boys. Callum is annoying, and Nick doesn't know I'm alive."

She waggled her eyebrows at me, Heather's way of trying to "get my goat," as she put it. She was good at it when I was in a certain mood. "Callum likes you," she said. "He keeps calling and texting you. Tell Nick about Callum and see if he gets jealous."

"How old are we? And boys are not your bailiwick, remember?"

She just smiled, and I turned away. I'd given Callum my number after I'd met him at the library—he said he wanted to send me any other articles he came across—and he'd used it frequently. He texted things like *I found the 1982 Greyhound bus schedule. What if Vivian took the bus out of town?* or *I found the ownership records for the motel at the courthouse. Here you go.* It was a little weird, frankly, that a guy as attractive as Callum took such an interest in me. That wasn't a self-confidence thing—it really *was* weird. I preferred to think of it as purely an intellectual interest, one geek to another.

We asked at the front desk for Jenny Summers, and a few minutes later a woman came out to get us. She was in her late fifties, whip-thin, with blond hair in a stylish short cut. She wore burgundy scrubs, Crocs, and very little makeup. She was a woman who had obviously always been pretty, and age had served only to sharpen her features and give her a harder, I-don't-give-a-crap expression. "Come with me," she said.

She led us down a hallway to a room that said PRIVATE BREAK ROOM on the door. Inside were a small fridge, a coffeemaker, a few chairs, and two sofas. The sofas had blankets folded on them, pillows on top. It was obviously used as a nap room for some of the shift workers.

Jenny motioned us briskly to sit, then went to the coffeemaker. "Which one of you is Carly?" she asked.

I raised my hand. "Me. This is my friend Heather."

Jenny nodded. "I could have guessed it. You look a little like Vivian. So you're her niece, huh?"

I felt a fizzle of excitement, like Alka-Seltzer in my blood. This woman,

right here, had known Vivian. Talked to her. Lived in the apartment
Heather and I shared right now. It was like a door back to 1982 had opened
a crack, letting me peek through. "My mother was Vivian's sister," I said.

"Sister!" Jenny leaned a hip against the counter as she poured her coffee. She shook her head, staring down at her cup. "She never mentioned
a sister. Then again, it was so long ago." She turned to us. "You know I
might not be able to help you, right? It's been thirty-five years."

"Anything you can remember," I said. "I want to know."

Jenny took her coffee and sat across from me, crossing one scrub-clad
leg over the other. "You weren't even born when she disappeared, right?
So you never knew her. Jesus, I'm old."

"What was she like?" I asked.

She looked thoughtful. "Viv was moody. Quiet. Lonely, I thought."

"The papers called her vivacious."

Jenny shook her head. "Not the Viv I knew. Maybe she was vivacious
back home in Illinois—I wouldn't know. But here in Fell, she kept to herself. She told me her parents were divorced and she wanted to get out of
her mother's house. She only talked to her mother once or twice that I
knew of, and she didn't seem happy about it. She worked nights at the
motel. No boys, no parties. We worked the same schedule because I was
on nights, so I knew her social life. She didn't go on dates. Though in the
weeks at the end she was gone a lot during the day. She said she had a hard
time sleeping so she'd go to the library."

I glanced at Heather. "What did she want at the library? Was she a big
reader?"

"Well, she never checked anything out. I remember telling the cops all
of this at the time and they couldn't even find a library card. Though a
few of the librarians remembered seeing her, so she wasn't lying. They
said she liked to read in the archive room."

So I'd been sitting exactly where Viv had been, maybe. Somehow that
didn't surprise me anymore. "Did she go anywhere besides the library?"

"That, I don't know. I mean, she was gone quite a bit near the end as far as I remember. Though I can't be sure, because I slept days. I had my first nursing home job then and I didn't rotate off nights until the following year." She looked around the break room. "I thought it was a temporary job to make a little money. Goes to show how much I knew. I'm retiring next year."

Maybe Viv would be retiring soon, if she'd lived. It was so strange to lose someone, to feel their life cut short, even if you didn't know them. Viv had only been as old as I was now. "It's strange, though, isn't it? That Viv wasn't home much in her last few weeks? She could have met someone."

"I suppose she could have." Jenny shrugged. "That's what the cops thought at the time, but they never could find anyone Viv knew. They kept asking me if she could have met some guy, like that would solve the whole thing. I kept telling them no, and they hated it. But they didn't know how deep inside her own head Viv was. I know what a girl looks like when she's met some new guy. I've *been* that girl. That wasn't Viv. She didn't look happy those last few weeks—she looked determined, maybe. Grim. I told the cops that, but they didn't really care. Viv was twenty and good-looking. They figured she must have run off with Mr. Right—or Mr. Wrong. Case closed."

Heather pulled her chair up next to mine. "How did they look for her?"

"As far as I know, they asked around," Jenny replied, sipping her coffee. "They did a search around the motel, but that only lasted a few hours. They talked to her parents. They searched her car and pulled our telephone records."

"Pulled telephone records?" I asked.

Jenny looked at me. "You remind me of my daughter. You kids don't know a damn thing. We only had a landline back then, of course. The records were kept by Ma Bell, and the cops got a big printout. Old school, as you would put it."

I wondered where that phone record was, and if I could get my hands on it. "She didn't mention anyone else to you?" I asked her. "Not necessarily a man, but anyone? A hobby? An interest? Anything at all?"

Jenny leaned forward, and I could see in her expression the weary look of a woman who had spent thirty-five years caring for people. "Honey, we weren't really friends. We were roommates. We didn't swap secrets or go on double dates. We just chatted while we got ready for work from time to time, that's all."

I looked her in the eye. She could tell herself whatever she wanted, but the truth was the truth. "Viv was gone for four days before someone called the police," I said, my anger humming beneath my words. "Four days."

Jenny closed her eyes briefly and her shoulders sagged. "I know. I went to see my parents for a few days. When I got back, I thought maybe she'd gone home for a visit. I figured wherever she was was her business. I was wrapped up in my own bullshit and drama, and I didn't think. It's bothered me for three and a half decades, but that's what I did." She sat back in her chair. "I think to myself, what if I had called the police that first night I got home? Would she be alive? I'll never know. But it was me who called them, though I did it too late. So on other nights I lie awake thinking, what if I never called the police at all? How long would it have taken for someone to notice that Viv was gone?" She ran a hand through her short hair. "A week? Two weeks? Her stuff was in the desk drawer in the motel office, and no one who worked there gave a shit. Literally no one cared that Viv's purse was sitting there and she was nowhere to be seen. That's worse, you know? That's fucking worse. Poor Vivian."

I didn't want to be here anymore. I didn't want to be in this place, in this depressing break room, smelling these depressing smells. How Jenny had done this job for thirty-five years, I had no idea. "You think something happened to her," I said. "You don't think she ran away."

"I *know* something happened to her," Jenny said. "The police can say whatever they want to make themselves feel better, but I *know*." She pointed to Heather. "If Heather dropped off the planet for four days, what would you think? What would you *know*?"

I clamped my teeth together as a chill went down my spine. I didn't answer.

"We were single girls who worked at night," Jenny said. "Do you think we didn't know the dangers, even back then? Christ, sometimes I think back to the fact that we had a conversation about Cathy Caldwell, of all things, a few weeks before Viv died. Cathy fucking Caldwell. How could I be so stupid?"

"Who is Cathy Caldwell?" I asked.

Beside me I felt Heather sit up straight, her narrow body tight as a bowstring. "She was murdered," she said, answering my question. "Dumped under an overpass in the late seventies." She looked at Jenny. "You knew her?"

"No," Jenny said. "She lived on my parents' street, and after I moved out and started working nights, she was my mother's favorite bogeyman. 'Be careful or you'll end up like Cathy Caldwell!' 'Don't talk to strange men on the bus or you'll end up like Cathy Caldwell!' That sort of thing. Cathy loomed large in my mother's mind—those were simpler times, you know? She was big about Victoria Lee, too."

"Killed by the jogging trail off Burnese Road," Heather said.

"'Don't take up jogging, Jenny! You'll end up like that girl!'" Jenny shook her head. "My poor mother. She grew up when these kinds of things didn't happen, or so she thought. She never did understand what the world was coming to. But she wasn't wrong. I was always careful, and so was Viv. We talked about it one night not too long before she disappeared. I think that's part of the reason I assumed Viv had gone somewhere sensible. Viv knew the dangers of working at night. She was careful. And she definitely wasn't stupid."

I thought of my brother, Graham, telling me stories about the man with a hook for a hand when we were kids. Bogeyman stories. Jenny's stories were different, though. I'd been dealing with creeps since I'd opened my first forbidden MySpace account at ten—strangers, people pretending to be other people, people trying to get you to do things, whether it was to buy something or sign a petition or send them a photo. When my mother caught me, she didn't know what to do or how to punish me—or if she even should punish me. She had been utterly lost. Viv, in her way, had known more about danger than her sister had decades later.

I glanced at Heather. She was perked up, her face tight and serious. *There are so many of them*, she'd said when I first met her, and when I asked her what she meant, she said, *Dead girls*.

"Is there anything else you can tell me?" I asked Jenny, because I sensed her break was almost over and our time was almost up. "Anything at all?"

Jenny looked thoughtful, and for a second I pictured her thirty-five years ago, wearing high-waisted jeans and a puffy blouse, her hair teased out. "Viv was beautiful," she said at last, surprising me. "I remember she said something about acting. She was originally going to New York, but she wasn't serious about it. She just wanted to get away. She didn't have the crazy beauty that models have. She was one of those girls who was beautiful the more you looked at her, if that makes sense."

"Yes," I said.

"It was something about her face, the stillness of it," Jenny said. "She was sad—at least the Viv I knew was sad. Nowadays she'd probably be a perfect candidate for therapy, but we didn't have that option then. And she was also angry, especially toward the end. I do think she was hiding something, though I suppose I'll never know what it was now. Oh, and one more thing." She pushed away her coffee cup and looked at me, her eyes hard. "Since they pulled our phone records and all, I always wondered why the police never asked me about the phone calls."

Fell, New York
October 1982
VIV

Jenny never spent her days off at home. She talked a lot about sitting in front of the TV eating candy as her perfect day off, but when the day came she never did it. Instead she spent her days off at the mall, spending her small paycheck on records or makeup or new shoes—loafers or low, pointy heels in rainbow colors like bright red or bright yellow, shoes she couldn't wear to work at the nursing home but wanted to have for "going to a party." Viv had never seen Jenny go to a party, but then again she hadn't been living with her all that long.

Today she was at the mall again, probably to see a movie or drink an Orange Julius or do any of the things Viv would have done at the mall back in Illinois six months ago. Instead of sleeping, Viv used the time home alone to find the traveling salesman.

She pulled the phone over to the kitchen table, using its extra-long cord, something Jenny had so she could wander and talk at the same time. Next to the phone she thumped down Fell's phone book and her notebook with a pen. Then, still in her terry bathrobe, Viv went into the kitchen, took out a box of Ritz crackers and a jar of Velveeta cheese with a knife, and sat down to work.

She flipped to the back of her notebook and took out the photographs

Marnie Mahoney had given her. There were only three that had what she wanted in them, but three was plenty. They all showed the Sun Down Motel at night, the lights on the corridors contrasting to the dark. One showed Mr. White opening the door of his room with a key. The second showed Helen entering that same room. The third showed Viv herself, leaving the AMENITIES room with a chocolate bar in her hand, walking back to the office.

Viv looked at herself in the photo, the girl she couldn't quite believe was her. She had a nice profile, clear pale skin, her hair pushed back from her face and clipped into a barrette. Anyone would think she was a nice enough girl, a pretty girl, if a little sad. Viv thought, *Who am I?*

But the girl wasn't what was valuable about the photo. All three pictures had caught a car in the parking lot, the back end of the car cut off by the frame. If you put the first and third photos together you could piece together the license plate number. The second photo, framed just right, caught the entire thing.

The traveling salesman's car.

Viv glanced at the telephone. She should call Alma Trent; she had promised she would. Alma had told her get *something, anything,* and she'd help identify the man who checked into the motel. But Alma also hadn't believed Viv. She'd thought the entire thing crazy.

Viv spread some cheese on a cracker and flipped through the Fell phone book. She closed her eyes and summoned the acting classes she'd taken after high school. She'd been good at acting, good at being someone else. It was one of the few things that made her feel better, being another person for a while.

She got into character. Then she called the DMV.

"Hello," she said when she got someone on the line. "I've just received a call from my insurance company that there's a problem with my husband's registration. Can you please help me?"

"Ma'am, I don't—"

"He's away on the road," Viv said. "My husband. He's traveling for work, and if he comes home and finds our insurance canceled, he'll be so angry. So angry." She tried channeling Honey from *Who's Afraid of Virginia Woolf?*—helpless, sweet, a little pathetic. "I don't know what to do. I don't even know what the problem is. Can you please just check?"

"It isn't—"

Viv interrupted by reciting the license plate number and the make and model, which she got from the photo. "That's the one. We've had it for years. *Years.* I don't know how there could be a problem all of a sudden. My husband says—"

"Please hold, ma'am."

There was a click, and silence. Viv held the receiver, her hand slick with sweat.

There was another click. "Ma'am, I don't see a problem with this registration."

"Are you sure?"

"There's nothing wrong at all. It's registered to Mr. Hess with no changes."

Mr. Hess. Viv felt light-headed, but she forced herself to keep calm, stay in character. "Oh, thank God," she said. "And you're sure the address is right?"

"You're still on Fairview Avenue?" the woman said.

"Yes. Yes, we are."

"It all looks fine to me."

Viv thanked the woman and told her she'd call the insurance company back to work it out. Then she hung up. She had cold sweat running down between her shoulders, beneath her bathrobe. Her mouth felt dry and hot.

She ate another cracker and drank some milk, then flipped through the phone book again, breathing deep. She let Honey go and let her mind travel, thinking up a new character.

There were only two Hesses in the phone book, and only one was listed on Fairview Avenue. Viv got into character again—tougher, brassier this time—and called the number.

A woman's voice answered. "Hello?"

"Mrs. Hess?"

"Yes."

"This is your husband's scheduling service." Viv tried to sound brisk, professional, like a secretary in an office. "We're not sure if we've made a mistake over here. Do you know if your husband is on his way to New York today?"

"New York? I don't think so. He told me he was going to Buffalo two days ago. But perhaps his plans changed." The woman laughed. "I guess you'd know that better than I would, right?"

"Like I say, Mrs. Hess, we may have had a mix-up. We're waiting for Mr. Hess to check in, but we thought we'd call and ask."

"That's all right. Westlake's scheduling service isn't usually this concerned."

Westlake. Viv flipped madly through the phone book. "We try to keep our salesmen organized. Sometimes things fall through the cracks."

"Well, I haven't talked to Simon today. If he calls I'll be sure to tell him to check in."

"We appreciate that, ma'am. Mr. Hess is always punctual about calling in. I'm sure we'll hear from him soon."

Viv said good-bye to the woman and hung up. She ate another cracker. She opened her notebook and picked up her pen. Turning to a blank page, she wrote:

Mr. Simon Hess

373 Fairview Avenue

Salesman for Westlake Lock Systems

She added his home phone number, Westlake's phone number, and his license plate and car.

And beneath that, she couldn't help but write:

That was easy.

She stared at the words for a minute. She looked back at the phone book and flipped back through the pages, finding the *W* section. She was thinking about her father, about the divorce. About the angry meetings with lawyers, about her mother coming home and throwing things, telling Viv she wasn't good enough.

You probably shouldn't do this, a voice in her head said.

And then, another voice: *I really don't care.*

She ran her finger down the *W* names until she found the one she was looking for. *White.* There were a dozen Whites in Fell, but only one was listed as *R. White.*

Again, easy.

She dialed the number. She didn't bother getting into character this time.

Again, a woman answered. "Hello?"

"Mrs. White?"

"Yes."

"Your husband is cheating on you," Viv said, and hung up.

Viv's head was throbbing by the time she got to Fairview Avenue, driving her Cavalier. She was supposed to be asleep right now; she'd only had a brief nap at eight o'clock this morning. It was two o'clock in the afternoon now, and she felt like she'd never sleep again.

Fairview Avenue was pretty, at least for Fell: bungalows with lawns, trees that would be leafy in summer. Viv drove the street slowly, peering at the house numbers in the gloomy October afternoon light. Number 373 had a car in front of it—a Volvo, the wife's car.

It was here that she had to admit she didn't know what exactly to do next. The traveling salesman was supposed to be in Buffalo; she didn't have a picture of him or know anything about him except where he lived. She had no answers to why he checked into the Sun Down with false names, or what he was doing there when he already had a home in Fell. She didn't know where he came from or who his friends were. She didn't know if he had children.

She didn't know whether he had anything to do with Betty or Cathy or Victoria. All she had was a man's name and address.

She should probably give up. Instead she parked around the corner, next to a small park. From her window she could see the driveway of the Hess house. She turned off the car and rubbed her face. *I should take out my notebook,* she thought, *and write some notes about what to do next.*

She leaned back in the driver's seat and was asleep before she could finish the thought.

When she woke, it was dark. She had a brief, disoriented flash in which she thought it was the middle of the night and she was supposed to be at the Sun Down. She looked at her watch and saw that it was only six o'clock, the early dark of the end of the year. She was shivering, and a cold wind buffeted the car.

She sat up and smoothed her hair, and then she went still.

There was a second car in the Hess driveway. The traveling salesman's car.

Without thinking she opened the driver's door and got out. If she hesitated, she would never do it. *Go, just go.* She walked around the corner toward the Hess house, trying not to flinch as a car drove past her on the quiet street, some nice man coming home from work. She waited until the taillights were in the distance and then she ducked around the side of the Hess house, crouching in the shadows of the garden.

This is crazy.

I don't care.

It was freeing, this not caring. She was unmoored from everything: family, friends, home, her real life. Even time had stopped having meaning since she started at the Sun Down, the days and nights jumbled into a long stretch that was as understandable as ancient Sanskrit. She looked at people anchored by time—get up in the morning, go to sleep at night, come home from work at six o'clock—as people she politely shared the world with but didn't understand. Why did people bother? The nights were so long now; it was night in the morning and it was night now. It was all darkness broken briefly by muddled gray light. Even now it could be three o'clock in the morning as she sat in the traveling salesman's garden. Who was to say it wasn't?

A light came on in a window a few feet away. Viv sidled toward it, listening. She didn't hear children's voices. Somehow it would make things worse to know that children lived with the traveling salesman, like seeing a toddler walk onto an empty road. *Move, move, run!* If the salesman was who she thought he was, he should live alone with his wife—Viv pictured a pale, wilted woman, long given up on life—and no one else. It fit.

Viv squat-walked toward the lit window, then carefully raised herself to peek into the corner. It was the kitchen, and a woman was standing at the sink, her back to Viv, the water running as she rinsed dishes. She wore pants that were elastic at the waist and a roomy T-shirt. With the practiced eye of a girl in theater, Viv noted that the woman's clothes were handmade on a sewing machine.

A man walked into the kitchen. He was of average height, average build, trim and clean-shaven with short hair brushed back from his forehead. He wore dress pants and a dress shirt with rolled-up sleeves and no tie. His face was square, his eyes small and nondescript. The last time she'd seen him, he'd smiled at her with a smile that didn't fit his face and made her queasy. *I guess I'm just that memorable,* he'd said. Without a word he put a plate on the counter next to the woman and left the room again.

Hello, Simon Hess, Viv thought.

The woman, she knew, would tell her husband about the strange phone call she got today. The scheduling service that had thought he was in New York. And the traveling salesman would look puzzled and say to his wife, *Of course they knew where I was. Why would they call?* Perhaps they'd already had this little exchange; a simple phone call to his company would tip him off that someone he didn't know had called about him. Viv had to move fast.

She ducked from the window again and squat-walked to the back yard, opening the latch to the backyard gate and peering in. It was a suburban fenced back yard, with a patio and a lawn in the dark. Still no sign of children's toys. Viv closed the gate again and backed out.

She had no idea what she was looking for—just *something*. Something that would put her closer to him, reveal something about him. She walked low against the house to the front again and saw the salesman's car in the driveway.

She crouched and moved to it. Peeked in the windows. The car was clean, as if he had bought it yesterday. No rips in the upholstery. No wrappers or junk. Nothing that said a man had just traveled in this car to Buffalo and back, that a man traveled in this car all the time.

She circled the car. If someone came by right now, she would be in plain view. The neighbor across the street could likely see her if he was looking out his window. The house across the street was dark with no car in the driveway. Still, she had to be fast.

The passenger seat had a few pieces of paper on it. Viv tried the passenger door and when it opened, unlocked, her blood went hot and pounding in her veins. She reached in and picked up the papers.

It was a schedule, typed up and run through a ditto machine. The ink smelled like school, and for a second Viv was dizzy with memories of class. Then she focused on what she was reading. It was a schedule, the words typed neatly.

Monday: Mr. Alan Leckie, 52 Farnham Rd., Poughkeepsie.

Wednesday: Terra Systems, Bank Street, Rochester.

Thursday: Monthly meeting at head office.

Viv almost laughed. This was from the salesman's actual scheduling department, the one she'd pretended to be a few hours ago. She flipped back and saw the schedule for the previous week, and the week before that. How long did they keep records? She wondered.

The schedule pages had letterhead, a contact name, a phone number. Viv slid the bottom page from the pile—maybe he wouldn't notice the bottom page gone?—and folded it into her pocket. She was just pushing the door shut when she looked up and saw the face in the living room window.

It was a girl, about ten, with long, straight hair tucked behind her ears. She was watching Viv with no expression.

Viv started. There had been no sign of kids anywhere. She should run, but instead she followed an impulse and met the girl's eyes through the window. She put a finger to her lips. *Be quiet, okay?*

The girl gave no indication of agreeing or not. Instead she lifted a hand and pointed silently in the direction of the front door. *He's coming.*

Adrenaline spiked straight through Viv's body, up the back of her neck and down into her gut. She ducked down the driveway and jogged to her car, trying to look casual in case anyone was looking—*I belong here! I'm just trotting down this street, no problem!* She got to her car and slid into the driver's seat as the front door of the salesman's house opened. She flattened herself down on the seat, trying to make the car look empty.

After a few seconds she dared a peek through the window. The salesman—Simon Hess—was standing in the driveway where she had just been, looking back and forth up the street. He was still wearing the pants and rolled-up dress shirt he'd been wearing in the kitchen. His gaze hit her car and passed over it, seeing it empty. Viv held her breath.

He turned back to his own car, circled it. He looked in the passenger window and opened the passenger door. He picked up the stack of papers.

Did I put them back in the right place? Did I?

He stared at the stack for a long time. Too long. Thinking, Viv knew. Trying to pin down what wasn't quite right. Trying to think of who had been in his car in his driveway—the passenger door had *thunked* shut when she closed it, she knew that, and now she knew he'd heard it. He was trying to put this together with the strange phone call. Trying to think of who it could be.

Slowly he put the papers back in the car and closed the door again. He turned and walked around the side of the house, disappearing.

Viv straightened quickly, turned on her car, and drove away. Her hands were slick and icy on the wheel.

Her mind raced. The salesman would see her footprints in the soft dirt of the garden at the side of the house: slim tennis-shoe prints. He would know it was either a boy or a girl who had been snooping at his house, not a large man. He'd figure a teenager. Viv's shoes were white unisex tennis shoes, and technically they could belong to a teenage boy. The salesman was more likely to believe a boy prowler rather than a girl.

That would work to her advantage—if the daughter didn't give her away.

She didn't think the daughter would give her away.

Still, the phone call had been from a woman. He would be suspicious, on his guard. Wondering what someone wanted from him. Because he knew, now, that someone wanted *something*.

I am hunting the hunter, and he suspects it.

The game is on.

She was afraid. Terrified, actually. But she was just starting.

Now she needed her next move.

The Internet was a gold mine of information on Cathy Caldwell. Whereas I'd spent months subsisting on the few paragraphs I could find about my aunt Viv, Cathy Caldwell was a whole different ball game. Cathy Caldwell was famous.

She hadn't always been famous. My first search for her name brought up a list of articles from the last few years—true-crime blogs, a podcast, and a Reddit thread with dozens of posts. Google showed me a photo, a 1970s color snapshot of a pretty woman with sandy brown hair standing in a sunlit back yard somewhere, smiling with a small baby on her hip. She was wearing short shorts and a turquoise halter top, her face a little blurry the way old snapshots always are from the days of film cameras with manual focus. The picture looked like the kind that was stuck in those old photo albums with plastic film that you smoothed over each page.

"I can't believe you didn't tell me about Cathy Caldwell," I said to Heather as I sat glued to my laptop after we got back from talking to Jenny Summers.

I was half joking, but Heather answered me seriously. "I told you we have a lot of dead girls in Fell."

"You weren't kidding. What was the other name she said? Victoria something?"

"Lee." Heather was standing in the kitchen, like she'd gone in there for something and then forgot what it was. She zipped the collar of her zip-up hoodie all the way up her neck, as if she was cold. She looked blankly at the closed door of the fridge. "That one was solved, and then it wasn't."

I frowned at her, though she wasn't looking at me. "What does that mean?"

"Her boyfriend was convicted, and then it was overturned a few years later. He was proven innocent."

"Truly?" I opened a new tab and started a new search. "That's incredible."

Heather turned and looked at me, her face still set in serious lines. "I can't talk about this anymore."

I took my hands from my laptop keys. "What?"

"The dead girls. I spent too much time reading about them a few years ago. It put me in a bad place. I'm not supposed to read about them anymore, you know?"

"Depression?" I asked her. "Anxiety?"

"A mix." She shrugged. "They go together. They bring the insomnia. And the bike accident I had—there was trauma from that." She glanced down at her zipped-up hoodie. "I have other issues, too, I think you may have guessed. My therapist says I have to work through it, but I can't get . . . fixated on negative things." She glanced at me. "I guess I'm not as much help as I thought I was. Sorry."

"No, I'm sorry," I said. "I showed up in your life and brought my problems. It's my fault."

She rolled her eyes and waved her hand. "It's fine. Just do the searches yourself. I'm going to go study. Maybe have a nap." She walked toward her bedroom, still hunched into her sweatshirt. It was so big, and she was so small, that she looked like a young girl in it. She got to her bedroom doorway, then put her hand on the frame and looked back at me over her shoulder. "Look up Betty Graham," she said. "And when you're done, help yourself to my meds." Then she went into the room and closed the door behind her.

Cathy Caldwell. Young, married, mother of a baby, her husband deployed. Left work one day and never came home; her body was found under an overpass, dead of stab wounds to the neck.

It happened in 1980. There was a sensation in the local newspapers for a while, and then, with the case ice-cold, the attention dropped off. Within a few years Cathy was forgotten—until a popular true-crime podcast revived the story in 2016. Then there was a rash of attention again, a new generation of amateur sleuths trying to put the pieces of the puzzle together. Cathy's baby son, now grown, did interviews, supplied photos. He talked about the unique pain of growing up knowing a monster had murdered your mother, knowing that whoever that monster was, he was still walking free.

But for all the Internet's attention, the case was still unsolved. There was DNA but no match in any system. There was nothing else to go back to, no other leads that new technology could magically exploit. Memories were rusty. A growing number of people, like Cathy's husband, were now dead. The only paper-thin theory, backed by zero proof, was that the husband hired someone to do it for the life insurance money. Otherwise, nothing.

There was less about Victoria Lee. She'd been strangled and dumped off a jogging trail in 1981, and her boyfriend was quickly arrested and convicted of the crime. Unlike the lengthy odes to pretty, sweet Cathy, there was no one to talk about how wonderful Victoria was. Instead there was a cropped, blurry photo of her face, obviously chopped from a group picture, and the caption *Murder victim Victoria Lee*. Cathy was a wife, a mother, beloved and kind and innocent. Victoria was just a murder victim.

In 1988 Victoria's boyfriend got a new legal team and won a second trial, based on a technicality in the first trial. In the new trial it came out that Victoria had been wearing a thin gold chain around her neck when she was strangled. The chain had been buried in the flesh of her neck, and whoever strangled her would have had marks on his hands. Victoria's boyfriend had no marks on his hands. His conviction was overturned and he was set free.

Which meant that Victoria's murder, initially solved, was unsolved again.

I didn't know why I was reading this. I didn't know what it had to do with my aunt Viv. But I couldn't stop.

Betty Graham was next. She had been murdered in 1978 and dumped on a construction site. Betty was a schoolteacher with no husband and no kids, and she'd kept to herself. A neighbor had seen a traveling salesman knock on Betty's door and get let in. No one saw her alive again.

Betty had had her own small Internet revival, though not as big as Cathy's. A few armchair sleuths had written about her, including a well-researched long-form article on a true-crime website. The details of the murder were scarce, but they made me go cold.

Betty had fought.

It wasn't released at the time, but the article's author had dug it out of the coroner's report decades later. Betty's body had bruises on the arms, the back, the shoulders. Her fingernails were torn and bloody. Her knees were swollen and damaged. There were scrapes on her leg and her hip, as if she'd been dragged. Her knuckles were bloody—her own blood—and four of her fingers were broken. She was missing two teeth. The coroner posited that she had been put somewhere, likely the trunk of a car, and had fought the whole way in. Then fought to get out. Then fought some more before her killer raped her, then stabbed her five times in the chest and finally killed her.

Then he'd dumped the body on a heap at a construction site—the site of the future Sun Down Motel.

My head went light. The Sun Down. A woman's body had been dumped at the Sun Down.

I scrolled through the article and found a photo of Betty Graham. She had a conservative haircut and wore a high-necked blouse, but there was no hiding that she was a beautiful woman. She was sitting for a formal portrait photo, likely for the school where she worked, her head tilted at that specific angle they always used in old school photos, her hands folded demurely in front of her, a polite smile on her face. She was beautiful but she was closed off, her eyes and demeanor saying *don't approach*. She looked like the kind of woman who could be polite and pleasant to you for years, and decades later you realize you don't know a single personal thing about her because she's never told you.

If you looked at her face, you wouldn't see a woman who would fight and bleed to her dying breath. You saw a woman who would lead a boring spinster existence to the end of her days, not someone who scratched her nails off and crawled on her knees in an effort not to die. You wouldn't see someone who wanted to live so badly, so desperately that she would do anything.

Then again, maybe you might.

Maybe you saw a woman who hated dying so much that she refused to do it all the way. Maybe you saw the woman in the flowered dress at the Sun Down Motel. Because I had. It was definitely her.

And if I had seen Betty, then it was possible Viv had seen her, too.

Five minutes later I was in the bathroom, sweating and gripping the counter with icy hands, hoping I wouldn't faint.

We had a conversation about Cathy Caldwell a few weeks before Viv died.

The woman in the flowered dress, looking down at me from the upstairs level.

Betty Graham, fighting and dying and getting dumped in the place where I now worked. Where Viv had worked.

We were single girls who worked at night. Do you think we didn't know the dangers, even back then?

Cathy fucking Caldwell. How could I be so stupid?

I bent over the sink and turned the cold water on. I put my hand under it, meaning to splash it on my face, but I couldn't quite do it. I just stood there, staring down at the water going down the drain.

This was the connection. It had to be. Viv had known about Cathy Caldwell in 1982—she had had a conversation about her with her roommate. If Viv knew about Cathy, it was entirely possible she knew about Betty Graham. Especially since Betty's body was dumped at the Sun Down construction site. It was one of those things you'd hear about when you'd worked in a place for a while.

If the woman in the flowered dress was Betty—and she was—then Viv had seen her. Known who she was. She could have figured it out, just like I did.

And it had something to do with her disappearance. It had to.

I spent too much time reading about dead girls a few years ago. It put me in a bad place.

Viv was sad. And she was also sort of angry, especially toward the end.

Viv had been out a lot at the end. Out pursuing something that wasn't a man. Something that made her angry.

The water still running, I raised my gaze to the shelf next to the medicine cabinet. I took in Heather's line of medications, arranged just so.

Betty, Cathy, Victoria. They were dark things, and following them led to a dark place. I could see it so easily, how you could walk through that door and never come out. How reading about the dead girls would lead to thinking about them all the time, to obsessing about them. Because after all this time, after decades and overturned convictions and reams of Internet speculation, no one knew who freaking killed them. No one at all.

If I was going to solve this, I was going to have to go through the door. So I went.

Two days later I was back in the archives room at the Fell library, going through old newspapers again. This time I bypassed the microfiche and went straight to the paper archives.

I read every article about Betty Graham's body being found in 1978. The murder had been the top story in Fell that year, a terrifying mystery in a town that had thought itself innocent up to then. There were anxious updates about how the police had nothing new, and the Letters to the Editor columns were filled with letters like *Should we lock our doors at night?* and *Are our streets safe anymore?* "I don't even want to let my daughter go to the roller rink," one woman—I pictured her in a sharp pantsuit with feathered hair, carefully hanging her macramé plant holder—complained. A man wrote, "I will not let my wife stay home alone." I pictured his wife popping Valium, thinking, *Please leave me home alone. Just for ten minutes.* Another man wrote, of course, that it must have something to do with black people, because who else could it be?

There was nothing anywhere about Betty's injuries. The police hadn't released that information. Was it too graphic for the public in 1978? Or did they withhold it because it was something only the killer would know about? Probably both.

I flipped forward to 1980. That was the year of Cathy Caldwell, and for the first time I wondered if the same killer could have done both. It didn't look like it on the surface: Cathy and Betty had been taken differently, killed differently. Cathy didn't have injuries like Betty did. But both were pretty; both had been raped, stabbed, and dumped; and it was too much of a coincidence that a place as small as Fell would have *two* vicious killers. I'd seen speculation about this from the armchair sleuths on Reddit, but the Fell police had nothing to say. Besides, if the same man had done both murders, he'd either stopped or moved away after Cathy. Or died.

Or he'd stayed, and he'd killed Viv in 1982.

"Hey," said a voice at my shoulder. "It's you again."

I jumped and looked up. It was Callum MacRae, the guy who spent all of his time in the archives room, digitizing everything. "Hi," I said.

"It's almost six," he said, smiling at me. "The library's about to close. They'll do an announcement in a minute or so."

"Oh, right." I looked around. "I should probably go."

"How's it going?" he asked as I stood up. "The search for your aunt, I mean."

He was wearing jeans and a zip-up hoodie today, both of them new-looking and not cheap. He knew how to dress, even if his social life seemed to be lacking. "I haven't found her yet," I said. "I haven't even gotten close."

"That's too bad. Anything I can do to help?"

I gestured to the archives behind me. "You already helped by showing me how to go through the old papers instead of relying on the microfiche. So thanks for that. I found things I wouldn't have found otherwise."

"Really?" His eyebrows went up. "Like what?"

I couldn't say why I felt uneasy, but I did. He was a nice guy in nice clothes taking an interest in my project, and yet I had the urge to sidle away. "Just the history of this place, I guess," I said. "There seem to be a lot of murders here."

"Ah." Callum smiled again. "I warned you about that. So I guess you see what I mean."

"Yeah, I guess so. How is the digitizing going?"

Callum spread his hands out, as if to show me they were empty. "I'm done for the day. And the place is about to close. What are you doing right now?"

I gaped at him because I was a dork. "What? Why?"

"We could go get dinner."

"I can't." It was a lie, but I pulled my phone from my pocket and saw that I'd had a phone call while I had it on silent. I recognized the number: Alma Trent, the retired cop that Nick Harkness had suggested I contact. I'd left her a message a few hours ago. "I have an appointment," I said to Callum, hoping that it was true.

"Oh, really? Where?"

I blinked at him but he waited for an answer, as if unaware he was on the edge of rude. A lifetime of training—*be nice!*—rose up and I said, "Um, I think I'm going to talk to Alma Trent, who was a police officer back when my aunt disappeared."

The librarian made the announcement about the library closing, and I started toward the doors. Callum followed.

"That sounds interesting," he said, unbelievably. "Can I come?"

"It isn't a good idea," I said, fumbling, as I pushed through the doors. "I promised I'd go alone."

His voice went a notch darker. "The cop made you promise that?"

We were outside the library now, and I could see my car parked in the pay spot at the curb. "Yeah," I said. "Thanks for offering, though. Talk to you soon, okay?" I gave him a fake-cheery wave and got into my car. Before I turned the key I pulled out my phone and listened to the message Alma had left.

She told me she was retired—I knew that from Googling her, like I knew her number from the good old Fell phone book—but she would be happy to talk to me. She had a pleasant, no-nonsense voice, a plain way of speaking. She told me I should just let her know when I could visit and she'd put some coffee on.

I called her back and told her I was coming, and she gave me her address. When I hung up, I gave in to impulse and texted Nick Harkness. *You up?* I wrote, because I was never sure when Nick was sleeping.

There was no answer. I stared at my phone for a minute, and then I added, *I'm going to see Alma Trent, the cop you told me about.*

I paused just in case. Still nothing.

I felt lame now, but I finished: *I'll tell you about it tonight.*

Not that he cared, of course. Why would he? I didn't even know what he did with his time besides sleep. The only reason I had his number was that he'd told me to text him when his pizza arrived last night.

I didn't know why I was texting him, except that I didn't want to see Alma Trent alone. And I didn't want to ask Heather because she was fragile about the whole thing right now. The last thing I needed was to worry that I was damaging Heather's mental health.

Still no answer. I sighed and put my phone down. I'd go alone.

I looked out the window. Callum was still standing in front of the library, his hands in the pockets of his hoodie. Watching me. When I looked at him, a slow smile touched his mouth, and he gave me a wave.

I started the car and drove.

Alma lived outside Fell, on the opposite side of town from the Sun Down, on a two-lane road that led to a well-kept old farmhouse. It was fully dark now but I could see that the house was of white clapboard, the shutters painted dark green. Pots, now filled with dead plants, lined the front porch, and as I approached the door a dog started barking. I knocked at the screen door, since the dog had obviously given me away.

"Hold on," came Alma Trent's voice from inside. Then, in a lower voice: "Stop it, you crazy thing. Honest to God, you're an idiot."

The dog kept barking, and a minute later the front door opened. Alma was in her late fifties, with gray-streaked brown hair tied back in a ponytail and no makeup on her pleasant face. She wore old jeans that bagged a little and a plaid flannel shirt under a brown cardigan. She was still fit and looked strong, and she gave me a kind smile. "Carly?" she said.

"Hi." I held out my hand. "It's nice to meet you. Thanks for taking the time."

We shook, her hand going easy on mine, though I could tell she could crush me if she wanted. "Come in," she said. "I put the coffee on, like I said. I know it's late for coffee, but I'm a night owl. Comes from doing all those years of night shift."

"Right," I said, following her down the front corridor and into her kitchen, which was dated but cared for. A small dog, some kind of terrier, barked his authority at me and then joyously smelled the cuffs of my jeans, dancing around my shoes. "I'd love some coffee. I'm a night person myself."

"Watch your step. My dog's an idiot." She led me through the cozy house into the small kitchen, where she gestured for me to take a chair. She paused, looking closer at me in the light. "You look a lot like her," she said.

I didn't have to ask who *her* was. I felt a zap of excitement again. I was in the presence of someone who had seen Viv, known her.

I opened my mouth to ask a question, but Alma started first. "Can you tell me something? What is it that brings you here looking for an aunt who died before you were born?"

"Technically she might not be dead," I said.

Alma's eyebrows shot up politely. "Okay."

"I mean, she is," I said. "She probably is. But they never found a body. Though she left her wallet and her car behind and everything." I trailed off. I sounded like a ditz.

If Alma agreed, she didn't say it. She opened a cupboard and took out two mugs. "It was a terrible night," she said. "I remember it well. The night I found out she was missing, of course. She'd been gone for four days by then." She paused by the coffeepot, lost in thought. "That shouldn't have happened, that lag. But it did."

"How?" I asked. It was like she was reading my mind.

"No one was paying attention, that's how," Alma said. "Vivian was quiet and kept to herself. She didn't invite attention. Her roommate was away, I seem to remember. But she was far from anyone who cared about her. The owners of the motel didn't even notice when she didn't show up to work. If you want to meet people who make an art of not being curious, go to the Sun Down Motel."

I watched her as she poured coffee into two mugs. She had a calm about her, an unhurried quality that wasn't tentative. I hadn't known what to expect, but I could picture this woman scraping up a drunk, teen-aged Nick Harkness at a party. Giving him a lecture and sending him on his way. In her decades as a cop, she must have seen a lot worse. "How did you know Viv?" I asked her.

She looked at me, her eyebrows up again. "How do you take your coffee?" When I asked for cream, she turned back to the cups. "I was Fell's night-shift duty officer for thirty years. I got called out to the Sun Down from time to time. Viv called me once or twice—truckers arguing in the parking lot, I think was the first one. You got petty disturbances like that at the Sun Down. It was just that kind of place. Still is."

"I know," I said as she set my mug in front of me. "I work there."

For the first time, I surprised her. She paused, her hand still on my mug of coffee. "I beg your pardon?"

"I work the front desk," I said. "Nights, just like Viv did. I went out there to ask a few questions, and there was a Help Wanted ad, and I just . . ." I watched as she pulled a chair back and sat down. "What?"

Alma shook her head. "The Sun Down isn't a safe place to work, that's all. It never has been. I worried about Vivian working there alone at night. Now it looks like I'm going to worry about you."

She knows about the ghosts, I thought, but when I looked at her face, I wasn't sure. She would make a great poker player. And I wasn't going to bring up ghosts with anyone except Nick, who had seen what I had seen. "I guess the Sun Down has always had bad luck," I said. "I mean, Betty

Graham's body was found there while the motel was being built. And there was a boy who died in the pool."

Alma sipped her coffee and looked at me as if she might be reassessing. Maybe she'd expected an airheaded twenty-year-old dunce who liked to Twitter. Who knew? Most people expected that. "How do you know about that?" she asked.

"The Fell library archives."

She put her mug down, her expression calm. "Okay. What do you want to know from me?"

I pulled my own mug toward me. I didn't sip it yet, though I'd barely slept today and I needed the caffeine. "Can you tell me anything about Viv's case file? What was in it?"

"I was just the night shift duty officer, not a detective. I didn't work missing-person cases."

"But you saw the file," I insisted.

She sighed and lowered her hand below the seat of her chair in the absent way that dog owners do. Her dog pushed his nose into her palm. "I read the file," she admitted. "I knew Vivian. It bothered me that she would go missing. She wasn't wild, and she wasn't on any drugs. And she wasn't stupid." She scratched the dog's head. "It was like the newspapers said, I guess. It seems that she went to work, because her car and purse were at the motel and she talked to the man on shift before her. But she vanished sometime during her shift, leaving everything behind."

"Her roommate says that Viv was out a lot during the day in her last weeks. That she seemed down or angry about something. She also said that when she got their phone bill after Viv disappeared, there were phone calls on it that she didn't make. She says she gave the phone bill to the cops but never heard from them again. It was like they didn't even follow up."

Alma shook her head. "I don't remember that."

"Jenny says she doesn't think there was a boyfriend, but there was something going on."

"Jenny didn't know her very well." Alma's voice was slightly clipped.

"Considering she sat in an empty apartment for two days and didn't wonder where her roommate had gone. Whether she was even all right."

"Okay," I said. "The newspapers all described Viv as pretty and outgoing, but Jenny says she wasn't outgoing at all."

"Pretty, yes," Alma said. "She truly was. That was one of the reasons I worried about her working alone at the Sun Down every night. But no, she wasn't outgoing. She was quiet, a little intense. She could light up when she was talking about something she was interested in. But I never heard about her having any friends."

"What was she interested in?"

"I beg your pardon?"

"You said she'd light up when she talked about something she was interested in. I just wondered what that was."

Alma paused, still stroking her dog. "You know, I don't remember. A movie or a TV show, maybe. We passed the time chatting. Like I say, I was worried about her."

"No one at the motel knew her?"

"Like who?" Alma said. "There's no one around on the night shift. I knew Jamie Blaknik was one of the regulars out there, and he'd definitely met her, but that was all I could get out of him."

"Jamie Blaknik?" I asked.

"He was a pot dealer in those days. Uppers and downers, too, when he could get his hands on them. That seemed like a big deal in 1982, before the harder drugs started coming in. He did some of his business out of the Sun Down, which meant he would have at least talked to Vivian. He was at the motel the night Viv disappeared."

"He was?"

"Yes. I questioned him myself. He told me he was only at the motel for a few hours, doing business, and then he left. He had more than one alibi, too. It seems he had customers between eleven and twelve, and more customers after he left and went to a bar. If he killed Viv, he would have had to do it in a ten-minute span between one customer and the next. The PD could never pin it on him. He wouldn't break."

"You questioned him," I said. "I thought you weren't a detective."

Her expression turned defensive. She pulled her hand from her dog's head and put it back in her lap. "I asked around. That isn't the same thing. There wasn't a lot to do on the night shift unless someone was drunk and disorderly. And I knew a different set of people than the day shift guys. Not that any of them wanted to listen to me anyway."

"Because you were just the duty officer."

She gave me a smile that had a layer of complexity behind it I couldn't read. "Because I was the Fell PD's only female officer," she said. "You think I did thirty years on nights by choice? That was the only shift they would give me. It was either take it or quit. And boy, were they mad when I worked it instead of quitting."

"That's crazy. Isn't it illegal or something?"

She laughed, a real laugh that came from her belly. "You're a smart girl, but you're so young," she said. "I started on the Fell PD in 1979. I was lucky to be able to get a credit card in those days without a husband. My coworkers called me 'Dyke' instead of my name, right to my face. I could have dated Robert Redford and they still would have called me that. If I got married and had babies, I was weak. If I stayed single, I was a dyke. I learned to appreciate the night shift because I didn't have to listen to pussy-eating jokes. If I'd complained, I would have been ridiculed and probably fired." She shrugged. "That was the way it was in those days. I wanted to be a cop, and I wanted to be in Fell. This is my town. So I took the night shift and I did things my way when no one was looking. And that included asking around after Viv disappeared."

I leaned back in my chair. "If I ever get a time machine, remind me not to go back to the seventies."

"It wasn't so bad," Alma said. "We had Burt Reynolds and no Internet and no AIDS. We didn't know how much fun we were having until the eighties came and it started to dry up." She sipped her coffee. "Jamie was around Viv's age and not bad-looking. He would have noticed a girl as pretty as Vivian. But I knew him most of his life, and he wasn't the violent type."

I pulled out a pen. Anyone who had met Viv was still on my list. "Do you know where I can find him?"

"Dead," she said bluntly. "Ran his car off the road and wrapped it around a tree. Gosh, when was that? The early nineties."

"Okay." I clicked the pen. "Who else did you suspect? Who else did you talk to?"

"There weren't a lot of options. I did talk to Janice McNamara, who owned the place and hired Viv."

I thought of the picture I'd seen in the newspaper in 1979, of the woman with her husband and son standing in front of the brand-new Sun Down Motel. "I work for her son, Chris," I said. "He says he doesn't spend any time at the motel if he can help it."

Alma gave me a look that was almost speculative, and for a second I wondered if she was going to bring up the topic of ghosts. "Janice was the same," she said. "There was an accident at the motel soon after it opened."

"The boy in the pool."

"Right. The boy died in the pool, and Henry, the motel employee who called the accident in, died of a heart attack in the office six months later. Janice and Carl never really wanted to be in the motel business in the first place—they thought it would be easy money with the amusement park that was supposed to come here, and that the land would appreciate in value. When the park fell through and the deaths happened, they both lost their steam. Carl got sick and couldn't work the place. Janice worked the front desk, but she didn't care much. She sure as hell wasn't there the night Viv disappeared. Chris took over after both of them died, but he doesn't want it, either." She shook her head. "It's just a place that's never been wanted from the first, you know? Right from the time Betty Graham's body was found at the construction site. I don't believe in curses, but the Sun Down is just one of those unloved places."

My stomach had fallen and I felt light-headed. "Someone . . . someone died in the *office*?"

"Yes. Oh, Jesus, I'm sorry." Alma shook her head. "I spent too many years as a cop, and we talk about this stuff. I forgot that you work in that office. Yes, Henry died of a heart attack. He was under stress after that boy died. I guess it caught up with him."

Was he a smoker? I thought wildly. *Because I think he still is.*

"It wasn't a big loss," Alma said when I didn't speak. "Henry, that is. He was a bit of an asshole, honestly. When I called his ex-wife after he died—she was still listed as next of kin—she said he could rot in hell and hung up on me. We'd had complaints from her over the years about him threatening her, but nothing ever came of it. She always dropped the charges. Henry wasn't much of a charmer." She picked up her cup and sipped her coffee. "I'm talking your ear off. You're a good listener."

"It's fine," I said. "Thank you." I looked down at the paper I was supposed to be taking notes on, which only had the name *Jamie Blaknik* on it. "Who else was staying at the Sun Down the night Viv disappeared?"

"Just Brenda Bailey," Alma said. "She was an alcoholic. Her husband would go through a phase of trying to make her quit, so she'd check into the motel to do her secret drinking. She was in her room that night, passed out. The detectives questioned her, and then I questioned her myself off the record. She didn't see or hear a thing." She nodded toward my paper. "And Brenda's dead, too. She passed in '87. Jesus, it seems like I know a lot of dead people, doesn't it? I promise there are still a few people alive in Fell."

I wrote down *Brenda Bailey*, because it seemed like I should. "What about the man who worked the shift before Viv's? He might be the last person to see her alive."

"Johnny? Sure, you can talk to him if you want. He's in his seventies now. Lives in an old folks' home in New Jersey, where his niece put him so he can be close. He never had anything to say about that night except that Viv showed up and he went home. His mother confirmed he was home by eleven fifteen."

This was hopeless. I was getting nowhere, so I changed the subject. "Did you work the Cathy Caldwell case?"

I looked up and saw that Alma's face looked shocked, like someone had given her bad news. "There is no connection between Vivian's disappearance and the Cathy Caldwell case." The words came out of her automatically, like the Snickers bars in the Sun Down's semifunctional candy machine.

"But we don't know that," I said. "They were around the same time. Cathy's murder is unsolved. So was Betty Graham's. And there was Victoria Lee, which everyone thought was solved, but it turns out it wasn't. So all three are open cases."

Alma's voice was firm. "Like I say, there's no connection."

"Isn't it too much for coincidence?" I insisted. "All these girls dead right before Viv? And then it stopped?"

Alma shook her head as I spoke. "Damn the Internet, honestly. Carly, honey. I know it's tempting. But we had detectives working those cases— good ones. They wanted to solve those murders, and if there was any connection with Vivian's disappearance, they would have jumped on it. But they couldn't find that connection. Without a body, there's nothing to go on."

She sounded so firm, so confident. And she had that cop's voice, the one that said *I know what I'm doing, so just do as I say.* But still. All of those women, murdered and unsolved around the same time. What were the odds that they were all different killers? And that Viv had crossed paths with yet another killer? This place would be worse than the town in *Murder, She Wrote.* Didn't the cops see that? Shouldn't they be the first ones to see it?

But from Alma's expression I knew I was trying to dig on stony ground. "Okay," I said. "It was just a thought." I closed my notebook. "Thanks for your time."

"I'm sorry," Alma said. "It's just that those cases are near to me. I'm not a detective, but we were all hands on deck after Betty and Cathy. People were scared. It was a difficult time." She pressed her lips together. "We had a strange run of deaths in the late seventies, early eighties, I'll give you that. But it stopped, and Fell was quiet for a long time. We didn't have any more headline-grabbing cases until the Harkness murder."

Nick. His father shooting his brother, then coming up the stairs as Nick jumped from the window.

"I'll tell Nick you said hello," I said.

Alma's eyebrows went up. "Nick is back in town?"

Oh, shit. Was that supposed to be a secret? *Don't mention my name,* Nick had said. I was such an idiot. "I guess so," I hedged. "I met him at the Sun Down." I put my notebook in my lap.

"Nick Harkness is staying at the Sun Down?"

"Just for a little while, I think." Why hadn't I kept my mouth shut? Nick wanted his privacy. Maybe he didn't want it all over Fell that he was back. "He's the one who gave me your name and suggested I talk to you."

"Yeah, he'd remember me," Alma said. "I dumped him in the drunk tank to sleep it off enough times." She pushed her chair back. "He isn't a person you want to get too close to, Carly. Take it from me."

"He's grown up now," I said, even though I didn't know Nick all that well. "He doesn't get in trouble anymore."

"Or so he says." Alma looked at me thoughtfully. "You know, we could never prove anything, but I always wondered if Nick was really upstairs in his room like he said he was. Tell him I say hello."

Fell, New York
November 1982
VIV

Without sleep, the nights were long. It felt like Viv lived in an endless stretch of darkness, punctuated only by fleeting daylight in which she dozed, her eyes restless behind her closed lids. Tonight she was at the Sun Down, sitting in the office alone. Her limbs ached and her eyes were half closed. She'd come in to find a single white envelope on the desk marked *Paycheck*—Janice's only interaction with her employee.

What if I didn't show up at all? Viv wondered to herself. *Would anyone notice? Would Johnny tell anyone? How many nights could I simply not come to work before someone wondered where I was?*

It was a lonely thought, and for a second she felt soft and bruised by it. She should call her mother sometime, maybe. Her sister. Try talking to her roommate, Jenny, again, even. How long had it been since she talked to someone? She rubbed her eyes and stretched her cramped legs beneath the desk.

There was no one at the motel tonight. Literally no one. For the first time since starting this job, Viv felt so empty and so achingly lonely she found herself near tears. She wished Jamie Blaknik would show up with his tousled hair and his strangely kind smile. She wished anyone would show up at all.

The phone rang, the noise loud in the silence. Viv picked it up. "Sun Down Motel, can I help you?"

"Viv, it's Marnie."

Tears stung the backs of Viv's eyes at the sound of a familiar voice. She needed to get a grip on herself. "Marnie," she managed.

"Yeah. Look, I was out on another job and I drove by your suspect's house. His car is in the driveway and the windows are dark. Looks like he's sound asleep."

Viv sat up straighter, the loneliness dissipating. Marnie did this for her sometimes—followed the traveling salesman when Viv couldn't. "Thanks."

"I also talked to a cop I know on the Fell PD. I told him I'd met a girl who thought she might be Betty Graham's cousin. I asked him if the cops think Betty and Cathy Caldwell could have been killed by the same man."

"And?" Viv asked.

"He didn't say much," Marnie said. "He was tight-lipped about it. He said they'd looked at that and haven't found any evidence. I have to be honest, Viv. The more I get into this, the more I think your theory is wrong. Those women didn't know each other, didn't travel in the same circles. Betty was a spinster teacher and Cathy was a married mom. My contact wouldn't even talk to me about Victoria Lee, because her case is closed. And Cathy's injuries were different from Betty's. Very different."

"Tell me what Betty's injuries were," Viv said. "I know you know. The papers wouldn't say."

She heard Marnie sigh. "This is just cop talk. But Betty had a lot of bruises. Like she fought hard. And she was raped."

Violated, Viv thought.

"Cathy was raped, too, and Victoria wasn't," Marnie said. "You see what I mean. It's too random. And this salesman—I've never seen him do anything except go to work and back. You're barking up the wrong tree, honey."

"He might hunt them all differently," Viv said. "It's how he works. He likes it. But you're right, he finds them somehow. There has to be a connection."

"Jesus, you're obsessed," Marnie said. "I worry about you. You spend too much time alone at night. You need a boyfriend, bad."

Viv laughed. "Do you have one?"

"Always. I don't need a man, but I like one. They come in handy sometimes. You should try it. Leave behind all this darkness-and-death stuff. It's no good for you. Never mind the fact that you could get yourself killed."

"I'll be careful," Viv said.

"You better," Marnie said. "If something happens to you, whoever does it is going to have to deal with me."

The cigarette smoke was pungent tonight. After she hung up the phone, Viv stood with her palm pressed to the office door, her eyes closed as she took breaths. It was definitely the smoking man, the man who had walked behind her the first night the ghosts came, his footsteps crossing behind her back as if he walked past an open door. There was another footstep on the walk, and with an inhale of breath Viv turned the doorknob and pushed open the door.

There was no one there, just the frigid cold darkness, the air that was starting to smell like snow. The wind hushed in the naked trees beyond the motel, and on a far-off street a siren wailed, the sound carrying high and faint.

I could disappear. I could die. Who would look for me?

Victoria's own parents hadn't thought to look for her because they assumed she was at a party. No one knew Betty was missing until she didn't come to work.

There has *to be a connection.*

There was a distinct crunch of gravel in the parking lot, and Viv heard the *snick* of a door opening. Then another, and another.

Betty was awake.

Viv had come to think of it that way. Betty slept, and the motel slept; but sometimes Betty was awake, which meant the motel was awake. Usually she awoke when the traveling salesman checked in, but he wasn't here tonight. Tonight there was no one here but Viv.

No one here but Betty and me.

Viv stepped out onto the walkway, past the AMENITIES room. Ahead of her, around the bend of the L, the doors were opening one by one, starting at the end and working toward her. She could hear them upstairs as well: *Snick. Snick. Snick.*

"Betty?" Viv said.

The sign flickered but stayed on, its garish neon colors strangely comforting in the darkness.

She pulled her collar up around her neck, let the wind lift her hair, and stepped off the walkway into the parking lot. The gravel crunched beneath her sneakers. *I could just disappear*, she thought. *Become one of the ghosts here. No one would ever know.* Maybe some future girl would work in the front office, and first she'd smell cigarette smoke, and then she'd hear the rumble of the ice machine, and it would start all over again. A year from now? Five? What would that girl look like? What would she think when she saw the ghost of Viv herself, scuffing gravel through the parking lot?

She turned away from the L, from the opening doors, and walked back to the office, though she didn't go in. That door was open, too, though she couldn't remember if she'd closed it behind her or not. Inside she was almost not surprised to see a man sitting at the desk she'd just left. He was older, skinny, and he was slumped over the desk, his head in his hands.

Viv stood in the doorway, her hand on the jamb to keep herself from falling. It felt like her breath was frozen in her throat. The air was suffused with the smell of cigarette smoke.

As she watched, the man raised his head and looked at her. His eyes were black and blazing.

"Goddamn bitch," he said.

Viv backed away and walked on shaking legs around the corner, toward the empty pool. It was nearly pitch-dark back here, farther away from the lights of the road and the sign, and Viv made out the black shape of the fence, the inky pool filled with leaves and garbage. Her tennis shoes scraped loudly on the broken concrete. Overhead there was a sliver of moon that gave barely any light.

She made herself take a breath deep into her lungs, letting the cold sting her chest. She tilted her head back and looked up at the sky. The exhaustion had left her and she only felt the pumping of her blood in her veins, the humming of her own skin. She closed her eyes, then tilted her head down and opened them again.

In front of the fence was a boy, sitting on the ground, his knees up, his back to the fence. His skin was pale and he was wearing a T-shirt and shorts in the icy cold. He was the boy who had hit his head and died. He, too, raised his head and looked at Viv, though his expression was helpless instead of angry.

"I don't feel good," he said, his voice high-pitched and insubstantial in the chilled night air.

"I can't help," Viv told him. "I'm sorry."

But the boy still watched her, unmoving, waiting, and Viv took a step back, unable to look at him anymore. "I'm sorry," she said again.

He was still watching her when she turned and walked back past the office, careful not to turn her head and look at the man inside. She rounded the corner and saw that the motel doors were open—every single door on both levels, ajar as if someone had forgotten to latch them closed. The lights at the end of the row blinked out, and then the next lights, and then the next. On the second level, a woman in a flowered dress appeared in one of the room doorways, then turned away again.

"Betty," Viv said, and this time it wasn't a question.

Behind her, the motel sign went out. Now there was only darkness, growing and growing as each light went out at the motel. *I'm alone in the dark*, Viv thought. *There's only me here.* But that wasn't quite true. And this time, she wasn't afraid.

She walked to the stairs and climbed them, her hand numb with cold on the railing. Her cheeks were losing sensation and her nose was starting to run. But she kept walking. She reached the doorway where she'd seen the woman and, with only the briefest breath of hesitation, she stepped inside.

It was dark in here, with a stuffy smell. Viv's tennis shoes went silent on the old carpet. The wind skirled in through the open door, but it was no longer cold. It was airless in here instead, unpleasantly warm like a chair that someone else has just sat on, the smell a little sickening, like a stranger's armpit. Viv made out a bed, a cheap nightstand, a mirror. And the woman.

It was the woman from that first night, the one who'd stood in front of Viv's car as she cowered inside. *Run*, she'd said then, and Viv had simply stared in terror, unable to process any other emotion. Now the woman stood with her back to her, wearing that same dress, and all Viv could feel was pain and a horrible, horrible kind of pity.

I couldn't just leave her, she thought.

"Betty," she said, the word coming out a rasp from her dry throat.

Slowly, the woman turned. Viv's eyes had adjusted to the dark—or perhaps it wasn't as dark as she'd thought—because she could see the woman so clearly, the line of her neck and the white of her skin. The hair that fell just past her shoulders, dark honey brown and carefully brushed, pinned back from her face. The way, Viv knew now, that Betty had pinned it back that final day before she opened the door to the wrong man.

Her stomach dropped because in the strange light she could also see Betty's scratches. The bruises and scrapes on her cheekbones. The deep marks on her neck. The blood smeared over her hands, over her fingers and palms, the nails ruined. Betty's lip was split and her left eye was swollen mostly closed. Below the hem of her dress, blood ran from her knees down her shins.

Horror came over Viv, so complete it was a wash of sensation crawling up her back and burrowing into her stomach, like cold hands on her neck and cotton in her throat. She stared with cold tears on her face as Betty spread her hands and looked down at them.

And then she spoke, like the man had spoken, like the boy. Her voice a far-off reedy sound in the wind. Coming from somewhere and nowhere at once.

"How did this happen?" she said.

Viv raised a hand to her cheek, smeared one of her tears with her icy fingers. "Betty," she said in a whisper.

Betty lifted her face and looked at Viv, and her expression was confusion and burning rage. "How did this happen?" she said again.

"I don't know," Viv said, and she had no idea if Betty could hear her or not, because she simply stood unmoving, her bloody hands held out. "Who was he? Tell me."

Betty stared with those blazing eyes, and through her terror Viv had the urge to step forward, get closer. Her feet wouldn't move. A plume of white rose in the air, and Viv realized it was her breath in the suddenly freezing air.

Betty's mouth moved. Her voice was fainter. "How did this happen?"

"Tell me!" Viv shouted. "I can fix it! Please!"

A horn honked from the parking lot and Viv jumped, a scream coming from her throat. Red and blue light briefly flashed through the window and the half-open door, and there was a *blip* of a siren.

Viv turned her head, distracted, and when she turned back Betty was gone.

On shaky legs, she walked to the door. In the parking lot below her was a police cruiser, parked diagonally in the middle of the empty space. Next to the driver's door stood Alma Trent, flashlight in her hand.

She looked up and saw Viv. "Jesus, you gave me a heart attack!" she said, her voice ringing clear through the night air. "The office door is wide open and there's no one inside. I couldn't find you anywhere. I thought some creep had stuffed you in his trunk and drove off."

Viv stood, staring down. Cold sweat trickled down her back, beneath her shirt and her sweatshirt.

"Aren't you cold?" Alma asked. "Why are the lights out? I didn't hear anyone call in a power outage." She flipped on the flashlight and raised it to Viv's face. "Are you okay? Why are all the doors open?"

Viv opened her mouth to say something—she had no idea what—and with an angry buzz the neon sign suddenly flipped on, the yellow and blue glowing in the darkness. Then the lights turned on, starting at the end of the L and moving up. One by one the doors clicked closed.

It took a silent stretch of minutes. When it finished, Viv still stood staring down at Alma, who had lowered the flashlight. The two women locked gazes for a long minute.

"Vivian," Alma said at last. "Come down here and we'll talk."

Fell, New York
November 2017
CARLY

I had been on shift at the Sun Down for an hour. It was midnight, and I was reading the old copy of *Firestarter* I'd found in the office. Drew Barrymore's baby face was on the cover, her hair lifting in the draft from the wall of flames behind her. Andy and Charlie had just been captured by the CIA, and things were about to get *really bad*. Then the office door opened and Nick walked in.

He was wearing jeans and a black zip-up hoodie. His hair was a little mussed and his beard was thicker. He looked like he just woke up. He carried a six-pack of beer, which he put on the desk in front of me.

"Hey," he said.

"What's this?" I asked from over the top of my book.

"Beer."

"I'm only twenty."

His eyebrows went up. "Are you for real?"

I put my book down, finding a Post-it note to use as a bookmark, because folding the corner of a page—even in a thirty-year-old book—is sacrilege. "Okay," I said. "I'm not a big drinker, though. What is this for, anyway?"

Nick walked to the corner of the room, pushed some old tourist brochures off a wooden chair, and pulled it up to the desk. "Because I didn't answer your texts earlier." He sat down and pulled a can from the pack.

"You were sleeping," I said.

"No, I was being an asshole." He popped the beer open and handed it to me. At the look on my face he said, "It's what I do."

"Okay," I said slowly, taking the beer from him.

He took his own beer and slouched back in the wooden chair, his big shoulders dwarfing the back. "It's a habit," he said. "I've been an asshole for a long time."

I sipped my beer politely and glanced at my book, like I was longing to get back to it.

"I'm not used to people being nice to me," he said.

"Um."

He waited a beat. "So I'm sorry," he said. "I apologize."

I lifted my glasses and scratched the bridge of my nose, then lowered them again. "Okay, I accept."

He let a breath out, almost like he was relieved. Which couldn't be right, but a girl can dream. "So what happened with Alma?" he said. "You wrote in your text that you would tell me."

I sipped my beer again, a tight knot forming at the back of my neck. I had said that, but now I didn't want to tell him everything that had happened with Alma. Because I'd told her that Nick was here, which I was now sure I wasn't supposed to. And she'd told me that Nick might not have been upstairs like he said he was.

This was awkward.

So I changed the subject. "I figured something out," I told him instead. "The woman who haunts this place was named Betty Graham."

Nick blinked. "The woman who sat on my bed?"

"Yes, that one. She was murdered in 1978 and her body was dumped here at the motel. It was a construction site at the time. She was a schoolteacher who lived alone. They never solved it."

Here was why I couldn't stay mad at Nick Harkness: He put all of the pieces together right away. "Your aunt disappeared only a few years later, from the same place. What are the odds it was two different guys?"

"Exactly." I nearly shouted it but kept my voice calm at the last second. "There are others, too. Cathy Caldwell."

Nick frowned, then closed his eyes briefly, remembering. "Girl left under an overpass?"

"That was two years later, Nick. Right in between Betty and Viv. And it was also unsolved."

"God, this town sucks," he said, running a hand through his hair and making it stick up more, which still didn't look stupid for some reason. "Believe me, if some scumbag decides he wants to murder people, the place he's going to come to is Fell."

"It seems like a nice place to kill someone," I said politely.

"There were no leads? Nothing at all?"

"Nothing that made it to the papers. It's frustrating. I thought Alma Trent might be able to give me some insight, but as soon as I mentioned Cathy and Betty she went quiet and closed me down." *And then she told me not to talk to you.* I bit my lip.

"What?" Nick said, watching my face.

I sipped my beer again.

"What?" he repeated. Then he frowned, figuring it out. "She said something about me," he said slowly, as if he were reading the words in writing across my forehead. "Something bad."

"Not really."

"Carly."

"I let it slip to her that you're here," I confessed. "She seemed so friendly. I'm sorry."

Nick frowned slowly, as if computing this. "Alma knows I'm here? At the Sun Down?"

"Sort of. Yes."

"Shit," he said softly. "I'm going to get a visit. Probably soon."

"I'm sorry."

"It's fine." He shook his head. "It wasn't going to be a secret forever. I mean, what was my plan? Stay at the Sun Down until I'm sixty? I'll go crazy before Christmas."

"She's not a fan of yours. Like you said." I put my beer down. "She says there's a theory that you weren't in your room when your brother was killed."

Nick went very, very still. He looked at me for a long moment, his expression going as quietly blank as a blackboard being erased.

I didn't want to feel nervous, but I did. The nerves made my throat dry and my back tight, made cold sweat start under my T-shirt. "Nick," I said finally, unable to take the silence.

"Yeah," he said as if he hadn't paused. "That was a theory. I remember."

I swallowed. "I didn't say I believed it."

"No, you didn't." He swigged his beer, then put the can down. For a second I thought he was going to say he was leaving, that it was over. He even leaned forward in his chair. Then he said, "Who's the kid? The one I see running around in shorts?"

It took a second for me to realize he meant the ghost. "He hit his head on the side of the pool and died," I said. "The year the motel opened."

Nick nodded, as if this made sense. "And the skinny old guy with the cigarette?"

I started, shocked. "You've seen him? The smoking man?"

"In the parking lot. He stands there and stares up at my room, smoking. Then he's gone."

"He was the one who called the ambulance for the kid. He died six months later. In this office." Now I swigged my own beer, remembering.

Nick's eyebrows went up. "Well, that's just fucking great," he said succinctly. "So what do we do next?"

We? Was there a *we*? I didn't know he was helping me with this. I had opened my mouth to answer—I had no idea what—when the office door swung open and Heather walked in.

"Hi," she said. And then she saw Nick and said, "Oh."

She was wearing skinny jeans, Uggs, and her big parka. Her hair was in its usual bobby pin, her cheeks red with cold. Her eyes were bright like they were the first day I met her and she brought a wash of the cold night air through the door with her. She carried a plain manila file folder under her arm, stuffed with papers. She stopped short and looked at us.

"Heather," I said as Nick turned in his chair to look.

"You're Nick," Heather said, fixing him with her gaze.

"You're the roommate," Nick said.

Heather nodded. Her eyes were slightly wide, the only tell she gave that she knew who he was. Only someone who knew her like I did would see it. Without another word to Nick, she turned to me. "I couldn't sleep, and you don't get any cell signal here. I have a bunch of stuff for you."

"Are you okay?" I asked her. "Are you sure you should be doing this?"

"I'm okay now, I promise." She put her file folder on the desk in front of me, next to the six-pack.

"Want a beer?" Nick asked her.

Heather shook her head and pointed a finger to her temple. "Messes with the meds," she said, then turned back to me. "I've been on the Internet for hours. I went into some of my old files and on the message boards I know. Check out what I found."

I opened the folder. The papers were printouts from websites: photos, articles, conversation threads on message boards. I saw Betty Graham's formal portrait, her lovely and reserved face tilted to the camera. Cathy Caldwell at a Christmas party. Victoria Lee's high school senior photo. And one other face I didn't recognize. "Who is this?"

"This is the big find," Heather said. "This is the one even I didn't know about." She pulled out the photo. The girl was obviously a teenager, smiling widely for the camera for her school photo. I felt my heart thud in my chest and my stomach sink. A teenager.

"This is Tracy Waters," Heather said. "She lived two counties over. She disappeared on November 27, 1982. Her body was found in a ditch two days later." She pushed the photo to the middle of the desk, so we could all see it. I felt horror creeping into the edges of my vision as I stared.

"November 29," Nick said.

"Exactly," Heather said. "Tracy's body was found the same night that Vivian Delaney disappeared."

The problem with the traveling salesman was that he didn't have a routine. Aside from the single page of schedule she'd seen in his car— *Mr. Alan Leckie, 52 Farnham Rd., Poughkeepsie; meeting at head office*— she had no idea where he was headed or when. He certainly didn't leave home at eight and get back at six like every other working man. That made him harder to follow.

When Viv awoke—whatever time of day that might be—she got into the habit of dressing, running a brush through her hair, and driving to the salesman's house. First she'd cruise by at regular speed just to see if his car was in his driveway. If it was, she'd park around the corner near the park, sink down in her seat, and wait for him to leave. If it wasn't, she'd drive on to Westlake Lock Systems on the other side of town to see if his car was in the lot. If it wasn't there, either, she knew he was on the road.

Those were the three things he did: went home, went to Westlake, and went on the road. He never had a day off, a Saturday where he did errands. Viv knew because she'd spent a day observing Mrs. Simon Hess, who was much easier to follow. Mrs. Hess took their daughter to school, then did all of the family's shopping and errands, then picked their daughter up again.

That part was simple: Mr. Hess worked and brought home the money, and Mrs. Hess did everything else.

After two fruitless days when he wasn't in town, she finally got a break. She found his car in the parking lot at Westlake Lock Systems, and as she sat low in her seat at the back of the lot she saw him come out of the building. He was wearing a suit, a navy blue overcoat, and shoes that were shined. He carried a briefcase. He was the perfect figure of a traveling salesman.

I guess I'm just that memorable, he'd said, and then he'd asked her name.

He acted normal and didn't change his routine, but Viv knew better. She was tracking a hunter, a predator. There was no thought in her mind anymore that she could be wrong, that this maybe wasn't the man who had killed Betty Graham at least, and probably others afterward. There was no thought that Simon Hess was just a blameless man going about his workday. There was no thought that she might be crazy.

Hess stopped next to his car and fished in his pocket for his car keys. As he did so he turned his head in a slow, methodical arc, taking in every corner of the parking lot. His eyes in that moment seemed dark and dead, like a shark's. It was the same look he'd done after he'd almost caught her in his driveway. He was looking for something. For her.

Viv sank lower in her seat and tilted her head to the side so he couldn't see the top of her head over the dashboard. She even closed her eyes and held her breath, as if that would help.

There was a long pause, thirty or maybe even sixty seconds. Then she heard the *clunk* of a car door closing and the turn of the motor. She peeked over the dashboard to watch Hess drive smoothly out of the lot.

I have to be careful, she thought, so she counted to sixty. Then she started her car and followed him.

He left Fell and took the interstate, exiting after an hour and coming to a town called Plainsview. She followed him down a suburban street, and when he pulled over she passed him, accelerating away. She circled until she found a spot on a side street and parked. She pulled a hat from her purse—a dark blue knit cap that she'd found in Jenny's closet. She put it on, got out of the car, put her purse over her shoulder, and walked, like any girl walking down a sidewalk.

She spotted his car, parked in the small lot of a strip mall that had a portrait studio, a hair salon, and a closed-up dentist's office. She zipped her coat up against the wind, dug her hands deep into the pockets, and kept walking, her eyes ahead and a small frown on her face as if she were thinking about something far away.

She couldn't see him; she didn't know where he'd gone. Then, with a jolt that almost startled her, she saw him only twenty feet away, ringing the doorbell of the house she was passing. The hedge had hidden him from view. His back was to her, and for a second she couldn't help but stare at him as she walked. His body turned, and she realized he could see her reflection in the glass of the storm door. She ducked her head and darted past before he could turn and see her in full.

It was close. She quickly walked around a corner, then another. There was a bus stop with a bench and three people already waiting. Viv tugged the hat down on her forehead, sat on the bench, pulled her notebook from her purse, opened it to the blank pages in the middle, and stared at it as if reading. She kept her face relaxed even when she saw the traveling salesman come around the corner at the edge of her eye.

He paused at the head of the street and stood there, looking at the bus stop. Looking at her. He wanted to know why she had stared at him in shock as she'd walked past him, wanted to know who she was. Viv didn't look up and she didn't tense as he watched her. She kept her face blankly intent on her notebook and her breathing even. She knew he was hesitating, not certain he wanted to approach her at a crowded bus stop in the middle of the day.

He was still undecided when the bus pulled up. Her face still blank with boredom, Viv closed her notebook, stood in line with the others, and got on. She paid her quarter in fare and took a seat as the bus pulled away from the curb. She didn't risk a look at him through the window.

Sloppy. He's too smart for that. Be more careful next time.

She waited two stops—one seemed risky—and got off, circling back on foot to the place where she had seen him. This time she didn't walk the street directly but circled behind a row of houses, where she found a walking path. She stood at the edge of the path, took out her notebook—it was useful for all sorts of things, it turned out—and fished a pencil out of her purse. She stood and faced the trees, the pencil moving over her page, so anyone out for a walk would see a pretty girl sketching a nature scene.

But in the wedge of space between two houses, she could see him. He was on the other side of the street, standing on a front porch, talking to the woman who had answered the door. Their conversation was swift and uneventful. The woman closed the door and Simon Hess pulled a folded piece of paper from his pocket. He took out a pencil—the fact that he was now in Vivian's own pose was not lost on her—and made a note, then looked at the page intently. He turned the page sideways and back again, and Viv realized he was looking at a map. He had a map of the neighborhood and was making sure he hit every house.

She watched as he moved to another door, and then another. A traveling salesman doing what he was hired to do, cover a neighborhood knocking on doors. After each door he took out his map and pencil and made another mark. Viv edged along the walking path, her own paper and pencil in hand, keeping him in view. He wasn't being careful. He wasn't looking around to see if he was being watched. He'd seen her get on the bus, and she knew she had caught the hunter in a rare slip-up. His guard was down. He hadn't matched the girl waiting for the bus with the footprints in his garden weeks ago. She was watching him unseen.

I've never seen him do anything except go to work and back. You're barking up the wrong tree, honey.

Part of her knew that anyone would think her crazy. *He's just a salesman going about his job!* But he wasn't. She knew that.

His head turned, and Viv took a step back, out of view. A man with a dog on a leash walked by, and she took her pencil to paper, sketching the trees. The man gave her a smile as he passed. "Nice day," he said.

Viv smiled back. "Yes, it is."

That made him smile more—men loved it when a girl smiled back at them, answered them as if whatever they'd said was the most wonderful thing. She even saw his step slow as he considered stopping and talking to her.

Move on, she thought. *Move on.*

The salesman could be walking away. Changing neighborhoods, maybe. Or getting back in his car.

The man's foot paused, and then the dog pulled on his leash, barking at a squirrel. The moment broke.

"Good luck with your drawing," the man said, following the dog and walking away.

"Thank you!" Viv said cheerfully, as if delighted he would say so. When he was a safe distance away she moved position again, looking for the salesman.

He had moved down the sidewalk and was standing with his map and pencil again. But he wasn't looking at the map. He was standing very still, his chin raised just enough to look ahead. His gaze was fixed on something, unmoving.

Viv changed position again, trying to see what he was looking at. It was a typical quiet suburban street; a car passed in one direction, then another in the other direction. A woman stood on a driveway, bundled into a winter coat, helping her toddler onto a tricycle. An elderly man with a newspaper under his arm crossed at the end of the street.

The traveling salesman was unmoving, and something about his gaze was hard, cold. Viv moved again, trying to see.

A girl was standing on the curb several houses ahead, where the street curved, holding the handlebars of her bike. She looked about sixteen, tall and slim, wearing dark jeans and a waist-length hooded coat zipped tight. Her dark blond hair was pulled back into a careless ponytail and she wore chocolate brown mittens. She was unaware of the man looking at her. As Viv watched, the girl swung one leg over the seat of the bike and put her foot on the pedal. She adjusted her balance and pushed off in a graceful motion, putting her other foot on the pedal and powering up. She biked away, her legs pumping, her body pushed forward. After a few moments, she was gone.

Simon Hess watched her, standing on the sidewalk with his map in his hand. It flapped softly in the cold wind. The hem of his long wool coat flapped, too, the gust of November wind rolling up the street and the sidewalks.

At last, as if in slow motion, he folded the map and put it in his pocket, along with the pencil. He blinked his eyes as if waking up. Then he turned and walked toward his car.

He's hunting, Viv thought.

She ran to her car to follow him.

An hour later, she gave up in despair. She couldn't find the salesman's car or the girl on the bike. She'd tried going in the direction she'd seen them go, but nothing. She'd tried the side streets to no avail. She'd ended up in downtown Plainsview, a main street with a grocery store, a diner, a hardware store, and a broken-down arcade. Simon Hess and his car were nowhere to be seen, and so was the girl.

He wouldn't do something today. Would he?

Panicked, Viv circled back to the street where she'd first seen the girl, parking where she'd parked before. She got out and walked past the house in front of which the girl had been getting on her bike. Did she live here? Was she visiting here? Or had she only stopped briefly while riding her bike down the street, on her way from somewhere else?

Viv wrote the address in her notebook, then walked back to her car and waited, watching. It was now nearly four o'clock in the afternoon; she should be exhausted. But she was wide awake, her blood pounding shrilly in her veins.

The traveling salesman was following his next victim. She was sure of it.

The question was, what was she going to do?

The house on German Street was at least sixty years old, a post–World War II bungalow with white wood siding and a roof of dark green shingles. This was a residential street in downtown Fell, a few blocks from Fell College in one direction and the huge Duane Reade in the other. In this small knot of streets, everything had been tried at one point or another: low-rise rental apartment buildings, corner stores, laundromats, a small medical building advertising physiotherapists and massage. In between these were the small houses like this one, the remnants of the original neighborhood that had been picked apart over the decades. This one was well kept, with hostas planted along the front and in the shade beneath the large trees, a fall wreath of woven branches hanging on the door.

There was a car in the driveway. That was a good sign, because Heather and I were dropping in unexpectedly.

"You're up for this?" I asked Heather for the third time.

She gave me a thumbs-up, and we got out of the car.

We could hear the doorbell chime through the door. After a minute the door opened and a woman appeared. She was black, in her fifties, with gray hair cropped close to her head. She wore a black sweater, black leggings, and white slippers.

Her eyes narrowed at us suspiciously. "Help you?"

"Mrs. Clark?" I said. "I'm Carly Kirk. We talked on the phone."

"The girl asking me about the photograph," Marnie said. "I already told you I have nothing to say."

"This is my friend Heather," I said. "We just have a few questions. We'll be quick, I promise."

Marnie leaned on the door frame, still not stepping aside. "You're persistent."

"Vivian was my aunt," I said. "They never found her body."

Marnie looked away. Then she looked from me to Heather and back again. "Fine. I don't know how I can help, but you get a few minutes. My husband is home in half an hour."

She led us into the front living room, a well-lived-in space with a sofa, an easy chair, and a big TV. A shelf of photos showed Marnie, her husband, and two kids, a son and a daughter, both of them grown. Heather and I sat on the sofa and Marnie took the easy chair. She didn't offer us a drink.

"Listen," she said. "I told you that photo was just something I got paid for. I don't know anything about your aunt disappearing all those years ago."

Heather pulled a printout of the article about Vivian from her pocket and unfolded it. There was Marnie's photo, Vivian with her lovely face and curled hairdo, her head turned and her expression serious. "Do you remember taking this?" Heather asked her.

Marnie glanced at it and shook her head. "I was a freelance photographer in those days. I shot anything that would pay. I took pictures of houses for real estate agents. I did portraits. I worked for the cops a few times, taking shots of burglary scenes." She put her hands on the arms of the easy chair. "When I met my husband, I took a job with the studio that worked for the school board. I did class photos. It didn't pay a whole lot, but the hours were easy and I had my son on the way. I couldn't run around taking pictures at all hours anymore."

"You said on the phone you've lived in Fell all your life," I said.

"That's right."

"Do you know the Sun Down Motel?"

Marnie shrugged. "I suppose."

"Here's the thing," Heather said. "I took this photo and enlarged it. You see this in the corner here." She pointed to the corner of the photo of Vivian. "When the picture is enlarged, that's a number—actually, it's two numbers, a one and a zero. Like the numbers on the front of a motel room door." She pulled out her phone. "So I went to the Sun Down and looked at their room numbers. The rooms on the bottom level all start with a one, and the rooms on the upper level all start with a two. And the door numbers look exactly like the numbers in your picture."

Marnie had gone still, her gaze flat. "What exactly are you saying?"

"The Sun Down hasn't changed its door numbers since it opened," I said. "This picture"—I pointed to the photo of Viv—"the one you took, was taken at the Sun Down Motel. Do you remember why you were taking pictures there?"

Marnie barely glanced at the photo. She shook her head. "What do you think is going to come from this?" she asked, looking from me to Heather and back. "Nancy Drew One and Nancy Drew Two. Do you think you're going to catch a murderer? Tackle him down and tie his hands while the other one calls 911? Do you think some photo pulled out of a thirty-five-year-old newspaper is going to be the smoking gun? Real life doesn't work that way. I've seen enough of it to know. Gone is gone, like I told you on the phone. I look at you two and wonder if I was ever as young as you are. And you know, I don't think I ever was."

Her dark brown eyes looked at mine, and I held her gaze. We locked there for a long second.

"You took pictures at the Sun Down in 1982," I said. "Tell me why."

Still she held my gaze, and then she sighed. Her shoulders sagged a little. "I took a side job for a lawyer. Following his client's wife. I followed her around and took pictures for evidence. She was cheating on him, just like he thought, and she met the other man at the Sun Down. So the pictures I took were not exactly for public use." She leaned back in her chair. "That job paid me a hundred and seventy-five dollars, and I paid the utility bill for almost a year with it. I was on my own back then, paying for myself. I needed the money."

I felt a tickle of excitement in the back of my mind. "What was the client's name?" I asked.

"Bannister, but it was thirty-five years ago. They might both be dead by now, for all I know."

"So you were taking pictures at the Sun Down while Vivian was there. Did you ever talk to her?" I asked.

"I had no reason to talk to her," was the reply. "I was in my car in the parking lot. I wasn't really advertising myself."

Which wasn't an answer. "So you didn't meet her?"

"Did I go in and introduce myself to the night shift clerk while I was following someone? No."

"You knew what she looked like," Heather chimed in. "When she disappeared, you knew you had a photo of her and you offered it to the newspapers."

"I knew what she looked like because her picture was already in the papers," Marnie corrected her. "When I saw her face, she looked familiar. The articles said the Sun Down, so I checked my photos and I saw the same face."

"Where are those photos now?" I asked her.

Marnie looked at me. "You think I kept photos from 1982?"

I looked at my roommate. "Heather, do you think she kept photos from 1982?"

"Let's see," Heather said. "A divorce case, valuable pictures that could be used as blackmail. I'd keep them."

"Me, too, especially if there was a known murder victim in them. You might be able to sell the pictures all over again if her body is found."

"Double the money," Heather agreed.

"You two are a piece of work," Marnie said. "I ought to smack both of you upside the head." She lifted herself out of the chair and left the room.

We waited, quiet. I didn't look at Heather. When I heard the sounds of Marnie rustling through a closet in the next room, I tried not to smile.

She came back out with a stack of pictures in her hand, bound together by a rubber band. She tossed the stack in my lap. "Knock yourselves out," she said. "The last time I looked at those was 1982, and they weren't very interesting then. I doubt they're any more interesting now. If you think your aunt's killer is in there, you can do the work yourself."

I picked up the stack. It looked like a hundred or so pictures. "Has anyone else seen these?"

"The lawyer I worked for back then got copies. I kept my copy just in case, for insurance. I even kept the negatives—you can have those, too." She dropped an envelope on top of the photos. "Like you said. When I sold the picture of Vivian to the newspapers, the cops didn't even call me. They didn't come to my door asking for that stack. So no, no one else has seen them."

We thanked her and left. When we got into the car and slammed the doors I said to Heather, "Okay, how many lies did she tell, do you think?"

"Three big ones and a bunch of little ones," she said without a pause.

I thought it over. "I missed a few. Tell me the ones you know."

She put up an index finger. "One, someone else has definitely seen the photos. They were the last known photos of a missing person. The cops must have at least looked at them, though I don't know why she'd lie."

I nodded.

"Two"—Heather put up a second finger—"her old client, Bannister, is definitely not dead. She was trying to discourage us from finding him."

"I caught that one," I said.

"And three . . ." Heather opened her file of newspaper clippings. "I've seen every mention of Vivian's disappearance in every paper. The first mention of it on the first day was a paragraph of text." She pointed to a few sentences in the *Fell Daily*. "It just says that local girl Vivian Delaney is thought to be missing, blah blah. Call the police if you know anything. There's no picture. But the next day, Marnie's photo runs in the paper. Which means Marnie didn't match the name and the photo to the girl from the Sun Down. When she sold her photo to the papers, she knew Vivian's name and her face."

"So she didn't just sit in the parking lot," I said.

"No." Heather snapped her file shut. "She knew Vivian, and she isn't admitting it. What I want to know is why."

Fell, New York
November 1982
VIV

Viv sat at her kitchen table again with the telephone and the phone book. Next to her—beside the box of Ritz crackers and the jar of cheese—was her notebook. It was open to the pages with the information she'd mapped out last night. She'd sat in the office at the Sun Down for her long, dark shift and made a list of dates.

Betty Graham: November 1978.

Cathy Caldwell: December 1980.

Victoria Lee: August 1981.

Viv tapped the end of her pencil against the table and went over the list again. If Simon Hess did all of these murders—and Vivian was personally sure he had—then there were gaps. Between Betty and Cathy. Between Victoria and now. Unless there were other dead girls she didn't know about.

She pulled out the sheet of paper from Simon Hess's scheduling office that she'd stolen from his car. She took a deep breath, got into character, and dialed the number at the top.

"Westlake Scheduling," a woman answered.

"Good afternoon," Viv said, lowering her voice to the right tone and letting the words roll. "I'm calling from the Fell Police Department."

The woman gave a disbelieving laugh. "You're having me on, right? There aren't any women police."

"I assure you, ma'am, that there are," Viv said. "At least, there's one, and that's me. My name is Officer Alma Trent, and I really am a police officer."

It was the best impression she'd ever done. She sounded competent and older than her years. She put her shoulders back and her chin up to make the sound coming from her throat deeper and rounder.

"Oh, well," the woman on the other end of the line said, "I had no idea. I've never had a call from a police officer before."

"That's okay, ma'am. I hear it all the time. I'm looking into a small matter here at the station, and I wonder if you could help me."

"Certainly, Officer."

She felt a little kick at that. It must be fun to be Alma sometimes. "We've had a few break-ins on Peacemaker Avenue," Viv said, naming the street that Victoria Lee had lived on. "Nothing too bad, just people breaking windows and jimmying locks. Trying to grab some cash. The thing is that some of these break-ins happened during the day, and one person mentioned seeing one of your salesmen on his street."

"Oh." The woman gave a nervous, defensive titter. "You don't think one of our men would do that, do you? We hire professionals."

"No, ma'am, I do not think that," Viv said with the straight seriousness that Alma would give the words. "But I would like to know, if one of your men was in the area, if there's anything he remembers seeing. Strangers or suspicious folks hanging around, if you know what I mean."

"Oh, sure, I get it." Viv heard the rustle of papers. "Did you say Peacemaker Avenue? We keep records of which salesman covered which territory. It's important to keep it straight so they aren't overlapping and the commissions are paid right."

"I'm sure you keep good records, ma'am, and I appreciate anything you can tell me."

There was more rustling of papers, the sound of pages turning in a scheduling book. "Here it is. You say someone saw one of our salesmen there?"

"Yes, ma'am."

"Well, I don't know what they were talking about. We haven't had a salesman cover Peacemaker Avenue since August of last year."

Viv was silent, her blood singing in her ears, her head light. Victoria Lee, who lived on Peacemaker Avenue, had been killed in August of '81.

She had just connected the traveling salesman with Victoria Lee— whose boyfriend was in prison for the murder.

"Hello?" the woman on the other end said. "Are you still there?"

Think, Viv. "Yes, sorry," she said, channeling Alma again. "Can you let me know which of your salesmen that was? I'd still like to talk to him. Maybe he's been back to the area and it isn't in the schedule."

"That's true," the woman said to Viv's relief. "He may have made a follow-up call. That wouldn't be in the book." There was a pause. "Well, darn. We do the schedule in pencil because there are so many changes, but someone's gone and erased the name right out of the book."

"Really?" *Checkmate, Simon Hess*, she thought. "That's strange."

"It sure is. Maybe two of our men were going to trade and the new names didn't get written in."

Viv thanked the woman and hung up. So Simon Hess was covering his tracks. But it was something. She was closing in. She wrote a check-mark next to Victoria's name.

She flipped to another phone number she'd pulled from the phone book. It was time to put Simon Hess and Cathy Caldwell together.

"Hello?" an older woman's voice said when Viv had dialed the number.

She didn't use Alma's voice this time. Instead, she used the voice she'd just heard at Westlake Lock Systems. "Hello, is this Mrs. Caldwell?"

"No, I'm not Mrs. Caldwell. I'm her mother. Mrs. Caldwell is dead."

Viv's throat closed. *Stupid, so stupid.* She'd assumed that Cathy's mother would also be Mrs. Caldwell, though of course Caldwell was Cathy's married name. "Ma'am, I'm so sorry," she managed.

The woman sighed wearily. "What are you selling?"

"I'm not—" She had to get a grip. "I'm, um, calling from Westlake Lock Systems. I wanted to know if you're satisfied with the locks you bought two years ago."

It was a long shot. But all the woman had to say was *I don't know what you're talking about* and the conversation would be over. *I wish I really were a police officer*, she thought. *It would be so much easier to get people to answer questions.*

But the woman replied with, "I suppose they're fine. I remember when Andrew and Cathy bought them. They didn't want to spend the money, but your salesman convinced them. With Andrew gone so much, they thought it would make Cathy safer. It didn't work."

Viv's hand was shaking as she put a checkmark next to Cathy's name. "Ma'am, I think—"

"You're one of those ghouls, aren't you?" the woman said. "You aren't from the lock company at all. Then again, I wonder how you knew about the locks Cathy put in. You're likely not going to tell me. So let me tell you something instead."

"Ma'am?" Viv said.

"You think we haven't had dozens of phone calls at this house? Hundreds? I moved in after Cathy died because my grandson was left without a mother. Andrew is deployed again so it's just my boy and me. And I'm the one who answers the damn phone calls. They've tapered off over the past two years, but we still get them. I can tell a ghoul from the first minute I answer the phone."

Viv was silent.

The woman didn't need an answer. "I've heard everything," she continued. "Cathy was a slut, Cathy was a saint. Cathy was targeted by Communists or Satanists. Cathy was killed by a black man, a Mexican. Cathy was having a lesbian affair. Cathy got what she deserved because she had left the path of God. I've told Andrew to unlist the number, but he won't do it. You ghouls have all the answers, except one: You can't tell me who the hell killed my daughter."

The woman's voice was raw with pain and anger. It came through the phone line like a miasma. Viv still couldn't speak.

"It's never going to happen," the woman said. "Finding him. Arresting him. Letting me watch him fry. I thought for a long time that I would get that chance. But it's been two years, and they still don't know who took my girl. Who stripped her, put a knife in her, and dumped her. A sweet girl who wanted to earn her next paycheck and raise her baby. Do you know who killed her? Can you end this for me?"

The words were right there. Sitting in her throat. *His name is Simon Hess.* But something stopped her; maybe it was the knowledge that saying it wouldn't end this woman's pain. "I—"

"Of course you don't know," Cathy's mother said. She sounded angry and tired, so tired. "None of you people ever know."

"He won't get away forever." Viv's voice was hoarse with her own emotion—anger and a different kind of exhaustion. She was tired, too, though she couldn't imagine how tired Cathy's mother must be. "He can't. He'll make a mistake. He'll come into the light. There will be justice, I swear."

"No," Cathy's mother said. "There won't. I'm going to die not knowing who killed my baby. He's going to walk free."

There was a click as she hung up.

Viv sat silent for a long time after she put the phone down. She wiped the tears from her cheeks. Then she got up to get dressed.

"Thank you for meeting me," Marnie said to Viv the next day as they sat on a bench in a park in downtown Fell. "During the day, no less."

Viv picked at the French fries she'd bought from a fast-food counter on her way here. Vaguely, she realized that she didn't eat real meals anymore; she snacked on crackers and coffee during the day and ate bologna sandwiches at night. She couldn't remember when she'd last slept eight hours.

"You look terrible," Marnie said, reading her mind.

Viv shrugged. "I feel fine." It was the truth. She had pushed past tiredness some time ago and now existed on a plane of exhaustion that floated her through the day.

Marnie did not look terrible. She looked great. She wore khaki pants with a pleated waist and a navy blue blouse beneath her wool pea coat, and she had a matching navy knit cap on her head. It was four o'clock in the afternoon, and a few of the people passing through the park looked twice at the black woman and the white woman sitting together.

"Okay, I came to tell you two things," Marnie said, leaning back on the bench next to Viv. "The first is that I had some downtime today, so I followed your salesman. He's in Plainsview again."

Viv straightened. Plainsview, where she'd seen him watching the girl. "Right now?"

"Yes, right now. I followed him to the exit, and then I kept going. Because if I follow him too close and too often, he'll see me. Which leads me to the other thing I want to say. I quit."

"What do you mean, you quit?"

"All of this," Marnie said, waving between the two of them. "The intrigue we have going on. I'm quitting. I'm done. I'm not following this man anymore. I'm not even sure he's a murderer."

Viv blinked at her. "There was a salesman from Westlake Lock Systems going door-to-door on Victoria Lee's street the month she was killed. And Cathy Caldwell and her husband bought locks from a Westlake salesman before she was killed, too."

Marnie's lips parted. She looked like someone had slapped her. "Oh, honey," she said in a rough voice, and Viv thought she was going to say *You're crazy* or *It doesn't prove anything*, but instead she said, "You need to stop before you get yourself killed."

"He doesn't know I'm investigating him," Viv said.

"The hell he doesn't. A man does crimes like this, he's looking over his shoulder. Covering his tracks. Waiting for someone to come up behind him."

Viv thought of the name erased from the Westlake schedule book and didn't reply.

"You're going to get hurt," Marnie said. "I know you think you won't, but you will. If he can hurt those girls, then he can hurt you. You need to talk to the police and tell them what you've found."

Viv licked her dry, chapped lips and ate a cold French fry.

"Promise me," Marnie said. "You owe me, Vivian. Promise me you'll talk to the police. That you'll try."

Viv forced the words out. "I promise." She didn't want to, but she meant it. She promised it to Marnie, and she would do it. "Please don't quit."

Marnie shook her head. "Sorry, but I am. I don't want to do this any-more. It's too dangerous. I have a man I'm seeing, and he says he wants to marry me. I can get married and start a family instead of doing this. I'm done."

"But you're the one who showed me everything," Viv said. "You're the one who took the photos and took me to the murder sites."

"I was trying to help you, because you were a clueless girl working in the middle of the night. I was trying to show you that there are predators out there. That you have to be careful." She gave a humorless laugh. "Looks like it backfired on me. How was I supposed to know you'd start hunting the hunter?"

"Maybe you were trying to help, but you knew all about the murders. It interested you, too."

"Maybe. Yes, okay. But I wasn't interested like you are now." Marnie leaned forward, her elbow on her knee, and looked Viv in the eye. "I'm all about survival. That's how I work. Knowing about the girls getting killed in this town was a part of that survival. Following a killer around is not." She pressed her lips together and sighed. "I like you. I do. But I have more to lose than you do. I'm not jeopardizing everything I have, everything I've worked for, my *life*, for something I can't prove, that no one will believe. I'm not willing to do that and I never was. Do you understand me?"

Viv dropped her gaze to her fries and nodded.

There was a second of silence. "You're going to Plainsview, aren't you?" Marnie said.

Viv nodded, still staring at her fries.

"I know I can't stop you, and you have some serious spine. But be careful, for God's sake. At least be ready to defend yourself. Don't be alone with him. All right?"

"I'll be careful."

"Damn it," Marnie said. "If I read about you in the papers, I'm going to be so damn mad at myself."

But she still rose from the bench, picked up her purse, and walked away.

The trail had gone cold in Plainsview. Viv circled the streets, looking for Hess's car. She started with the neighborhood she'd last seen him in, then widened out to the next neighborhood and the next. Plainsview wasn't a very big place, and soon she'd covered it pretty thoroughly.

She ended up at the town's only high school, Plainsview High. It was a new building, and even though it was dinnertime, the parking lot was full of cars, the lights on in all the windows. Viv saw a handmade sign that said, CHOIR NIGHT TONIGHT!!

She parked on the street and scanned the cars in her view. The girl she'd seen on her bicycle was high school age, which meant she might be here, or her hunter might come to this place. After a minute she got out of the car and looked up and down the street. He wouldn't park in the lot, but nearby. That was what she would do.

She shoved her hands in the pockets of her coat and walked toward the school. Nothing moved; choir night was still happening. But when she stepped on the edge of the school's concrete tarmac, the school doors opened and parents and students began to file out. The performance was finished.

There was the sound of a motor, and a car pulled away in the edge of

Viv's vision. She turned and squinted. It was the same make and model as Hess's car, but at this angle she couldn't see the driver. She took a step forward as the car receded, trying to read the license plate, but she could only catch a nine and a seven before the car disappeared.

Simon Hess's license plate had a nine and a seven.

She walked through the small crowd. She looked like someone's big sister, or maybe even a senior, so she blended in. Moving against the flow of people leaving, she walked through the school's open doors. On a folding table was the night's program, now over. She picked it up.

On the front was a list of the songs in tonight's performance. On the back was a list of the members of the Plainsview High School Choir. There were fifteen girls.

She folded the page in her pocket and wandered farther down the hall, passing teachers and parents chatting in knots. The school was small, and the crowd was rapidly dispersing. There were other folding tables here, advertising other things: the football team, the science fair. One of the tables had a handmade sign that said ORDER YOUR 1982–83 YEARBOOK NOW! Next to it was a copy of the 1981–82 yearbook on display.

This is so easy, Viv thought as she picked up the yearbook, slid it in her coat, and walked back out the door with the rest of the crowd.

Downtown Plainsview was closing, but a hardware store was still open.

Viv went in, thinking of that car driving away tonight. Thinking of Marnie's advice: *At least be ready to defend yourself.* And that stupid news item on safety tips for teens: *Use a buddy system. Never get into a stranger's vehicle. Consider carrying a whistle or a flashlight.*

Viv walked up one aisle of the small store, then down the other. A whistle was not much use at the Sun Down, where there was no one around for miles. If she ever used it, she'd be whistling into the wind. As for a flashlight, she pictured shining one into the traveling salesman's face. That wouldn't do much, either.

"Excuse me, miss?"

Viv turned to see a boy of about eighteen standing at the end of the aisle. He had pimples on his cheeks and a red apron on. He gave her a smile that was friendly and a little embarrassed. "We're closing now," he said.

"Oh," Viv said, looking around. "I was just—"

"Is there something I can help you find?"

"Maybe." She smiled back at him. "I was just thinking that I should carry something to defend myself. Because I work nights."

"Jeez, sure," the guy said. "We don't carry Mace, though. You'd be surprised how often we get asked for it."

"Right." Viv had never actually thought about how to defend herself. Could she punch someone, kick them? Growing up in suburban Grisham, the idea was absurd. Now she glanced at the darkening windows outside and wondered exactly what she would do.

What would you do if you ever saw real trouble? her mother had said.

"There's a baton thing you can carry," the hardware guy told her. "It gives a good whack, I think. But it's big and heavy for carrying around every day." He turned the corner to the next aisle, and Viv followed him. "Personally, if I were a girl and I wanted to defend myself, I'd carry this." He reached onto a shelf and put a thick leather holder into her hand.

Viv pulled the handle. It was a knife—not the retractable switchblade kind, but a regular knife with a wooden handle and a wicked silver blade. The blade itself was about three inches long and looked like it could cut glass.

"Wow," Viv said.

"I told you, we get asked a lot," the guy replied. "This is a hunting knife, but it works for what you want. Small enough to fit in a purse. Sharp enough that you mean business." She looked up to see that he was smiling at her. "You can even take it jogging in the park. Some pervert comes up to flash you—*boom!* At least, if I were a girl, that's what I would do."

She blinked up at him, and she smiled at him. She watched him blush.

"I'll take it," she said.

Fell, New York
November 2017
CARLY

A few thin flakes of snow swirled in the air, white against the darkness. They flitted in front of the blue and yellow of the motel sign like fireflies, looking almost pretty. Thanksgiving was coming, and I'd had an email from Graham a few hours ago, asking if I wanted to spend the holiday with him and his fiancée back home.

I pictured an awkward dinner at Graham and Hailey's apartment, football on TV. It was the second Thanksgiving since Mom died, and my brother and I should probably spend it bonding and supporting each other. But we didn't have particularly warm memories of the holiday—Mom always cooked a big Thanksgiving dinner, but she worked and sweated over it for days, making a meal for the three of us that didn't matter much in the big scheme of things. By the end of it she was always too exhausted to be much fun, and if Graham and I either offered to help her or told her to keep it simple, she got defensive and angry.

She'd even cooked Thanksgiving dinner for us when she was sick. She was still on her feet then, trying to convince herself that she could do everything she used to do. She'd waved us off, gone shopping for a load of groceries when Graham and I weren't looking. She'd fallen asleep while the turkey was in the oven. Just thinking about it now made me sad. I had no idea what old idea buried in my mother's psyche made her crazy at Thanksgiving, and now I would never know.

I loved Graham. He was my big brother, my only sibling, my protector and my torturer for as long as I could remember. The one who didn't let bullies tease me for being a dorky bookworm, but who also believed that making me watch horror movies at age nine would "toughen me up" and had snuck me my first copy of *Pet Sematary*. But now he was twenty-three, working in an office, and practically married. While I stood here in the parking lot of the Sun Down at three in the morning, watching the snow, it felt like Graham was on Mars.

I held the photo in my hand out at arm's length, matching the image to the motel. It was one of Marnie Clark's stack of photos, taken from the parking lot of the Sun Down in 1982. This shot was taken from near where I was standing, at the edge of the parking lot, facing the motel. I moved the photo until I had it exactly matched—the real motel outside the frame, the 1982 version inside. There was almost no difference at all.

In a weird, scary way, this place was almost magical, stuck in time.

I lowered the photo and picked up the next one from the stack. It was taken from the same angle. There were two cars in the parking lot in the picture, parked in front of rooms 103 and 104. They were boxy, early-1980s cars, ugly and oddly retro-attractive at the same time. A woman was getting out of one of them. She was young and dark-haired and beautiful, sexy and maybe a little mean. Or she just had resting bitch face, perhaps. This was the woman Marnie had been paid to follow and catch cheating. Bannister, Marnie had said the name was. This was Mrs. Bannister, on her way to an assignation at the Sun Down.

I switched to the next photo. My hands were getting cold in my mittens, but I didn't care. There was no chance that I would be needed inside the Sun Down office anytime soon, because we had no customers, and I liked looking at the photos out here, seeing where Marnie had been when she took them, the real spot where Mrs. Bannister had parked. It was like a door through time.

The next photo showed the door to room 104 opening and a man standing in the gap. He was smiling at Mrs. Bannister. He was fortyish, with salt-and-pepper hair. Not bad-looking, I thought, but it was a mystery why a woman so young would cheat with him at a down-and-out motel. Then again, I was the last person to understand anything about sex.

I looked more closely at the photo of Mrs. Bannister and her lover. Marnie had been at the back of the parking lot, and she'd gotten a lot of the motel into the frame. On the upper edge I could see the second level of the motel, the bottoms of the line of doors through the slats of the second-story railing. There was a dark shadow on the second floor, as if maybe someone was standing there. But then again, it could be anything.

Inside the motel office, I heard the desk phone ring. I jogged back toward the motel, putting the photos in my coat pocket. The ringing stopped as someone picked up the phone, and then the office door opened. Nick stepped out and motioned to me. He'd been in the office going through the rest of the stack of Marnie's photos. "It's Heather," he said.

"Thanks." My glasses fogged as I walked back inside, and when I pulled my hat off my hair probably looked comical. I continued to make an excellent impression on Nick Harkness in my campaign for seduction.

"Hey," I said, picking up the receiver he'd left on the desk. It was sort of a thrill, using an old-style telephone. It felt like it weighed five pounds.

"Okay," Heather said on the other end of the line. "I've been researching the Bannisters for the last hour and I'll tell you what I've found: nothing."

"What do you mean, nothing?" I pawed at my hair with my free hand, trying to pat the flyaways back down. I heard Nick sit, though I couldn't see him through the fog.

"I mean nothing," Heather said. "There's a mention of a Steven Bannister winning a high school high jump contest in 1964, and that's it. I have no idea if it's even the right person. No other mentions of either husband or wife at all. And they're not in the Fell phone book."

The frustrations of tracking people who didn't live their lives online.

"Okay. It was a long shot anyway that either of them would have met Viv. What about the man Mrs. Bannister was cheating with?"

"Aha," Heather said. "Now you'll see how clever I am. Because I truly am fiendishly clever."

"Fiendishly?" My glasses cleared, and I glanced over to see Nick sitting in one of the office chairs, leaning it back with his feet pressed against the desk. He was wearing jeans and his black zip-up hoodie, his hair pushed back from his forehead as if he'd pushed it with his fingers. He had Marnie Clark's photo negatives in his hand and was looking at a strip in the overhead light, squinting a little, his body balanced easily. Even in that pose he looked awesome, scruff on his jaw and all.

"Yes, fiendishly," Heather said as I watched Nick put down one strip and pick up another. "I talked to a guy online who can do DMV lookups. Those photos of Marnie's have license plates in them. It cost me seventy bucks, but now I know who owned the cars in those pictures."

"You're right—that is fiendish."

"I know. So here goes: The Thunderbird in the photos belonged to none other than Steven Bannister, high school high jump star. He moved to Florida in 1984 and dropped off the map. The second car belonged to a Robert White, who died in 2002. He would have been forty-one in '82, so that probably makes him Mrs. Bannister's lover."

"Okay," I said. Nick started to lower his chair, so I stopped staring at him and moved my gaze to a spot on the wall.

"There's a third car, too. That one belonged to a fellow named Simon Hess. Here's where it gets interesting."

"Go on."

Heather paused, purely because she loved the anticipation. "Two things about Simon Hess. First, he worked as a traveling salesman."

That made a bell ring deep, somewhere in my brain. "Where did I read about a traveling salesman?"

"When you read about Betty Graham," Heather said. "She was last seen letting one into her house."

Now the back of my neck went cold. "Oh, Jesus."

"It gets better," Heather said. "I looked up old Simon Hess to see if he was dead yet. And I found something interesting. It seems he left on a sales trip sometime in late 1982 and he never came home."

"What? That makes no sense. What do you mean he never came home?"

Nick was sitting up and watching me now, trying to follow the conversation. I wished like hell this ancient phone had a speakerphone option, but I'd just have to tell him everything after I hung up. How did anyone before 1999 do anything at all?

"He just left and never returned," Heather said. "And get this. His wife didn't even call the police. She eventually declared him dead *five years later*, when she tried to claim his life insurance money. She said she thought he'd abandoned her for another woman, but eventually she figured he might have died, so she wanted to sell their house and get the money."

"Could she just do that?"

"It seems like it. There's a time period someone has to be missing before they can be declared dead. In New York it's three years. I couldn't access the file, but they must have investigated it and decided that Simon Hess was dead and Mrs. Hess got her money."

I rifled through the pile of photos with my free hand, pulling out the one that had Hess's car in it. "So his wife said he went missing sometime in 1982, but she didn't know when?"

"She last saw him in November."

"These photos are from October. So he was still around." I brushed my finger along the edge of the photo, then picked up the next one in the sequence, which showed my aunt Viv walking along the walkway from the AMENITIES room to the office. It was the shot Marnie had cropped and sold to the newspapers, showing Viv's face. Hess's car was in the corner of the frame.

"What are the odds that we have two people who went missing around the same time in one photograph?" I said.

"I don't think it's a coincidence," Heather said. "And if Simon Hess was Betty's killer, then I'd say it isn't a coincidence at all."

"So he killed Viv and fled town."

Nick was listening, but he leaned his chair back again, balanced it, and picked up another negative, looking at it through the light. For the first time, I wondered what he was looking for.

"You have to admit, it's a pretty great theory," Heather said. "But Simon Hess seems like a dead end. No one's seen him since 1982 and he's legally dead."

"Maybe Alma Trent can help."

"She isn't a cop anymore. Do you think we should go to the cops with this?"

I was starting to think so. This was looking less and less like an amateur attempt to satisfy my curiosity and more like something the police could actually use.

I thought of Betty as I'd seen her, tormented and terrifying and somehow still beautiful. Her body dumped here at the Sun Down. Simon Hess's car here. Simon Hess vanishing. Did he leave town before he could be arrested for murder?

It couldn't be a coincidence that Hess had come to the motel sometime in October 1982. But what was he doing here?

I smelled cigarette smoke and glanced at Nick again. He wasn't smoking, of course. He was still looking at Marnie's negatives, but now he was frowning at them, pulling the strip in his hand closer to see it better.

"I'm going to call Alma tomorrow," I decided. "I'll tell her what we have. She'll know what to do."

I hung up and dropped into the office chair. "You're not going to believe this," I said to Nick.

He righted his chair again and raised his eyebrows at me. "I've been here for weeks. I'll believe a lot of things. Including the idea that the smoking guy is around somewhere right now."

I met his gaze. It was strange, so strange to have someone share your crazy delusion. Someone who saw the same ghosts you did.

"This is even weirder than that," I said.

"Hit me."

I told him everything. Nick did what he always did, no matter how crazy the story: listened without judging, laughing, or scoffing. All he said at the end was: "Interesting."

"*Interesting?* That's it?"

"Yes. If he killed Betty and dumped her here, then he was familiar with this place. Maybe, once it was built, he stayed here on his sales trips. Maybe he'd seen Viv and was watching her. Planning." He tapped his fingers on the arm of his chair, his gaze moving past me to look at nothing. "They said my father snapped the day he killed my brother, that he went crazy all of a sudden. But it wasn't true. He planned it."

I held my breath and waited, listening.

"He'd had the gun for over a week," Nick said. "He'd never owned a gun before. He went through the process of getting it legally. He spent some time figuring out what he was going to do and putting the plan into motion. He'd even called our high school and said we were taking a family vacation, so both of his sons would be out of school for a while." His blue gaze was remote. "The only reason Eli was home at all was because his basketball practice had been canceled. He called Dad at work and asked him where he kept the stash of gas money, because he needed to put gas in his car. So Dad knew we were both home. He gave Eli an answer, then left work and came home to kill us."

I didn't know what to say to that. "I'm sorry," I said.

"He said at the trial that he heard voices telling him to do it. But my father was a lawyer. He may have been trying for an insanity defense. I don't know whether he was lying about the voices or not. In any case, the defense didn't work." He looked at me calmly, holding my gaze. "I got asked a lot if I was really in the bedroom when it happened. I was."

I dropped my gaze to the desk in front of me.

"I spent a lot of time wondering if I should have stayed. If I could have gotten past Dad without being killed, gone downstairs and helped Eli. But he died so fast, and no ambulance could have saved him. I think, deep down, that I knew that. Dad had been quiet in the last few weeks, so quiet. He wasn't a violent person, but somehow, when I heard the shots and the screaming, I knew. I knew that Dad had shot Eli, and that it would be over in minutes if I didn't run. I don't know how it's possible, but I think I expected it."

"You had a gut feeling," I said. "An instinct."

Nick pressed his fingertips to his forehead and rubbed it tiredly, his eyes closing for a minute. "Maybe. But if I had an instinct, then why didn't I act on it? Why didn't I say something? Do something? I know I was a fourteen-year-old kid, but this is the kind of thing that goes through your head when your dad tried to kill you. It's why I don't sleep."

"I bet you could sleep in the right place," I said. "Not just at the motel. You can't spend the rest of your life here. I bet you could sleep if you were in a place that made you happy. Where you knew you'd wake up to something good."

He gave me half a smile. "You think that place exists?"

"Sure it does. There are good places, Nick. They're different for everyone. I think you'll find yours."

"You're way too nice to me," he said.

I shrugged. "I have ulterior motives. I have to sit at this desk all night and I have no one to talk to."

"Maybe, but your theory doesn't explain the fact that I can sleep in this shitty motel out of all the places on Earth. Because this is definitely not a good place."

"No. The Sun Down is not a good place. But you can sleep in it because it suits you—at least right now. I know because it suits me, too."

Nick frowned. "That's truly messed up."

I held up the book I'd brought to read tonight—Ann Rule's classic *The*

Stranger Beside Me. I'd read it so many times it was falling apart. "Have you met me?"

He laughed, which gave me a rush of pleasure. Which I tried to ignore. "So what do we do next?" he said.

I put the book down. "We talk to Alma tomorrow about whether any of this should be turned over to the Fell PD. And we try to find out everything we can about Simon Hess. He could be my aunt's killer. And we know he crossed paths with her at least once." I slid the photo across the desk that showed Viv at the motel with Hess's car in the corner of the frame. "He disappeared around the same time she did. I think if we know why, we can solve what happened to her."

"I have another question to add to the pile." Nick put the strips of negatives he'd been looking at on the desk. "Why do we have more negatives than we have prints?"

I sat up straighter. "We do?"

"Yes. I've been looking at the negatives, matching them up. There are four photos in the negatives that we don't have prints of." He pointed to them, though lying on the desk they just looked like splotches of nitrate. "It looks like some kind of outdoor shot—trees or something. What is it, and where are those photos, and why didn't Marnie Clark give them to you?"

I looked at the strip of negative and bit my lip. "I guess I'll get out the phone book. There must be somewhere in town that develops old negatives. After all, this is Fell."

"You're right, there is," Nick said. "You don't need the phone book. I know where it is. And guess what? It's open twenty-four hours."

Maybe this was how the police did it. Viv had no idea—no movie or TV show she'd ever seen showed her how the police really worked. It was all car chases and shootouts with a background of sexy music. Whereas Viv had a choir list, a yearbook, and her trusty telephone.

She went down the list of names of the girls in the choir, looking each of them up in the yearbook. The seventh girl was the one: The face in the yearbook was that of the girl she'd seen pedaling away on her bicycle, the traveling salesman watching her. The girl's name was Tracy Waters, and she was a senior.

Viv didn't have a Plainsview phone book, so she called directory assistance and asked for the number for Plainsview High School. The operator gave her the number for the main office, and Viv dialed it and listened to it ring as she flipped the page in the yearbook, looking for a likely name.

She got a secretary and asked to please speak to the principal. "Who may I say is calling?" the secretary asked.

Viv put her finger on a face in the yearbook—an unattractive girl with a bad perm and glasses that seemed to take up most of her face. *CAROL PENTON*, the name said. "I am Carol Penton's mother," Viv said, making her voice sound older, lower, slightly aggrieved. "I have a concern about my daughter's security."

To her surprise, after a few minutes of holding she was put through to a man who sounded about sixty. "How can I help you, Mrs. Penton?"

"I was at Choir Night last night," Viv said, "and I saw a strange man there. He was looking at the girls."

"Excuse me? Looking at the girls?"

"Yes. He was there alone." She described Simon Hess. "He was just standing there by himself—he didn't have a wife or a child that I saw. I thought it was strange. And when the show was over and everyone was leaving, I saw him again in the hallway. Just standing by himself. He was *staring*. The look in his eyes when he looked at those girls—I didn't like it one bit. If any man looked at my daughter that way, I'd call the police."

"Well." The principal sounded flustered. "That's certainly a concern, Mrs. Penton. Though perhaps he was an uncle or a distant relative of one of the girls. I'm sure he meant no harm."

Viv ground her teeth together. *How are you sure? How?* "I thought Carol was attending a school that took the students' safety seriously."

"We do, we do." Now he was placating. "Let me look into the matter. See if anyone knew who this fellow was."

"He was staring at Tracy Waters," Viv said. "She walked past and he couldn't take his eyes off her." She said it so convincingly that she could see the imaginary scene in her head. "Tracy was with her parents, and none of them acknowledged him. He certainly wasn't a relative."

The principal sighed. "Mrs. Penton, what would you have me do?"

"*Pay attention*," Viv said, tempted to shout. "Look out for your students, especially the girls. Tell your staff to keep their eyes open. Tell them to look out for Tracy especially. She might be in danger."

"Mrs. Penton, I'm sure you're overreacting. We haven't had a complaint from Tracy's family. He was likely an innocent fellow who means well."

No. He is a hunter. There is a hunter after one of your students, you fool. "If anything happens to Tracy, it's your fault." Viv hung up the phone.

She sat for a minute, fuming. She wouldn't be *overreacting* if she were a cop. If she were a man.

She was so limited, sitting here trying to warn people over the phone. No one would listen. She needed to warn Tracy, and she had to do it right.

She switched tactics, pulled out her stationery, and picked up a pen to write.

At midnight that night, she sat in a chair in the Fell police station, trying not to stare. She'd never been in a police station before. From what she could see, it was an open space with a few scarred desks and telephones. They were all unoccupied in the middle of the night except for Alma Trent's. At the front was a desk facing the door, where presumably a cop usually sat to direct people who walked in. There was no one there, either. The entire space was dim and empty except for Alma at her desk, the circle of light from her desk lamp, and Viv herself.

Alma turned the page in Viv's notebook, reading. Viv wanted to get on the phone and call all of these sleeping cops, get them out of bed. *There's a man named Simon Hess who is going to kill a girl named Tracy Waters. Why is everyone sleeping?*

But she had to wait. She chewed her lip and tried not to jiggle her knee in impatience as Alma read her notes.

"Okay, wait," Alma said, pointing to a page. "What's this about Cathy Caldwell and door locks?"

"Cathy and her husband bought door locks before she died. From a door-to-door salesman."

Alma looked up, her face pale. "You can verify this?"

"I don't know the exact date, but Cathy's mother remembers it. The locks were bought from Westlake Lock Systems." She reached over the desk and turned the page. "Westlake Lock Systems also had a salesman scheduled on Peacemaker Avenue, which is Victoria Lee's street. He was scheduled to make calls there in August of last year."

"This can't be," Alma said, almost to herself. "It isn't possible."

"It's very possible," Viv said, trying not to sound impatient. "When I asked the Westlake scheduling service what the salesman's name was, she said it had been erased from the scheduling book. He's covering his tracks. That means he knows there's at least a possibility that someone is onto him."

"A line erased from a scheduling book doesn't mean anything," Alma said, but the no-nonsense confidence was gone from her voice. She was almost whispering. "It could be a random mistake."

"But matched with everything else, it isn't," Viv said. "I've connected him to Cathy and Victoria for you. We already know that Betty saw a traveling salesman before she died. I can only get so much information by myself, but I bet if you requested all of Westlake's records, you could find something I couldn't. The connection between Betty and Simon Hess."

Alma was staring at her. "You've done a lot of work on this," she said. "Dozens of hours."

Viv shrugged. "I thought about applying for a job in Westlake's scheduling department to get access to the book, but it would take too long and it would be too risky. They might put me in another department. Plus I'd actually have to work there all day when I have other things to do. So I can't get full access to the books on my own, and there are only so many times I can phone them, pretending I'm you."

"You did what?"

"It isn't important."

"It's important," Alma said. "Vivian, it's illegal to impersonate a police officer."

Viv wanted to scream. "Simon Hess killed Victoria Lee, and her boyfriend was put away for it. And you're going to put *me* in jail?"

Alma held up a hand. "Back up here," she said. The firmness was back in her voice, as if she was getting control of the situation. "I took a look at the Betty Graham file after the last time we talked. And one of your premises here is actually wrong. Since Betty was last seen letting a salesman into her house, there was a thorough investigation done into every company that employs door-to-door salesmen. They couldn't find any company that had a salesman in the area."

Viv felt her pulse pound. She was so frustrated, so angry. She didn't know that. She didn't know anything, because she didn't have the access to what she needed to put all the pieces together. She was just a twenty-year-old motel clerk. If only she could see everything she needed.

But she thought it over and shook her head. "It doesn't matter."

"Vivian, please. I'm trying to work with you here. But with no salesman in Betty's neighborhood that day, it means that whoever killed her came to her door *pretending* to be a salesman. Which puts you back to square one."

"No, it doesn't. Did they look at the month before the murder? Two months before? The woman in the scheduling department told me that sometimes the salesmen go back for follow-up visits on their own, and those visits aren't recorded in the schedule book. He could have seen her earlier and gone back."

Alma looked shocked again. "They said that?"

"Even if he didn't sell her locks," Viv continued, "Betty was a teacher. Simon Hess has a daughter who is about ten. Maybe his daughter goes to Betty's school—but I can't access the school records. You can. He lives ten minutes away from Betty's house. He could have seen her in the market, the park. Anywhere." She pointed to the book. "You have his name. You can find the connection. I can't."

Alma frowned. She still wasn't sold; Viv could tell. She had no idea what else to do, what else to say.

"This is all based on the idea that this man, Simon Hess, checks into the motel where Betty's body was dumped," Alma said. "That doesn't make him Betty's killer, especially if he isn't the salesman who came to her house." She gestured to the notebook, the motel photos from Marnie, other papers Viv had brought. "You've done amazing work here, Vivian. You could be an investigator. But I'm just the night duty officer, and you're just a motel clerk. If I am going to the higher-ups with a killer this dangerous, like Fell has never seen, I need something so concrete it can't be argued."

Viv swallowed. She looked at the desk, at the papers and photos scattered there, her eyes burning.

"This is compelling," Alma admitted in her kinder voice. "But it's also full of holes. Big ones. Any case I take up the ladder has to be airtight. *Completely* airtight. I'm already no one on this force. Not a single one of these guys will take me seriously. It'll be an uphill battle before I even open my mouth, and if I fail, I'll probably lose my job. They're just looking for a reason."

It was a refusal. A kind one, but still a refusal. Viv would weep if she could summon any tears. She would scream if she could find her voice.

"You're saying the risk is too great," she said.

"That's exactly what I'm saying. You're young, Viv, but I think you're getting the idea. I'm the night duty officer in a small town—and I've worked for *years* just to get this far. I've fought tooth and nail. I've taken insults and abuse, and I'll take more. I'll take it for my whole career. I do it because being a cop is who I am, no matter who tries to tell me differently. But this . . ." She gestured to the papers. "I could lose everything with this. At least, the way it is now. I need more. I need physical evidence. I need eyewitnesses, confessions. No cop could take any of this to court, which means no cop is going to risk his career on it. Including me."

Viv was numb. It was like Marnie, telling her the risk was too great. *I quit.* She'd promised Marnie she'd go to the police, get help, stop putting herself in danger. But Alma wasn't going to help her, either. No one was.

She was in this alone.

"He's going to kill her," she said, her voice a murmur.

"You saw a man looking at a girl, that's all," Alma said. "It doesn't mean anything. Men don't go to jail for looking at girls. And you have nothing else you can prove. You saw a car you thought was his, driving away from the high school. You didn't see who was in it—and even if you had, you still have nothing."

"Okay." Viv leaned forward and gathered up her notebook and papers, her maps and photos. "I appreciate you taking the time. I have to go to work now."

"I've upset you," Alma said.

She couldn't take that. She couldn't take Alma's kindness, her pity that was big-sisterly, almost motherly. It meant nothing if the traveling salesman still walked free, if Tracy died. "He comes to the motel and he checks in under a fake name," Viv said. "He has no reason to do that because he lives in town, but he does. And every time he does it, Betty Graham wakes up and goes crazy."

Alma was silent.

"That's how I know," Viv said, standing up. "I've worked there every night for months, and that's how I know he killed Betty. Because she tells me every time he's there. Her body got dumped at the Sun Down, and she never left. You know that's true as much as I do, except you don't want to admit it."

"Honey," Alma said, "I think it's time you considered seeing a doctor."

Viv kicked her chair back and walked to the door. "That's a lie and you know it," she said, meeting Alma's eyes. "You've seen her. So have I. The difference is that I listen when she tells me what she has to say."

She left and closed the door behind her. Her only hope was the letter she'd sent. It was the only way Tracy Waters was going to stay alive.

Fell, New York
November 2017
CARLY

Tracy Waters was murdered on November 27, 1982," Heather said. "She was last seen leaving a friend's house in Plainsview, heading home. She was riding a bicycle. She was eighteen, and even though she had her driver's license, her parents only rarely lent her their car and she didn't have her own."

I sipped my Diet Coke. "I know that feeling," I said. "I didn't have a car until I was eighteen, when my mother sold me her old one. She charged me five hundred dollars for it, too."

"I'm a terrible driver," Heather said. "I could probably get a car, but it's best for everyone if I don't."

We were sitting in a twenty-four-hour diner on the North Edge Road. It was called Watson's, but the sign outside looked new while the building was old, which meant it had probably been called something else a few months ago. It was five o'clock in the morning, and Watson's was the only place we could find that was open. We were both starving.

"So," Heather said, taking a bite of her BLT. She was wearing a thick sweater of dark green that she was swimming in. She had pulled the top layer of her hair back into a small ponytail at the back of her head. She flipped through some of the articles she'd printed out. "Tracy was a senior in high school, a good student. She didn't have a boyfriend. She only had a few girls she called friends, and they said that Tracy was shy and introverted. She had a summer job at the ice cream parlor in Plainsview and she was in the school choir."

I looked at the photo Heather had printed out. It was a school portrait of Tracy, her hair carefully blow-dried and sprayed. She had put on blush and eye shadow, and it looked weirdly out of place on her young face. "She sounds awesome," I said sadly.

"I think so, too," Heather said. "She went to a friend's house on November 27, and they watched TV and played Uno until eight o'clock. Oh, my God, the eighties. Anyway, Tracy left and got on her bike. Her friend watched her pedal away. She never got home, and at eleven her parents called the police. The cops said they had to wait until morning in case Tracy was just out partying or something."

I stirred my chicken soup, my stomach turning.

"The cops came and interviewed the parents the next morning, and they started a search. On November 29, Tracy's body was found in a ditch off Melborn Road, which is between Plainsview and Fell. At the time, Melborn Road was a two-lane stretch that no one ever drove. Now it's paved over and busy. There's a Super 8 and a movie theater. It looks nothing like it did in 1982." She turned the page to show a printout of an old newspaper article. *LOCAL GIRL FOUND DEAD* was the headline, and beneath it was the subhead *Police arrest homeless man.*

"A homeless guy?" I asked.

"He had her backpack. He seems to have been a drifter, passing through from one place to another. He had a record of robberies and assaults. The thing is, he actually went to the police to *turn in* the backpack when he heard the news. They kept him on suspicion, and when he couldn't provide an alibi for the murder, they charged him."

"That's it? They didn't look at anyone else?"

"It doesn't seem like it. He said he found her backpack by the side of the road, but who was going to believe him? His fingerprints were all over it, and there was a smear of Tracy's blood on one of the straps. There were no other suspects. Her parents were beside themselves. They said they'd had a warning that someone had been following Tracy. The whole story fit." She held up a finger, relishing the story in her Heather way. "But. *But.*"

"You like this too much," I said, smiling at her.

"Whatever, Dr. Carly. You're not listening. The next part gets interesting."

"Like it wasn't interesting before. Go ahead."

"The homeless guy was never convicted. He never even went to trial. It seems that even though he was homeless, he had some kind of access to a good lawyer. Everything was hung up for over a year, and then the charges were dropped and he was set free. The case was opened again, and it's still open. Tracy's parents eventually got divorced, but her mother has never given up on solving the case. She started a website for tips on Tracy's murder in 1999. She still has it, though from what I can tell it's mostly run by Tracy's younger brother now. There's a Facebook page and everything. And remember how I said that someone had been following Tracy? They knew because they got an anonymous letter in the mail the week before she was killed. And now that letter is posted on the Facebook page and the website." She took a sheet of paper out of her stack and handed it to me.

It was a scan of a handwritten letter. I read it over.

This letter is to warn you that I've seen a man following Tracy Waters. He was staring at her while she got on her bike and rode away on Westmount Avenue on November 19 at 2:20 in the afternoon. After she rode away he got in his car and followed her.

I know who he is. I believe he is dangerous. He is about 35 and six feet tall. He works as a traveling salesman. I believe he wants to kill Tracy. Please keep her safe. The police don't believe me.

Keep her safe.

I pushed my soup away. "This is the saddest letter I've ever read in my life," I said.

"The mother was worried when they got it. The father thought it was a prank. The mother decided that the father must be right. A few days later, Tracy was dead. Hence the eventual divorce, I think."

"A traveling salesman," I said, pointing to the words. "Like Simon Hess."

"Who disappeared right after Tracy was murdered. But if you can believe it, it gets even better."

I sat back in my seat. "My head is already spinning."

"Tracy's mom always felt that the letter was real," Heather said. "She thought it was truly sent by someone who saw a man following Tracy. And it wasn't a homeless drifter, either." She tapped the description of the salesman. "This letter is part of why the case against the homeless guy was eventually dropped. But get this: In 1993, over ten years after the murder, Mrs. Waters got a phone call from Tracy's former high school principal. He told her that he had a phone call a few days before Tracy's murder from someone claiming to be another student's mother. The woman said that she'd seen a man following Tracy, and that she thought the school should look out for her."

"And he didn't tell the police?" I said. "He didn't tell anyone for ten years? Why not?"

"Who knows? He was probably ashamed that he didn't do anything about it at the time. But he was retired and sick, and he felt the need to get it off his chest. So this was a preventable murder. Someone warned both Tracy's parents and her principal about it. And if either of them had listened and kept Tracy home, she wouldn't have died."

I blinked at her. "A woman," I said. "The person who called the principal was a woman." I picked up the scan of the letter and looked at it again. "This could be a woman's handwriting, but it's hard to tell."

"It's a woman's," Heather said. "Tracy's mother had a handwriting expert analyze it."

There were too many pieces. They were falling together too fast. And the picture they made didn't make any sense. Who knew that Tracy was going to be killed? How? It couldn't possibly be Vivian, could it?

And if Vivian knew that Tracy was going to be murdered, why couldn't she save herself?

"Did you call Alma?" Heather asked.

"I sent her a text," I said. "She said she was a night owl, but it's still sort of weird to call someone you barely know in the middle of the night when it isn't an emergency. I'm not even sure she texts, to be honest. If I don't hear from her this morning, I'll call her." I looked at the time on my phone. "I should probably get back to the Sun Down. Not that anyone would know I've been gone."

"Where's Nick?"

"Off somewhere getting those negatives developed. He said there's an all-night place in Fell."

"That would be the ByWay," Heather said, gathering her papers. "I think they still rent videos, too."

"Fell is officially the strangest place on Earth." I looked at Heather as she picked up her coat. "What would you say if I told you the Sun Down was haunted?"

She paused and her eyes came to mine, her eyebrows going up. "For real?"

"For real."

She watched me closely, biting her lip. Whatever expression was on my face must have convinced her, because she said, "I want to hear everything."

"I'll tell you."

"And I want to see it."

I rubbed the side of my nose. "I can't guarantee that. She doesn't come out on command."

"She?"

"Betty Graham."

Heather's eyes went as wide as saucers. "You're saying that Betty Graham's ghost is at the Sun Down."

"Yeah, I am. Nick has seen her, too."

"Is she . . . Does she say anything?"

"Not specifically, but I think she's trying to." I thought of the desperate look on Betty's face. "There are others. There's a kid who hit his head in the pool and died. And a man who died in the front office."

"What?"

"Keep your voice down." I waved my hands to shush her. "I know, it's weird, but I swear I really saw it. Nick is my witness. I didn't say anything before because it sounded so crazy."

"Um, hello," Heather said. She had lowered her voice, and she leaned across the table toward me. "This is big, Carly. I want to stake the place out. I want to get photos. Video."

I looked at the excited splotches on her cheeks. "Are you sure that would be good for you?"

"I've read and seen every version of *The Amityville Horror* there is. Of course it's good for me. I'm better with ghosts than I am with real life."

"This is real life," I said. "Betty is real. She's dead, but she feels as real as you and me. And the first night I saw her, there was a man checked in to the motel, except he wasn't. His room was empty and there was no car. I know—maybe he left. But I keep thinking back to it, and I'm starting to wonder if he didn't leave at all."

"If he didn't leave, then where did he go?"

We looked at each other uncertainly, neither of us able to answer. The door to the diner opened and Nick walked in. He brushed past the dead-eyed truckers and exhausted-looking shift workers without a sideways glance. He had an envelope in his hand.

"Photos," he said.

He sat on my side of the booth as I scooted over, as if he was already learning to stay out of Heather's no-touch bubble. He brought the smell of the crisp, cold morning with him, no longer fall but heading for winter. He opened the envelope and dumped the photographs onto the table.

We all leaned in. There were four photos, each of the same subject from a different angle: a barn. It was old, half the roof fallen in. The photos were taken from the outside, first in front, then from farther back, then from partway down a dirt track.

"Why would Marnie take these?" Heather asked.

"Why didn't she have prints?" Nick added. "Either she never made any, or she made them and gave them to someone."

"It's a marker," I said, looking at the photos one by one. "This barn is important somehow. She wanted a visual record in case she ever needed to find it again."

We stared at them for a minute. The barn looked a little sinister, its decrepit frame like a mouth missing teeth. The sagging roof was sad, and the front façade, with its firmly shut doors, was blank. It looked like a place where something bad had happened.

"Where do you think it is?" Heather asked.

"Impossible to tell," I said. "There aren't any signs. It could be anywhere." I peered closer. "What do you think this is?"

In the farthest angle, something was visible jutting over the tops of the trees.

"That's the old TV tower," Nick said. "It's gone now. They took it down about ten years ago, I think."

I looked at him. "But you know where it was?"

"Sure I do." He was leaned over the table, his blue gaze fixed on the picture. "It's hard to tell what direction this is taken from, but it can't be more than a half mile. These farther shots are taken from a driveway. A driveway has to lead to a road."

I grabbed my coat. "We can go now. The sun's starting to come up. We have just enough light."

"Don't you have to be at work?" Heather asked.

"They can fire me. I came to Fell for this, remember? This is all I want."

"But we don't know what this is," she said, pointing to the pictures.

I looked at the pictures again. "It's the key." I pointed to the barn. "If Marnie wanted to be able to find that barn again, it's because there's something inside it. Something she might want to access again."

"Or something she might want to direct someone else to," Nick added.

I looked at both of them, then said the words we were all thinking. "What if it's a body? What if it's Vivian's body? What if that's what's in the barn?"

We were quiet for a second and then Nick picked the photos up again. "We'll find it," he said. "With these, it'll be easy."

It took us until seven. By then the sun was slowly emerging over the horizon, hidden by a bank of gray clouds. All three of us were in Nick's truck. We'd circled the area where the TV tower used to be, driving down the back roads. We were on a two-lane road to the north of the old tower site, looking for any likely dirt driveways.

"There," I said.

A chain-link fence had been put up since the photos were taken, though it was bent and bowed in places, rusting and unkempt. A faded sign said NO TRESPASSERS. Behind the fence, a dirt driveway stretched away. I dug out one of Marnie's pictures and held it up.

The trees were bigger now, but otherwise it looked like the place.

Nick turned the engine off and got out of the truck. Heather and I got out and watched him pace up the fence one way, then the other. Then he gripped the fence and climbed it, launching himself over the top. His feet hit the ground on the other side and he disappeared into the trees.

He reappeared ten minutes later. "The barn is there," he said. "This is the place. There's no one around that I can see—there hasn't been anyone here in years. Come over."

Heather climbed the fence first. I boosted her over and Nick helped her down. Then I climbed, waiting every second for a shout, the bark of a dog, the scream of an alarm. There was only silence. I swung my leg over and Nick took my waist in his hard grip, lowering me down.

"This way," he said.

The foliage had grown in over the years, and we fought our way through the naked branches of bushes until we found the path of the driveway. It was overgrown, too, washed over with years of snow and rain. There were no tire tracks. I could see no evidence of human habitation at all. The wind blew harsh and cold, making sounds in the bare branches of the trees.

"What is this place?" I asked.

"I have no idea," Heather said. She was walking as close to me as she could, her cheeks deep red with cold. "It looks like someone's abandoned property."

How old were Marnie's photos, I wondered? If they had been taken at the same time as the Sun Down pictures, they were thirty-five years old. Had no one really been here for thirty-five years? Why not?

We picked our way over the uneven drive, and the barn appeared through the trees. It wasn't even a barn anymore; it was a wreck of broken boards, caved in and rotted. There were dark gaps big enough to let a full-grown man through them. The front doors looked to be latched closed, but with the state of the rest of the walls, it wasn't much security.

"Wait here," Nick said. He circled the barn, disappearing around the corner. We heard the groan of rotten wood snapping. "I found a way in," he called.

On the side of the barn, we found he'd snapped some rotten boards and opened the hole wider for us. He looked out at us. "It's dark in here, but I can see something."

I looked at Heather. She had gone pale, her expression flat. Gone was the girl who had wanted to spend the night at the Sun Down, taking pictures and videos of ghosts. I didn't have to touch her to know that her skin would be ice-cold. "You don't have to come in," I said.

She looked at me, her gaze skittish as if she'd almost forgotten I was there. "I should go in."

I stepped closer to her. "This isn't a contest. You don't win a prize for going in there. She's my aunt, not yours. This is my thing. Just wait and I'll tell you if it's safe."

I thought she'd argue with me, but instead she hesitated, then gave a brief nod. I wanted to touch the arm of her coat, but I didn't. Instead I turned back to the barn.

The hole gaped at me, deep black. I could see nothing inside, not Nick, not even a shadow. A dusty, dry, moldy smell came from the hole, and dust motes from the disturbance swirled in the air.

"Carly?" Nick called from the dark.

Down the rabbit hole, I thought, and stepped through.

The light inside came through the gaps in the walls, soft slices of illumination from the gray sky overhead. I could see the four walls, junk tossed against them, dark shapes in the corners. An old bicycle, tools, scattered garbage. As my eyes adjusted to the dark I caught sight of Nick, who had walked to the other end of the barn. He was standing right behind the closed doors. He turned and looked at me. "Hey."

I came closer to him. Behind him was an old green tarp thrown over what was obviously a car underneath. I paused at Nick's shoulder, looking at it.

My mind spun. The newspaper reports had said that Viv's car was left in the Sun Down parking lot the night she disappeared. Wherever she'd gone, she hadn't taken it.

But what had happened to her car after the investigation? Where had it gone? Where did a missing person's car go, long after they went missing?

"Uncover it," I whispered to Nick.

He didn't hesitate. He grabbed one end of the tarp and tugged it, stepping back and letting it fall to the dirty floor. Underneath it was a car, boxy and decades old. The color was indistinguishable in the dim light. The tires were flat. The windows were opaque with dust.

Nick stepped over the tarp and brushed the side of his hand along the passenger window, smearing the dust. "No one's been near this thing in ages, maybe years," he said. He leaned forward and peered through the clear hole he'd made.

Don't, I wanted to shout. *Don't*. I jumped at the sound of flapping in one of the barn's upper corners, cold sweat rising between my shoulder blades as I realized it was a bird somewhere up there in the shadows. I made my feet move, made myself circle the car to the driver's side and wipe my own spot, peer through it.

The driver's seat was empty, tidy. I straightened and tried the door handle. It opened, the click loud in the silence. Inhaling a breath, I pulled the door open.

A rush of stale air came out at me, laced with something sour. Dust motes swirled in the air. On the passenger side, Nick opened the door and leaned in. We both craned our necks, peering around the empty car.

Nothing. No dead body. No sign of Viv—no clothing, no nothing. There was no indication that anyone had ever used this car at all. Nick opened the glove box, revealing that it was completely empty.

"Cleaned out," he said.

"Maybe it's nothing," I said. "Maybe it's just a coincidence. It's some old car that someone didn't want to use anymore, and they parked it here and left it. It happens all the time, right?"

"Why did Marnie have photos of this barn, then?"

It didn't feel right. My stomach was turning, my head pounding. "Maybe Viv stole the car," I said. "Maybe she stole it and stashed it."

"Maybe whoever killed her stashed it," he countered.

"We don't know that. We don't know anything." I sighed. "This is a crazy dead end. We've done all this work, and we aren't any further along than we were. It's a red herring, Nick."

"What's that smell?" he asked.

There was definitely a smell. Sour and rotten, but old. "Garbage?"

"Worse than garbage." He straightened and stepped back, leaving the front passenger door open. He opened the back passenger door and peered in. "Nothing back here. But the smell is worse." He straightened again, leaving that door open, too.

We walked to the back of the car. The trunk had a keyhole in it, the way all old cars did. We'd seen no sign of a key.

"How do we get that open?" I asked as Nick bent his knees, lowering himself to a crouch.

"We don't open it," he answered me. "We call the cops." He pointed to the floor beneath the trunk. "Either that's oil or it's very old blood."

I crouched and followed where he was pointing. There was a large pool of something black beneath the trunk. It was dry and very, very old.

The blood rushed from my head, and for a second I thought I would faint. The pool was definitely too big to be oil. I gripped my knees and tears came to my eyes, too swift and hard for me to stop them. "Viv," I said. I started shaking. My aunt was in the trunk, her body a foot from me, behind metal and cloth. She was dead in this car. She had been here for thirty-five years, her blood pooling, then drying and darkening on the floor. So lonely and silent. I inhaled a breath and a sob came out. "He killed her," I said, my voice choked. "He did it. He killed those others. He killed Viv."

I felt a hand on the back of my neck—large, warm, and strong. "You've got this, Carly," he said gently. "You've got it."

I inhaled again, because I couldn't breathe. Another sob escaped my throat. My cheeks were soaked with tears now, my lashes wet, getting water on my glasses. "I'm sorry," I managed as I cried. "I didn't—I didn't expect—"

"I know," he said.

I'd been so in control. I'd been able to handle everything—ghosts, mysteries, this strange and crazy place. It wasn't a game, exactly, but it was a project. A quest for justice. A thing I had to do in order to get on with my life. And if I did it, I would be fine again. I would know.

I hadn't expected that being at Vivian's grave would break my heart. I hadn't expected the grief. It was for Viv, and it was for my mother, who had lived the last thirty-five years of her life not knowing this car was here, that her sister's body was alone and silent in the trunk. My mother had lived three and a half decades with grief so deep and so painful she had never spoken about it. She'd died with that grief, and now she would never feel any better.

I sobbed into my dirty hands, crouched on the floor of the barn. I cried for Viv, who had been so beautiful and alive. I cried for the others—Betty, Cathy, Victoria. It was over for them, too. I cried for my mother and for me.

Nick moved closer, put his arm around my shoulders. He knew exactly how I felt—of course he did. He knew how this kind of thing rips you in pieces from the inside out, changes the makeup of who you are. He was the only person who could be here and actually understand. He held his arm around my shoulders and let me weep. He didn't speak.

After a minute I heard Heather's voice from the other end of the barn. "What's going on?"

"There's a car," Nick called to her, his voice calm. "There's old blood pooled under it. We think there's a body in the trunk. Can you call the cops?"

Heather didn't say anything, and I assumed she'd stepped back out to pull her phone out of her pocket. I wiped my eyes and mopped the snot on my face, attempting to get a grip.

"I'm okay," I said.

"We should go," Nick said quietly. "This is a crime scene."

He was right. Thirty-five years old or not, this was the site of my aunt's dumped body. We needed to get our footprints and our fingers and our hair fibers out of here. Even the rankest amateur knew that, let alone a true-crime hobbyist like me.

I straightened, Nick keeping his hand on my elbow to help me keep balance. He'd know all about crime scenes, since his childhood house had been one. Nick had real-life experience of crime instead of just in books and on the Internet. Well, now I had experience, too.

Vivian was dead. But Simon Hess had been at the Sun Down. He'd seen Viv. And he'd disappeared at the same time. I knew now what had happened to Vivian, and I knew who had done it. My next job was to track down Simon Hess, wherever he was, and make him pay.

It was past noon when a cop came out of the barn and down the drive to where I was standing. The gates to the rusty fence were thrown open now and the dead foliage had been crushed with tire tracks. A single uniformed officer had been sent out first, and then a short stream of vans and unmarked cars had arrived. We had been shooed off the property from the first, and we hadn't been able to see anything that was going on. We'd been questioned, together and separately, over and over. It was freezing and damp. When the cops finished with us, Nick had driven Heather home because she was nearly shaking with cold and shock. I hadn't been able to leave. Not until someone told me something—anything.

In my pocket was a photo. One of the pictures from Marnie's stack, showing Simon Hess's car parked at the Sun Down. It was exactly the same make and model as the car we'd seen in the barn. The size and shape were burned into my mind, and I knew, in my heart, that we'd found Simon Hess's car.

Nick came back in his truck, bringing me hot coffee and something to eat. I'd sipped the coffee and forgotten the food. My phone was long dead. I stood on the dirt road, as close to the gates as the cops would allow, simply waiting. I was going to wait for as long as it took.

The police knew my situation, that I was looking for my aunt who had vanished in 1982. After a while someone inside the barn must have taken pity on me, because a man came down the dirt drive to the gate. He was about fifty, a black man with close-cropped graying hair. He was wearing jeans and a thick black bomber jacket, which meant he wasn't a uniformed officer. I had no idea who he was. His face was stern, but when he looked at me I knew he had seen people like me before, desperate family members waiting for any word at all.

"Are you Miss Kirk?" he asked me.

"Yes."

He introduced himself—garbled a name and a title that I didn't hear or retain. The blood was rushing too loudly in my ears.

"I understand you're looking for your aunt, Vivian Delaney," the man said.

I nodded.

He looked at me closely. "Listen to me, okay? I understand you're in a weird place. But listen to what I'm saying."

He did know. He understood what it felt like. I felt my shoulders relax, just a little.

"Two things," the man said. "There is a body in that car. It's been there a long time."

My fingernails dug into my palms. I barely felt it.

"The second thing," the man said, "is that it isn't your aunt."

My lips were numb, barely working. "How do—how do you know?"

"Because it's a man," he said. He shook his head as I opened my mouth again. "No. I've got nothing else to say. We're conducting an investigation, and I have no information yet. But I can tell you definitively that we do not have Vivian Delaney in there. I'm sorry for the loss of your aunt. But we have your contact information if we need you, and you need to go home."

He waited, his eyes on mine, until I'd nodded a brief assent before he turned his gaze to Nick. "Make sure she gets home," he said, underscoring the message. Then he turned and walked away.

My head was spinning, my brain feverish. Nick took my elbow again and led me back to his truck. He helped me in, then circled to the driver's side, getting in and slamming the door.

He turned the key and the truck's heater came on, a blast of warm air on my face. My cheeks and lips tingled as the cold left them. I flexed my frozen fingers.

Nick didn't put the truck in gear. He just sat there, his dark eyes on me, his expression unreadable. He was wearing a coat, but once again he didn't seem cold. I thought he must be like a human furnace, not to be cold after all these hours. I wondered what that was like.

"Carly," he said.

"It's Simon Hess," I said.

His eyes narrowed and he didn't speak.

"I thought he was a monster," I said, more easily now that my face was thawing. My brain thawing, too. Everything was thawing. "I thought he killed her and got away with it. But he didn't, did he?"

"No," he said. "He didn't get away with it. At least, not in the end."

I scrubbed a hand over my cheek, beneath the rim of my glasses. My cheek was starting to feel warm now. I was light-headed from the shock and the crying and the coffee and the lack of food. But at the same time I was thinking more clearly than maybe I ever had.

"It doesn't answer the question of Vivian," Nick said. "Where is she?"

And I knew. I simply knew. I didn't know everything that had happened, and I didn't know all of the details, but I knew. Because after all this time, living this life here in Fell, I *was* her.

I looked at Nick, right into his blue eyes, and said, "I think my aunt Viv did a very, very bad thing."

Fell, New York
November 1982
VIV

The night it all ended, Vivian was alone.

She woke from a restless doze fully clothed on her bed. It took her a second to orient herself; she was in her apartment on Greville Street. Her window was a square of darkness; the sun must have set.

She swung her legs off the bed. When had she come home and lain down? She couldn't remember anymore. She'd left Alma's office and everything else was a fog of exhaustion. Was that yesterday? The day before?

She was wearing jeans and a white T-shirt, now slightly wrinkled. Her sneakers were still on her feet, navy blue and white. The slender watch on her wrist said that it was ten twenty at night. She glanced in the mirror over her dresser and saw that her face was pale, her hair mussed. Her mouth was parched, as if she'd been sleeping for days. She opened her bedroom door and walked out into the apartment.

There was no one here. Jenny had gone away somewhere—to visit her parents, maybe. There had been no one in the apartment for days, not even the small signs of life with another human: empty glasses on the counter, a purse tossed on the sofa, the TV left on. There was only darkness until Viv flipped the light switch, blinking. She walked to the kitchen

sink and poured herself a glass of water. She downed it, and then, unable
to bear the silence, she turned on the TV.

". . . now told us that the body found on Melborn Road is positively
identified as that of Tracy Waters, a high school senior whose parents
reported her missing two days ago. There are no other details at this time,
but we will update you at eleven—"

Viv's knees gave out. She sank to the floor. "Tracy," she said.

Her letter. Her phone calls. All for nothing.

He'd taken her. He'd killed her. He'd dumped her. And she'd slept the
entire time.

Viv's stomach turned, and for a minute she thought she'd throw up.
Spots danced behind her eyes. She knelt on the floor with her hands on her
stomach and the blood rushing in her ears, her eyes closed. The TV had
gone back to its regular programming, but it was just noise. *I failed. I failed.*

What had she done wrong? Were the phone calls not good enough?
Was it the letter? Should she have included Simon Hess's name? She'd
almost done it, and at the last minute she'd heard Alma saying, *I need more.
I need physical evidence. It has to be airtight.* After everything, after all these
weeks, she'd had one wavering second of doubt, so she'd settled for describ-
ing him instead. Had it cost Tracy her life?

This was all her fault. All of it.

She stayed on her knees for a stretch of minutes, then got to her feet.
She turned the TV off. She walked to the bathroom and washed her face.
Then she brushed her hair and sprayed it. She changed her clothes, put on
makeup, eye shadow in purple and blue. She made herself look nice.

She put on a navy blue sweater and her nylon jacket. She picked up her
purse and her car keys. She knew what the eleven o'clock news would say:
There was a killer on the loose. People should lock their doors. Women
should look over their shoulders, try not to be alone at night. Parents should
look out for their daughters and always know where they are. Women
should carry a whistle or a flashlight. Because if you were a woman, the
world was a dangerous place.

Viv unzipped her purse and pushed aside the contents. She picked out the hunting knife she'd bought at the hardware store in Plainsview, pulling it out of its thick leather sheath. She looked at the blade, silver and sharp in the light, then slid it back into its place. She put the knife back into her purse.

She'd been carrying it for days now. She only wished she had given it to Tracy Waters instead.

She was alone in the dark, just like she always was. But now it was time to go to work.

"I wrote a note to Janice about the door to number one-oh-three. There's something wrong with it. It keeps blowing open in the wind, even when I lock it," Johnny said.

Viv's mind was still reeling over Tracy's murder. She watched Johnny leave, then sat at the desk and pulled out her notebook.

Nov. 29

Door to number 103 has begun to open again. Prank calls. No one here. Tracy Waters is dead.

The ghosts are awake tonight. They're restless. I think this will be over soon. I'm so sorry, Tracy. I've failed.

There was the sound of a motor in the parking lot. It cut out, a door slammed, and Jamie Blaknik walked through the door to the office. He was wearing his usual jeans and faded T-shirt under a sweatshirt and a jean jacket, his hair mussed.

"Hey, Good Girl," he said. "I need a room."

Viv blinked at him. He was so real, snapping her out of her fog of a dream. He smelled like cold fall air and cigarette smoke. A lock of hair fell over his forehead. He dug into his back pocket, peeled a few bills out of a folded-up wad, and dropped them on the desk. Then he pulled the guest book toward him, picked up the pen, and wrote his name.

"Quiet night, huh?" he said as he wrote.

"I guess so," Viv said.

He finished writing, put down the pen, and smiled at her. She felt herself go warm from the shoulders down, all through her chest and her stomach. She couldn't remember the last time she felt warm. Maybe it was the last time Jamie had smiled at her. She really liked his smile. Maybe some girls wouldn't look twice at Jamie, but his smile was really, really nice.

"You're staring at me," he said, breaking the silence. "Not that I mind."

She blinked, then leaned back in her chair. She pulled open the desk drawer with the room keys in it. "Sorry," she mumbled, embarrassed.

"It's nice," he said, taking the key from her. "Come knock on my door if you need me, Good Girl. The invitation's open as always." He turned and walked out. Her eyes followed him of their own accord, the easy way he moved, the way he looked in his worn jeans. *I'm going to die a virgin*, she thought.

But that was a weird thought, because she was only twenty, and she wasn't going to die.

The time was eleven forty-five.

At twelve fifteen, the silence was broken again. It wasn't the door to 103 banging in the wind this time; it was actual banging, someone pounding a fist on one of the doors. "Helen!" came a ragged male voice. "Helen!"

Viv grabbed her purse, put her hand on the hunting knife. She edged to the office door, looking out the window. She could only see wet, hard rain coming down, spattering the concrete. The angle didn't let her see the man who was pounding the door.

She put the purse strap over her shoulder and edged the door open, looking out. There was a man standing on the walkway, banging his fists against the door to 112. "Helen!" he shouted. "If you're in there, you bitch, open the fucking door!"

Viv put down the purse with the knife in it, because she recognized him. It was Robert White, the man who was cheating with Helen. Except he didn't look like his usual self right now. Instead of a crisp, handsomely aging businessman, he was bedraggled now, his salt-and-pepper hair mussed and damp in the cold rain. He wore khakis with spattered cuffs and a zip-up nylon jacket. He banged on the door again, shouting and swearing, but when Viv stepped out onto the walkway, he paused and looked at her, his eyes lighting up with recognition.

"Where is she?" he said in a voice that was ragged with shouting. "Is she in there? Tell me the truth."

Viv shook her head. "She isn't here."

"Bullshit," Robert said. He looked around. "Her car isn't here, but I'm not fooled. She got dropped off by her husband, didn't she? That god-awful bitch."

Viv rubbed her sweating palms on her jeans. She wished that Jamie hadn't gone to his room, or that he would hear and open his door. "Mr. White, I don't—"

"So you remember my name." Robert turned and took a step toward Viv. "I guess you remember everyone who comes here, don't you? You know all of their secrets. Including mine."

"That isn't true," Viv said.

"Sure it is." He took another step toward her. "Did you know about it from the beginning? Did Helen tell you? Or did you just guess?" He looked at Viv's expression and shook his head. "No, she wouldn't tell you. She's too smart, too criminal. Why would she tell the little mouse working at the motel about her blackmail scheme?"

Blackmail? Viv pictured Helen, her easy confidence and her short, stylish hair. Marnie saying, *Damn, that woman is cold.* And, *Sounds to me like that bitch is going to get put out on her ass. And for what? A few nights with Mr. White in there?*

"I don't know anything about blackmail," Viv said. If Helen was setting up Robert to blackmail him, why was her husband having Marnie follow her?

"'I don't know anything about blackmail,'" Robert said snidely, mocking her. "That's a likely story. You're so innocent, right? You just sit behind your desk and watch a man like me get *fucked*—and I don't just mean in bed. You watch Helen and her husband pull a number on me like it's a TV show. 'Here's the scene where she lures him to the motel. And here's the scene where someone takes pictures of them.'" His expression changed as an idea occurred to him. "Who took the photos? Those fucking photos of me and Helen that were sent to my goddamn *office*? It was someone at this motel, wasn't it?" He took another step toward her. "Maybe it was even you."

Viv shook her head. She'd had it wrong. She'd thought that Helen was the one being investigated, that she would lose her marriage and her easy life. But Helen and her husband must have arranged it. They must have arranged the photos for blackmail. If they were running some kind of con, that was why they'd used an intermediary to hire Marnie—to keep Marnie in the dark.

Viv wasn't about to give Marnie away. Not to anyone, and certainly not to this enraged man. "I didn't take the pictures," she said, her voice coming out surprisingly calm.

He was still coming closer to her. She could only back up so much before she was in the office, and she wasn't sure she wanted him in the office with her. "Those photos got sent to my office," Robert said. "My assistant handed me the envelope. For God's sake, she's worked for me for a decade. If she'd seen what was inside, my career would be finished— which is what Helen wanted, isn't it? For my assistant to see the photos and the blackmail letter."

Viv put her hand on the frame of the office door. She might be able to duck back inside and close the door on him.

"But that wasn't good enough, was it?" Robert continued. "Not for greedy Helen. No, she had to call my wife and tell her I'm cheating on her. My goddamned wife. I came home to find her in tears, and when I told her it wasn't true, she didn't believe me. She's moved into her sister's house and taken our kids with her. All because of a fucking *phone call*."

He was livid. Viv felt the chill of fear go down her spine. *I made that phone call*, she thought. *It was me.* She hoped her thoughts didn't show on her face. She felt like they were floating in the air, the words easy to read. She pressed her lips together so she wouldn't speak.

"I've got her goddamned money," Robert said. "She told me to meet her here in room one-twelve. But you say she isn't here. Why wouldn't she be here to collect her paycheck? That's what this whole thing was about, right? Helen has to be here. Unless you're lying, you little bitch."

He was fast. She thought she had time to duck, but she didn't. Robert grabbed her wrist in a hard grip and yanked her forward, pulling her off-balance. He pushed her into the vinyl siding of the motel, shoving her wrist into the middle of her chest and jerking her like a doll. The back of Viv's head knocked against the wall. She opened her mouth, but Robert already had one hand over her throat, his grip strong and male, willing to do anything.

"Don't scream," he said.

Viv gasped as his grip tightened just a little.

Robert's eyes looked into hers. They were hard with fury. He didn't look like a normal, rational man. He looked crazy.

"Tell me the truth or I'll kill you," he said.

Viv felt her breath saw in her throat. "I don't know anything."

He squeezed a little, his fingertips digging into her flesh. "You think I won't kill you? You think I can't? There's no one here, bitch. I can choke the life out of you and leave you in the parking lot."

She had left her knife in her purse in the office. Six feet away, but it might as well be on planet Mars. She was never making that mistake again. "Please don't," she said.

"'Please don't,'" he said in that mocking voice of his. "You're pathetic. The more I look at you, the more I know that you're covering for her. She was too afraid to meet me in person, wasn't she? She knew how angry I'd be. She knew I'd hurt her. So she sent you instead. What did she promise you? A cut of the money? She's a lying bitch. She doesn't intend to give you a penny. You're as stupid as I was. It would probably be a mercy to strangle you right now."

"You're wrong," Viv managed. She had to convince him. She had to get out of his grip, get to her knife. If she could get to her knife, this would never happen again. "You have it all wrong. I don't know what you're talking about."

There was the hum of a car motor, and headlights appeared on Number Six Road. The approaching car slowed, and Viv realized that even through the rain, she and Robert were clearly visible under one of the motel lights, Robert with one hand on her wrist and the other on her throat, pinning her against the motel siding. Whoever was in the car could see them.

She opened her mouth to shout for help, then realized that the person in the car was Helen.

For a second, their eyes met. Robert squeezed Viv's throat, and she gasped for breath. His back was to the road, Helen behind him. Viv stared at Helen, silently begging her.

Helen's face held no expression. She hit the gas and the car sped away, off down Number Six Road again.

"No!" Viv rasped, struggling to get free.

"Shut up," Robert said. He took his hand from her wrist, keeping the other on her throat. He reached into the breast pocket of his Windbreaker and pulled out an envelope. "Take it," he snarled. "Take her fucking money. She's your problem now, her and her husband. Tell her if I ever see her bitch face again, I'll kill her with my bare hands. You know I can."

He yanked at the neck of Viv's sweater, pulling it roughly down. He shoved the envelope down her shirt, the paper cool against her bare skin, the edges and corners scraping her. The only sound was their heavy breathing and the crinkle of the envelope as he pushed it on her.

Then he used his grip on her neck to pull Viv forward. She overbalanced, and he used the momentum to shove her to the ground. She landed hard on her back, her wrist and the back of her head hitting the pavement. *This is what it was like for Victoria Lee*, she thought as her vision flashed white. *Falling on the ground of the jogging path in the rain.* She thought of Betty Graham. *Betty had a lot of bruises. Like she fought hard.* She wondered if cops would see the bruises on her body someday.

Upstairs, one of the motel doors flew open with a bang. Then another.

Robert White bent down, his hands out, and grabbed the front of her jacket. Viv tried to fight him off, but he was strong. She opened her mouth to scream.

"Excuse me."

White flinched in surprise at the voice. It was male, calm, coming from a few feet away. When White turned his head, Viv pushed her heels into the pavement and scrambled away, scraping her back and her elbows. She turned to see the person who had interrupted them and went very still.

Simon Hess, the traveling salesman, was standing at the edge of the parking lot. His car was parked a few feet behind him, close to the dripping trees. He wore a dark gray overcoat and carried a small suitcase in one hand. His expression was utterly calm, only a small line of consternation between his eyebrows giving anything away.

"Are you assaulting that young lady?" he asked White, as if he were commenting on the weather.

White straightened up. His face was splotched red, his hair messed. Still, he managed to look the other man in the eye and say, "It's a private matter."

Hess looked at Viv on the ground, then back at White. His expression was blank. "I think she works here," he said to Hess as if Viv weren't there. "I need a room."

"This is none of your business," White said.

"Obviously not. It doesn't change the fact that I need a room. I'd appreciate getting one and getting out of this rain. It's been a long day, and I'm really quite tired."

Viv couldn't take her eyes off him. His smoothly combed hair, his large and capable hand holding the handle of his suitcase. Tracy Waters was dead in an ice-cold ditch, her family in ruins. *It's been a long day, and I'm really quite tired.*

White smoothed the front of his jacket, and Viv felt a bolt of panic. *Don't leave me here alone with him*, she silently begged the man who had just assaulted her. *Please don't go.*

"I'm leaving," White said. He looked at Viv, wet and cold on the ground. "If I were you, I wouldn't say a fucking word." He stepped over her like she was garbage and walked across the parking lot to his car. Viv heard a motor start, saw the stripes of headlights against the motel wall.

A hand came into her line of vision. Simon Hess was offering to help her up.

By instinct she scrambled away from him again, getting her feet under her. She was scraped and bruised, getting wet in the spitting rain. The envelope was still inside her shirt, against her skin. She brushed her hands together, wiping the dirt and gravel off her palms. Hess waited.

"My room?" he said after a minute.

She could scream. She could run to Jamie's door and pound on it.

"Do you remember me?" Hess asked. He gave her a smile. "I'm a traveling salesman. The one who's so memorable."

Don't show fear. Don't let on.

"I, um." Her voice was a rasp. She was almost glad White had attacked her, because she had a reason to look terrified, which she was sure she did. "I remember," she managed.

"That's good. I need to stay tonight, possibly tomorrow night as well. I'm waiting for a phone call." He smiled again. "It's my usual routine."

"Okay." She thought of the knife in her office. If she screamed, he could attack her out here in the dark. She made her feet move toward the office, giving Hess a wide berth. Her calf stung and her ankle ached when she put weight on it, so she limped a little.

Hess followed her. "Are you all right?"

"Yes," she said.

"I suppose I didn't need to intervene," Hess said. "I know you keep the keys in the drawer. But that didn't seem right. I should check in properly." He paused. "You seem to have made him very angry."

"Yes. I did." Viv stepped into the office and grabbed her purse. She clutched it to her chest as if it were the most precious thing in the world. The gesture made the envelope crinkle under her shirt. One of her shoelaces was wet and untied and made a slapping sound on the cheap carpet.

She rounded the desk and sat in the chair. Hess put his suitcase down.

She pulled open the drawer with a numb hand and picked out a key. Number 212, upstairs. She kept her other hand on her purse, which she held in her lap. Ready to pull the knife out if she needed it.

She slid the key over the desk. Hess looked at her scraped hand as he picked it up. "Perhaps you could use some antiseptic," he commented. "The skin is broken."

"Yes," she said. Her eyes were trained on the desk, but she made herself raise them to his face. She looked him in the eye.

Hess was looking at her closely in the unflattering light of the office. "I know you from somewhere," he said.

Cold panic tried to crawl up her spine. "You know me from here," she said. "Like you said, you've been here before."

"Yes, yes." He nodded. "I have. That's not it, though. I know you from somewhere else." He gave her his smile again, which made her skin crawl. "When I think of it, I'll let you know. I never forget a face. Especially a pretty female one."

Viv wanted to scream, but she knew what was expected of her. She tried to give him a smile, which was probably ghastly. He didn't seem to notice. "Thank you. It's probably from here, though. I've never seen you anywhere else before."

Hess paused, as if he didn't believe her and wasn't sure what to say. The lie hung in the air between them. *Buy it*, Viv thought. *At least for now.*

Finally he looked down at his key, reading the number. "Two-twelve," he said. "Home sweet home. Good night."

"Good night," she managed to say as he walked away and closed the door behind him.

When he was gone, she sat for a long moment in the silence, trying not to panic. A door slammed upstairs, then another.

"Betty," Viv said out loud. "He's here."

Silence.

She glanced at the guest book and realized Simon Hess hadn't signed it.

Viv reached into her shirt and pulled out the envelope there. She pried it open. It was stuffed with bills, a thick stack of them. Hundreds of dollars. Maybe thousands.

It didn't seem real. It seemed like fake money, Monopoly money. No one had money like this. It was bewildering; Helen had gone to great lengths to get this, yet she'd driven off without it. Was she coming back for it? She'd seen Viv with Robert, and she'd seen Viv's face; she must know Viv knew about the blackmail scheme, at least, if she didn't have the money.

Viv put the envelope in the key drawer. Maybe Helen would show up, looking for it. Or maybe her husband, whoever he was, would come. She didn't want the money, and her hands were shaking from the attack. She couldn't think about it right now. She closed the drawer and pushed the money out of sight.

Cigarette smoke wafted to her nose, pungent and thick. The lights flickered out, then went back on again.

Viv got up from her chair and looked out the office door. In the dark above Number Six Road, the Sun Down sign went dark with a zapping noise, then buzzed on again, shouting its endless message: VACANCY. CABLE TV!

Tracy Waters was dead. Her killer was here. And Betty Graham was very, very unhappy.

Vivian closed the door behind her and hurried for the stairs.

. . .

She started at Mrs. Bailey's room on the second floor. It was dark, with no sign of life. Viv had to glance at the parking lot to see that the woman's car was in fact there before she knocked on the door.

"Mrs. Bailey?"

No answer. How many times, now, had she seen Mrs. Bailey come to the Sun Down to drink herself into oblivion? Four times? Five? The routine was always the same: She arrived sober, then made a run to the liquor store. Next came the calls to the front desk with drunken requests—a taxi, some ice, a phone book. Sometimes the calls were abusive; other times Mrs. Bailey was laughing to herself, the TV on in the background. Eventually came the silence as she drank herself out of consciousness.

Viv peered through the window. She couldn't see any sign of the TV flickering past the sheer drapes. She knocked on the door, again, and then a final time, banging on it loudly. There was still no answer.

At the end of the row, the door to 201 clicked and drifted open, showing a sliver of the empty darkness inside. Then the door of room 202.

Viv ran down the corridor and banged on the door of room 210. Jamie Blaknik's room. After a minute, he opened it. He had taken his jean jacket off but was still wearing his sweatshirt.

He looked at her face and said, "You okay, Good Girl?"

"Is there anyone in there with you?" she asked him.

"No."

Viv glanced down the corridor. The door to room 203 clicked open. The lights flickered again.

"What's going on?" Jamie asked.

The air was heavy with electricity, like the moments before a lightning storm. And suddenly, Viv knew it: This would end tonight. Here, now. After months of waiting and wondering, it would all be over. One way or another.

Now or never, she thought.

She turned back to Jamie. She put a hand on the back of his neck, rose to her toes, and kissed him on the mouth. His lips were warm and as soft as she'd thought they would be. He tasted like Doublemint.

She let him go and pulled back. His eyebrows went up and a smile crooked the corner of his mouth. "Well?" he asked her.

"Will you do something for me?"

"After that? Fuck yes."

"You need to leave," she said. "Go and don't come back tonight."

"Should I ask why?"

"No."

The smile left his lips. "Something's wrong, isn't it?"

Viv bit her lip. She could still taste him. As scared as she was, the pleasure of it would keep her going for a while. "Something bad is going to happen, but I can handle it. It's best if you're not here."

Jamie seemed to think it over. He walked back into the room and picked up his jean jacket. The lights flickered out again.

When they came back on, the door to room 205 was open and Jamie was back in his doorway, shrugging on his jacket. "You know I'd help you if you wanted me to, right? I have some experience kicking ass."

Viv stepped back as he came out of the room. He locked the door and dropped the key into her hand. He looked down the corridor at the open doors. "Damn," he said. "I'm not leaving you in this."

"You have to go. But you can do one favor for me."

He turned back to her. "Anything. Tell me what it is."

So she told him.

It was one o'clock a.m.

Jamie's car was gone, and the motel had gone ominously quiet. The wind kicked up outside, howling over the parking lot and shushing the empty trees. In the office, Viv sat behind the desk as the lights flickered yet again.

She was waiting. If Jamie did what he had promised, it would happen any minute.

The phone rang. Viv started in her chair and stared at it, sweat prickling her neck. This was the plan, but still she felt the jolt of terror. She was jumpy.

"Hello?" It wasn't the greeting she'd been trained to give.

It wasn't who she expected. There was silence on the other end of the line. Soft breathing. Someone listening and waiting.

These calls were routine at the Sun Down. *Kids*, the other clerks grumbled. *Teenagers. Don't they have anything better to do?*

But now, listening to the breathing in the waiting silence, Viv wondered how they could all have been so stupid, herself included. The sound on the other end of the line wasn't the comical kind of heavy breathing particular to pranking teenage boys. It was simply breath, the sound of another person living, existing.

Someone who wanted to talk. Who maybe couldn't.

"Betty?" Viv said.

Still, the breath. No pause, no hitch.

"He's here," Viv said, letting her voice fill the silence. "I know it upsets you. I know it makes you angry and sad. But I'm going to take care of it tonight. I promise."

Still nothing. Just breath.

"I've been living with this for so long," Viv said. "I don't think I have a life anymore. I don't know that I want one. I don't really see the point anymore. Do you?"

Did the breathing change its rhythm? Even for a second? She couldn't be sure. She didn't know if what she was saying could even be heard by whatever was on the line. But she said it anyway.

"I'm sorry. I'm so sorry. I don't think anyone has been as sorry for you as I am. I looked at your picture, and you could be me. You could be any of us. You didn't deserve it—none of us do. It's wrong. I don't know what else to do except try to make it right. I think it might cost me everything, and I don't care. I don't matter, really."

Still quiet. Why did she feel like the other person was listening? There was no indication. Still, the feeling was there.

"That's the best way to fix this," Viv said. "The only way. I'll take someone who doesn't matter and trade her for the rest of you. I'll trade myself for the rest of you. To stop him. I think it's the only thing strong enough to end this. I know who he is now. He won't be stopped by anything halfway."

The next breath on the other end of the line was a sigh, and then a single word, spoken on the breath: "Run." Then the line went dead with a click.

Viv put the phone down. While her hand was still on the receiver, the phone rang. She picked it up again. "Hello?"

"Room two-twelve," a familiar voice said.

Viv pressed the button and put him through. She watched as the button on the phone lit up with its soft *click*. Then she listened with the receiver.

"Hello?" came Simon Hess's voice.

"I know you," the other voice said. "I know what you've done."

There was a pause. Then Hess again. "I don't know what you're talking about."

"Yes, you do." Viv closed her eyes. He was doing such a good job. It was Jamie Blaknik saying the lines she'd given him. "Meet me at the corner of Derry Road and Smith Street. I'm calling from the pay phone there. I saw you with Tracy. If you aren't there in twenty minutes, I'll tell everyone what I saw, what I know. Not just about Tracy. About the others, too."

Silence on the line. Viv held her breath. This was the moment of truth. Then Simon Hess spoke. "You're the one who's been following me, aren't you?"

"I saw you in Plainsview, watching her," Jamie said, following the lines Viv had written for him. "I saw you at the high school choir night. I know everything. And I'm going to tell."

"Is this blackmail?" Hess said. "Do you think you'll get money out of me?"

Viv bit her lip hard, trying not to sob. *I was right*, she thought. *I thought I was crazy, but I was right. I was right.*

"You won't know what I want until you meet me," Jamie said. "Twenty minutes or I go to the police." He hung up.

Hess breathed into the phone for a second, then hung up as well. Viv put the receiver down. Her throat was tight, her eyes burning.

A minute later, a car motor started in the parking lot. She walked to the door and watched Hess drive away. Now, except for the passed-out Mrs. Bailey, Viv was alone at the Sun Down.

She waited fifteen seconds in case Hess changed his mind. Then she opened the bottom desk drawer and rifled through it until she found what she was looking for: a key labeled *MASTER*. Janice had shown her the key briefly on her first night. *If someone's passed out or dead in one of the rooms, you might need this.*

Viv took the key and stood, hesitating. Then she dug in her purse and put her knife in its leather holster under her sweatshirt. She had left the office unarmed once, and it had nearly cost her. She wasn't doing it again.

She left the office, walking quickly to the stairs. She had needed Jamie to make that phone call; Hess would never have believed a woman. He'd expect his blackmailer, the mastermind who had put all the pieces together, to be a man. He would have hung up on a woman—and then he would have remembered Viv, that he'd seen her somewhere.

So she'd enlisted Jamie, and he had done his part. It wasn't bad for the price of a kiss.

Viv climbed the stairs and walked to the door of room 212. Put the key in the lock. The doors up here were closed again, as if Betty had tidied up after herself. But as Viv opened the door to 212, the lights flickered.

The room was like all the rooms at the Sun Down: bed, nightstand, small dresser. A TV sat dark in the corner, the famously advertised cable TV on the sign. On the bed was the small suitcase Simon Hess had been carrying. It was closed. Nothing in the room was touched. It seemed as if Hess had checked in and simply sat, doing nothing until he got Jamie's phone call.

What goes on in his mind? Viv wondered. *Everything? Nothing?* Hess had killed Tracy Waters either this morning or last night. Her death would be fresh to him. Was he reliving it in his mind, the memories vivid? Or had he forgotten about it already?

She walked to the suitcase and flipped the latches, opening it. She turned on the bedside lamp. Inside the case were neatly folded clothes: shirts, ties. A toothbrush, a shaving kit. Everything was tidy and clean. If Viv had hoped for bloody clothes and a murder weapon, she was out of luck. The problem was, she didn't know *what* she was looking for.

At the bottom of the case was a folder, neatly tied shut, full of papers. She pulled it out and untied it, leafing through the pages. These were the neatly dittoed lists of Hess's schedule, his maps, his sales receipts.

There was the map of the neighborhood in Plainsview where Viv had seen him. It diagrammed the street and each house with its number. In the square of each house Hess had handwritten a symbol, the language not hard to figure out. An *X* meant he had been turned down at that house. An *O* meant no one was home. And a *Y* meant he had made a sale.

Tracy's house was blank. What did that mean? Viv flipped through the pages, hoping for something else. Something concrete. Pictures of Tracy, maybe, or notes to her. She wanted to call Alma Trent and get her to arrest Simon Hess right now, tonight. But Alma would have to call in other cops to do that, and she wouldn't do it without a reason. *Get me something, anything*, Alma's voice said in Viv's head. *Get me something, Viv.*

"I know," Viv muttered to Alma in the dark silence. "I know you would help if you could. You just don't understand. And now Tracy is dead."

At the bottom of the file was a second map. This one was hand-drawn in pencil on a piece of lined paper. Viv held it under the lamp and saw a row of houses, a laneway between two of them, a square at the end of the lane labeled *Park*. In front of the houses, on the other side of the park, was a street that curved in a C shape. Viv turned the page one way and then another, trying to see if the map was familiar. Her brain paged through its mental images of Cathy's street, Tracy's, Victoria's. The map didn't match any of them.

What was it a map of? A victim Viv didn't know about? Was this a map of something in Fell, or in another town? There were no street names written anywhere. She flipped the page over and studied the back, but there was nothing there, either.

This meant something, she was sure of it. She just had no idea what.

"Close," she said to herself, to Alma, to Betty. "I'm so damned close."

She went through the papers again. Then the suitcase, the clothes. She circled the room, looked in the trash can, the dresser drawer, the nightstand drawer. All were empty. She walked into the bathroom. It was dark and silent, untouched. She looked at the shower curtain, the single thin towel hanging on a rail.

The lights flickered again, a few quick blinks this time, on and off, like someone flipping a switch. Except there was no switch that would turn the entire motel on and off in an instant.

Betty.

A warning.

Viv turned from the bathroom and stepped out into the main room again. She patted her pockets for her key. The suitcase was sitting open on the bed, the contents obviously rifled through. Viv straightened the clothes quickly and flipped the lid of the case closed. She was fastening the latches when a voice in the doorway said, "What are you doing?"

Simon Hess was damp now, the shoulders of his overcoat wet with rain. Water had splashed the hems of his trousers. The bedside lamp lit his features, his even and regular face. He had brown eyes, Viv realized for the first time. He looked very calm.

Still, her gut turned and her blood pumped, every nerve ending screaming *danger*. "I—I'm sorry," she stammered.

The words hung there, inadequate. Hess looked at the suitcase she was closing, then back up to her face. He blinked. "You," he said, his voice soft with surprise. "It was you."

Viv took her hands off the suitcase and turned to face him. He blocked the doorway and there was nowhere to run. "I don't know what you mean."

"Yes, you do." He took a step into the room and closed the motel door behind him. As he did, Viv could hear the click and bang of one of the doors slamming open. Then there was no sound as Simon Hess closed the door, trapping them in his room.

"I don't," Viv insisted. Cold sweat was beading under her clothes.

"Then why are you here?" The question was asked calmly, as if he were a doctor or a teacher, but Viv could see the splotches of red on his cheeks that meant anger. "In my room, going through my things? You were at that bus stop. Your footprints were in my garden."

Viv couldn't look away from him. This close, she could see the beginnings of stubble on his jaw and his neck. Five o'clock shadow, his mother had always called it when her father hadn't shaved. Her parents were very far away now.

She was afraid, and yet she wasn't. She'd been following him for weeks now. Part of her was ready.

"I'm going to call the police," Viv said. "You killed Tracy."

He didn't flinch. "Who did you tell?"

She shook her head. "No one."

"You told someone," Simon Hess said. "The boy who called me on the phone just now, for example. You told him, did you not, when you asked him to lie to get me out of my room?"

He put emphasis on the word *lie*, as if that mattered. As if he were offended by dishonesty after what he'd done. He looked at her with a tinge of disgust, and Viv felt the anger flush hot in her own cheeks.

"You're just angry because you got caught," she said. "You thought no one would ever do it, but I did."

"Wrong," Hess spit back. "You haven't caught me yet. I'm still standing here. Call the police if you want. What can you prove?"

"I saw you with her." She was angry, so angry. "I saw you with Tracy. Watching her. Following her. Why did you do it?" The words were wild, unwise, but they came out of her anyway. They had been dammed up for too long. "She never did anything to you. None of them did. Why did you have to kill her? And why do you keep coming back here?"

Outside in the corridor, a door blew open with a loud bang. It was the door to the next room. Then something soft hit their closed door, one thud and then another. A palm.

"Help me," came a woman's voice from outside, raspy and hoarse. "Help me!"

Viv's hands went cold. The voice was the most terrifying and the saddest thing she'd ever heard. It was the voice of someone who knew she was dying, that after a long fight it was going to be over. That she would never win.

"Help me!" the voice screamed hoarsely, the palm hitting the door again, weaker this time.

Viv looked at Simon Hess and saw that he had a dreamy smile on his face. "Betty," he said. "That's why I come here. Because she's here. I can't . . . I go as long as I can without seeing her, but I always have to come back."

Outside, the voice sobbed. "Help me. Please. *Please*."

She sounded like that, Viv thought, *when he did whatever he did to her. What does* violated *mean?*

"She was in my trunk," Hess said, his voice a calm counterpoint to Betty's screaming. "I thought she'd be quiet, but that was a mistake. She wasn't quiet at all." He shook his head. "I never made that mistake again. I learned my lesson. They aren't quiet when you want them to be."

Viv thought of the Betty she'd seen in the photo, calm and confident. A teacher. *Spinster* was the word the papers had used, even though she was only twenty-four when she died. "Why Betty?" she asked Hess.

"I loved her," Hess replied. "I've never loved anything in my life, but I loved Betty. I just had to make her see."

Betty screamed again, her palms pounding on the door, and Hess smiled. Betty had sounded like that in his trunk. She'd screamed like that, pounded on the trunk lid like that. To Hess, it was a lullaby. Her stomach twisted and she thought she was going to be sick.

She walked toward the door. She had to brush past him to do it, but he didn't move. She tried not to recoil as she got near him.

"What are you doing?" Hess asked.

"Letting her in," Viv said. She put her hand on the doorknob—it was ice-cold, so cold it almost burned her fingers—and wrenched it. The door opened and the cold, wet wind blew in. There was no one in the corridor.

She looked at the outside of the door. There were bloody palm prints on the cracking paint. Viv opened her hand and placed her palm over one of the prints, feeling the cold blood against her skin. *It's almost like it's real,* she thought crazily. Her palm fit perfectly over the print on the door.

Run, Betty had told her, standing in front of her windshield while Viv crouched in the car. *Run*.

She could run now. She had the door open. She had no doubt Hess would chase her; he might even win. He was older than her, less agile, but he was a hunter who had chased down his prey many times. Maybe she'd never know how many times. He'd chase her down, and then she'd be the next one on his list.

He had the same thought. "Do you think you're going somewhere?" he asked calmly, even though she stood in an open doorway, ready to run.

She could do it. Get down the stairs, get in her car. Drive away from this place, from this killer. Tell the authorities.

What good would it do?

Nothing would happen. No one would believe her. Simon Hess would seem like a reasonable, law-abiding person who was falsely accused by a crazy girl. And it would start all over again.

Or he would kill her, and he'd get away with it. Again.

She stepped back from the doorway and turned around to face him. "No," she said. "I'm not going anywhere."

Three things happened.

All of the lights, including the sign, went out and everything went dark.

Betty screamed.

And Viv pulled the knife from her sweatshirt, slid it from its holster, and sank it into Simon Hess's chest.

Fell, New York
November 1982
VIV

It was surprisingly hard. Putting a knife in a man's chest was like pushing it through thick cardboard, the blade punching through cloth and muscle. But the hunting knife was sharp, and Viv was full of adrenaline. She felt numb and strong and outside of her own body. She felt terrified and pure.

The wind howled through the open door, and footsteps ran past in the dark, heading for the stairs. "You got him!" the little boy's voice cried out. "You got him!"

She could see nothing in the darkness. She heard a deep, gasping breath from Simon Hess, the sound of his footstep as he backed away. She let go of the knife handle and left it stuck in his chest as he moved. *This isn't happening*, she thought wildly. *It isn't real.*

All of the doors in the corridor were open now, and she could hear them banging. She blinked in the darkness, unsure whether she should step forward or retreat. There was a thump in the empty air of the room, then another, harder one. Simon Hess hitting the floor.

He was still breathing. She could hear it. Heavy, shaking, slow breaths. *He might stop*, Viv thought. *He might die. Here, now.* She didn't want that yet. She stepped forward into the blackness, following the sound of his breathing. She knelt on the floor and crawled toward it, her eyes adjusting so she could barely see the shapes of her hands.

She reached out and touched something covered in fabric. Something hard, the bone of a knee perhaps. A hand shot out and grabbed her wrist, jerking her off balance. The hand was big and soft and cold, so slick with chilled sweat she almost slid out of its grasp. But Hess was still strong, and he shoved her so she landed on one side, her hip hitting the floor and her head banging against something hard—the edge of the bed, or maybe the nightstand. *This is the second time I've been attacked tonight*, she thought. *I'm going to have bruises.*

They wrestled in grim silence for a minute, Hess trying to grasp her with his slick hands, the strength in his arms faltering, Viv thrashing back and kicking him. Hess gave a dark grunt and grabbed at her again, his neat, trim fingernails trying to dig into her flesh. Outside, there was the slow *click* of high heels in the corridor and a strange, rotten smell.

She kicked Hess away again and then his hands were gone. There was a wheeze as he seemed to fall back to the floor, weak. She flipped her body and put her hands on him again, feeling numbly along his torso. Her fingers hit warm blood.

"Tell me," she said urgently. "Why Betty? Why?"

He reached up and grabbed her hair, twisted it, but his strength was failing. "Betty was mine," he said, his voice a harsh whisper as if he were telling her a secret. "I loved her. I just wanted her to see."

She had so much she needed to know. There was no time. She went still as his hand twisted harder in her hair. "And Cathy?"

"My daughter went to the dentist's office where she worked." He wheezed, and she recognized the sound as a sick sort of laugh. "She meant nothing to me. She was so obviously alone. So easy. I wanted to know if I could do it again. It turned out I could."

She was so obviously alone. That was what they had in common. Not hair color or age or build. Betty, living her spinster life. Cathy with her husband deployed. Victoria with her fights and her anger. Tracy with her parents who didn't keep her home.

Viv thought of Cathy's baby, of her grieving husband, of her mother on the phone. *A sweet girl who wanted to earn her next paycheck and raise her baby. Do you know who killed her? Can you end this for me?* Her fingers gripped Hess's shirt, soaked in blood. She wished she could see his face— and yet she didn't want to see it at all. "Victoria?" she asked, her voice cracking.

"A mistake," Hess replied. He cleared his throat. His hand was still wound in her hair, his grip surprisingly hard, and Viv stayed braced in case he attacked her again. They were in a strange embrace, here in the dark, fighting and telling each other secrets. "She was there when I sold her mother a lock system. I thought she wouldn't be a challenge. But she fought me. She bit me, that little bitch. And the location wasn't right. It was hasty and too exposed. I had to cut my losses."

Cut my losses, to Simon Hess, meant strangling a teenaged girl and throwing her in the bushes in the rain. The tips of Viv's fingers touched the handle of her knife, still sticking out of his chest. She gritted her teeth as bile rose in her throat. Or perhaps it was tears. She made herself say the final name, grind it out of her furious throat. "Tracy Waters."

Hess coughed, the sound wet. "What do you think?"

"She was good and sweet," Viv said. "Innocent. She had a family who loved her. She never did you any harm."

Hess laughed. "You haven't caught on. None of them did me any harm."

"She wasn't beautiful," Viv said. "She wasn't sexy or cruel. She'd never even met you. She was a girl. Why did you do it?"

His hand twisted in her hair, and his grip was strong but she could feel him trembling. "Because no one ever stopped me," he said. "Because I could."

"How many others are there?"

He was quiet. She could hear his breathing. She knew this was a game—he had something she wanted, knew something she wanted to know. And she desperately wanted to know. *Did I miss someone? What girl didn't I see?*

"The map in your suitcase," she said, more urgently now. "What is that?"

He didn't answer, torturing her.

She struggled in his grip, changed her angle, and grabbed the handle of the knife. She gave it a shove, tried to twist it. It was stuck solid, as if in thick glue. Simon Hess gave a low groan of pain.

"Tell me," she said.

Behind her came the *click* of heels from the corridor, turning to soft footsteps on the cheap motel carpet. Ice-cold air touched Viv's back.

"Betty," Hess said, his voice high with fear.

A low moan came behind her, the sound unearthly. Viv wondered if Betty was wearing her purple dress, if her hands were bloody. *How did this happen?*

"She doesn't love you," Viv said to Hess, pushing on the knife. "She never did. She hates you. She haunts this place because she hates you so much. You come here and she gets so furious I can feel it, taste it. She makes me furious, too. Do you understand me? *Betty hates you.*"

That low moan behind her again, and she felt the rise and fall of Hess's chest. Slower and slower by the minute. "I can see her," he said softly. "I watched her for so many weeks. I memorized her face. She's mine. She's still mine."

"She isn't yours," Viv whispered back. "It's the other way around. You're hers, or you're going to be."

His voice was trembling now. He let go of her hair and traced his hand over Viv's face, his fingertips cold and clammy. "I know you from somewhere," he said. "Where?"

Viv went still, feeling his touch on her skin. He was touching her. *Touching her.* She tightened her grip on the knife handle.

Hess's fingers brushed over her mouth, traced her lips in the dark. "I don't remember," he said, his voice faint and vague now. "There are so many. I know all of their faces. But I can't see you. Which one are you?"

"I'm the one you didn't kill," Viv said. She pulled the knife out of his chest. And as he took in a breath of pain, she plunged the knife back down.

Fell, New York
November 2017
CARLY

Was I awake or asleep? I didn't know. I was somewhere dark, and my phone was ringing.

I opened my eyes. I was on the sofa in my apartment, where I had sat down a long time ago—for just a minute, I'd thought. Now I was slumped against the arm of the sofa, fully dressed. My cheek ached and my throat was dry. It was dark outside the windows and there was no sign of Heather.

I picked up my phone from the coffee table and answered it, picking up my glasses with my other hand and putting them on. "Hello?"

"Carly, it's me. Callum MacRae."

I cleared my throat. "Um."

"I'm sorry. Were you asleep? It's only six thirty."

I glanced at the dark windows. Night came early this time of year. "I'm fine," I said. "I work nights. What's up?"

"I got some news," he said. His low, pleasant voice was excited. "They found a body in an old barn just outside of town. It was just this morning. And I know you're looking for your aunt, so I checked it out for you."

I scrubbed a hand under my glasses, rubbing my eye. "It isn't her," I said. "I already asked. It's a man."

There was a beat of silence. "Oh, okay." He laughed. "You're good. I called some of my contacts, and the word from the Fell PD is that they have an identity and a cause of death."

"Already?" We'd found the body just this morning.

"Well, it isn't one hundred percent yet. They won't announce it until they know for sure. But yes, they have preliminary findings already. Why don't you come meet me?"

"Meet you where?"

"There's a coffee shop just down the street from the central library. It's called Finelli's. It should be open for another hour or two. Come down and I'll tell you what I know."

I looked around the darkened apartment. Where was Heather? She'd gone to bed when we got home; I wondered if she was still asleep. Nick had said he was going back to the Sun Down to try to sleep, too.

"Carly?" Callum said.

"Yes," I said, getting my thoughts on track. "Um, sure. Yes, I'll meet you."

"Great. Twenty minutes. I'll see you then."

I hung up and stood, stretching my aching neck. "Heather?"

There was no answer. I turned on a lamp and saw a note on the kitchen table.

Gone to see the rents. I need to retreat for a while. Don't worry, I took my meds. I don't really know when I'll be back. But I left you this present, which I got from the depths of the Internet. Don't ask questions. Here you go.

In my half-asleep state, it took me a minute to translate that Heather had gone to her parents'. I picked up the sheet of paper she'd left with the note. It was a printout of an old scan. A list of numbers.

I pulled out a kitchen chair and turned on the light, studying the page. I was looking at a phone record, I realized. Just like Viv's roommate Jenny had said. *The cops would get a big old printout.*

Heather had circled the name at the top of the report: Sun Down Motel. And the date: November 1 to November 30, 1982.

I scanned the numbers. There weren't many; the Sun Down didn't make or receive a lot of phone calls in 1982, a situation that hadn't changed in thirty-five years. Some of the calls were marked as incoming, others as outgoing. Near the bottom of the list were the calls made on November 29 and the early hours of November 30.

Just after one a.m. on November 30 was an incoming call. The record didn't show which room it was routed to, if any. Heather had circled the number the call came from and written a question mark next to it. That meant she hadn't been able to identify the number.

At 1:54 a.m. was an outgoing call. Again, there was no record of whether it came from the motel office or one of the rooms. Heather had circled this number, too, but next to it she wrote *Fell Police Department*.

There were no other calls that night.

I stared at the numbers for a minute. Someone had called in to the motel just after one. Maybe that was a coincidence, a fluke, or a wrong number. Maybe not.

But just before two, someone at the Sun Down had called the police.

Was it Vivian? Simon Hess? Someone else?

I put the note down.

My aunt Vivian killed Simon Hess.

She must have. There was no other explanation. Or was there? I didn't really know what had happened that night in 1982. But someone—a woman—had warned Tracy Waters's parents about Hess. And Tracy had been killed, her body found the same day Viv disappeared.

Had Hess killed Viv, then been killed by someone else?

Callum's information would answer some of my questions. An ID on the body in the trunk in the barn and a cause of death, even a preliminary one, would put some of the pieces together. I went into the bathroom and cleaned up, then changed into clean clothes. I had a text on my phone from my brother, Graham, but I ignored it. My old life seemed so far away.

I texted Heather quickly so she wouldn't worry. *Callum has info from the police. Going to meet him.* As I hit Send, the phone rang in my hand. I didn't recognize the number.

I bit my lip for a second, undecided. Then I answered. "Hello?"

"You found him." The voice on the other end was female, older than me, and familiar.

"Marnie?" I said.

Marnie sighed. "You're a smart girl. We hid him good, and he stayed gone for a long time. But it looks like you dug him up after all these years."

I shook my head. "You lied to us. But you took a photo of the barn where you left him."

A pause. "Yes, I suppose I did."

"Why did you take the picture?"

"I wanted to be able to find the place again. I don't think I ever believed he'd stay buried forever. We thought maybe we'd have to go back and move him, but we lucked out. For a while, anyway. Now is as good a time as any for all of it to come out. It was going to happen whether I wanted it to or not."

"Who killed him?" I asked. "Was it you? Was it Viv?"

"It's a complicated story."

"Not really. Someone put Simon Hess in a trunk and left him in a barn. Was it you? Or her?"

"You didn't find the notebook, did you?"

I stood straighter, my skin tingling. "Notebook?"

"It was left for you," Marnie said. "You're missing so much of the story. It's why you're confused. Read the notebook and you'll understand."

My mind raced. *It was left for you.* What did that mean? "Where is the notebook?" I asked Marnie.

"Tell me," Marnie said. "Did you ever try to get candy out of the candy machine?"

I froze, remembering the broken candy machine. Nick saying, *I can't believe this even works.*

"Read the notebook," Marnie said again, "then meet me at Watson's Diner."

"When?"

"Tonight," Marnie said. "When you're there, I'll be there. Don't worry." She hung up.

Finelli's was a beacon of yellow light on the dark downtown street, where a lot of businesses were already closing for the night. Fell wasn't a late-night town. At least, not here. At the Sun Down, it was an all-night town.

Callum was sitting at one of the small tables, a coffee in front of him. He was wearing a button-down shirt, a zip-up sweater, and a fall jacket. The guy knew how to layer. His hair was neatly combed and he smiled when he saw me.

He held up his mug when I sat down. "Decaf," he said. "Want one?"

I blinked at his cup, still groggy. "I want the most caffeine this place can supply."

Callum smiled again and signaled for the waitress. "Right, you work nights. I guess this is morning for you."

"To be honest, I don't know what time of day it is. I haven't in a while."

"Interesting," Callum said. "And kind of freeing, I guess." He put his cup down. "The rest of us are stuck in time. You know—you do one thing in the morning, this other thing in the afternoon, go to sleep at night. The same thing every day. But that isn't real, is it? It's just something we construct for ourselves. If we wanted to, we could let it go."

I sipped the coffee the waitress had brought and tried to follow what he was talking about. "A lot of people work nights."

"Sure they do." Callum smiled again. "Thanks for meeting me."

Now I was perking up. I took another swallow of coffee. "You said you have information."

Callum's gaze dropped to his coffee cup, then wandered around the room. "Do you want to know something strange?"

That was when it clicked. Something was off. I'd been too distracted, too tired and overwhelmed, to notice it before. "Callum," I said. "You told me you had information from the police."

"Do you want to know something strange?" Callum said again. "I mean, really strange. Like the craziest strange thing you've ever heard."

I went still. I was suddenly aware of the coffee shop around me, how nearly empty it was. How dark it was outside. How I was alone here with him.

"You have this big mystery in your family," Callum said. If he was aware I was uncomfortable, he didn't show it. "You came all the way here to solve it, and you met me in the library. But I have a family mystery of my own. Isn't that crazy?"

"Sure," I said slowly, putting my cup down.

"I have a family disappearance, too," Callum said. "My grandfather. He went to work one day and never came home. No one ever saw him again."

My mouth went dry. It couldn't be.

"My grandmother never even called the police," Callum went on. "Crazy, right? Mom says that my grandmother always assumed that my grandfather left her for another woman. She found it so humiliating that she never considered filing a missing-person report. She never wanted to talk about it, all the way to the day she died five years ago. Those were different times."

I licked my lips and swallowed.

Callum turned his gaze back to my face. It was hard and unreadable. "Imagine that. Just imagine it. Your husband of fifteen years goes to work one morning and never comes home, and you just live with it. You pretend everything is fine and he didn't just vanish. You pretend everything's fine for the rest of your life. No wonder my mother is so screwed up." He smiled, but now I could see it was forced. "Everyone has a screwed-up family, but I think yours and mine win some kind of award, don't they?"

He stared at me, expecting an answer, so I said, "I don't know."

"I've asked my mother about it, of course," Callum said. "I mean, I grew up with a long-gone grandfather. So I was curious. My mother wasn't as closemouthed as my grandmother was. She was a kid when he left, so she wasn't subject to the same shame. She told me that the topic of her father was completely taboo in her house growing up. Once he left, she wasn't supposed to talk about him, even to admit he had ever existed. My grandmother was too proud." He shook his head. "So I have this family mystery, and so do you. And both of those mysteries happened around the same time. The first thing I thought when I saw the article about your aunt was, *Maybe she ran off with Granddad*. She was a lot younger than him, but it isn't impossible. My grandfather was a traveling salesman—he met all kinds of people. He met people all day, every day. Maybe he met your aunt, and in a fit of passion they drove away together to start a new life."

The coffee shop seemed too empty, too quiet. One of the few customers had left, and the young man working behind the counter was starting to clean up to prepare for closing, one eye on us, hoping we would leave.

Maybe in a fit of passion they drove away together to start a new life.

I thought of the car in the old barn, the dried blood on the ground beneath it.

I pushed back my chair. "I need to go."

"You just got here," Callum said.

"You said you had information from the police." I picked up my purse. It suddenly seemed urgent that I get out of here, get away from him. "You lied to get me here. I'm going."

Callum watched me, and his handsome face was unreadable. "I don't need information from the police," he said. "I already know who the body is in that trunk. Do you?"

I didn't answer. I turned and left.

"Call Alma Trent," Callum called after me. "She knows who it is, too. Maybe she'll tell you."

Outside, I got in my car, started it, and hit Dial on my phone. Nick's phone went to voicemail.

"Nick," I said after the beep, "I got a call from Marnie. She says there's a notebook hidden in the candy machine we need to see. I'm coming to the motel to find it."

Through the windshield, I watched Callum come out of the coffee shop. He gave me a little wave, as if nothing were wrong. He got in his own car.

I hung up and tossed my phone on the passenger seat. I pulled out of the parking lot and headed through town.

I wasn't surprised when I looked in the rearview mirror and saw Callum right behind me.

Fell, New York
November 1982
VIV

There was a moment, a few minutes after it happened, when Viv thought of the little girl she'd seen through Simon Hess's front window. When she thought of Simon Hess's wife, in her homemade clothes from a Butterick pattern, washing his dishes and keeping his house. What would those two do now?

But she had to confess: The thought didn't last very long. Maybe he would have killed them. Maybe not. And right now there was too much to do.

The lights were back on. Betty was gone. And Viv was left with a dead body on the motel room floor.

She picked up the room phone, realizing when she heard the dial tone that she'd half expected the phone to be dead. Betty was unpredictable, especially when she was angry.

But the phone worked, so she dialed the number she had learned by heart because she'd stared at it so often on long night shifts, on a piece of paper tacked to the wall.

"Fell PD," came a bored voice on the other end of the line.

Viv made her voice the drawl of a girl who was both bored and stupid. "Alma there?"

"Maybe. You have a problem, dear?"

"I can make one up." Viv gave an empty giggle. "I'm working the Sun Down tonight. Honestly? I just want to know if she's free to come visit me. I'm bored." She glanced down at the floor, where Simon Hess lay still, her knife still in the side of his neck. He'd died quickly in the dark, a gasp and a thrash and a few twitches. Then it was over. His eyes were half closed, as if he were drowsy.

As soon as it was over, Betty was gone—as if that was what she wanted all along. But it wasn't that simple. Betty hadn't left the motel; Viv could feel her watching. She was no longer sure Betty *could* leave the motel.

"You girls," the cop said, disgusted. "This is a job, not a gossip session. Hold on."

A few seconds later, there was a click and Alma's voice came on the line. "Viv?"

Viv was speechless for a second. She had never in her life been so overwhelmed with relief at the sound of another person's voice. "Alma," she said, her voice cracking and the bored façade breaking down. "Slow night."

"Is it?" Alma said, because Viv was phoning her, and Alma wasn't stupid.

"Sure," Viv said. She glanced at the body again. Her first thought when she picked up the phone had been *Alma will understand*. Because she would, right? She knew what Viv had been investigating. She knew the evidence. She knew what Simon Hess was. She would know that if Simon Hess was dead, it was because Viv had no choice.

Now she wasn't so sure. Alma might come out here and arrest her. In fact, she most likely would.

I should be arrested. I should go to jail.

Logically, she knew that. But deep in her heart, she wasn't going to let it happen.

"Viv?" Alma said.

"It's nothing," Viv said. "I just got sick of having no one to talk to. I can't even tell you how bored I am. I finished my novel and I don't have another one. I didn't even like it very much."

There was silence on the other end of the line.

"You're working," Viv said. "I forgot. It's fine. I'll talk to you later." She hung up.

Shit.

She'd just called the police on her own crime, because she thought Alma would understand. She wasn't thinking like a criminal. Because she *wasn't* a criminal—she was a sheltered girl from suburban Illinois.

Not anymore. Now you're a murderer. Start thinking like one.

What would you do if you ever saw real trouble? Viv's mother had said. *You think you're so damned smart.*

She turned and looked at Simon Hess, lying on the floor. "You're the expert," she said. "What's the best way to hide a body?"

He was silent.

She thought that was kind of witty. There was something terribly wrong with her.

She stepped forward and took a closer look. He'd bled into the rug beneath him, but it was a small bedside rug placed over the carpet. If she could get rid of him and the rug both, there might be minimal cleanup in the room. But how would she lift him? And where would she put him? Panic fluttered deep in her belly as she started to truly realize what she'd done. Alma would come and find this mess. Viv would go to prison. Her parents, her sister would be mortified. She'd get old in prison. She might even die there.

It didn't matter that Simon Hess was a killer—she'd still go to jail.

She'd told Betty on the phone that she was willing to sacrifice herself. That she didn't matter. But now, faced with life in prison, she was starting to think differently.

She stared at his still face, at his hands curled lifeless on the rug. Hands that had killed so many and would never kill again.

It was worth it, she thought. It would be worth it even if she went to prison.

But she wasn't in prison yet.

She gripped the edge of the rug and pulled at it. Squatted on her hamstrings and put her weight into it. The rug with the body on it slid one inch, then another. She stood and realized the lamp was on, shining a beacon out the room's window, so she walked to it and turned it off. She opened the room door in the dark and looked out. There was still no one in the parking lot, no one for miles. The corridor lights were back on, the room doors all innocently closed, the road sign lit up as usual. Betty was quiet, but Betty was watching.

"I did it," Viv said out loud. "Are you happy?"

There was no answer.

"Of course you're not happy," Viv said. "You're still dead. You'll always be dead. But now so is he."

She turned away from the open doorway and started pulling the rug again. There was nothing for it but to get Simon Hess out of here.

He was impossible to move. He lay as a dead weight, his blood soaking the rug. The knife was still in his neck, and when Viv looked at it her stomach turned. She didn't quite have the nerve to pull it out.

Time was running out; someone would come sooner or later. Either a customer or Alma Trent, dropping by to find out why Viv had sounded so strange on the phone. Viv pulled harder, got the rug slid halfway across the floor to the doorway. She was so focused on her task that she didn't hear the car pull up in the parking lot.

But she heard the footsteps as they came up the stairs. She froze with her hands gripping the edge of the rug. The room was dark, but the door was open. It was the only open door in the entire motel.

The footsteps got closer, and Viv silently let go of the rug, inching back, away from view of the doorway. There was no way to close the door now. The instinct to get out of sight was overpowering.

She was trying to silently crawl back in a crab-walk when a voice called, "Vivian? Is that you in there?"

Marnie.

Viv opened her mouth to shout something—she had no idea what—but there was no time. The footsteps came to the open doorway and Marnie appeared. She went very still, and Viv knew that she could see enough from the light in the corridor: the body, the knife, the blood, the rug, and Viv herself, crouched on the floor, most likely looking wild and insane.

"Vivian," Marnie said. "What the hell have you done?"

"What a mess," Marnie said over and over again as they folded up the edges of the rug around Simon Hess's body. "What a damn mess. You couldn't do it in a way with less blood? Hit him over the head or something?"

Viv shook her head numbly, as if this question required an answer. She was still in shock over how quickly Marnie had adapted to the situation—and how in control she seemed to be. The entire night was seeming more and more like a crazy dream.

"Hold on, Viv," Marnie said darkly, as if reading Viv's mind. "No spacing out. What did he say to you?"

Viv felt tears sting her eyes, but she breathed deep and blinked them back. Her emotions were running wild, trying to get out of control. Panic, anger, hopelessness. "Everything," she said to Marnie. "He told me everything." She blinked harder, the body going blurry in her vision. "He thought he was in love with Betty. He kept saying she was his."

Marnie was quiet for a second. "Somehow I doubt Betty agreed," she said, her voice even. "Why bother telling a girl you love her when you can stuff her in your trunk instead? And the others?"

Viv shook her head. She couldn't repeat the horrible things Simon Hess had said, not right now. *A mistake. I wanted to know if I could do it again. She was so obviously alone.*

"Damn," Marnie said, again as if Viv had spoken.

"Why are you here so late?" Viv asked. "I thought you were done. Why did you come to the motel?"

"I heard about Tracy Waters. I had the radio on, and they said they found her body, and I thought . . ." Marnie looked down. "I knew it was him. We could have stopped it. *I* could have stopped it."

"I tried," Viv said. "I called the school. I wrote her parents. It wasn't good enough. I failed."

"At least you did something," Marnie said. "Now I get to do something. Did you ever see *Psycho*?"

Viv felt her eyes go wide. "Are you saying I'm Norman Bates?"

Marnie said, "Go get the shower curtain from the bathroom."

Viv did. They wrapped the rug in it, with Hess inside the rug. They were about to drag the entire package through the doorway when Marnie paused again.

"The knife is still in him with your fingerprints on it," she said.

Viv swallowed. "Should I take it out?"

"Take it out and get rid of it."

Viv put down her end of the shower curtain. Hess was curled in on himself, twisted to one side, his body undignified. She had to move him to get at the knife. It slid out easily, though the sound it made would haunt her for the rest of her life. Hess's blood was cold now, and none of it spilled when she pulled out the blade.

"Wrap it in a towel," Marnie said. "We'll deal with it later."

Viv carried the knife to the bathroom and wrapped it in one of the thin, rough hand towels. She would have to figure out where the spare towels were kept, and whether there were spare shower curtains. She was thinking like a murderer now. She put the knife in its towel on the shower curtain next to Hess.

"We need his keys," Marnie said. She was good at this. "They're probably in his pocket. And I'm not doing it."

Viv gritted her teeth and bent to the body again. She had to touch it—touch him. Even after he was dead, touching Simon Hess made her recoil, as if she could smell all the dead girls on him, as if he'd reach up and put a hand on her that had beaten Betty Graham, that had pushed Cathy Caldwell into her car, that had strangled Victoria Lee and thrown her in the bushes. A hand that had stripped Tracy Waters and left her in a ditch after violating her.

Still, she patted his trousers, his skin ice-cold through the fabric, feeling his pockets. His keys were in the inside pocket of his jacket, and when she felt them she had to pull the lapel away from his shirt and put her fingers in the pocket. She could feel the soft, dead flesh of his chest, the pucker of a nipple. She grabbed the keys and yanked her hand back.

They checked through the open door. There was still no one in the parking lot.

It was hard work getting Hess down the corridor and the stairs, but Viv was ready now. She held up her half of the wrapped-up shower curtain as she and Marnie maneuvered it. Grunting and panting, they worked with the speed of the panicked. They carried him to the car, and Viv used Hess's key to open the trunk. They dropped one end of the shower curtain and rolled him in, inside the rug. The knife tumbled out, hitting the bottom of the trunk.

"Put it in the back seat," Marnie said. "We'll dump it."

Hess didn't quite fit, and Viv had to push his feet in, tuck them under the edge of the trunk while Marnie folded up the shower curtain. Viv was reaching up to the trunk lid to close it when headlights swept across the parking lot.

Marnie swore and dropped the shower curtain. Viv slammed the trunk.

The car stopped and the headlights went out. A door slammed.

"Alma," Viv said.

"Oh, Jesus," Marnie whispered. "A cop."

Alma approached them. She was alone, in uniform, one hand on her hip. She looked back and forth from Viv to Marnie.

"I know you," she said to Marnie. "You're one of the photographers we sometimes use."

Marnie said nothing.

Alma looked at Viv again. She took in Viv's disheveled appearance, her flushed face lined with cold sweat. "Vivian," she said. Her voice was strangely flat, empty of its usual Alma confidence. "Tracy Waters is dead. We found her body early this morning."

"I know," Viv said.

"I think . . ." Alma looked away, closed her eyes for a second. She opened them and turned back to Viv and Marnie. "I think I was wrong. I think you might have been right when you came to me, but I didn't listen. So I did something that I don't normally do. When I heard they'd brought Tracy's body in, I looked up Simon Hess's phone number and called to see if he'd come to the station for an interview."

Both women were silent. The only sound was the wind howling through the trees.

"He wasn't home," Alma said. "His wife said he'd gone out very early this morning, before six, and she hadn't seen him since. She doesn't know his schedule. She thinks he might be home tomorrow."

She looked at the closed trunk. Viv felt her hands clench, felt cold sweat on her back and in her armpits.

"I would have called Simon Hess's scheduling service, but they were closed for the day," Alma said, still looking at the trunk. "I was going to call first thing in the morning to ask if they know where he is."

Then, finally, her gaze wandered to the shower curtain, crumpled in Viv's hands. There were thick smears of blood on it.

Alma's face went very still. She raised her eyes to Viv's. "Vivian," she said, echoing Marnie. "What did you do?"

"He told me everything," Viv said, as if that explained.

Alma was quiet for a long minute. "He checked in here?" she asked finally.

"Yes."

"And he did all of them? He told you that?"

"Yes. Betty, Cathy, Victoria. Tracy. Maybe more. I couldn't get it out of him. He was laughing at me, because to him it was a game."

Alma flinched a little. "Did he say why?"

"Because he liked it," Viv said. "Because it was fun. A challenge. Because all of them were lonely. Because no one stopped him. Because he could."

"Goddamn it," Alma swore softly. She sounded nothing like she usually did; she sounded sad and almost broken. She lifted her gaze to Viv again, her face. "Did he hurt you?"

"No."

"You're not going home."

Viv blinked. "What?"

"You're not going home," Alma said again. "Not tonight, and not for a long time. If we get rid of this"—she motioned to the trunk—"and we will, then it can't be traced back to you. We can't take that chance."

"He's a murderer," Viv said. "A killer."

"It's that simple, is it? That cut-and-dried?" Alma's voice was regaining its usual tone. "You have proof? Irrefutable evidence?"

"He told me he was."

"And you think that's good enough? That's why you're in this parking lot, doing your best to get rid of the body." Alma shook her head. "I'll tell you what's going to happen. Simon Hess isn't going to come home. His wife is going to report him missing. The police are going to investigate. And at some point their investigation is going to lead here. To tonight. To you. Tell me, did anyone else see Simon Hess here tonight?"

Viv remembered Robert White, his hands on her throat. The way he'd thrown her to the ground. And then—Simon Hess, standing there. *Are you assaulting that young lady?*

White would remember Simon Hess. The question was, would he say anything?

Helen, driving up, slowing her car. Had Hess been there then? Had Helen seen him?

And then there was Jamie Blaknik. He technically hadn't seen Hess, but he'd made that phone call. Viv had trusted him. But could he be trusted when he learned that Hess was dead?

"Two people saw him," Viv said, because she wasn't sure about Helen. She felt compelled to add, "It isn't likely that either one will say anything. And he didn't sign in. His name isn't anywhere. It isn't likely that anyone will know he was here."

"Anything is likely," was Alma's reply. "Anything at all. They'll come back to you, Vivian. And it will be over."

"What about me?" Marnie said.

"You were never here." Alma was in control now, the shock wearing off. "No one can put you at the Sun Down tonight except us, and hell, we might be lying. You should go home now and get out of this."

Marnie looked from Viv to Alma. "I don't think I can do that. There's too much to do, and it has to be fast. And I have an idea of where we could put him."

Were they really talking about doing this? Was this really happening? Were they going to put Simon Hess somewhere and hope no one found him? And what was going to happen to her?

Was Alma, a cop, really going to go along with it? She looked at Alma's face and saw determination. Anger. And there had been that moment of shock that had almost undone her. This was affecting Alma; it had dealt her some kind of blow. For whatever reason, Alma was in.

Alma glanced out at the parking lot, which was still empty. But for how long? "Where do you think we should put him?" she asked Marnie.

"Martin Greer on Weston Road is in his eighties. His kids are putting him in a home. They don't want the property, and he doesn't maintain it. It's huge and it's empty."

Alma thought it over and nodded. "I know the place. It'll work for a few weeks, at least. If we come up with something better, we'll move him."

"You'll move him," Marnie corrected her. "I'm seeing this through, but I'm done after tonight."

Alma looked at Viv, assessing her. "You're still good for this? If not, speak up."

"I'm good," Viv said, though her face felt numb.

"We'll need a plan for you. It needs to look like you left suddenly, and maybe not willingly. It can't look like you decided to skip town."

"What if I just stayed and pretended nothing happened?" Viv said.

"You, being questioned by police?" Marnie broke in, shaking her head. "You wouldn't last a minute. The whole thing unravels if that happens, and you put all of us in danger. No, I like her idea." She motioned to Alma. "You're gone, but you didn't skip town. You're just gone."

You're just gone. What about her parents? Her sister? "Won't the cops look for me?"

"Sure we will," Alma said. "We'll look in the wrong places. And not right away." She turned to the car and pulled the keys from where they were hanging in the lock of the trunk. "Leave your purse. Leave everything. Where is that file and notebook you showed me?"

"In the office."

"Go get it. Don't bring your wallet or anything else. Leave your car, everything in your apartment." When Viv hesitated, she said, "You did this. You killed him. The consequences follow from that. Do you understand? There's before tonight, and after. That's what your life is from now on."

Viv nodded. *There's before tonight, and after.* She'd made a decision in that motel room. Now she was living the aftermath.

While the others put the shower curtain in the trunk and closed and locked Hess's room, Viv jogged back to the office. The lights were on, the door unlocked. Her jacket hung from the hook. Her purse sat next to the desk.

She went into it and got out her notes, quickly, trying not to touch anything in her purse. If she touched her things, she'd pause and rethink. She couldn't stand to see or feel her wallet, her ID, her keys. The makeup she kept in her purse. *Those belong to a dead girl. I am starting everything over.*

She walked to the desk and opened the key drawer. The envelope of Robert White's money was still there, stacked with bills. She took it and stuffed it in the back pocket of her jeans. She was starting everything over, but she had a little money to do it. White would never know where his money went. The thought made her feel a little better.

She took a last glance at the guest book. Jamie's name was in there, and Mrs. Bailey's. Both of them would be questioned. But Mrs. Bailey was passed out, and she didn't think Jamie would talk.

Actually, she was sure he wouldn't. Because she'd ask him not to.

Turning her back on her old life, she left the office. Alma was behind the wheel of Simon Hess's car; she was wearing some kind of plastic doctor's gloves, her hands on the wheel. Marnie got in her own car and motioned to Viv.

"Come with me," she said. "Let's take a ride."

Viv walked to Marnie's car and got in.

Callum's car followed in my rearview mirror as I drove out of downtown Fell, onto the back roads. I gripped the wheel and my mind spun as I wondered what I should do. Pull over? Try to lose him? Call someone? Who?

What did Callum want?

He can't possibly want to hurt me. That was the first thing that came to mind. Did a man just follow a woman around in order to hurt her?

Yes, you idiot. He could.

He had invited me out by lying to me. He had told me a crazy story about his grandfather—who, if Callum was telling the truth, was serial killer Simon Hess, formerly of Fell and now long dead in a trunk. And then Callum had followed me. He wasn't friendly or nice. Whatever he wanted, I didn't want to know.

And suddenly I knew what to do. I left Fell and took the back roads to the west, away from the Sun Down. The sky was dark and, except for the odd car, the roads were quiet. There was just me and Callum. He wasn't even trying to hide that he was following me.

I turned onto another familiar road, and then another. I sent up a silent prayer that the person I was going to was home. And then I pulled into Alma Trent's driveway.

I turned off the ignition. A dog barked wildly in the house, and the front porch light switched on. I sagged in relief.

Alma Trent opened her front screen door and walked out onto her porch. She was wearing jeans and a navy blue sweatshirt, her hair tied back in a ponytail. She looked at me, still sitting in my car, and then her hard gaze moved to the car still on the road at the foot of the driveway, idling. She watched it for a long minute, and then Callum's car pulled away.

I opened my driver's door with a shaky hand and got out.

"Evening, Carly," Alma said, her voice its usual unhurried speed. "Were you having a little trouble?"

Her tone said that trouble didn't scare her. That she'd spent decades walking toward it instead of walking away.

"Maybe a little," I said. "A guy was bothering me."

"Well, that's goddamned rude," Alma said. "I can talk to him if you like. Some guys don't get the message until they get a talking-to from me."

"His name is Callum MacRae," I said.

Alma went very still. For the first time, I saw a crack in her cop's façade. "I see," she said. "I didn't realize you knew Callum."

"It's strange," I said. "I first met him at the Fell Central Library. I was doing research there, and he introduced himself. I'm wondering now if maybe he found me."

"Callum can seem nice enough, but sometimes he's a little unstable," Alma said. "Do you want to come in for a cup of tea?"

I took a step forward, but I didn't answer her question. "You were on shift the night that my aunt Viv disappeared, right?"

Alma hesitated for the briefest second. Then she nodded. "I was."

"But you didn't know she was missing until it was reported four days later."

"How would I know she was missing?"

It was a hunch. Only that. But every instinct in my body and my brain told me I was right. "I'm wondering now if maybe my aunt didn't die that night," I said. "I'm wondering if maybe she lived and someone else died."

"Carly," Alma said, "you should really come in for a cup of tea."

"I don't think so. I don't think I'm going anywhere with you. Or Marnie Clark. I'm sure you heard about the body I found in a trunk this morning?"

Alma's eyes were fixed on me, but I couldn't read them. Pity? Kindness? Fear? I realized now that to survive decades as the only female cop on a male police force, Alma had become very, very good at hiding what she was thinking. "I heard about it, yes," she said.

"I thought it was my aunt, but the police told me it was a man," I said. "And then Callum called me and told me this crazy story about how his grandfather disappeared around the same time my aunt did. And I know he's telling the truth, because a man named Simon Hess disappeared sometime around November 1982. His wife was too embarrassed to report it because she thought he'd left her. Simon Hess worked as a traveling salesman. Just like the last man seen with Betty Graham."

"Callum gets fixated on things," Alma said. "His grandfather's disappearance is one of them. He's never been quite right. We think he has borderline personality disorder."

"Who's *we*?" I asked.

"He's had more than one run-in with police," Alma said, ignoring my question. "Usually for bothering girls. He stops when he gets a talking-to. He'll stop bothering you if I talk to him."

"Not if he thinks my aunt murdered his grandfather and stuffed him in a trunk," I said.

Alma was quiet.

"Did she?" I asked her.

"You know I can't answer that," she said.

"Then I'll answer it myself. Marnie says there's a notebook at the Sun Down that I need to read. I think I'll go read it."

"You talked to Marnie?" Alma said, her voice shocked. "You have the notebook?"

"I'm going to get it now. And then I'm going to meet her."

Alma hesitated, then nodded. "She's right," she said. "It's time."

Now is as good a time as any for all of it to come out, Marnie had said to me on the phone. *It was going to happen whether I wanted it to or not.*

Why now? Why me?

"What am I going to find in the notebook?" I asked her.

"You'll see," Alma said. She turned toward her door, then back to me. "Go meet her," she said. "Do whatever she asks. Maybe you don't want my advice, but that's it." Then she turned, went into the house, and closed the door behind her.

No one followed me on the dark roads as I drove across town from Alma's to the motel. Was I supposed to be working tonight? I didn't even remember anymore. Maybe I was quitting. Maybe I was fired. It didn't matter.

The road sign was lit up, the familiar words blinking at me: VACANCY. CABLE TV! Nick's truck was in the parking lot, and the office was closed and dark. I parked and got out of my car, letting the cold wind sting my face. There was no sound but the far-off rumble of a truck farther down Number Six Road. I could smell dead leaves and damp and the faint tang of gasoline.

In a crazy way, I belonged here more than I'd belonged anywhere in my life. The Sun Down was the place I was supposed to be.

And yet I had the feeling that I was here at the end of the Sun Down's life. That it wouldn't be here much longer.

I walked to the stairs and climbed them, the feeling of being watched crawling up the back of my neck. Betty, maybe. Maybe one of the others. I no longer really knew.

I reached Nick's door and banged on it. It opened immediately and he was there, big and tousled, in a dark gray T-shirt and jeans, a worried look on his face. "Thank fucking God," he said. He took my wrist and gently pulled me into the room, closing the door behind him.

I paused, looking around. I'd never been inside Nick's room before. There was a suitcase with clothes strewn over it, a wallet and a phone on the nightstand. The gun was nowhere to be seen. The bed was rumpled and slept in, a fact that would have embarrassed me except for the fact that it was also strewn with papers, a spiral notebook lying open in the middle of it.

"The notebook," I said.

"I got your message," Nick said. "It was in the candy machine, just like you said. Behind the panel I was working on, jammed into the machine's works. She must have put it there recently. There was no way it was in there for thirty-five years."

I looked down at the papers strewn over the bed. They were all inked with the same hand: pages of writing, lists, maps, diagrams. "Marnie must have put it there after I started working here. I wonder how much she knows."

"Everything," Nick said. "Carly, I've been reading through this. I've barely started. But it's incredible." He picked up a piece of paper. "This is a map of Victoria Lee's street. Her house, the jogging trail, the place where her body was found. See this *X*? She's put a note saying that from this spot you can see Victoria's house and you can access the jogging trail at the same time. This was most likely where the killer was standing."

He put that down and flipped a page in the notebook. "These are her notes about Simon Hess's sales schedule at Westlake Lock Systems. It says he was in Victoria's neighborhood the month she was killed. He sold locks to Cathy Caldwell. And this here"—he picked up another sheet—"these are her notes about the day she followed Hess to Tracy Waters's street and watched him follow her."

"What? She *saw* him stalk her?" I looked at the notes. "She must be the one who wrote the letter to Tracy's parents. She must also be the one who phoned the school principal. There's no other way."

"This, here," Nick said, turning to yet another page, "is her diary of

Simon Hess's movements. His address, his phone number, the make and model of his car, his license plate. When he left the house every day and what he did. Where he went. Vivian was following him. For weeks, it looks like."

He was right. I scanned the notes and saw day after day listing the times Simon Hess left his house and where he went. There were gaps in the timeline, with notes: *Not sure—missed him. Fell asleep. Lost him somewhere past Bedford Rd.* But there was no mistaking that Vivian had been following Simon Hess. Stalking him.

On the bottom of a note listing Hess's name, address, phone number, and place of work was a note: *That was easy.*

Whatever had happened to Simon Hess, it hadn't been an accident. He had been targeted for a long time.

Maybe my aunt Viv was crazy.

I pulled up the room's only chair and sat down. I put my head in my hands.

"Marnie had all of this, all this time," Nick said.

"She must have," I said. "But where is Viv?"

His voice was gentle. "Dead, maybe. It's been thirty-five years."

"She left that night," I said, still staring down between my knees as I cradled my head. "She ran. She wasn't abducted. She killed Hess and took off without her car or her wallet. Without money. How?"

I heard Nick move to the bed and move the papers. "She had help."

"Which means Marnie, and maybe Alma, have been hiding her all these years. Maybe supporting her. Why? Why not turn her in?" I shook my head. "Hess was a serial killer. The pattern is right there in Viv's notes. He was dangerous. Why not call the police and claim self-defense?"

"Because she'd still go to jail," Nick said. "No matter who she killed, she's still a killer. The circumstances could be mitigated a little, but that's the best-case scenario. The worst case is that there's no evidence at all that Hess killed anyone—at least nothing that can be proved in court. So Viv goes down as a crazy girl who decided to commit murder one night and chose an innocent man as a victim. Either way, she goes down."

Maybe she should have, I thought. I'd seen the car parked in the old barn, the dried blood on the ground beneath it. Maybe the person who did that should go to trial. To prison. If she didn't, what was to prevent her from doing something like that again?

"Do you smell smoke?" Nick asked.

I lifted my head and realized I did. Cigarette smoke, fresh and pungent. The smoking man, though I'd never felt him up here on the second floor before.

"Henry," I said.

"What?" Nick asked.

I stood up. "Henry. That's the smoking man's name." I walked to the door and opened it, looking over the dark parking lot. Waiting for the lights to go out.

The lights stayed on. Nick's truck and my car were the only cars in the lot. But standing in the middle of the lot was the figure of a man. He was thin, cloaked in shadows. I watched him raise a cigarette, watched the smoke plume around him. He was facing my way, and I was sure he was watching me.

Then he lifted a hand and pointed down Number Six Road. I froze still. There was a figure on the side of the road—a man, walking quickly along the shoulder, his hands in his pockets, his head down, his shoulders hunched. I peered into the darkness, trying to decide if I recognized him, trying to see if he was a living figure or a dead one. I didn't know the difference anymore.

But before I could decide either question, the man approached the motel and ducked around the corner toward the office, out of sight.

I looked back at the parking lot, looking for Henry. But the parking lot was empty. He was gone.

The office was dark, but someone had kicked the door. Nick and I had heard the thumps as we left his room. Now even in the reflected light from the road sign I could see the marks of a shoe where it had hit the wood.

"What the hell was he thinking?" Nick said, his voice low. "Did he think he could get in?"

I stared at the shoe marks, unsettled. "Callum MacRae followed me from town," I said. "I had to drive to Alma's place before he left me alone."

"MacRae," Nick said. "Do I know him? His mother is a professor at the college, right? What does he want with you?"

"I'm not really sure." Callum's interest in me had sometimes seemed personal, sometimes not. "But tonight he wanted to tell me that he's Simon Hess's grandson."

Nick paused, then shook his head. "Fuck it, I've been gone too long. I don't know all the town gossip anymore. If I ever did." He stepped back and looked around. "If he followed you, then he was driving."

"Yes." Though that didn't explain why he was walking along the side of Number Six Road now. Or kicking the office door. If it was even Callum at all.

"He didn't go back to the parking lot. He must have gone this way." Nick walked around the corner toward the empty pool.

I followed him, shoving my hands in the pockets of my coat. It was darker back here, on the other side of the building from the corridor lights. The dark made it seem colder. I kept close to Nick as he walked toward the broken-down chain-link fence around the pool, his boots scuffing in the layers of dead leaves.

"MacRae!" he shouted.

There was no answer.

"Let's just go back," I said.

Nick held up a hand. "I hear him." He took a step and paused. "MacRae!"

I looked around, trying to see in the darkness. The empty pool with the fence around it. The broken concrete walkway that had once been the path that guests would take to the pool. The back doors that led to the utilities room and the storage room. From the other side of the building a truck went by on Number Six, making a loud, throaty barreling sound. There was the faint click I recognized as coming from the ice machine in the AMENITIES room, forever making ice that no guest ever used.

"There's a break in the fence," I said. I picked my way toward it, trying not to trip on the broken concrete. It was on the far side of the pool.

"Wait," Nick said. "Be careful. Let me check it."

"I can't tell if it's recent or not," I said, touching the edge of the break without going through it toward the pool. "This fence is so old it might—"

A shadow came out of the darkness. Big hands grabbed me and shoved me through the break. I stumbled back toward the pool, letting out a scream.

"Carly!" Nick shouted.

The hands shoved me farther. My ankle bent and I tried to keep my balance on the broken concrete. Whoever it was was in shadow and I couldn't see his face. But when the voice spoke, I recognized it.

"Fuck you, bitch," Callum MacRae said, and pushed me backward into the empty pool.

**Fell, New York
November 2017
CARLY**

I landed hard on the concrete, and everything happened at once. Pain lanced up my back and my shoulder, reverberated through my chest. My head hit the ground and my glasses came off. The breath left me in a *whoosh* and for a second I was curled up and gasping, trying to breathe.

"Carly!" came Nick's panicked voice. "Carly!"

I opened my mouth. *I'm okay. I don't think anything's broken.* The words were just a thought, a whisper of breath. I couldn't make anything come out of my lungs and into my throat.

"Carly!"

"Nick," I managed. I was lying in a pool of garbage and leaves, old beer cans and fast-food wrappers. I couldn't see much in the dark without my glasses. Pain was throbbing through my body, from the back of my head and down to my tailbone. I managed a deep breath and tried again. "Nick. I'm okay."

I heard him at the edge of the pool above me, the rustle of his footsteps. "Are you hurt? Do you need help?"

The only thing I could think of was Callum MacRae running off into the trees, getting farther with every second. The thought put me into a dark, black rage, and for a second I was more furious than I had ever been in my life. More furious than I had ever imagined being.

"Go get him," I shouted at Nick. "Don't let him go."

He must have heard something in my voice that said I wasn't helpless, because he swore and the next thing I heard were his boots taking off over the concrete, swift and hard.

I wondered if Nick would catch him. I wondered if Callum was armed. I wondered if Nick had his gun.

Fuck you, bitch, Callum said in my head.

"Fuck you, bitch," I said back to him, my voice throaty as I still gasped for breath. I rolled onto my back and took stock.

I had a bump on the back of my head. My shoulder was screaming with pain, and when I rotated it, it made a sickening *click* sound that said it had been dislocated. I screamed through my gritted teeth, then took more breaths as the pain eased a little.

I had taken most of the impact on my back, and it throbbed from top to bottom. I moved gingerly, patting the leaves and garbage around me, looking for my glasses.

Feet shuffled in the dead leaves next to the pool, a few feet behind me.

I went still. At first I couldn't see anything in the out-of-focus world around me; then I saw a smudge move from the corner of my eye, like someone shifting position.

"Nick?" I said.

There was no answer. I was cold, so cold. Trying to keep an eye on the blur, I felt for my glasses again.

A voice came, high and sad, almost faint. "I don't feel good."

My mouth went dry with fear. It sounded like a child—a boy. The boy I had seen. The boy who had hit his head in this pool and died.

I felt for my glasses again. They hadn't fallen far. I ran my fingers over them. They were wobbly, but they weren't broken. I picked them up and listened to them click as my hand shook.

"I don't feel good," the boy said again.

Slowly, I put my glasses on. I made myself turn around and look. He was standing at the far end of the pool, wearing shorts and a T-shirt. His arms and legs were thin and white in the darkness. He was looking at me.

"I—" I made myself speak. "I have to go."

He started to walk toward me, the leaves rustling at his feet.

I sat up fast. I was bruised and filthy. When I moved a foot I heard a *clink* and knew there was broken glass in here somewhere. I tested with my palms before I put them down and pushed myself up, getting into a standing position as fast as I could as the pain moved through me.

The only way out of here was to climb the rusted old ladder that hung from the edge on the other end of the pool. I started toward it as the footsteps came behind me.

"Why don't I feel good?" the boy asked, making me jump. But I moved one foot after the other, shuffling and limping, trying to gain speed, dirt and leaves on my clothes and in my hair. I likely looked like an extra in a zombie movie, but I kept moving. Slowly, too slowly, I climbed the incline from the deep end toward the shallow end and the ladder.

"I'm sorry," I said as I walked. "I have to go. Maybe you'll feel better soon."

"Help me, please," he said, still behind me, his footsteps still moving in the leaves.

"I can't," I said, my voice nearly a whisper of fear. "I really can't."

"Help me, please!"

The bolts on the ladder had nearly rusted to dust in the decades since the pool had last been used, and the ladder wobbled dangerously when I grabbed it. I swung my weight onto it and climbed out. Gritting my teeth in pain, I moved as fast as I could toward the break in the fence, but I couldn't resist looking back over my shoulder.

The boy was standing at the bottom of the ladder, still watching me. I turned back and half ran toward the motel.

I could hear nothing from the direction Callum and Nick had run. No shouts, no gunshots. I felt in my pocket for my cell phone, then remembered I'd left it in my car because there was no service here. I needed to call the police.

My keys were in my coat pocket, and I fumbled them in the dark until I opened the office door. I flipped on the overhead light and walked around the desk. I picked up the desk phone.

Now is the moment when you realize someone has cut the phone line . . . someone who hasn't left the motel.

"Shut up," I croaked aloud to my overactive brain. "This isn't a horror movie." And it wasn't. The dial tone came loud and healthy from the clunky old handset.

I dialed 911 and looked down at myself in the fluorescent light. I was streaked with dirt and old leaves, and there was a bloody scrape on my left wrist that I hadn't even felt yet. My body begged me to sit in the office chair, as uncomfortable as it was, but I was afraid if I sat down I'd never manage to stand up again.

I told the 911 dispatcher what had happened: that I'd been followed, that I'd been assaulted and pushed into an empty pool by a man named Callum MacRae, that my friend Nick had taken off after my assailant. The dispatcher asked if I was injured, and I said, "Probably," as pain ran up and down my spine. He asked if I could stay on the line as he sent police and an ambulance, and as he spoke the words I heard footsteps walking up the corridor toward the office.

The air went icy cold and I smelled pungent cigarette smoke.

"Miss Kirk?" the dispatcher said. "Are you still there?"

The footsteps came closer. Paced, measured. Not a soft tennis shoe or a woman's high heel. A man.

I could see a plume of my own breath in the air.

"Miss Kirk?" the dispatcher said again.

"I can't stay on the line," I said, feeling bad about it. He was being so nice to me. "I really have to go."

I hadn't closed the office door behind me, and as I hung up the phone a man walked in.

He was wearing dress pants and a long, dark wool coat. His shoes were shined. He was a white man of about thirty-five, with dark hair neatly combed and a clean shave. An average face with even features. I could see the knot of his tie where it disappeared into his buttoned-up coat. He was carrying a small, old-fashioned suitcase.

And something about him scared me so much I almost screamed.

He looked at me for a moment. I couldn't see the color of his eyes—gray, perhaps, or brown. All of the details of him—the composition of his face, the exact color of his clothes—seemed to roll off, to not quite take, like water that has been dropped onto a pool of oil. I blinked and my eyes watered. My stomach clenched in terror. My fingers were numb with cold. The smell of smoke was heavy and sharp.

"I need a room, please," the man said.

His voice was like water on oil, too—what exactly did it sound like? I couldn't say. I couldn't even say if I had really heard it or if it was only in my head.

And somehow, I knew it: I was looking at Simon Hess.

Should I run? Was he a figment of my imagination? I had to get past him to get out the door. If I came close to him, would he vanish into noth-ingness, or—worse—would I feel something, as if he had some kind of corporeal body? I couldn't get near him. So I stood there frozen as he looked at me. And he *saw* me—I was sure of it.

"May I have a room?" he asked me again. He held out a hand, palm up.

A key. He was asking for a key. I didn't even think as I reached down and opened the key drawer. I picked a key without looking, the leather icy in my cold hand. I was too afraid to circle the desk and hand it to him, so I put the key on the desk, pushing it all the way to the edge farthest from me.

Simon Hess stood there for another moment, his hand held out. Then he dropped it to his side again. "Room two-oh-nine," he said in that voice that was real and yet not real. "Home sweet home."

I glanced down and saw the number 209 on the leather tab of the key on the desk.

"Thank you," Hess said. He turned and left the room.

I heard his footsteps walk away down the corridor toward the stairs.

The office door blew shut with a loud slam, making me jump. A terrified whimper left my throat. And the lights went out.

Somewhere in the dark, in the office, a man coughed.

Outside the office door, I saw the sign go out.

Betty, I thought.

She was here. And so was her killer. I'd just given him a room.

I circled the desk, making my legs work as fast as they could. Something brushed me as I ran for the door, the feeling faint and cobweblike. I was too busy escaping to scream.

The doorknob wouldn't turn under my hand. "No," I moaned, jerking it and shoving at it, trying to force the door open. "No, Betty, no, no, no . . ."

Behind me, in the dark office, the desk phone rang, the sound shrill and screaming. I jerked the doorknob again and this time it turned. I burst out onto the walkway, my breath sawing in my lungs. I ran for my car.

Upstairs, the motel doors banged open one by one. The lights went out. The phone shrilled behind me. And when I got to my car, I realized I didn't have my keys. They were back in the office.

"No," I said again. I couldn't stop saying it; it was the only word that would leave my throat. "No, no." I wrenched at the car door handle and the door opened. I'd left the car unlocked, but I had no way to start it and get out of here.

I ducked into the car anyway. It felt safer than standing out in the open, waiting for whatever Betty Graham had planned. Or whatever Simon Hess had planned. Or both of them.

I dropped into the driver's seat, but when I tried to pull the door closed, something resisted. I used both hands, crying out as the motion wrenched my aching back, but I couldn't pull the door closed.

In the passenger seat, my cell phone rang. I jumped, my sweaty hands slipping from the door handle. It wasn't possible; there was no reception here. Yet the phone lay faceup on the passenger seat, buzzing and ringing. The call display said *NICK*.

I let go of the door and grabbed the phone, swiping at it. "Nick?" I called. "Nick?"

There was no answer. Just a second of silence, and a click.

"Nick!" I shouted. I tried redialing his number, but nothing happened. No signal.

The wind gusted into the car through the open door. I had tears on my face, running down my cheeks, cold and wet. Even from here I could hear the phone ringing in the motel office, over and over, on and on. I tried to redial my phone.

Then there was the hum of a car motor, the crackle of tires on gravel. I lowered the phone and watched as a car pulled up next to mine.

The woman inside—I recognized her. Even thirty-five years later, her hair grown long down her back, a knit cap on her head. I knew that face. I'd looked at it so many times, I'd know it anywhere.

My aunt Viv leaned over and opened the passenger door. "Get in, Carly," she said. "It's time to get the hell out of here."

Fell, New York
November 2017
CARLY

The night roads flew by out the window. My body throbbed with pain, and my phone was hot and silent in my hand. Vivian Delaney sat next to me, driving in silence.

She looked older, of course. Her cheekbones had thinned and her face was harder, tougher. Her hair was grown long, the 1980s perm long gone. She wore jeans, boots, and a practical zip-up jacket, a knit cap on her head. She wore barely any makeup. She smelled faintly fruity, like cherry body wash.

"I'm not taking you far," she said at last. "But it's best to get out of the Sun Down, at least for a little while."

"The ambulance is coming," I said, my voice raspy. "The cops. Nick . . ."

"What happened, exactly?"

I made myself look at her. Really look. "You're alive," I said.

Viv said nothing.

"You've been alive for thirty-five years."

She pulled into a parking lot. I recognized the sign for Watson's Diner. "I couldn't go home," she said. "I had to run."

I watched as she parked the car, turned off the ignition. My emotions were like blinking lights behind my eyes. Shock. Fear for Nick. Excitement. And anger. So much anger, quick and hot. "My mother died grieving for you," I said.

Viv froze, her jaw working, and I realized she hadn't known her sister was dead.

That told me everything I needed to know. I opened the door and got out.

"Okay, listen," she said, following me into the diner. "I deserved that. You can be mad at me. I had to move on and cut ties completely or I'd lose my nerve. But we have to talk about what happened tonight. What's still happening."

I kept my phone tight in my hand. When I walked into the diner I saw that I had bars of service, so I called Nick. It rang, but no one answered.

I hung up before the voicemail kicked in and sat in a booth, my legs and back groaning in complaint. Viv sat across from me as if she'd been invited, even though she hadn't. Part of me wanted to kick her out. But another part knew she was right: We had a lot to discuss. I had been in Fell for weeks now, living her old life. The least I needed to do was get answers.

I set my phone down on the table in front of me, faceup, in easy reach. I heard Viv order two bowls of soup from the waitress, but I barely paid attention. *Nick, where are you?*

But Viv's next words jolted me out of my stupor. "We'll start with Betty. What set her off tonight?"

"You've seen Betty," I said.

"I saw her in 1982, yes. Saw her, heard her." She picked up the cup of coffee the waitress had put in front of her. "In those days, she went crazy every time Simon Hess checked into the motel. But I haven't worked the night shift in a long time, so I don't know what did it tonight."

"He checked in," I said. I was talking about this like it was real. Because it *was* real. "He came into the office and asked for a room. I saw him. His voice was in my head. I put a key on the desk and he thanked me and left again."

Viv's knuckles were white on her mug, and she downed half the coffee in one swig. "You checked him in?"

I shrugged. "I suppose so."

"Well, Betty is going to be furious. Does the motel have any other guests?"

I shook my head, thinking back to the guest book when I was in the office. It was blank. "Unless they didn't sign the book. I haven't exactly been there very much tonight."

"Then no one else will get hurt, maybe," Viv said. "Whatever happens there, it's going to be bad."

"There will be cops and EMTs there, if there aren't already," I said. "And my friend is there somewhere."

The waitress put our bowls of soup in front of us as I called Nick again. No answer. "Eat," Viv said when I put the phone down again. "You need sustenance, trust me."

I put my spoon in my soup—chicken noodle, I realized. "I just saw Simon Hess," I said. "Except he's dead."

Viv took a swallow of her own soup. "Are you waiting for me to say it? Okay, I will. Simon Hess is very, very dead. I killed him in November 1982. I put a knife in his chest, and then I pulled it out and put it in his neck. Then I wrapped him in a rug, put him in the trunk of his own car, and left it in an abandoned barn." She put her spoon in her soup again. "I did it because he was a serial killer who killed four women that I knew of. I did it because he admitted everything to me that night before I put the knife in the second time. I did it because if I hadn't, he would have gone free and killed again. Most likely starting with me."

I watched as she took another swallow of soup. "You're so casual about it."

"Because I've had thirty-five years to come to terms with it. You're just figuring it out for the first time." Viv pressed her napkin to her lips. "If you want to call the cops on me, I won't stop you. I've had thirty-five years of freedom that I haven't really enjoyed and that a lot of people will say I don't deserve. I'm no danger to you, Carly."

This was the strangest conversation I'd ever had. I didn't know what to do, so I ate some soup. "You didn't do it alone," I said. "You had Marnie and Alma."

"I did it alone," Viv said.

I shook my head. "Marnie called me. She told me about the notebook in the candy machine. It was right where she said it was."

"Are you sure that was Marnie?"

I stared at her. When I thought back, Marnie hadn't actually identified herself. The call was from an unknown number. I had recognized her voice and assumed. And then Alma: *Go meet her. It's time.*

Damn it. "That was you? Why?"

"I haven't been an actress in a long time, but I can still do voices," Viv said. "You've met Marnie. She pretends she isn't a force of nature, but she is. Being her was the easiest way to get you to do something. Easier than doing it as me. There would be too much to explain if I'd told you who I really was. What I wanted was for you to find the notebook."

"Why?"

"Because it explains why I did what I did. It's all in there. Everything I found about Simon Hess and those murders."

"That still doesn't mean Marnie wasn't involved that night," I said.

"She wasn't. There was just me. Only me."

"Marnie took a photo of the dump site. I found it in her negatives."

"Maybe someone used her camera."

I gripped my spoon in frustration. "The phone records. They show that someone—you—made a call to the Fell PD that night. It would have gone through to Alma, the night duty officer. But those records were somehow never investigated."

"I don't know anything about the police investigation," Viv said calmly, finishing her bowl. "I didn't call the police that night. Maybe Mrs. Bailey did. She was passed out in her room, or so I thought. Maybe she woke up and heard something, but nothing came of it. Alma didn't come to the motel that night, and neither did any other cop. At least, not before I left."

"You were missing for four days before it was reported." The pieces were coming together in my mind, all of them moving into place. "Your roommate reported it after she came home from a weekend away. But Marnie and Alma both knew you were gone."

"No one knew I was gone. I killed Simon Hess, I dumped him, and I ran."

"Alone?"

"Alone."

No. No way would Viv, who was a hundred and ten pounds soaking wet, have been able to do everything alone—lift the body of a full-grown man into a trunk, clean up afterward, come up with the plan. Then she had to start a new life with no ID and no money. "Who are you now?" I asked her.

"Christine Fawcett," Viv said. "I have a driver's license and a birth certificate. I vote in every election. I picked Christine at random, but then Stephen King wrote that book, so I figured it was fate. And Fawcett is for Farrah Fawcett, who was my idol as a teenager."

It struck me again how casual she was. But as she'd said, she'd had thirty-five years to get accustomed to being Christine. I hadn't.

"You didn't do it alone," I insisted. It bothered me that I had come so far, was sitting across the table from the truth, and I still wasn't getting it. "You need resources and money to start over. To get fake ID. To get a birth certificate. You weren't a career criminal."

"No, but Jamie Blaknik was."

I knew the name. Alma had said he was at the Sun Down the night of the murder. "He was a pot dealer."

"A pot dealer who knew a lot of the right kind of people, and knew how to keep his mouth shut." Viv sat back in the booth, her eyes sad. "He died a long time ago, so nothing you do can hurt him."

"You cared about him," I said, seeing it in her face.

Viv glanced away, then nodded. "I asked a lot of him, but he never failed me. The cops questioned him as a suspect in my murder, but they couldn't get anywhere with him. He kept my secret when he could have saved himself by turning me in. To the day he died, I knew I could never repay him. He'll always be important to me." The corner of her mouth quirked in the ghost of a smile. "Besides, a girl has to lose her virginity somewhere, right?"

I gaped at her. "Are we actually talking about this right now?"

Viv laughed softly, amused. It made her even more beautiful than she was before. "It may be a different time, but you remind me so much of me at that age. Smart, resourceful, and very, very square."

"I am not square." The words leapt out in my defense. "Wait a minute, no one even says *square* anymore. And we are not talking about this."

"I got married once." Viv sipped her coffee. "After Jamie. It lasted eleven months, and then he left me. He said he could never really know me, that I kept too much to myself. *You're always so far into your own head, where no one else can go.* That's what he said, and he wasn't wrong. I liked him—loved him—but I can't let anyone in. My life doesn't work that way. It's the sacrifice I made." She looked at me speculatively. "You can choose differently, though. My sister's girl. I think I can take some comfort in that. How did she die?"

"Cancer," I said, my body aching all over again.

"It runs in the family, then. Get yourself screened, sweetheart."

"I know. My grandmother—your mother—died of cancer, too." I put my hands palm-down on the diner table. "Look, I'm glad we're having this little family heart-to-heart, but I have big problems to deal with. There are ghosts running around the Sun Down right now. My friend is out there somewhere and not answering his phone. And I got pushed into the empty pool by Simon Hess's grandson."

Viv put down her mug. For the first time, she looked shocked. "You had a run-in with Callum MacRae?"

"How do you know who Callum MacRae is if you worked alone and you haven't been to Fell for thirty-five years?"

"I said I ran that night," Viv said. "I said I've been Christine for thirty-five years. I never said I didn't come back to Fell."

"Wait a minute. I've been looking for you all this time, and you *live* here?"

"How do you think I knew you worked at the motel?" Viv bit her lip. "I couldn't stay away. I left for a few years, and then I came back. I love this place. What can I say? Fell is home." She shrugged. "I'm even in the old-fashioned phone book. And no, no one has ever recognized me. My disappearance didn't get much coverage. I live in a different part of town now, and I work from home as a tutor. I barely spoke to anyone when I worked the night shift, and no one remembered me after a few years. I even passed my old roommate, Jenny, on the street one day and she didn't look twice at me. It's amazing how quickly people forget."

I opened my mouth—to say what, I no longer knew—but my phone rang. It lit up and buzzed on the table, the ringtone high and sharp.

Nick.

I grabbed the phone and answered it. "Nick?"

"Carly," he said. "I came back and you were gone. Where the fuck are you? Where did you go?"

"I'm not far," I said. "I'm okay. What's going on? Are you all right?"

"I'm fine. I'm at the motel." Voices sounded in the background, and Nick replied something I couldn't hear. Then he came back on the line. "It's a little crazy here at the moment."

I was nearly woozy with relief at the sound of his voice, as deep and confident as ever. "Are the police there? The ambulance? Is Callum there?"

"They're here," he said. "But Callum is dead, I think. And the motel . . . I can't even describe it. I think you need to get back here right now."

I t was chaos at the Sun Down.

There were police cars and an ambulance. The red and blue lights flashed, bouncing off the front of the building, the corridors, the stairs, mixing with the yellow and blue of the road sign—which was lit up again.

Viv pulled into the edge of the parking lot, in a spot that didn't block the official vehicles. When I got out of the car, she followed me.

There was yellow police tape pulled across the second-floor corridor, and several police were there. More police were on the ground level outside the office, surrounding Nick, who was standing with his arms crossed.

When I tried to approach, a policeman stopped me. "I'm the night clerk," I said. "I'm supposed to be here."

"You work here?" he asked.

"Yes." I gave him my name. "I'm the one who called 911."

He glanced past my shoulder at Viv. "Who is this?"

"My aunt." The words came out before I could even think them. "Her name is Christine Fawcett. She picked me up after Callum MacRae attacked me, and then she took me for a bowl of soup."

The cop was reluctant, but he allowed us through and brought me to another cop, a big, sixtyish man who seemed to be in charge.

As I answered his questions, I kept glancing at Nick. He was flanked by a policeman of his own, who was asking questions and taking down the answers.

"I had no idea the Fell PD even had this many cops," Viv said softly to me.

Nick raised his gaze and looked back at me. He looked unhurt, and his expression was intent and unreadable. Then his gaze moved to Viv, and I knew he recognized her. He looked almost angry. I wished to God I could get him alone and explain.

"Where's Callum?" I asked the cop.

He motioned toward the ambulance, which was starting up and pulling out of the parking lot. "From what we can piece together, after he pushed you into the pool, Mr. MacRae took off into the woods with your friend Nick in pursuit. Nick claims he lost Callum somewhere in the chase. After a while he gave up and came back to the motel. He found Callum on the second-floor corridor, unconscious. He was trying to wake him when we pulled up." He raised his eyebrows at me. "That's what he says, at least. Do you have anything to add to that statement?"

"I told you what happened," I said. "Callum attacked me. I called 911. I was afraid he'd come back. My aunt came and picked me up. She took me away, and then we came back here."

The cop's gaze flicked to Viv, then back to me. He obviously didn't recognize her. "Do you need medical assistance?" he asked me.

"No, I need to talk to Nick."

"That isn't possible right now. The fact is, we found him bent over Callum MacRae's body. Until we know exactly what has been going on, we are going to take him for questioning."

"He didn't do anything!" I heard my voice rising, cracking. "He only chased after the man who assaulted me! That's all!"

From where he stood, Nick shook his head at me, silent.

"We're going to have a paramedic look at you," the cop said, softer now. "You had a bad fall and you need to be checked out. We're going to go over your statement again. Miss . . ." He looked at Viv.

"Fawcett," Viv said. "Christine Fawcett."

"Miss Fawcett, I'd appreciate it if you'd wait over there until we're finished with your niece."

"Of course, Officer." She reached out and squeezed my hand. Hers was warm; mine was icy cold. "I'm not going far, sweetie. I'll talk to you soon."

They took Nick away. It wasn't an arrest; there were no handcuffs, no reading of rights like on TV. They took him for questioning and he went quietly, his eyes downcast. He was Nick Harkness, the son of one of Fell's most notorious murderers, the boy who may or may not have been in his bedroom. He was found crouching over a man who wasn't breathing. He was a suspect whether I liked it or not.

I answered questions as a paramedic checked my blood pressure, checked the bump on my head, shone a light in my pupils, had me follow her finger as she wagged it in the air, had me walk in a straight line. She didn't think any of my ribs were broken. She gave me some Motrin for the pain.

It seemed to take forever. Yes, I worked at the Sun Down. I had for a few weeks now. No, I did not know Callum MacRae very well; I had only met him a few times. Yes, Nick Harkness was a guest at the motel, even though his name wasn't in the guest book. He had a deal worked out with the owner.

"What about the damage?" the cop said, flipping the page in his notebook. "You say you've worked here a while. Did you notice it?"

"What damage?" I asked.

"The flooding, the leaks, the cracks in the walls." He looked curiously at me. "You say you've never seen it?"

I glanced past him to the motel. For the first time I noticed that there was water dripping off the second-floor corridor, as if the upstairs level had flooded. What I had taken for shadows on the walls in the darkness—they might be mold. Black mold. The office door was open, and there was water in front of it, too. I tilted my head back and saw that swaths of shingles were gone from the roof, the wood beneath dark with rot.

"I don't . . ." I was nearly speechless. There was no sign of Simon Hess or Betty Graham, the boy in the pool or Henry, the smoking man. Was the feeling of being watched gone, or was it just my imagination? "It wasn't like this when I left," I said.

"That's what your friend Nick said." The cop kept saying *your friend Nick*, as if that were an accusation in itself. "Funny that he's been staying here so long and hasn't noticed that the ceiling is so water damaged it's about to cave in."

"What?" I said.

"The flooding is bad, and old. The carpets in most of the rooms look wrecked. Same with the carpet in the office, even though we haven't had heavy rain in a long time. There are cracks in some of the load-bearing walls. There's mold all over the ceilings on the upper floor. Looks like there was a leak in the AMENITIES room, too, so the entire ceiling is almost black." He looked up from his notebook and at the motel, as if looking for answers like I was. "It's strange, but I guess you haven't been in the rooms very much. Neither has anyone else. No one really comes out here, do they?" He shrugged. "We can't say how it happened, only that it's there."

Betty, I thought, *what did you do?*

But she didn't have to tell me. I had checked her killer into the motel, after all. *Betty is going to be furious.* This was Betty's version of trashing the place.

As for Simon Hess . . . I had no idea what she had done to him.

"Can I get my things?" I asked the cop as the paramedic finished up. "They're in the office."

He nodded. "We'll have someone get them for you. Then I'll have someone take you home."

"I'll take her." Viv appeared at my side, putting her hand on my shoulder. "You can't drive, honey," she said to me, as if she'd been my aunt all my life. "I'll get you home."

When I had my keys and my bag back from my car, Viv led me away. "Viv," I said, "I appreciate this, but I don't—"

"Of course I'm not taking you home," she said. "We're going to the police station to get Nick out of there. This isn't over yet."

"Callum had no visible injuries," Viv said as we drove into town. "They're doing a full exam, of course, but it doesn't appear that he was attacked. They'll have to do an autopsy to be sure."

"So he's dead," I said numbly.

"As of a few minutes ago in the ambulance, yes," Viv said. "The official cause of death will likely be something natural, like heart failure or an embolism."

"And the unofficial cause of death?"

"Betty Graham." She glanced at me. "He was her killer's grandson. He should never have gone into that motel. God knows why he did it. Now we'll never know."

I looked out the window, wondering what Callum had seen in his last minutes, what had lured him up to the motel's second floor. His grandfather? Betty? Something else? Despite everything, I felt bad for him. It didn't seem like he'd had a very happy life. "How do you know he died?" I asked Viv. "You can't tell me you weren't talking to Alma Trent on the phone."

Viv smiled, as if she were a little amused. "Carly, I've been a vault for thirty-five years. You need to stop asking questions I won't answer."

But I had no intention of stopping. "How did you know that your mother died of cancer?" I asked her.

"What?"

"You didn't know that my mother had died, but you knew your mother had. When I told you that Mom died of cancer, you said . . ." I trailed off as it hit me. "You didn't say they died. You said cancer runs in the family."

"It does."

I felt my stomach lurch. This was too much, all in one night. "You have cancer." My voice was flat.

"I did have it," Viv said. "I beat it."

"And now?"

"Get yourself screened, sweetheart," she said as we pulled into the police station parking lot. "We're here."

They made us wait for two hours. We sat on hard chairs in the police station, watching people come and go. Every once in a while I'd go back up to the duty officer's desk and ask about Nick Harkness. He'd tell me that he'd let me know as soon as there was any news, and then I'd sit down again.

Viv got up twice and made a phone call, walking a few feet away for privacy. The second phone call was a disagreement—I could tell from her hunched posture, the way she spoke intently into the phone, the low, whispered sound of her voice. *I know. I know. I'm sorry.* Those were the only words I could pick out with my limited lip-reading skills.

"Who were you talking to?" I asked when she sat down again, though I knew it was useless.

For the first time since I'd met her, through everything that had happened tonight, Viv looked visibly upset. "No one."

"Right," I said. I was upset myself—tired, worried, in pain. "No one."

For a second she looked like she'd argue with me or say something hard. Then she sat back in her uncomfortable plastic chair and took my hand in hers. She held it there, her fingers strong and cool over mine. I didn't move my hand away.

"Do you think he needs a lawyer?" I finally asked, miserable.

"No," Viv said. "He won't need a lawyer. There wasn't a crime committed, unless they want to try pinning a stopped heart and a bunch of motel mold on him. They're questioning him extra long because of who he is."

Because he was Nick Harkness, whose father committed one of Fell's most famous murders, and who had made a lot of mistakes afterward. Who had been in and out of trouble until he finally left Fell. *We could never prove anything, but I always wondered if Nick was really upstairs in his room like he said he was.*

I didn't know why I felt I had to say it, but I did. "Nick was in his bedroom that day."

"Yes, I know," Viv said.

"Alma doesn't think so."

"Did she tell you that?" Viv looked at me, still holding my hand. "Alma likes to rattle people if she can. It's a cop reflex. You should take it as a compliment. It means you shook her up."

It was the first time Viv had admitted she even knew Alma, but I couldn't bring myself to feel anything. "He's not a criminal."

"No," Viv said. "I am."

I looked into her eyes. She really did have beautiful eyes, my aunt Viv. They looked like my mother's.

"They've identified Simon Hess," she said. "Dental records, though it isn't official yet. They're going to process the car top to bottom for evidence."

She squeezed my hand, then let me go and stood up.

"What are you doing?" I asked.

She didn't answer, but turned away. The door behind the desk opened, and Nick came out. His blue eyes lit briefly with surprise when he saw me, and then he came my way.

"Hi there," Viv said to the night shift desk clerk. "I need to talk to a detective."

Nick came toward me. Tears stung my eyes.

"No," I said softly, but I didn't stop her.

"What is it regarding?" the desk clerk asked.

Nick put his hand on my shoulder.

"The body they found in the trunk of a car this morning," Viv said. "I put it there. My name is Vivian Delaney, and I disappeared thirty-five years ago. I'd like to make a confession."

It was surprisingly calm, surprisingly civilized. The desk clerk made a phone call. Then he stood up and said, "Come with me."

Vivian didn't look back as she followed him into the police station. The door clicked closed behind her.

Fell, New York
February 2018
Three Months Later
CARLY

It got cold that winter. The snow started early in December and didn't let up. The winds were icy, the roads hard. I barely made it home to Illinois for Christmas.

I stayed with my brother, Graham, and his fiancée for three days. Then I got back in my car and drove back to Fell.

Graham and Hailey didn't understand it. Why I wanted to be in Fell, of all places. Why I didn't want to leave. Why Fell, the place where our aunt had committed murder and pretended to vanish, was home. But it was.

I stayed with Heather for another month, and then I moved into Viv's apartment on the other side of town. Most people would think it strange that I would take over my aunt's place after she was indicted for murder—specifically, voluntary manslaughter—but Heather didn't. "Why not?" she said when I suggested it. "It fits in with the rest of this weird story."

So I moved in. I quit college—another pissed-off lecture from Graham—and researched what I really wanted to do. For the first months of winter, I lived a quiet life. I read books. I walked. I hung out with

Heather. And I spent dozens of hours, days, in the Fell Central Library, reading and researching. Thinking.

Callum's autopsy showed that he had died of a brain aneurysm that night at the Sun Down. A quick and painless death, apparently. I was glad he hadn't suffered. There was a funeral, but it was small and private. I wasn't invited, and I didn't attend.

The body of Callum's grandfather, Simon Hess, was officially identified by police in early December. The cause of death was two stab wounds, one to the chest and one to the neck. The neck wound, said the coroner, had likely been the one to kill Hess, though if left untended the chest wound would have done it in time. The murder weapon was not found on the body, though it was determined to be a hunting knife, very sharp, the blade four to six inches in length.

Vivian Delaney's defense claimed she had killed Hess in self-defense when Hess admitted to her that he was a serial killer. It made state and national headlines when Hess's DNA was matched to the DNA found on Betty Graham, Cathy Caldwell, and Tracy Waters. There was no DNA found on Victoria Lee, since she was killed in haste and not raped.

Betty's, Cathy's, and Tracy's families found closure. Victoria's did not.

I didn't go back to work at the Sun Down after that night, and neither did anyone else. The building was damaged from the roof to the foundation. Chris, the owner, tried to keep it open, but there were no customers and a county health inspector informed him that he had to close it down. The mold and the damp were a health hazard, the plaster ceilings and walls were starting to crumble to inhalable dust, and the heat didn't work in the cold. The water pipes froze and the electricity went out, the sign going dark for good.

So Chris did what any sensible man, saddled with an unwanted and unviable business, would do: He got an insurance payout, put the land up for sale for next to nothing, and had the building condemned.

In late December, just after Christmas, a quick chain-link fence went up around the Sun Down, laced with signs that said PRIVATE PROPERTY.

The motel sign came down and was carted away in a specialized truck. And in February, when the sky was muddy gray and the ground was churned with dirty snow and slush, the bulldozers and other vehicles moved in.

I watched it. I parked my car on the side of Number Six Road and walked to the chain-link fence, my gloved hands in my pockets and a hat pulled over my ears, the wind freezing my nose and my cheeks, chapping my lips. It wasn't dramatic or even very interesting; there was no one else there to watch as the machines rumbled around the demolition site, pulling down walls and drilling into the concrete of the parking lot. There was no swelling music, no choir or curtain to fall. Just the streaked, darkening sky and the snow starting to fall as the crew worked day in and day out.

Betty Graham wasn't there. Neither was Simon Hess, or the little boy, or Henry the smoking man. They were all dead and gone.

My phone rang in my pocket as I stood by the fence, and I pulled it out and yanked off my mitten to answer it. "Hello?"

"Victoria's case is being reinvestigated," said the voice on the other end. "They've pulled all the evidence and are going over it again. Including reexamining her clothes for traces of the killer's DNA."

I turned and started walking back to my car. "Don't tell me how you know that," I said to Alma Trent.

"Don't worry, I won't," Alma said. "I managed to make a few friends on the force over the course of thirty years, despite my personality. That's all I'll say."

"If they can pull scheduling records, it will help. Viv's notebook says that Hess was scheduled on Victoria's street the month she died."

"I know. I've read the notebook."

"Not recently," I said. The notebook was mine now; I'd kept it. By now I'd read it a hundred times. "Have you called Marnie and told her?"

"I have no idea who you're talking about."

"Of course you did," I said as if she hadn't answered. "You called her first, before me."

"The name sounds familiar, but I can't say I place it. You're thinking of someone else."

"Tell her I said hello."

"I would if I knew who you mean."

I sighed. "You know, one of these days you're going to have to trust me."

"This is as trusting as I get," Alma said. "I'm just a retired cop who takes an interest in the Vivian Delaney case. Call it a hobby, or maybe nostalgia for the early eighties. Where are you? I can hear wind."

"On Number Six Road, watching the Sun Down get bulldozed into oblivion."

"Is that so," Alma said in her no-nonsense tone. "Do you feel good about that or bad?"

"Neither," I replied. "Both. Can I ask you something?"

"You can always ask, Carly." Which meant that she wouldn't always answer.

"Victoria's boyfriend was originally convicted of her murder. But his case was reopened and overturned. I looked it up, and it turns out that it all started when the boyfriend got a new lawyer in 1987. Do you know anything about that? I mean, something must have changed. There must have been some kind of tip that encouraged him to seek a new trial."

"I don't know any lawyers," Alma said.

Right. Of course. Except she knew for certain that the wrong man had been convicted, and that the right man was dead in the trunk of a car. "Here's the other interesting thing," I said. "Right after Tracy's murder, a homeless man was arrested because he tried to turn in her backpack. Everyone assumed he must be her killer. But the case was thrown out because it was circumstantial. And the reason he went free was because he had a good lawyer."

"Is that so?"

"Yes. That's kind of strange, isn't it? A homeless drifter who has a really good lawyer? It sounds like something someone would help out with if they knew for sure that the man was innocent."

"I wouldn't know. Like I say, lawyers aren't my thing."

I sighed. I liked Alma, but it was impossible to be friends with her. Heather was more my style. "I took pictures of the Sun Down being demolished on my phone. I think Viv would like to see them the next time I visit her."

"I hear they're giving her medical treatment in prison while she awaits trial," Alma said.

My heart squeezed. Despite everything, Viv was my aunt. "They're giving her chemo, but they don't know if it will work."

Viv had cancer again. She was going to either die of it or spend the rest of her life in prison. Maybe both.

Maybe neither.

Either way, there was nothing more I could do.

Did I feel good about that, or bad? It depended on the day, on my mood, on whether I felt anger at what Viv had put my mother through or the ache of missing family or admiration at some of the things she'd done. There were times I felt all three at once. This was going to take time— time that Viv, maybe, didn't have.

"She beat it once," Alma said. "She can beat it again. She can beat anything."

"Jeez," I said. "It almost sounds like you know her."

"I don't, of course, but she sounds like an interesting lady. Tell her I'd like to meet her someday."

I rolled my eyes. "Whatever."

"It's cold out on Number Six Road. Do you want to come by for a coffee? I don't care what time it is. I'm a night owl."

"Me, too," I said, "but I'm not coming today. I have plans."

"Is that so," Alma said again. "It's about time."

"What does that mean?"

"It means have fun," she said, and hung up.

Nick was wearing jeans and a black sweater. He had shaved and he smelled soapy. He had long ago moved into an apartment in a third-floor walkup, a small place that was sparse and masculine and somehow homey. He had started a partnership with an old high school friend in a renovation company, and he ran two renovation crews in town. Maybe some of the business came because he was notorious, but not all of it did. When Nick put his mind to something, he could do anything he wanted.

"I want to study criminology," I said to him as we ate a late-night dinner at a Thai place downtown. "I can start in the spring, get credits over the summer before I enroll for the fall."

He lowered his chopsticks. The restaurant lighting was dim, making his dark hair and his shadowed cheekbones almost stupidly gorgeous. I couldn't decide if I liked him better with his insomnia stubble or without.

"Are you sure about that?" he asked me.

"Yes." I poked at my pad thai noodles. "I think I'd be good at it. Do you?"

He looked at me for a long moment. "I think you'd be brilliant at it," he said, his voice dead serious. "I think the world of criminology isn't ready for you. Not even a little."

I felt my cheeks heat as I dropped my gaze to my plate. "You just earned yourself another date, mister."

"I have to earn them? This is like our tenth."

"No, it's our ninth. The time we ran into each other by mistake at CVS doesn't count."

"I'm counting it."

"I was in sweats," I protested. "I had a cold. Not a date."

"I sent you home, and then I bought all of the cold meds you needed and brought them to you. Along with food and tea," he countered. "It was a date."

I most definitely still had a crush on the former occupant of room 210 of the Sun Down Motel.

"Well, tonight is going to be better," I told him.

It was. We finished our dinner, then went to the revue cinema for a midnight showing of *Carrie*. There were exactly fourteen people there. I held his hand through the whole thing. When it was over and we went outside, it was snowing. We barely noticed on the drive back to his apartment. We were too preoccupied.

Like my aunt Viv said, a girl has to lose her virginity somewhere, right?

Hours later, when I lay warm in bed with Nick's arm over me, I turned toward the window in the darkness. I watched the snow fall for a long time before I finally fell asleep.

Acknowledgments

Thanks to my editor, Danielle Perez, for her sage help with this book, and thanks to the rest of the team at Berkley for their hard work and my amazing cover. Thanks to my agent, Pam Hopkins, for everything she does. Thanks to Molly and Stephanie, who read a draft of this book and told me it wasn't terrible. Thanks as always to my husband, Adam, who understands my need for writing time and makes sure I have it. Thank you to the booksellers and librarians who work so tirelessly to get the word out about my books. And thank you, readers, the ones who keep picking up my books and talking about them. Without you, none of this happens. Thank you so much for reading my stories.

The Sun Down Motel

SIMONE ST. JAMES

QUESTIONS FOR DISCUSSION

1. Why do you think the author chose to tell this story across two time periods and two points of view? Do you think it was effective? Why or why not?

2. Discuss how each of the victims were described in the media. Do you think the way the media characterized these women played a role in the overall investigation—and the failure by the police to catch the killer? How does their characterization compare to how victims are described by the media today?

3. From the beginning, Viv is determined to uncover who the female ghost is and why she's haunting the motel. Why do you think this was so important to her? Why do you think she didn't just flee Fell, New York, and the motel?

4. Viv, Carly, and Heather all have a somewhat morbid curiosity surrounding both the Fell, New York, murders and true crime in general, which reflects the fact that young women tend to be the biggest consumers of true crime content. Why do you think this is?

5. Discuss the ghosts that haunt the motel, especially Betty. What do you think each of them represented, if anything?

6. There are multiple instances where the women of this novel discuss what women should be doing to protect themselves, although as Viv notes: "It was always girls who ended up stripped and dead like roadkill. . . . It didn't matter how afraid or careful you were—it could always be you." What do you think the author is saying about the experience of being a woman? Do you think the novel might have been difference if Viv and Carly were men? If so, how?

7. How are the concepts of female rage and empowerment explored in this novel, if at all?

8. Consider Alma and Marnie, and the relationships they formed with Viv and with each other. Why do you think they allowed themselves to become involved with Viv's investigation?

9. Multiple characters throughout this novel end up returning to the small town of Fell, New York, or choose to remain there despite many reasons—and opportunities—to leave. Why do you think they are drawn to the town?

10. Building off the previous question, why do you think the author chose a remote town—and an even more remote roadside motel—for the setting of this novel? How do you think the story would have changed with a different setting?

11. Discuss the way the killer was finally stopped. Do you think those involved did the right thing? Do you think, especially with consideration of the time period, that they could have done anything differently?

KEEP READING FOR AN EXCERPT FROM
ANOTHER CHILLING NOVEL FROM
SIMONE ST. JAMES

The Broken Girls

AVAILABLE NOW FROM BERKLEY

Barrons, Vermont
November 1950

The sun vanished below the horizon as the girl crested the rise of Old Barrons Road. Night, and she still had three miles to go.

The air here went blue at dusk, purplish and cold, a light that blurred details as if one were looking through smoke. Squinting, the girl cast a glance back at the road where it climbed the rise behind her, the breeze tousling her hair and creeping through the thin fabric of her collar, but no one that she could see was following.

Still: *Faster,* she thought.

She hurried down the slope, her thick schoolgirl's shoes pelting stones onto the broken road, her long legs moving like a foal's as she kept her balance. She'd outgrown the gray wool skirt she wore—it hung above her knees now—but there was nothing to be done about it. She carried her uniform skirt in the suitcase that banged against her legs, and she'd be putting it back on soon enough.

If I'm lucky.

Stop it, stupid. Stupid.

Faster.

Her palms were sweaty against the suitcase handle. She'd nearly dropped the case as she'd wrestled it off the bus in haste, perspiration stinging her back and armpits as she glanced up at the bus's windows.

Everything all right? the driver had asked, something about the panic in a teenage girl's face penetrating his disinterest.

Yes, yes— She'd given him a ghastly smile and a wave and turned away, the case banging her knees, as if she were bustling off down a busy city street and not making slow progress across a cracked stretch of pavement known only as the North Road. The shadows had grown long, and she'd glanced back as the door closed, and again as the bus drew away.

No one else had gotten off the bus. The scrape of her shoes and the far-off call of a crow were the only sounds. She was alone.

No one had followed.

Not yet.

She reached the bottom of the slope of Old Barrons Road, panting in her haste. She made herself keep her gaze forward. To look back would be to tempt it. If she only looked forward, it would stay away.

The cold wind blew up again, freezing her sweat to ice. She bent, pushed her body faster. If she cut through the trees, she'd travel an exact diagonal that would land her in the sports field, where at least she had a chance she'd meet someone on the way to her dorm. A shorter route than this one, which circled around the woods to the front gates of Idlewild Hall. But that meant leaving the road, walking through the trees in the dark. She could lose direction. She couldn't decide.

Her heart gave a quick stutter behind her rib cage, then returned to its pounding. Exertion always did this to her, as did fear. The toxic mix of both made her light-headed for a minute, unable to think. Her body still wasn't quite right. Though she was fifteen, her breasts were small and she'd started bleeding only last year. The doctor had warned her there would be a delay, perfectly normal, a biological aftereffect of malnutrition. *You're young and you'll recover,* he'd said, *but it's hell on the body.* The phrase had echoed with her for a while, sifting past the jumble of her thoughts. *Hell on the body.* It was darkly funny, even. When her distant relatives had peered at her afterward and asked what the doctor had said, she'd found herself replying: *He said it's hell on the body.* At the bemused looks that followed, she'd tried to say something comforting: *At least I still have all my teeth.* They'd looked away then, these Americans who didn't understand what an achievement it was to keep all your teeth. She'd been quiet after that.

Closer, now, to the front gates of Idlewild Hall. Her memories worked in unruly ways; she'd forget the names of half the classmates she lived with, but she could remember the illustration on the frontispiece of the old copy of *Blackie's Girls' Annual* she'd found on a shelf in the dorm: a girl in a 1920s low-waisted dress, walking a romping dog over a hillside, shading her eyes with her hand as the wind blew her hair. She had stared at that illustration so many times she'd had dreams about it, and she could recall every line of it, even now. Part of her fascination had come from its innocence, the clean milkiness of the girl in the drawing, who could walk her dog without thinking about doctors or teeth or sores or scabs or any of the other things she had buried in her brain, things that bobbed up to the surface before vanishing into the darkness again.

She heard no sound behind her, but just like that, she knew. Even with the wind in her ears and the sound of her own feet, there was a murmur of something, a whisper she must have been attuned to, because when she turned her head this time, her neck creaking in protest, she saw the figure. Cresting the rise she'd just come over herself, it started the descent down the road toward her.

No. I was the only one to get off the bus. There was no one else.

But she'd known, hadn't she? She had. It was why she was already in a near run, her knuckles and her chin going numb with cold. Now she pushed into a jog, her grip nearly slipping on the suitcase handle as the case banged against her leg. She blinked hard in the descending darkness, trying to make out shapes, landmarks. How far away was she? Could she make it?

She glanced back again. Through the fog of darkness, she could see a long black skirt, the narrow waist and shoulders, the gauzy sway of a black veil over the figure's face moving in the wind. Unseen feet moving beneath the skirt's hem. The details were visible now because the figure was closer—moving only at a walk, but already somehow closing in, closer every time she looked. The face behind the veil wasn't visible, but the girl knew she was being watched, the hidden gaze fixed on her.

Panicked, she made an abrupt change of direction, leaving the road and plunging into the trees. There was no path, and she made her way slowly through thick tangles of brush, the dead stalks of weeds stinging her legs through her stockings. In seconds the view of the road behind her disappeared, and she guessed at her direction, hoping she was heading in a straight line toward the sports field. The terrain slowed her down, and sweat trickled between her shoulder blades, soaking into the cheap cotton of her blouse, which stuck to her skin. The suitcase was clumsy and heavy, and soon she dropped it in order to move more quickly through the woods. There was no sound but the harsh rasp of her own breathing.

Her ankle twisted, sent sharp pain up her leg, but still she ran. Her hair came out of its pins, and branches scraped her palms as she pushed them from her face, but still she ran. Ahead of her was the old fence that surrounded Idlewild, rotted and broken, easy to get through. There was no sound from behind her. And then there was.

Mary Hand, Mary Hand, dead and buried under land . . .

Faster, faster. Don't let her catch you.

She'll say she wants to be your friend . . .

Ahead, the trees were thinning, the pearly light of the half-moon illuminating the clearing of the sports field.

Do not let her in again!

The girl's lungs burned, and a sob burst from her throat. She wasn't ready. She *wasn't*. Despite everything that had happened—or perhaps because of it. Her blood still pumped; her broken body still ran for its life. And in a moment of pure, dark clarity, she understood that all of it was for nothing.

She'd always known the monsters were real.

And they were here.

The girl looked into the darkness and screamed.

Barrons, Vermont
November 2014

The shrill of the cell phone jerked Fiona awake in the driver's seat. She lurched forward, bracing her palms on the wheel, staring into the blackness of the windshield.

She blinked, focused. Had she fallen asleep? She'd parked on the gravel shoulder of Old Barrons Road, she remembered, so she could sit in the unbroken silence and think. She must have drifted off.

The phone rang again. She swiped quickly at her eyes and glanced at it, sitting on the passenger seat where she'd tossed it. The display glowed in the darkness. Jamie's name, and the time: three o'clock in the morning. It was the day Deb would have turned forty if she'd still been alive.

She picked up the phone and answered it. "Jamie," she said.

His voice was a low rumble, half-asleep and accusing, on the other end of the line. "I woke up and you were gone."

"I couldn't sleep."

"So you left? For God's sake, Fee. Where are you?"

She opened her door and swung her legs out into the chilly air. He'd be angry, but there was nothing she could do about that. "I'm on Old Barrons Road. I'm parked on the shoulder, at the bottom of the hill."

Jamie was quiet for a second, and she knew he was calculating the date. Deb's birthday. "Fee."

"I was going to just go home. I was." She got out of the car and stood, her cramped legs protesting, the cold air slapping her awake and tousling her hair. She walked to the edge of the road and looked up and down, shoving her free hand into the pocket of her windproof jacket. Back the way she'd come, she could see the road sign indicating thirty miles to Burlington and the washed-out lights of the twenty-four-hour gas station at the top of the hill. Past the hill, out of her sight, she knew there was the intersection with the North Road, with its jumble of fast-food restaurants, yet more gas stations, and a couple of hopeful big-box stores. In the other direction, ahead of the car's hood, there was only darkness, as if Old Barrons Road dropped off the face of the earth.

"You didn't have to go home," Jamie was saying.

"I know," Fiona replied. "But I was restless, and I didn't want to wake you up. So I left, and I started driving, but then I started thinking."

He sighed. She could picture him leaning back on the pillows, wearing an old T-shirt and boxer shorts, the sleek muscles of his forearm flexing as he scrubbed a hand over his eyes. He was due on shift at six thirty; she really had been trying not to wake him. "Thinking what?"

"I started wondering how much traffic there is on Old Barrons Road in the middle of the night. You know, if someone parked their car here and left it, how long would it be before someone drove by and noticed? The cops always said it wasn't possible that Tim Christopher could have left his car here for so long, unseen. But they never really tested that, did they?"

And there it was: the ugly thing, the demon, coming to the surface, spoken aloud. The thing she'd become so good at keeping buried. The idea had been niggling at her for days as Deb's birthday approached. She'd tried to be quiet about it, but tonight, as she'd lain sleepless, her thoughts couldn't be contained. "This isn't healthy," Jamie said. "You know it isn't. I know you think about your sister a lot. I know you mourn her. But actually going to Idlewild—that's different, Fee."

"I know," Fiona said. "I know we've been over this. I know what my therapist used to say. I know it's been twenty years. I've tried not to obsess about this, I swear." She tried to keep the pleading from her voice, but it came out anyway. "Just listen to me, okay?"

"Okay," he replied. "Shoot."

She swallowed. "I came here and I parked by the side of the road. I sat here for"—she checked her watch—"thirty minutes. Thirty *minutes*, Jamie. Not a single car passed by. Not one." By her calculations, she'd been here for forty-five minutes, but she'd been asleep for fifteen, so she didn't count those. "He could have parked here and done it. The field at Idlewild Hall is only ten minutes through the trees. He would have had plenty of time."

On the other end of the line, she heard Jamie breathe. They'd been together for a year now—a fact that still surprised her sometimes—and he knew better than to say the usual empty words. *It doesn't matter. This won't bring her back. He's already in prison. It was twenty years ago; you need to move on.* Instead, he said, "Old Barrons Road wasn't the same in 1994. The old drive-in was still open on the east side of the road. It didn't do much business by the nineties, but kids used to party there, especially around Halloween."

Fiona bit back the protest she could feel rising in her throat. Jamie was right. She swiveled and looked into the darkness across the road, to where the old drive-in used to be, now an abandoned lot. The big screen had been taken down long ago, the greasy popcorn stand razed, and now there was only a dirt clearing behind the trees, overgrown with weeds. She remembered begging her parents to take her and Deb to the drive-in as a kid, thinking with a kid's logic that it would be an exciting experience, a sensory wonder. She'd soon learned it was a fool's quest. Her intellectual parents would no sooner take them to the drive-in to see *Beverly Hills Cop II* than they would take a walk on the moon. Deb, three years older and wiser, had just shaken her head and shrugged at Fiona's disappointment. *What did you expect?* "There wouldn't have been many kids at the drive-in on a Thursday in November," she said.

"But there *were* kids there," Jamie said with the easy logic of someone whose life hadn't been ripped apart. "None of them remembered seeing Christopher's car. This was all covered in the investigation."

Fiona felt a pulse of exhaustion behind her eyes, countered by a spurt of jagged energy that wouldn't let her stay still. She turned and paced away from the hill and the lights of the gas station, toward the darkness past the hood of her car at the other end of Old Barrons Road. "Of course you think they covered everything," she said to Jamie, her voice coming out sharper than she intended. "You're a cop. You have to believe it. In your world, a girl gets murdered, and Vermont's greatest minds come together to solve the case and put the bad guys away." Her boots scuffed the gravel on the side of the road, and the wind pierced through the legs of her jeans. She pulled up the collar of her coat as a cold shudder moved through her, an icy draft blasting through the layers of her clothes.

Jamie wasn't rising to her bait, which was one of the things that drove her crazy about him. "Fiona, I *know* they covered everything because I've been through the file. More than once. As have you, against all the rules and regulations of my job. It's all there in the murder file. In black and white."

"She wasn't your sister," Fiona said.

He was quiet for a second, acknowledging that. "Tim Christopher was charged," he said. "He was tried and convicted of Deb's murder. He's spent the past twenty years in a maximum-security prison. And, Fee, you're still out there on Old Barrons Road at three o'clock in the morning."

The farther she walked, the darker it got. It was colder here, a strange pocket of air that made her hunch farther into her coat as her nose grew numb. "I need to know how he did it," she said. Her sister, age twenty, had been strangled and dumped in the middle of the former sports field on the abandoned grounds of Idlewild Hall in 1994, left lying on one side, her knees drawn up, her eyes open. Her shirt and bra had been ripped open, the fabric and elastic torn straight through. She'd last been seen in her college dorm thirty miles away. Her boyfriend, Tim Christopher, had spent twenty years in prison for the crime. He'd claimed he was innocent, and he still did.

Fiona had been seventeen. She didn't much like to think about how the murder had torn her family apart, how it had affected her life. It was easier to stand on the side of the road and obsess over how Christopher had dumped her sister's body, something that had never been fully understood, since no footprints had been found in the field or the woods, no tire tracks on the side of the road. The Idlewild property was surrounded by a fence, but it was decades old and mostly broken; he could have easily carried the body through one of the gaps. Assuming he came this way.

Jamie was right. Damn him and his cop brain, which her journalist brain was constantly at odds with. This was a detail that was rubbing her raw, keeping her wound bleeding, long after everyone else had tied their bandages and hobbled away. She should grab a crutch—alcohol or drugs were the convenient ones—and start hobbling with the rest of them. Still, she shivered and stared into the trees, thinking, *How the hell did he carry her through there without leaving footprints?*

The phone was still to her ear. She could hear Jamie there, waiting.

"You're judging me," she said to him.

"I'm not," he protested.

"I can hear it in how you breathe."

"Are you being serious?"

"I—" She heard the scuff of a footstep behind her, and froze.

"Fiona?" Jamie asked, as though he'd heard it through the phone.

"Ssshh," she said, the sound coming instinctively from her lips. She stopped still and cocked her head. She was in almost complete darkness now. Idlewild Hall, the former girls' boarding school, had been closed and abandoned since 1979, long before Deb died, the gates locked, the grounds overgrown. There were no lights here at the end of the road, at the gates of the old school. Nothing but the wind in the trees.

She stiffly turned on her heel. It had been distinct, a footstep against the gravel. If it was some creep coming from the woods, she had no weapon to defend herself with. She'd have to scream through the phone at Jamie and hope for the best.

She stared into the dark silence behind her, watched the last dying leaves shimmer on the inky trees.

"What the fuck?" Jamie barked. He never swore unless he was alarmed.

"Ssshh," she said to him again. "It's no one. It's nothing. I thought I heard something, that's all."

"Do I have to tell you," he said, "to get off of a dark, abandoned road in the middle of the night?"

"Have you ever thought that there's something creepy about Old Barrons Road?" she asked. "I mean, have you ever been *out* here? It's sort of uncanny. It's like there's something . . ."

"I can't take much more of this," Jamie said. "Get back in your car and drive home, or I'm coming to get you."

"I'll go, I'll go." Her hands were tingling, even the hand that was frozen to her phone, and she still had a jittery blast of adrenaline blowing down her spine. *That had been a footstep. A real one.* The hill was hidden through the trees from here, and she suddenly longed for the comforting sight of the fluorescent gas station lights. She took a step, then realized something. She stopped and turned around again, heading quickly for the gates of Idlewild Hall.

"I hope that sound is you walking toward your car," Jamie said darkly.

"There was a sign," Fiona said. "I saw it. It's posted on the gates. It wasn't there before." She got close enough to read the lettering in the dark. ANOTHER PROJECT BY MACMILLAN CONSTRUCTION, LTD. "Jamie, why is there a sign saying that Idlewild Hall is under construction?"

"Because it is," he replied. "As of next week. The property was sold two years ago, and the new owner is taking it over. It's going to be restored, from what I hear."

"Restored?" Fiona blinked at the sign, trying to take it in. "Restoring it into what?"

"Into a new school," he replied. "They're fixing it up and making it a boarding school again."

"They're *what*?"

"I didn't want to mention it, Fee. I know what that place means to you."

Fiona took a step back, still staring at the sign. *Restored*. Girls were going to be playing in the field where Deb's body had lain. They would build new buildings, tear down old ones, add a parking lot, maybe widen the road. All of this landscape that had been here for twenty years, the landscape she knew so well—the landscape of Deb's death—would be gone.

"Damn it," she said to Jamie as she turned and walked back toward her car. "I'll call you tomorrow. I'm going home."

Photo by Perryvinkle Photography

Simone St. James is the *New York Times* bestselling and award-winning author of *The Sun Down Motel*, *The Broken Girls*, *Lost Among the Living*, and *The Haunting of Maddy Clare*. She wrote her first ghost story, about a haunted library, when she was in high school, and spent twenty years behind the scenes in the television business before leaving to write full-time.

CONNECT ONLINE

SimoneStJames.com

SimoneStJames

Simone_StJames